DEATH IN A GREEK LABYRINTH

The first round went wide, nicking the edge of the dolphin fresco. Vance listened, startled, at the explosion, at first thinking it was a sharp crack of thunder from outside. Then he heard the bullet sing into the dark, a high-pitched hiss. For a moment he wondered if he was dreaming, his mind adrift in the bloody myths of the palace. Then a second explosion flared from the direction of the archway, the round grazing his neck.

"Eva!" He threw his body across hers, slamming her against the alabaster portico. His free hand slapped awkwardly at the candle, crushing out the last sputter of flame. As he swung around, the empty ouzo bottle clattered into the dark, spinning, its revolving sound a beacon. Get it, he thought, and stretched across the stone to grope in the dark. Finally he felt the smoothness of the glass gliding at the edge of his reach. Slowly, carefully, his fingers circled the neck and he pulled it toward him.

Still grasping the neck of the bottle, he moved silently across the floor. He pressed against the wall, feeling for the doorway until he sensed a shadow slip past, slowly edging into the room. The muzzle of a pistol glinted against the flare of lightning outside, and he realized it was no more than a couple of feet away.

Now.

He swung the empty bottle with all his might, aiming for the tip of the muzzle. The impact coursed up his arm as the bottle splintered against the metal.

Books by Thomas Hoover

Fiction
Project Daedalus*
The Samurai Strategy*
Caribbee
The Moghul

Non-Fiction
The Zen Experience
Zen Culture

* Published by Bantam Books

Project Daedalus

A Novel

Thomas Hoover

BANTAM BOOKS

NEW YORK · TORONTO · LONDON · SYDNEY · AUCKLAND

PROJECT DAEDALUS
A Bantam Falcon Book / August 1991

FALCON and the portrayal of a boxed "f" are trademarks of Bantam
Books, a division of Bantam Doubleday Dell Publishing Group, Inc.

Grateful acknowledgment is made to the following for permission to
reprint previously published material.
Ovid: The Metamorphoses, translated by Horace Gregory. New
American Library. Copyright © 1958 by The Viking Press, Inc.
Reprinted by permission of Viking Penguin, a division of Penguin
Books USA, Inc.

ISBN 0-553-29108-4

Published simultaneously in the United States and Canada

Bantam Books are published by Bantam Books, a division of Bantam
Doubleday Dell Publishing Group, Inc. Its trademark, consisting of the
words "Bantam Books" and the portrayal of a rooster, is Registered in U.S.
Patent and Trademark Office and in other countries. Marca Registrada.
Bantam Books, 666 Fifth Avenue, New York, New York 10103.

PRINTED IN THE UNITED STATES OF AMERICA

RAD   0 9 8 7 6 5 4 3 2 1

PROLOGUE

So Daedalus turned his mind to subtle craft,
An unknown art that seemed to outwit nature.
                                        Ovid, *The Metamorphoses*

Thursday 8:40 A.M.

*G-load is now eight point five. Pilot must acknowledge
for power-up sequence to continue.*

The cockpit computer was speaking in a simulated female voice, Russian with the Moscow accent heard on the
evening TV newscast *Vremya*. The Soviet technicians all
called her Petra, after that program's famous coanchor.

Yuri Andreevich Androv didn't need to be told the force
weighing down on him had reached eight and a half times
the earth's gravity. The oxygen mask beneath his massive
flight helmet was crushed against his nose and the skin
seemed to be sliding off his skull, while sweat from his
forehead poured into his eyes and his lungs were plastered
against his diaphragm.

*Auto termination will commence in five seconds unless
you acknowledge.* Petra paused for a beat, then spoke
again: *Four seconds to shutdown . . .*

He could sense the blood draining from his cerebral
vascular system, his consciousness trying to drift away. He
knew that against these forces the human heart could no
longer pump enough oxygen to the brain. Already he was
seeing the telltale black dots at the edge of his vision.

It's begun, he thought. The "event." Don't, don't let it
happen. Make your brain work. *Make* it.

Three seconds . . .

The liquid crystal video screens inside his flight helmet

seemed to be fading from color to black and white, even as his vision closed to a narrow circle. The "tunnel" was shrinking to nothing. The first stage of a G-induced blackout was approximately two and a half seconds away.

You've done this a hundred times before at the Ramenskoye Flight Test Center, he told himself. You're the USSR's best test pilot. Now just *do* it.

He leaned back in the seat to lower his head another few millimeters, then grasped for the pressure control on his G-suit, the inflatable corset that squeezed critical blood paths. He ignored the pain as its internal pressure surged, gripping his torso and lower legs like a vise and forcing blood upward to counter the accumulation at his feet.

Two seconds . . .

With his right hand he rotated a black knob on the heavy sidestick grip and turned up the oxygen feed to his mask, an old trick from fighter training school that sometimes postponed the "event" for a few milliseconds.

Most importantly, though, he strained as if constipated in the snow, literally pushing his blood higher—the best maneuver of all. He liked to brag that he had upped his tolerance three G's through years of attempting to crap in his blue cotton undersuit.

It was working. The tunnel had begun to widen out again. He'd gained a brief reprieve.

"Acknowledged." He spoke to Petra, then reached down with his left hand and flicked forward the second blue switch behind the throttle quadrant, initiating the simulated hydrogen feed to the outboard scramjet tridents, portside and starboard. Acceleration was still increasing as the flashing green number on the video screens in front of his eyes scrolled past Mach 4.6, over four and a half times the speed of sound, already faster than any airbreathing vehicle had ever flown.

Only a few seconds more.

He had to stay conscious long enough to push his speed past Mach 4.8, raising the fuel-injector strut temperature of the scramjets to the 3,000-degree-Fahrenheit regime and establishing full ignition. If the scramjets failed to stabilize and initiated auto shutdown, he would flame out—at almost twenty-five hundred miles per hour.

You are now experiencing nine G's, the female voice continued, emotionless as ice. *Pilot will confirm vision periphery.*

The fucking computer doesn't believe I can still see, he thought.

Most men, of course, would have been functionally blind by then. Prolong the experience of ten G's and you went unconscious: the event.

Confirm, Petra's voice insisted.

"Thirty-eight degrees." He read off the video screens inside his helmet, temporarily quieting the computer. But now he had a demand of his own. "Report scramjet profile."

Inboard tridents at eighty-two percent power. Outboard tridents at sixty-eight percent power, the voice responded.

Get ready, Petra. Spread your legs. I'm coming home.

The velocity scrolling on the right side of his helmet screen was about to pass through the barrier. Strut temperature was stabilizing. With engines in the scramjet mode, the vehicle should be able to push right on out to Mach 25, seventeen thousand miles per hour. From there it was only a short hop to low orbit. If—

Inboard tridents at eighty-eight percent power. The voice came again. *LAC compression nominal.* The liquid air cycle equipment would be using the cryogenic hydrogen fuel to chill and liquefy the rush of incoming air; oxygen would then be injected into the scramjets at pressures impossible to achieve in conventional engines.

With a sigh he eased back lightly on the throttle grip in his left hand. As he felt the weight on his chest recede, the pressure in his G-suit automatically let up. He smiled to think that a less experienced pilot would now be slumped in his seat, head lolling side to side, eyes wide open and blank, his bloodless brain dreaming of a lunar landscape. He knew; he'd been there often enough himself. In the old days.

System monitors commencing full operation.

Good. From here on, the fuel controls would be handled

by the in-flight computer, which would routinely monitor thrust and temperature by sampling every two milliseconds, then adjusting. But that was the machine stuff, the child's play. He'd just done what only a *man* could do.

Power-up complete for inboard and outboard tridents, portside and starboard, Petra reported finally. *Hydrogen feed now in auto maintenance mode.*

She'd taken full charge. He was out of the loop.

But I just rode this space bird up your ice-cold *peredka,* silicon lady.

He felt a burst of exhilaration and gave a long, basso whoop. It was a crow of triumph, a challenge to every male ape in the forest. Yuri Andreevich Androv lived for this, and only felt alive when he'd just pushed his body to the limit. He needed it, lusted for it. It was all he'd ever really cared about.

It was, he knew, his primal need to dominate his world. He knew that, but so what? Other men merely dreamed it, played at it—in games, business, even politics. He *did* it. And he fully intended to go on doing it.

"Roll down her audio, dammit," he yelled into his helmet mike. "She's driving me crazy."

"She's supposed to," a radio voice sounded back in his ear. "Ramenskoye says all test pilots—you included, my friend—pay more attention to a female voice." A laugh. "Come to *matya,* darling."

"I'd like to see her and—*Nayarevayet!*—just once." He smiled in spite of himself as the tunnel widened more and the screens before his eyes began to recolor, pale hues gradually darkening to primary shades. The blood was returning to his brain. Acceleration was stabilizing now, down to 4.7 G's.

"She'd be a cold-hearted piece, Yuri. Guaranteed."

"It's been so long, I probably wouldn't notice." That's what he really needed now—a woman.

"You would, believe me," the radio continued. "By the way, congratulations. Your alpha was right across the oscilloscope, as always. Zero stress response. How do you do it, *tovarisch*? I think Petra was more worried than you were."

"Shut off the tape, and cut the 'comrade' crap," he

barked back. "Sergei, I nearly lost it there at nine point five."

"No indication on the physio monitors." The flight technician sounded unconvinced.

"The hell with the wavy lines. I know what was happening," he snapped again, still wired with tension. "Can we get another fifteen percent tilt out of this damned seat, help lower my head. There're no windows anyway, so who cares *where* I'm looking?"

"We can send a memo to Engineering," the radio voice replied. "Though there may not be time."

"Tell them they'd better *make* fucking time. Say I want it done." Not enough time? What in hell was going on?

He took one last look at the high-definition video screens —one for each eye—inside the helmet that would be the vehicle's "windscreen," then flipped the snap and began shoving it up. He hated the damned thing, thought it made him look like a giant high-tech moth.

"Shall we power-down the centrifuge now?" the voice continued, unfazed.

"Take it down. I'm ready for lunch. And a bottle of juice. *'Peit budu ya!'*"

"I read you," the radio voice chuckled once more, knowing there wasn't any vodka to be had for a hundred miles around the facility. Reports were the project director had heard too many stories about Russian drunkenness and somehow always forgot to include liquor in the supply requisition. "I hear there's borscht again in the mess today. Petyr just came in from the North Quadrant. Said it tastes like piss. Bastards still haven't learned—"

"Pomnyu, pomnyu." He found himself longing for real food, seemingly impossible to produce here. Just like a drink.

He waited a few seconds longer, till the huge white centrifuge had come to a complete stop, then shoved down the metal hatch release and stepped out. He looked up at the high-impact glass partition of the instrument room, waved to the medical team, and began unzipping his flight suit. It was only half open by the time the technicians marched in, anxious to remove quickly the rubber

suction cups and wires he was wearing on his head and
chest, the instrumentation probes for their body monitor
system. They wanted to reclaim them before he ripped
them off, something he frequently had been known to do.
Androv always said he was there to fly whatever plane
nobody else had the balls to, not take a physical, so he
wanted the goddam things off, and fast.

Air Force Major Yuri Andreevich Androv was thirty-
seven, tall, with the studied swagger all Soviet test pilots
seemed to acquire after a few years. His dark eyes and hair
were set off by a high forehead and long, lean cheeks, and
behind those cynical eyes lurked a penetrating intelligence. There was something else too, the most vital attri-
bute a test pilot can have: a perfect, natural integration of
the two sides of his brain.

Soviet medical studies had shown that the best pilots
were artists, because handling a plane at three times the
speed of sound was primarily a function of the intuitive
right side of the brain, the side that provides the instincts,
the seat-of-the-pants judgment. The left brain, in contrast,
handled a pilot's rational functions—it was his data management system, his computer.

Flight instructors for tactical aircraft at the Ramenskoye
Flight Test Center south of Moscow knew that a pilot lost
his edge when his brain started getting its signals mixed,
when it was no longer sure which side was in control. They
called it the biology barrier. The result of information
overload in a stress situation, it could lead to a total break-
down. The brain went haywire.

Yuri Androv was one of the few Soviet test pilots who
never reached the biology barrier. He was, in fact, the
best.

He knew that his gift was one of the reasons he had been
specially selected for this project. Another was experience.
Over the years, he'd flown them all—the Tupolev Black-
jack, the MiG 25 *Foxbat*, even the ultra-secret new MiG 31
Foxhound. But this hydrogen-fueled, scramjet-powered
monster opened the door to another world. Above Mach 5,
you were no longer merely supersonic, you were *hyper-*
sonic—where no air-breathing vehicle had ever ventured.

Could it be done? He had to admit the technology was awesome—all the aerodynamic design by supercomputer, the new ceramic composites for the leading edges, the Mach 13 burst-tests in the hypersonic wind tunnel, the scramjet static-test power-ups at the aeropropulsion facility. . . .

This was supposedly just a space-research vehicle, for godsake. But it had *twelve* engines. And whereas the MiG 25, the USSR's fastest fighter-interceptor, topped out well under two thousand miles per hour, this space-age creation was capable, theoretically, of speeds almost ten times that.

The schedule agreed upon called for the certification of both the prototypes in their lower-speed, turboramjet mode, and then the commencement of hypersonic flight tests in the scramjet mode. That second phase wasn't supposed to begin for three months.

But now the project director had ordered the test program accelerated, demanding the hypersonic test flights begin immediately with the one prototype now certified— in ten days.

Maybe, just maybe, it could be done. Of course, everybody else would be sitting safely in Flight Control there in the East Quadrant when he kicked in the scramjets at sixty thousand feet. *His* ass would be the one in the cockpit.

This was the riskiest project of his life. Until the operational shakedown, nobody actually knew whether or not those damned scramjets would produce a standing shock wave in their combustion chamber, creating a supersonic "compressor" the way the supercomputer promised they would.

And what about somebody's brilliant idea of using the plane's liquid hydrogen fuel as coolant for the leading edges, to dissipate the intense heat of hypersonic flight? Had to do it, they claimed. Computer says there's no other way. But that was about as "brilliant" as filling your car radiator with frozen jet fuel! He'd be flying in a cocoon of liquid hydrogen . . . and, even scarier, he'd be doing it blind, with no windscreen. If he burned up he'd have to watch it on television.

He glanced back one last time at the white centrifuge, a fifty-foot propeller with the simulated cockpit on one blade and a counterbalancing weight on the other. The centrifuge itself was pure white enamel, spotless, just like the room. A little honest Russian dirt would actually have made him feel better. Riding in that "cockpit" was like being strapped inside a video game, all lights and nothing real.

Frowning, he shrugged and passed on through the door, greeted the milling technicians, and tossed his crumpled flight suit toward two medics from the foreign team who caught it in midair, bowed, and hurried it into the medical lab for . . . the devil take it, he didn't know and he didn't care.

The fluorescent-lit hall was crowded with white-shirted technicians returning from the morning's test in Number One, the big hypersonic wind tunnel. Everybody was smiling, which told him the final run-up of the model must have gone without a hitch.

That was the last segment of the revised schedule. The hypersonic test flight was on, in eighteen days.

What in hell was the sudden rush? What was everybody's real agenda? Nobody was talking.

That was what really bothered him, had bothered him from the start. This top secret vehicle wasn't destined to be some kind of civilian space-research platform, regardless of what anybody claimed. Who were they fooling? The ultimate weapons delivery system had just been built here, a high-tech behemoth that married advanced Soviet thruster and guidance technology with a hypersonic airframe and scramjets created by the world's leading manufacturer of high-temperature alloys and supercomputers. And it was all being done here, the one place on earth with the technology.

Here. The trouble was, this wasn't the Soviet Union.

So Daedalus devised his winding maze;
And as one entered it, only a wary mind
Could find an exit to the world again. . . .
                    Ovid, *The Metamorphoses*

BOOK ONE

CHAPTER ONE

Wednesday 7:33 A.M.

"You're lucky I love this spot," Vance said, gazing out over the city. "Nothing else on the planet could have got me up this early in the morning."

"It's the one place I thought I could persuade you to meet me." The bearded man sighed, his dark eyes grim. The accent was Russian, the English flawless. "I have a problem, a very big problem."

"The Cold War's over, Alex, or maybe you hadn't heard." He strolled on, tugging his trench coat tighter. "What have we got left to talk about?"

"Please. We both did what we had to."

"I still do. Life's too short for anything else." He turned back. "Now how about telling me what's on your mind."

Vance was firm-muscled and lean, with the leathery skin of a man who drank his tequila straight and preferred spending his days in the sun, two habits that also had bestowed a network of threadlike smile lines at the corners of his sea-blue eyes. Aleksei Ilyich Novosty had phoned him at the Athenaeum Inter-Continental half an hour earlier, begging to meet him, saying it was of the utmost importance. A cab was downstairs. The driver had taken him to the old flea market at Monastiraki Square, where Alex's own black limo waited. But now Novosty was playing games, and the days for KGB games were supposed to be in the past. What did the man want?

"My friend, give me a moment. . . ." Novosty wiped his brow, manicured nails glistening, then looked up and pointed. "By the way, I've always believed that one is the most exquisite female in the world. That one there. What do you think?"

"Sexy, plenty of style." Vance swept his eyes over the figure, loving how the cloth was shaped by her breast, the vague hint of thigh as one leg brushed against the gauze of her tunic. "But the lady next to her's a looker too. Always seemed a tough call."

Above them, the stone caryatids smiled down, their pale faces timeless and ethereal. They were Greek statues that served as columns for the south porch of the Erechtheum, the Ionic temple standing across from the Doric Parthenon. Down below the steep north wall of the Acropolis, the dark-glazed rooftops of Athens, city of Pericles, droused mutely in the early haze.

"Yes, perhaps you're right." Novosty brushed awkwardly at his patchy stubble, searching for an opening. He knew Vance never made the first move, always waited for the other side to show its cards. "Michael, I . . . is it true you occasionally still take an assignment? I mean, outside the usual work for ARM. I made some inquiries in Geneva last week. The word is—"

"Hang on. I think you're getting your team colors mixed. I work for the other side, remember?" He stooped and picked up a handful of the grainy red soil at their feet, massaging it in his fingers and wondering why it had taken him so long to get back here, to Greece. This was where he belonged. This was the place, the ancient people, he still dreamed about. But could he fit in again after so many years away? Yes, he'd *make* it work.

Michael Vance, Jr., had the sangfroid of one who moved easily among the decisionmakers of two continents. He was to the manner born—Yale—and he'd long since concluded it was the way man was meant to live. In years past he'd been a field archaeologist, and a good one; then he'd had a brief consulting stint for the CIA. These days, he lived at the Nassau Yacht Club marina, where he moored his restored forty-four-foot Bristol racing yacht, the *Ulysses,* headquarters for his three-boat charter operation. He was mortgaged to the hilt, but he didn't really care. When things got tight, he could always take on a quick money job for the Association of Retired Mercenaries, ARM.

"The situation is not necessarily what you're thinking," Novosty pressed. "So perhaps you would consider—"

"Whatever it is, the answer's still no. The next three weeks are going to be spent working on a tan."

Why tell Alex the facts? Today he was in Athens for only a few hours, a stopover on the way to Crete. He glanced at his watch—an old Eterna Chronomatic, the 1946 classic he loved—and calculated that the flight for Iráklion left in less than four hours. This time tomorrow morning he would be looking in on the crew from the University of Stuttgart's dig for the German Historical Society, part of the restoration of a Minoan palace near Crete's southern shore. Novosty and all he stood for were the last thing he needed right now.

"Then at least let's have coffee," the Russian said finally, pointing. "I brought some. There in the bag."

Vance needed it, to cut his hangover. Without a word he turned to the marble steps, pried open the white paper, and reached in.

"Plastic." Dismay filled his voice as he lifted out one of the smooth Styrofoam cups and examined it, like an insect. "This nails it. Game over. Our side won all the chips. Now even Greek coffee comes American style." He frowned as he pried the white lid from the cup. "What's left?"

"It's everywhere. Perhaps they'll wrap these statues in cellophane next, who knows."

"I fear the worst." He took a sip, relishing the first hit of the dawn. It was dark and sweet, the real thing despite the container.

"Michael, please . . . at least hear me out." He reached for a cigarette, extracting it filter-first from his trench coat.

"I have a serious personal problem, and I don't know where else to turn."

Could it be true? Vance examined him more closely. The beard wasn't the only change. The left side of his gray coat bulged as he searched for his lighter. Alex had never bothered to carry his own protection. At least never before.

He knew Alex Novosty was part of KGB's T-Directorate, the USSR's special organization for high-tech theft. In the old days he operated out of Sophia, arranging the laundering of underground Soviet funds by mingling them with the flight capital and drug money that made its way between Turkey's Ziraat Bank, the Vatican's Istituto per le Opere di Religione, and Geneva no-questions fronts with names like the Banco di Roma per la Svizzera.

The truth was, Michael Vance, Jr., and Aleksei Ilyich Novosty had, over the years, often traveled the same paths. They used the same organizations and contacts—Novosty to conceal illicit monies, Vance to expose them.

"You know, I always enjoyed our games." Novosty looked out over Athens, his voice trailing off. "But, as you say, that was the old days. The world's changed. Now perhaps we can just be two professionals. Do some business."

He seated himself on a block of marble, still slightly moist with morning dew, and withdrew a wrinkled clipping. It was from *The Times* of London. "Here, read this, please."

Vance glanced down at it, then realized he had already read it on the Reuters satellite news service. He had looked it over, stored it in his news-update computer file, and promptly forgotten about it.

SOVIET PARTY OFFICIAL SOUGHT IN DISAPPEARANCE OF FUNDS

MOSCOW, Mar. 18—The Central Committee today lodged formal charges against a CPSU official, Viktor Fedorovich Volodin, First Secretary of the *oblast* of Sakhalin, in connection with his alleged embezzlement of government funds and subsequent disappearance.

The island of Sakhalin, together with the Kuril Islands, is an administrative district in the far eastern region of the Soviet Federated Socialist Republics. Since being taken from Japan in 1945, the southern Sakhalin *oblast* has been closed to all Western visitors. The island is said to have a major military airfield at Dolinsk and a naval base at Korsakov facing La Perouse Strait, the only year-round passage between Soviet warm-water ports in Asia and the North Pacific. It is an economically and strategically vital part of the Soviet Far East, with the only oil fields in the eastern regions.

The amount embezzled is reported at twenty million rubles, which would make Party Secretary Volodin responsible for the largest outright theft of state monies in the history of the Soviet Union . . .

Vance looked up. "The home team at play. Some ministry shell game, probably. Little budget scam. What's it got to do with you?"

"My friend, this thing is no game." Novosty crumpled his cup. In his other hand, the cigarette remained unlit. "I was . . . involved. Of course, I didn't know then. But if Dzerzhinsky Square finds out I stupidly let myself be—" He flicked his black Italian lighter, then inhaled. "KGB will post me to Yakutsk piece by piece. In very small boxes."

Vance stared into his dark eyes, trying to gauge the truth. None of it added up. "Alex, you're one of the sharpest guys in the business. So, assuming this is straight, why in hell would you let yourself even get *close* to it? The thing had to be some internal play."

For a moment the bearded man said nothing, merely smoked quietly on his cigarette. The sun was beginning to illuminate the cloud bank in the east, harbinger of the midday Athens shower. "Perhaps I . . . yes, it was an unknown, but what is life without unknowns? The job looked simple, Michael. I just had to launder it. Easy enough. Of course, if I had realized . . ." Again his voice trailed into the morning haze.

"So what's the inside story?"

Novosty drew once more on his cigarette. Finally he spoke. "All right. The number of twenty million rubles? Of course it's 'disinformation.' Typical. The real amount, naturally, is classified. There is even a formal directive, signed by Chief, First Directorate Gribanov."

"Guess KGB still has enough clout to write the rules."

"The old ways die hard. They, and the military, are fighting a rearguard action to protect their turf—just as your CIA and the U.S. Department of Defense are doing now. Which is why they are so concerned about this. If they don't get to the bottom of it, they will once again be proved incompetent . . . as well as overfunded." He scratched at his beard. "More to the point, this operation went around them. That's a very bad precedent, if you understand what I'm saying. And the money, Michael, was almost three times what they admitted. In dollars it was over a *hundred* million."

"Nice chunk of change." Vance whistled quietly.

"Even now, though, I have to admit it was brilliant. Flawless. Viktor Fedorovich Volodin, first secretary of the State Committee for Sakhalin, Far Eastern District, got authority signed off, got his passport stamped *vyezdnye*, or suitable for travel, and then wired the sixty million rubles not to the district, but to the state bank of Poland, with instructions for conversion. A lot of money, yes, but it was not unprecedented. And he did it late Friday, around two in the afternoon, after all the *nomenklatura* had left for their weekend dachas. By Monday morning he was in Warsaw, to clarify the 'mistake.' Next the money was sent to my old bank connection in Sophia . . . by then, of course, it's zlotis . . . I just assumed it was something KGB wanted laundered." He paused. "They claim sometimes things have to be handled outside the *nomenklatura*, to avoid the paperwork bottleneck."

"So how much did you end up cleaning?"

"All of it," he sighed. "I converted it to deutsche marks, then bought pounds sterling and used those to acquire British gilts, the long-term government bonds. They're currently parked in a dummy account at Moscow Narodny Bank, in London." The momentary lilt drained from his voice. "But now, now what can I do? The funds are just sitting there, waiting. But if I show up and try to wire them out, I'm probably as good as dead."

"The man who's tired of London is tired of life."

"Michael, the moment I'm seen in London, I may not have a life. I think KGB already suspects I was somehow connected. If they find me, they will turn me into sausages. I'm trapped. You've got to help me move it again, make the trail just disappear." He tossed away his cigarette and immediately reached into his overcoat for another.

"Seems to me the first thing you ought to do is try and locate Comrade Volodin. Maybe let a couple of your boys have a small heart-to-heart with him. Little socialist realism. Give him some incentive to straighten it out himself."

"Michael, first directorate is already combing the toilets of the world for him. He's vanished. The ministry of defense, and the GRU—"

"The military secret service."

"Exactly. The minute either of them finds him, the man's a corpse." He shrugged, eyes narrowing. "If I don't find him first."

Vance listened, wondering. "That's a very touching story. You could almost set it to music. Only trouble is, the punch line's missing. There's got to be more—too much money's involved. So who else is in on this? South Africa? Israel? Angola?"

"What do you mean? I've told you everything I know. Volodin, the bastard, used me as part of his swindle. But now he's lost his nerve and run, disappeared, and left me to face—"

"Sure, that's all there is to it." He cut in, laughing. "Incidentally, you take your standard cut up front? Back at the beginning?"

"Michael, please, I am a businessman. Of course. The usual percentage. But now—"

"Like you say, it's a problem."

He turned to stub out his cigarette. "A nightmare. Think

about it. A hundred million dollars U.S. That's starting to be real money, even for the USSR. Not even the czars ever managed to steal so much."

Vance looked him over. Novosty was telling the story backward, inside out. "Look, whenever somebody gives me only half a setup, I just—"

"Michael, no one knows better than you all the ways money can be moved in this world. Those funds must be made to just vanish from London, then reappear another place with no trail. I have already arranged for a bank, far away. After that the money can be returned, anonymously. What other solution is there?" He hesitated painfully. "You know, I have no friends I have not bought—the definition of a tragic life. But I remember you always were a man who kept his word. I can trust you. Besides, where else can I turn?"

"Alex, forget it. I've already got all the fun I can handle." Vance sipped his coffee, now down to the black grounds and undissolved sugar. It was both bitter and sweet, contradictory sensations against his tongue.

Just like Novosty's tale, part truth and part lie. Alex had no intention of returning the money, for chrisake. He was probably in the scam *with* Volodin. And now the hounds were baying. The main problem was, who were the hounds?

"Michael, do us both a favor. Help me move it." He pressed. "I'll take care of the rest. And I'll even give you half the two million that was my commission. Just take it. Gold. Tax free. It's yours. You'll be set for life. All you have to do is arrange to transfer the money to another bank I will tell you. I have an account already waiting, everything, but I can't do it myself. They're too close to me."

A million dollars, he thought. Christ, with that you could pay off the four hundred thousand mortgage on the boats, free and clear. You'd also be helping Alex out of a jam, and the man looked like he could use all the help he could get. He stared out toward the encircling mountains, now swathed in fleecy clouds. . . .

No. The deal had too many unknowns. The whole point

of working for yourself was you could pick and choose your jobs. If you ever started going with the highest bidder, you were a fool. Guys who did that didn't last in this business.

"Afraid I'll have to pass. There're plenty of other . . ."

That was when he absently glanced down at the early sun glinting off the windows of Athens. In the parking lot below, a tan, late-model Audi had just pulled in. He watched as it idled. "Incidentally," he said as he thumbed at the car, "friends of yours? more art lovers?"

Novosty took one look and stopped cold.

"Michael, I'm sorry, I really must be going. But . . . perhaps you might wish to stay here for a few more minutes. Enjoy the women. . . . Though I hear you like them better in the flesh. . . ." He reached into his breast pocket. "Think about what I've said. And in the meantime, you should have this." He handed over a gray envelope. "It's the original authorization I received from Volodin . . . when he transferred the funds to the bank in Sophia."

"Look, I'm not—"

"Please, just take it. Incidentally, it probably means nothing, but there's a corporate name there. I originally assumed it was KGB's cover. Who knows. . . ." He continued to urge the envelope into Vance's hand. "I've written the London information you will need on the back. The account at Narodny, everything." He was turning. "Be reasonable, my friend. We can help each other, maybe more than you realize."

"Hold on." Vance was opening the envelope. Then he lifted out a folded page, blue. "Good name for a dummy front. Nice mythic ring."

"What . . . ?" Novosty glanced back. "Ah, yes. From the old story."

"Daedalus."

"Yes, everything about this is a fiction. I realize that now. Of course The Daedalus Corporation does not exist." He paused. "Like you say, it's just a myth."

Vance was examining the sheet, an ice blue reflecting the early light. Almost luminous. Something about it was very strange. Then he massaged it with his fingertips.

It wasn't paper. Instead it was some sort of synthetic composition, smooth like silicon.

Saying nothing, he turned away and extracted a booklet of hotel matches. He struck one, cupped it against the light wind, and with a quick motion touched the flame to the lower corner of the sheet.

The fire made no mark. So his hunch was right. The "paper" was heat resistant.

When he held it up, to examine it against the early sun, he noticed there was a "watermark," ever so faint, an opaque symbol that covered the entire page. It was so large he hadn't seen it at first; it could have been reflections in the paper. He stared a second before he recognized—

"Talk to me." He whirled around. "The truth, for a change. Do you know where I'm headed this afternoon?"

"I confess my people did obtain your itinerary, Michael. But only in order to—"

"When?"

"Only yesterday."

"That was after you got your hands on this, right?"

"Of course. I just told you. That was the original authorization."

"The Daedalus Corporation?"

"That name is only a myth. Nothing but paper." He began walking briskly down the steps next to the Temple of Athena Nike, the Sacred Way, toward his black limousine in the parking lot. "We will finish this later. The final arrangements. I will be in touch."

Vance watched as the black limo backed around and quickly headed toward the avenue. After a few moments, the tan Audi slowly pulled out of the parking lot to follow.

He turned back to look at the temples, sorting through the story. Somebody in this world, this Daedalus Corporation or whomever it represented, had a hundred million dollars coming, dollars now all nicely laundered and ready to go. What did it add up to?

In years past Alex Novosty had moved money with total impunity. So why would he turn up in Athens, bearing an elaborate and patently bogus story, begging for help? It couldn't be for the boys back at Dzerzhinsky Square in Moscow. They *never* went outside with their own problems. Besides, they cleaned money all the time.

Somebody, somewhere, was pulling a fast one.

Don't touch it, he told himself. For once in your life just walk away. It's got to be hot. Bad news all around. Just forget it and go on to Crete.

He could hardly wait. Eva Borodin was meeting him there; a decade-late reunion after all the stormy water under the bridge. Or was it going to be a rematch? Whichever, *that* was going to be a scene. He had vague hopes they might put together a rerun of years past, only this time with a happy ending.

Still mulling over the pieces of Novosty's puzzle, he turned and headed for the northwest edge of the Acropolis. In the distance stood the ring of mountains that once served as Athens's natural fortress: Parnes, mantled in dark forests of fir; the marble face of Pentelikon; Hymettus, legendary haunt of the honeybee; Aigaleos, its noble twin crests rising up to greet the early sun. And directly below lay the excavated ruins of the ancient Agora, the city center where Socrates once misled the youth of Greece, teaching them to think.

Now Vance needed to think. . . .

Remembering it all later, he realized he'd been in precisely the wrong place to actually witness the accident. He just heard it—the screech of rubber, the sickening crunch of metal. He'd raced to look, but the intersection below was already a carpet of flame.

What had happened? There was a gasoline truck, short and bulky, wheels spinning in the air, its hood crumpled against the remains of an automobile.

He strained to see. Which was it? Alex's limo? the tan Audi?

Then came the explosion, blotting out everything, an immense orange ball that seemed to roll upward into the morning sky like an emerging sun.

Wednesday 8:23 A.M.

Viktor Fedorovich Volodin was amazed he'd managed to make his way this far, from the fiery intersection at the base of the Acropolis all the way down Leoforos Amalias, without his frayed facade of calm completely disintegrating. He bit his lip, using the pain to hold back the panic. Traffic on the avenue was backed up as far as he could see, and firemen were still trying to reach the charred remains of the truck. On his right, the new Zapio conference center and its geometric gardens were shrouded in smoke.

He scarcely noticed. Breathing was impossible anyway, since the diesel fumes of the bus settled in through its broken windows and drove out all oxygen.

How had it come to this? He'd spent his entire life in the party apparatus of Sakhalin, rubber-stamping idiotic economic plans concocted in Moscow, trying to survive the infighting and intrigue of the *oblast*'s State Committee. Then one day a personal aide of none other than the president, Mikhail Sergeevich himself, had secretly made an offer that sounded too good to be true. Help transfer some funds, do it for the Motherland. . . .

It would be simple. KGB would never know.

Nobody told him he'd be stepping into a nightmare. And now his worst fears had come true. To see your driver crushed alive, only inches away, then watch him incinerated. They were closing in.

Fsyo kanula ve vyechnost, he thought, *kak ve prizrachnoy skazke.* Everything is gone now, like a fairy tale.

He crouched down in the torn plastic seat as the ancient city bus bumped and coughed its way into the center of Syntagma Square. Around him were packed the usual morning commuters gripping briefcases and lunch bags, cursing the delays and blaming the incompetents in Parliament. The air was rank with sweat.

Finally the vehicle shuddered to a halt. End of the line. He rose, trembling, and worked his way to the forward exit, then dropped off. As his feet touched down on the

warm pavement, he quickly glanced right and left, searching the crowded midmorning street for any telltale signs
that he'd been followed.

There was nobody, he concluded with relief. The milling
Greeks didn't seem to notice he was there, or care. They
were too busy complaining about the traffic, the smog, the
latest round of inflation. Business as usual in Athens, the
timeless city. This place, he told himself, should have been
the perfect location to hide, to just disappear. Novosty was
supposed to handle the final delivery.

Maybe the crash had been an accident. Fate. *Sud'ba.*
Things happened that way.

He was sweating heavily now, whether from fear or the
early morning sun he wasn't sure. Already it was a nascent
ball of fire in the east, promising to bake the asphalt of the
square by noon.

He stepped over the curb and onto the sidewalk. The
outdoor cafés were all thronged with workers and tourists
having a quick coffee before taking on the city this spring
day. He felt his knees tremble slightly and realized he only
wanted to collapse. Any table would do. Just melt into the
crowd, he told himself, then nothing can happen. *Nichevo
nye sluchitsya.*

He wiped at his brow and settled nervously into the first
empty chair, plastic and dirty, hoping to look like just
another tourist. The café, he noted, was Papaspyrou, in
front of the American Express office. Perfect. Above all
else, he wanted to pass for an American. But he was still
trying to get it right. How did they look?

"*Ellenikó kafé,* my friend? Greek coffee?"

He jumped at the sound of the voice over his shoulder,
seizing the side of the table.

The voice was speaking English, he finally realized.
Maybe he did look American!

It was an accident, he kept telling himself. The truck
couldn't have— Relax. Novosty made the arrangement
with the American, didn't he? You saw him hand over the
letter. Now the trail will just vanish. KGB will never be
able to stop it.

He turned, casually flashed an empty smile for the small,

gray-haired waiter standing behind him, tray in hand, white towel over the sleeve of his tailored but frayed brown suit.

"Sure, thanks."

You're better every day, he told himself. You're even starting to get the accent right now. Keep working on it. The twang. And learn to saunter. The shoulders. Americans walk looser, swing their arms, seem not to have a care in the world. Learn to slouch. Act like you own the world, even if you no longer do.

He'd been secretly practicing for weeks, getting ready to disappear after his part was over. Of course, he'd originally planned to go back home afterward. But that was before he had a taste of this. The good life, the freedom. For that matter, maybe he'd go to America. Why not? He'd heard how it worked. Defection, so the stories went, could be very rewarding. They'd open the golden gates for him at Langley.

The tiny cup of murky black coffee appeared in front of him, together with the usual glass of tepid water. He reached for the water eagerly and drank it down. Something, anything, to moisten the cotton in his mouth.

There, that was better. Now the hard part: something to quiet his mind.

The cup rattled against the saucer as he gingerly picked it up. He could still see the cab of the truck coming out of nowhere, hurtling down on them, still feel the horror. Odd, but he couldn't remember anyone at the wheel. He wanted a face, but none was there.

His own driver, the Afghanistan veteran Grigor Yanovich, had tried to swerve, but he hadn't been quick enough. He'd caught the first impact, the grind of metal that whipped the tan Audi around, flung open the door . . .

Grigor, thirty years old, must have died without ever knowing what happened, if not from the impact, then from the wall of flaming gasoline that swept over the seat.

He marveled at his own luck, the hand of chance that flung him from the car only a second ahead of the explosion. He remembered skidding across the pavement on his back, then tumbling into the grassy ditch that separated Amalias Avenue from the tiny side road of Thrassilou. Some of the raw gasoline had drenched his sleeve, but he'd been safely out of the way, his face down, when the explosion came.

It *could* have been an accident. He swiped at his brow and told himself that anything was possible.

Don't be a fool. They're closing in. How much do they know?

He sipped at the gritty coffee and scanned the street.

Just get through the next few days, he told himself. Once the transfer's complete, your part's over.

He was reaching for his small white cup when he noticed the woman, striding directly toward his table, smiling, catching his eye. The way she was swinging her brown leather purse, the jaunty thrust of hips beneath the suede skirt, the carefully groomed auburn hair—all marked her as American. Rich American. Probably headed into American Express to cash a thousand or so in traveler's checks. America . . .

He lounged back in his chair with a rakish air. He was, he knew, an attractive man. He had deep blue eyes, sandy hair, a practiced smile, a trim figure far younger than his fifty-six years. He'd divorced his wife Natasha three years ago, after she discovered his lunchtime liaisons with one of the girls in the State Committee typing pool. He had experience handling women.

Three weeks in Athens, he thought, and maybe my luck is about to change. If you can get her, the nightmare could be over for a while. You can't go back to the hotel now; they may be watching. But if she's got a room somewhere? What better way to hide out till the transfer is complete?

He was still trying to make his ragged mind function. Now was the time for a "pick-up" routine. The lonely traveler . . . *Kak grussno mnye, tak zhalostno mnye* . . . no, damn, not the sentimental Russian, think American.

But where? He'd heard of New York, San Francisco, Miami, even Chicago. But what if she was *from* one of those places?

All the careful preparation and he still didn't dare put

himself to the test. So what would he say? Canada? Australia?

Her eyes held his, interest growing as she continued to approach. They were darkened with kohl, sensual, inviting. And she was still smiling, even as she placed her hand on the chair across from him.

Was this how the women . . . ? America *was* the Promised Land.

"Etot stolnik osvobodetsya, Viktor Fedorovich?"

It took a second for the language to register. She was speaking Russian, calmly inquiring if the table was free, but his mind was rejecting it, refusing to accept the implications.

"Perhaps you'd like to buy me a *kofye,* Comrade. I prefer it very sweet." Now she was settling her purse on the table, adjusting her tight skirt in preparation to sit. "Or would you rather take me shopping. I could help you spend some of the money."

He'd never seen her before in his life.

Your part will be routine. Somewhere in the back of his mind echoed the voice of the president's personal aide, the brisk young Muscovite who had come to his dacha that snowy evening last October. *We will take care of any risks.*

It had all been a lie. Every word. They must have known where he was every minute.

Then he spotted the two men approaching from opposite sides of the square. The suits that didn't quite fit, the trudging gait. Why must they always look like the stupid, brutal party hacks they are, he thought bitterly. The incompetent bastards.

Who betrayed me? Was it Novosty? Did he do this, to get them off his trail?

So be it. First I'll kill her, and then I kill him.

Seething, he pulled his body erect while his right hand plunged for the snap on the holster at his belt. Simple. He'd just shoot her on the spot, then make a run for it. Through the café, out the back. They wouldn't dare start anything here, in the middle of Athens, that would cause an international "incident."

The snap was open. He thumbed up the leather flap and realized the holster was empty.

The crash. It must have jarred loose. His new Walther automatic had been incinerated, along with the Audi.

His life began to flash before his eyes.

Make a run for it, he heard his mind saying, commandeer the first taxi, any taxi. He shoved back from the table, sending his chair clattering across the patched sidewalk.

She reached into her leather purse, now lying atop the table, next to his coffee. He heard the click of a safety sliding off. "Don't be impetuous, Viktor Fedorovich. You've been such a good boy this last week, showing us the sights. The perfect tour guide. But now your little vacation is over. We must talk."

"About what?"

She smiled. "Whatever you think we need to hear."

"I don't know anything." He could feel the cold sweat on his palms.

"Viktor Fedorovich." She brushed at her auburn hair as she continued in Russian. "You have the most valuable commodity in the world, knowledge. That makes you even richer than you think you are now."

They didn't try to kill me this morning, he suddenly realized. It was Alex they were— Is he planning to double-cross everybody? No, that's insane. He'd never get away with it. He has to deliver the payment.

KGB wants me alive, he thought with a wave of relief. They think I'm the one who knows where it is.

His pulse raced. "What do you want?"

"We need you to answer certain questions. But not here. At a place where it's quieter."

The two men were loitering closer now, only a few feet away, one on each side of the table. The first was overweight, with bushy eyebrows and pockmarked cheeks. He could be Ukrainian. The other was medium height, wearing a cheap polyester suit, balding and sallow. Neither looked as though he had smiled in the last decade.

"Where do you want to go?"

"We will take a stroll in the park." She gestured toward Amalias Avenue. On the other side was Ethnikos Kipos, the National Garden. Then she smiled again. "We thought you would like to take the morning air."

She rose, purse in hand, and tossed a wad of drachmas onto the wooden table. The coffee drinkers around them did not look up from their newspapers and tourist maps.

As they made their way past the Olympic Airways office on the corner and across the avenue, she said nothing. Her silence is deliberate, he told himself, part of a trick to unnerve me.

It was working. He was learning something about himself he'd never before known. He was learning he was a coward.

That was the reality. He wouldn't hold out. He'd tell them everything he knew, because they would hurt him badly. He couldn't bear pain; they probably knew that. And then they'd kill him anyway because he couldn't tell them the one thing they wanted to know. He didn't know it himself.

Viktor Fedorovich Volodin realized he was about to die. All the years of pointless intrigue in the party, the fudging of production figures, the father-in-law who'd made his existence wretched, it all added up to a lifetime of nothing but misery, with the payoff a bullet. *Rasstrel,* a KGB execution.

They were entering the national garden, a mirage of green in the desert of asphalt and cement that is central Athens. Its informal walkways were shady lanes of quiet and cool that seemed miles away from the smoke and glare and heat of the avenues.

Finally she spoke. "We're running out of time, and patience, Viktor Fedorovich. Let's start with the money. Where have you deposited it? Next, we want to know the names of everyone—"

"It—it's—I don't know where it is now."

"You're lying." She did not break her pace. "The time for that is over."

"But I don't have it. Someone else—" He heard himself blurting out the truth. "He's in charge of everything."

"You are lying, again. You are the one who embezzled the funds." She was walking by his side as they entered a secluded alleyway of hedges, the other two trailed only inches behind. There was no escape. "The criminal is you, Viktor Fedorovich."

"No, he—I—I don't know anything." How true was that? he asked himself. He knew where the money was supposed to go, but he didn't know what it was for, at least not specifically. That part had been classified. He had the small picture but not the big one.

"If you know nothing, then telling us everything you *do* know should not take very long." The calm, the assurance in her voice sent chills through him. He knew he would talk and they knew it too. "However, the more you have to say, the longer we can linger."

The early morning park, with its manicured footpaths and wandering cats, was empty except for a few gardeners trimming hedges, watering the grass, collecting loose papers. The sounds of the avenue were rapidly receding. Now the two men had moved directly alongside, one by each arm. He realized they were both taller than he was, and they smelled.

"Wait. I don't know where it's deposited now; I wasn't supposed to know. But there's still time. I can help—"

They were entering a long arbor, a high trellis bright with obscuring red flowers, when the first blow came into his left side, directly in his kidney. He groaned and sagged, breath gone, while the man on the right slipped an arm around and held him erect.

"Yes, Viktor Fedorovich," the woman continued tonelessly, "you will help us, because you will want to die long before we let you. So, shall we try again? Where is the money?"

"It's . . . I don't know, exactly. But—"

He gasped and sagged again as another blow came. Already he wasn't sure how much more pain he could tolerate. How long before he would just blurt out everything he knew?

A third blow, and his knees crumpled. He had never known the meaning of pain, or fear, until this moment.

Why not just tell them? his frightened mind was pleading. Alex has already set it up with the American.

"You are worse than a mere criminal," she went on, dark eyes filling with anger. "You are a traitor. You will tell us every detail of your involvement, from the very beginning."

How much did they really know? he wondered. Were they bluffing?

They *were* bluffing, he quickly concluded. Otherwise she wouldn't be asking him things she should already know.

If you talk, you'll jeopardize everything. The most important thing now is to keep KGB from discovering the scenario. If they do, they still could stop it.

Of course they were alarmed. They should be. In the New Russia being born, there was no place for them.

But I can't endure pain. I'll talk if there's pain.

He felt a surge of resolve. Whatever else happens, he told himself, I won't be the one responsible for making it fail. I can't let them know any more than they do now. I've—

Another blow struck him in the side and he felt his knees turn to butter. None of the gardeners in the park seemed aware that a man was about to be beaten to death. To them the four foreigners were merely huddled together as they strolled, enjoying the dubious beauty of modern Athens.

Another blow came and he wheezed. "Please, let me just—"

He'd been gathering his strength for this moment. Now he lunged forward, shutting out the stab of pain in his side, and wrenched at her open purse. The two men reached for him but not before he had it in his grasp. His hand plunged in as he rolled to the ground.

They were on top of him now, shoving his face against the loose pebbles of the walkway, but they were too late. He felt the smooth metal of the grip. It was what he wanted.

He recalled the triumphant words Fyodor Dostoyevski had uttered upon being released from prison. "Freedom, new life, resurrection. . . . What a glorious moment!"

Ya nye boyuc za sebya! he thought with joy. I have no more fear. . . .

He heard the shot, faintly, as the bullet ripped through

the back of his mouth and entered his brain. Viktor Fedorovich Volodin died with serene final knowledge. Daedalus, whatever it was, was still safe. And he was free.

CHAPTER TWO

Wednesday 3:29 P.M.

"Michael, you look marvelous. It's so good to see you again. I really mean that. The years have treated you well." Eva Borodin leaned back against the gray fabric of the Saab's headrest and appraised him.

"You don't look half bad yourself." Vance smiled to himself as he returned the favor. Vintage Eva, ladling on the flattery. But she was smashing, just as he remembered— the coal-black hair, the smoldering eyes, the high Slavic cheekbones. Then, too, her every gesture was spiked with the promise of Olympic sensuality; he remembered that as well. Everything about her spoke of a time and place far away, where there were no rules. Eva, the eternal Eva. With a Ph.D. "Everything's just the same."

That part wasn't entirely true. There had been some changes, probably for the better. Instead of a plunging neckline and a fortune in gold accessories, she was wearing a blue silk blouse, form-fitting designer jeans with an eighty-dollar scarf for a belt, and lambskin boots. Far more demure than the old Eva. What had happened to the dangling turquoise earrings, enough musky perfume to obscure radar, at least one endangered fur draped somewhere?

The years had definitely mellowed her. The Slavic passion seemed curbed today, the same way her hair had been trimmed down to a pageboy. Maybe, he thought, this was her new look: the Russian aristocrat of the nineties.

"No, Michael, I'm different now. Or I'm trying to be."

She laughed, flashed her come-on smile, and tried to toss her missing hair.

Whoops, he thought. Sure, you've changed.

"Being formally promoted to director of SIGINT brings responsibilities," she continued.

"Congratulations."

"It was two years ago."

"Well, congratulations anyway." He was beginning to wonder if she really had mellowed. Back in the old days her Russianness was her way of making a statement. An identity. How much could she change, want to change? She'd always been a firebrand: throwing things was her preferred mode of communication. Not to suggest she wasn't verbal: she was always passionately happy to see him, passionately sad when bad things happened, passionately angry when she didn't get her way. Everything she said was flirtatious, carrying a sexual innuendo. Sometimes he thought she made Jean Harlow sound like Jeane Kirkpatrick.

"Your call caught me a little off guard." He glanced over. "I never expected to hear from you again after you disappeared into the labyrinth of NSA." He knew she'd been with the National Security Agency for eight years now, but he hadn't heard that she'd been promoted to director of Soviet satellite intercepts. Of course, NSA didn't spend a lot of money on press releases. Still it was no surprise. Eva knew her stuff when it came to the Soviets, their satellites, their codes. "I must say, though, this is a hell of a long way to come for a catch-up chat."

"It's been way too many years since we've seen each other. I've missed you."

"Hope you mean that." Did she? he wondered. Even if she did, that wasn't the real reason she'd come. He knew her too well.

"Guess you'll have to try and find out," she said, her voice holding an instinctive, automatic invitation.

"Guess I will." Already it felt like the old days. *How* did she know so precisely where all his buttons were? "The only thing I'm sure of so far today is that this morning's little accident was no accident." He'd told her about seeing

Novosty, but not what they'd talked about. Why drag her into it? Besides, she'd known about Alex a lot longer than he had. Just one more piece of the past that didn't need to be stirred up. "Somebody got taken out. The question is, Who? We both know Novosty's a survivor, old school, but . . ."

"I probably shouldn't say this, Michael, but I assume you're aware he's KGB, part of T-Directorate." Her voice had grown serious. "That executive VP slot he has with Techmashimport is just his cover. We've had a file of intercepts on him for years."

"Of course I know about him. Good old Alex and I go back a while. You're slightly out of date concerning my most recent fun and games."

"All right. I mean, I wouldn't even bring it up, but I think you should be warned. KGB's in a big turmoil, looking for something . . ." She paused. "Whenever this happens, there're plenty of stray arrows sure to be flying. Just stay out of the crossfire. A word to the wise."

"I may already be in it. Thanks to Novosty's little 'welcome aboard' breakfast." He remembered the letter Alex had given him. "But I'm beginning to think I'd damn well better find out."

She looked around sharply. "What happened? Did he say something?"

"If you believe him, somebody in Moscow mislaid a few million dollars. Darndest thing."

"It's better left alone, darling."

"I'm on vacation, remember?" He winked at her. "With better things to do."

"I should hope so." She leaned back again and studied his profile. "Well, at long last it's happened. I finally have to admit I need you for something." Her long, dark lashes fluttered. Warming me up, he thought. Now we're getting down to business. "Which is why I wanted to meet you here."

They were five minutes out of Iráklion, on an unpaved back road he loved, headed for the palace at Knossos, and so far she'd done nothing but hint about what was on her mind. Everything was still a puzzle. For one thing, she never needed anybody. She was the stalwart Russian who'd ended their affair eleven years earlier just as casually as she had begun it. This afternoon, though, she seemed to be deliberately keeping the lid on, holding back. Uncharacteristic.

"The truth is," she went on, "I've been thinking about us, the old times, and the palace."

She'd called him in Nassau four days earlier, wanting to get together. It was the old Eva, darling this and darling that. When he said he was going to Crete, she'd grown strangely silent. Then she'd said—in a curious, tiny, voice—"Why don't I just meet you there? In fact, that's sort of why I rang. . . ."

"So why's the palace suddenly so important to you?" He examined her, still trying to read her mood. "I *need* to go back out today. Try and brush up a bit. But that place was part of our problem back when, not part of the solution."

She didn't answer. Instead she shifted the conversation sideways. "Speaking of the palace, I suppose I should congratulate you on finally being proved right. Did the Stuttgart team really ask you to look in on their dig?"

"Call it the ultimate capitulation," he grinned. "Remember, they were the ones who led the critical fusillade when the book first came out. That makes it doubly sweet."

"Right. I also remember that book of yours caused such a stink that no serious university would consider hiring you. Which, I assume, is why you ended up a part-time spook. Probably it was the only job you could get."

"You're closer to the truth than you know." He laughed, wondering for the ten-thousandth time if he should have stuck out the academic slings and arrows. No, the secret truth was he was bored with the university regimen. He yearned for the real world. He knew it then and he knew it now.

"Then the next thing I heard, you were down in the Bahamas, goofing off and renovating some old yacht." She looked him over once more, shaking her head. "What did you end up christening it? the *Fuck Everybody*?"

"Crossed my mind. But then I chickened out and called her the *Ulysses*." He leaned back and reflected momen-

tarily on the forty-four-foot Bristol racing sloop he'd restored, having picked it up for a song at a customs-house
sale on Bay Street. Formerly the possession of a Colombian
in the export business, it had a hull of one and three-
quarter inch planked cedar, with a trim beam, did an easy
fifteen knots in a decent breeze. He loved her. He'd installed a fortune in electronics, including a Micrologic
Commander LORAN and a Navstar satellite navigation
system. "It started out as a hobby, and three boats and a
mortgage later it ended up a business."

"And what do you do down there all day? Just sit around
and drink margaritas?"

"Sure. About once a month." He reached up and adjusted the open top of the car. "Hate to admit it, but on a
typical day I'm usually out of bed by sunrise. Check the
weather, then maybe take a short swim to get the oxygen
flowing. After that I go to work. The 'office' is up forward in
the *Ulysses*. My main discovery is that chartering is pretty
much like any other business. Mostly problems."

It was. There were always tourists who came to Nassau
thinking they wanted more than the standard hotels, top-
less shows, and casinos on Paradise Island and Cable
Beach. *They* wanted a taste of what it was like sailing
through the Family Islands, away from the glitz, a feeling
for the real Caribbean. Or so they thought. That was until
they discovered the hard way that the real thing included
broiling sun, jellyfish stings, nosy sharks, hangovers, sea-
sickness, close-quarters quarrels with spouses and significant others, snapped fishing lines, generator failures,
unexpected weather . . .

"And you manage to do okay, right?"

"Nobody ever got rich in the charter business, at least
the kind I'm in. If you're not running high-priced South
American produce, you have to do it for love, not money."

His real livelihood, which he didn't bother to mention,
came from elsewhere. In between managing Bahamian
skippers and crews he also kept a hand in another occupation. In years past he'd served as a financial consultant for
the CIA, helping monitor the flow of illicit drug and terrorist money passing through the banking laundries of Ge-

neva and the Caribbean. When the Company finally formed its own section to handle that work, he'd moved on and hired out his expertise to a free-lance organization called ARM, the Association of Retired Mercenaries. They were retired, all right, but only from the antiterrorist units of a half dozen European nations. They still saw plenty of covert action, squelching those terrorist activities European governments wanted dealt with outside official channels. He was their money man and they paid him well, which was how he kept his three vessels shipshape and lived a yachtsman's life of "ease."

"So after all these years, you ended up doing exactly what you wanted." She looked at him admiringly. "A lot of people would probably envy you that."

"I like taking my own risks, if that's what you mean."

"Well, all the same I suspect you're secretly very pleased with the fact you've been invited back to Crete. I always thought you'd return to archaeology sooner or later. If I know you, you couldn't stay away forever."

Was she right? Even now he didn't know. "One thing's for sure. Crete's a world apart."

That was an understatement. As he glanced back at the road, it was now blocked entirely by a herd of sheep, their shaggy brown fleeces suspended above dark, spindly legs. Around them the silence of the Cretan countryside was rent by bleats and the jangle of bells. The flock milled and darted about their rented Saab, but failed to move on down the road. Why bother? The shepherd, in dark hat and coat, lounged sidesaddle on his burro, oblivious, while his black-shawled wife trudged in his dusty wake, bringing up the rear. Strangers came, gazed upon the wonders of his land, then departed; he, possessor of donkey, sheep, and wife, would remain. And prevail. His weathered face contained all the worthwhile knowledge in the world. The parched hills and verdant valleys of Crete belonged to him alone. Now and forever.

"Okay," he went on, "you're here, I'm here. Now how about telling me what's going on?"

"That's just it. I don't know for sure. Everybody at NSA claims I'm starting to see things." She paused to examine a long red fingernail. "So don't you say it too. I need some moral support."

"Maybe I'd better hear this first."

"Michael, I . . . I don't want to talk about it yet. It's just—"

"Well, give me a hint at least."

"A few days back I decoded part of a transmission . . ." She leaned over and started to turn on the radio, then changed her mind and straightened. "Look, I just need you to help me get my thoughts organized."

"Is that why you came all the way here? to organize your thoughts? You'll forgive me if I'd hoped for a little more." In spite of himself, he felt mildly annoyed. The truth was, he'd been looking forward to a reunion that wasn't about business. "You know, I sort of had the idea you wanted to . . . well, maybe try and piece things back together." He looked her over. "Being with you wasn't exactly the worst experience of my life."

She sighed wistfully and smoothed back her hair. "Fixing Humpty Dumpty is tough work, darling. We both know that. It's been a long time. Life's never that simple."

"Maybe not for you. But it seems very simple to me. We just lose the past. Pretend it never existed." He felt his pique growing. "Or then again, screw it. What are we doing here anyway?"

Could it really work a second time around? he asked himself. Why not? Through all those years after things fell apart, he'd never once stopped remembering her. Her mind, her body, her excitement.

Those memories dogged him now as they drove down the road he knew so well, had traveled so many times in his long-ago life. At times the ancient palace here on Crete had seemed almost a second home. After the publication of his book about it, *Realm of the Spirit*—to universal denunciations—he even began to dream about it. He thought he'd never come back, and now here he was with Eva. Life took strange turns sometimes.

Eleven years ago in New Haven when he'd decided to work for himself, he'd actually been saying good-bye to this world and all it stood for. Back then it had seemed a golden moment to give academia the bird.

Had it all come full circle now? Fortunately he'd kept up with the journals when he had the chance, tried to stay on top of what was happening. With any luck he'd have the pleasure of watching a lot of academics eat crow. All he had to do was just deal with whatever was bugging Eva and then get on down to Phaistos. He hoped the Stuttgart crew wouldn't realize he was over a decade out of date.

"You know," she was searching in her purse, then stopped herself and looked up, "I always remember the palace when I think of you. It sort of tied us together."

"Best I remember, it's what finally drove us apart. It turned into our 'irreconcilable difference.'"

"Maybe you're right, and it was dumb of me. Given the lousy luck I've had with men, you're probably the best thing that ever came along. After that flap over your book, I let you get away."

"Hold on a second. You announced you had to live your own life, and I was getting too emotionally involved in my work and it would be better all around if we just shook hands and called it quits. No hard feelings."

"It wasn't quite like that." She laughed her alluring laugh, the one he remembered so well.

"Oh, no?"

"Okay, maybe it was a little like that." Out came the sunglasses. The old Eva again. "But I was changing, Michael, more every day. It was time to try and make it on my own."

That was definitely what she'd decided to do. He'd always thought she broke things off because she was obsessed with finishing her own Ph.D. Self-centered and self-indulgent, that's what he'd called her at the time, just another pampered Russian blue blood. Only years later did he realize how self-centered *he'd* been. Maybe she'd been right; maybe they weren't ready for each other yet.

She sighed, and then her voice came as a whisper. "You know, after you called this morning and told me about that nightmare with Alex, I just drank some retsina and went back to bed." She put on the shades, adjusted them, and looked his way. He thought they went well with her new forties hairstyle. "Michael, I know things I shouldn't. And the things I should know, I don't. The worse part of all is, none of it makes any sense." Her eyes seemed to soften behind the tinted plastic. "Do you remember the first time you and I talked about this place?"

"Like it was yesterday." Who could forget? It was just after *Realm* was published, relating his theory that the palace, whatever it may have been originally, had eventually become a ceremonial necropolis, an abode of the dead. "We ended up having a terrific argument over the book. Nobody wanted to believe me, including you."

"Come on, darling, it wasn't *my* opinion you cared about. It was your father's. The revered holder of Penn's Edelstein Chair of Classical Antiquities. Supposedly the world's living expert on Minoan Crete."

Did he really care what the old man thought? he wondered. Not in the way she meant. He would have liked it, though, if everybody had gotten along a little better. Michael Vance, Sr., never quite knew what to make of Eva's Slavic intensity, since it contrasted so vividly with his own up-tight Anglo-Saxon instincts. That was a repressive family strain Mike had fought—successfully, he hoped—to undo all his life. Eva had looked to be the perfect soul mate in that battle. She was born unrepressed.

Her own father, Count Serge Borodin, was president emeritus of the Russian Nobility Association in America, exiled aristocracy. They were a people apart. He recalled in particular a Russian Orthodox wedding they'd all attended once. The operative assumption that sunny afternoon in Oyster Bay was that the czar had been a living god, the Romanovs the world's last surviving cherubim. He still remembered the black-hatted Orthodox prelates and the incense and the tinny balalaikas and all the counts and countesses drunk and dancing and crying at the same time. Growing up in the middle of that, she *had* to be exuberant.

"You'd gone off on your own and set the world of archaeology on its ear," she continued. "Typical Michael. But your father refused to stick up for you when all the shit came down. I guess I didn't support you very well either, I admit now. I'm truly sorry, darling, looking back."

"No big deal. I could handle it."

"Sure." She reached over and patted his thigh. "You handled it just great. You were disgusted. At me, at him, at all the 'stuffed-shirt' academics who never went out on a dig and got their hands dirty. You practically dragged me here to show me you were right. You were obsessed with the palace, admit it."

"It wasn't that bad." He looked over at her. "Was it?"

"Let's not talk about it anymore, all right?" She sighed. "Christ."

"Fine with me." He was pulling off the main road, heading into the flower-lined trail, the arcade of magenta bougainvillea that led down toward the palace. "By the way, I brought along some ouzo." He indicated a pint bottle in his coat. "What's a picnic without a little rocket fuel?"

"You think of everything."

"I also think we should park up here, dodge the tour-bus mayhem. Keep the funny hats and loudspeakers to a minimum."

"Yes, please. Besides, I could use the air." She inhaled deeply.

Around them the few lingering white sprays of almond blossoms seemed like remnants of late spring snow, while the ground itself was blanketed with wild orchids, lavender and pink anemones, white narcissus. He watched as she climbed out of the car, then stopped to pluck a waxy yellow prickly pear flower, next an orange-blue *Iris cretica*. He loved the flowers of Crete, and the afternoon was fragrant with the scent of jasmine and lemon blossoms. Ahead, down the hill, was the parking lot for the palace, with two tour busses in attendance, one just pulling out.

"How long has it been since we were last here together?" She brushed her dark bangs back from her brow as she squinted into the waning sun, sniffing at her cactus flower.

"It's beginning to seem like forever. But I think it's about—what?—almost twelve years now."

"And how old is the palace supposed to be? I've gotten a little rusty."

"The latest theory going is that it was destroyed about fourteen hundred B.C. So we're talking roughly three and a half thousand years since it was last used."

"Guess our little decade doesn't count for much in the grand scheme."

"Time flies." He remembered how she'd been back then, that day so long ago when she had been in her mid-twenties, as inviting as the brazen ladies-in-waiting of the palace frescoes, and even more voluptuous. *Mais, ce sont des Parisiennes,* a dazzled French scholar had marveled. She was like that. Perfect sensuality. For a while he'd forgotten all about archaeology and just concentrated on beauty.

The place where all this occurred was the Palace of Knossos, lovingly restored in the early part of the twentieth century by the wealthy English archaeologist Sir Arthur Evans. There an almost modern civilization had flowered to magnificent heights, then mysteriously vanished. The path leading to the palace down the hill was becoming wider as they walked, opening on the distant olive groves in the valley. The vista was stunning, probably the reason it had been built here.

He looked over and noticed she was digging in her purse again. This time she drew out a pack of Dunhills. He watched while she flicked a gold lighter, the one he'd given her as a present so long ago, emblazoned with a lapis lazuli skull and crossbones. At the time, the hint had worked. She'd quit.

"The return of the death wish? When did you start that again?"

"Last week." She defiantly took a puff.

"Any particular reason?"

"No, darling, I just did it." She exhaled. "I'm wound up. I'm . . . I'm scared. Michael, for godsake, how many reasons am I supposed to need?"

"Hey, lighten up." He'd quit a month after they met, but it hadn't been a big deal. "I've mellowed out from the old days. Life is like most other things—a lot more fun when you don't take it too seriously."

They were moving across the empty parking lot, headed for the entrance to the palace. It had once been a twelve-hundred-room labyrinth, perhaps deliberately confusing. Now the upper courtyard and chambers lay exposed to the sky, their massive red-and-ocher columns glistening in the waning sunlight. The columns tapered downward, as though tree trunks had been planted upside down to prevent resprouting.

It was a poetic place to meet Eva again, he thought. And thoroughly bizarre as well. She'd gotten her Ph.D. in linguistics, specializing in ancient Aegean languages, then a few months later she'd surprised everybody by accepting a slot at the National Security Agency, that sprawling electronic beehive of eavesdropping that lies midway between Washington and Baltimore, on the thousand acres of Fort Meade. It'd seemed a startling about-face at the time, but maybe it made sense. Besides, it was that or teaching.

NSA was a midsized city, producing among other things forty tons of classified paper trash a day. Its official insignia, appropriately, was a fierce eagle clasping a key—whether to unlock the secrets of others or to protect its own was unclear. Eva's particular branch, SIGINT—for signals intelligence—was an operation so secret NSA refused even to admit it existed. Employing ten acres of mainframe computers, Eva's SIGINT group monitored and analyzed every Russian transmission anywhere: their satellite downlinks, the microwave telephone networks within the Soviet Union, the chatter of civilian and military pilots, missile telemetry far above the Pacific, the split-second bursts of submarines reporting to base, even the limousine radiophone trysts between Politburo members and their mistresses. The instant an electromagnetic pulse left the earth, no matter its form or frequency, it belonged to the giant electronic ears of the NSA.

So why shouldn't Eva end up as the agency's top Russian codebreaker? She was a master at deciphering obscure texts, and she'd spoken Russian all her life. Who better to make a career of cracking secret Soviet communications. Her linguistics Ph.D. was being used to real purpose.

"I want you to help me think some, love," she went on. "I know it may sound a little bizarre, but I'd like to talk about some of the legends surrounding this place. You know, try and sort out fact and fiction."

Now they were headed side by side down the stairway leading into the central court, an expanse of sandstone and alabaster tile glinting golden in the pale sun. On their left a flight of stairs seemed to lead out, but in fact they led right back in again. The deceptions of the palace began at the very entrance.

"The truth is, about all we have is stories, though sometimes stories can be more true than so-called history. The standard version is that this area was where the athletes performed ritual somersaults over the sacred bulls."

The restored frescoes around them showed corridors crowded with lithe Minoan priestesses, eyes rounded with green malachite, faces powdered white, lips a blood red. They all were bare-breasted, wearing only diaphanous chemises, while their jewels glistened in the sunshine as they fanned themselves with ostrich plumes.

There were no frescoes, however, of the powerful, bloodthirsty King Minos.

"Michael," she called out, her voice echoing off the hard walls, "you know, this place has always felt a little sinister to me. None of the lightness and gaiety in those frescoes seems real."

"That's part of what made me start wondering if the Minoans hadn't somehow managed to make a monkey out of every ponderous scholar on the planet." They were moving down the monumental grand staircase, three restored flights of which had originally been five, toward the rooms called the royal chambers. "Maybe the reason this place had no walls or fortifications was because you only came here when you were dead. Who the hell knows."

Whatever the truth was, the eerie feeling of the palace seemed to make the ancient stories even more vivid. The legends told that King Minos's wife, Pasiphaë, had a burning passion for one of the sacred white bulls he kept, so she arranged for his chief architect, Daedalus, to design a hollow wooden cow for her covered over with a hide. She concealed herself inside and, as luck would have it, lured one of the beasts. The progeny of that union was equally beastly—the Minotaur, a monster with a human body and a bull's head.

Now they were rounding a final corner in the twisting maze of stairs. Directly ahead was the boudoir of the queen. The past welled up for him.

The frescoes over the alabaster arches showed bold blue dolphins pirouetting in a pastel sea dotted with starfish and sea urchins. And just beneath them stood the famous bathroom of the queen, connected to the vast drainage complex of the palace, great stone channels curved in precise parabolas to control and dampen turbulence. Daedalus was an engineer-architect who had mastered the science of fluid dynamics thousands of years before the invention of wind tunnels and supercomputers.

"My favorite spot. The bedroom." He slipped the small bottle of ouzo from his trench coat pocket. In the dank of the palace's lower depths, he needed its warmth. "I've had unspeakably erotic thoughts about this place—now it can be told—with you no small part of them." He handed her the bottle. "Want a hit of high octane?"

"Glad to know I've had a place in your memory all these years, even if it was X-rated." She took the bottle with a knowing smile, then drank. "It's like licorice."

He laughed. "Blended with JP-7."

"Michael," she continued, looking around, "maybe this is the very room where Pasiphaë gave birth to the Minotaur. What do you suppose?"

"That would fit the story." He moved on, his eyes still adjusting to the shadows. "The only thing the legends actually say is that King Minos ordered Daedalus, resident genius, to create a secret labyrinth in the cellar of the palace to keep the beast. But nobody's ever located it."

"You know, I think the labyrinth was no myth. It was real, only it was here. All around us. We're in it now." She handed back the bottle. "It was this whole sinister palace, this realm of the dead. After all these years, I finally think maybe you were right."

Vindicated at last? Had even Eva come around? But why didn't he feel any satisfaction? Instead he found himself aware of the old chill, the almost occult intuition that had first told him the palace wasn't the happy playground everybody supposed it was. Once more it felt like death.

But now something else was entering his senses. Was it imagination? In the encroaching dark the lower levels of the palace seemed to be totally deserted, with only a couple of persistent German tourists arguing out near the parking lot, and yet . . .

They weren't alone. He could feel it. He *knew* it. Was it the spirits of the dead?

No, it was far more real. Someone was with them, somewhere. In the shadows. They were being watched.

He looked at Eva, trying to make out her eyes in the semidarkness. Did she sense it too? That somebody was nearby, waiting, maybe listening?

"Darling, let's talk some more about the myth of Daedalus. In the version I remember he—"

"Not much more to the tale. After a while a Greek prince called Theseus arrived, to brave the labyrinth and do battle with the man-eating Minotaur. When he showed up, King Minos's beautiful daughter, Ariadne, instantly fell in love with him, naturally."

"I love myths. They're always so realistic."

"Well, he dumped her later, so I guess he did turn out to be a creep. But anyway, she persuaded Daedalus to give him a ball of string. He attached it to the door of the labyrinth and unwound it as he went in. After he killed the beast, he followed the twine back out, and escaped. With Ariadne. Unfortunately, when Minos discovered what had happened, he was so mad he locked the great chief architect in a tower. But Daedalus managed to get out, hoping to escape from the island. However, it wasn't going to be easy, since Minos had clamped down on all the harbors, having the ships searched. That's when Daedalus declared, 'Minos may control the land and the sea, but he doesn't control the regions above.' And he constructed some wings, attached them to his shoulders with wax, and soared away into space. First human ever. Up till then, only the gods could just leave the earth anytime they wanted."

"What?" She'd stopped dead still.

"Daedalus. You remember. The first person to fly, mankind's ago-old dream. In fact, a few years back some Americans duplicated the feat with a human-powered glider. They made it from here on Crete over to the island of—"

"No, you said 'space.' "

"Did I?" He smiled. "Call it poetic license. But why not? Back in those days I guess the skies themselves could be considered outer space, if they even knew such a thing existed." Then he looked at her and sobered. "What's—?"

"It's—it's just something that's been in the back of my mind." She moved on.

With a shrug, he took another drink of the ouzo and followed her on down the hall toward the famous Throne Room. He was bracing himself now for what was next.

Its walls were decorated with frescoes of the massive Minoan body shields, shaped as a figure-eight, that signified the men's quarters of Knossos. And incised in stone above King Minos's wide alabaster throne was his fearsome emblem of authority, symbol of his domination of the ancient world.

There it was. He looked around, reassuring himself that it was everywhere, just as he'd remembered. He'd also been right about something else. It was precisely the same, right down to the smooth curves of the blade, as the "watermark" that had been on the sheet of "paper" Alex had given him. Almost four thousand years old, it was the insignia of the new Daedalus Corporation.

The Minoan double ax.

Wednesday 6:12 P.M.

The dusk was settling majestically over Tokyo, after a rare smogless day. The view was particularly inspiring from the fifty-fifth-floor penthouse of the granite-clad Mino Industries building. The corner office was an earth-tone tan, carpeted in a thick wool shag the color of elm bark. The heavy doors at the far end of the office were emblazoned with a two-bladed ax, and in the center of the wide expanse between the door and the single desk, on a gleaming steel pedestal, stood a meter-long model of an airplane more advanced than any the world had yet seen.

The temperature of the room was kept at a constant 59 degrees Fahrenheit, a frigid comfort-accommodation for the tawny, eight-foot snow leopard named Neko now resting on a pallet beside the window, gazing down. Remnant of an endangered species, she'd been rescued as a starving, motherless cub during an expedition in the Himalayas and raised for the past six years as a pampered pet of the penthouse's owner.

Along the sound-proof walls were gilt-framed photographs of a Japanese executive jogging with Jimmy Carter in Tokyo, golfing with Ferdinand Marcos in Manila, receiving an accolade from Linus Pauling in San Francisco, dining with Henry Kissinger in Paris. He was the same man now sitting behind the massive slate desk.

"You believe he was an American?" Tanzan Mino, president and CEO of the Daedalus Corporation, a paper creation of the Mino Industries Group, adjusted his pale silk tie and examined the subordinate now standing before him. He had just turned seventy-three, but the energy in his youthful frame made him seem at least a decade younger, perhaps two.

"*Hai*, Mino-sama." The other man, in a dark suit, bowed. "We have reason to believe the Russian has . . . they were seen exchanging an envelope."

"And your people failed to intercept either of them?"

The man bowed again, more deeply. "An attempt was made, but unfortunately the Soviet escaped, and the American . . . my people were unsure what action to take. We do know the funds have not been deposited as scheduled."

Tanzan Mino sighed and brushed at his silver temples. His dark eyes seemed to penetrate whatever they settled upon, and the uncomfortable vice-president now standing in front of him was receiving their full ire.

Back in the old days, when he directed the Mino-gumi clan's operations at street level, finger joints were severed for this kind of incompetence. But now, now the organization had modernized; he operated in a world beholden to computers and financial printouts. It was a new age, one he secretly loathed.

He'd been worried from the start that difficulties might arise. The idiocy of Japan's modern financial regulations had driven him to launder the payoffs thoroughly. In the old days, when he was Washington's man, controlling the Liberal Democratic Party, no meddling tax agency would have dared audit any of his shadow companies. But after a bastard maverick named Vance—with the CIA, no less!—had blown the whistle on his and the Company's clandestine understanding . . .

He had arranged the initial financing for the project, as well as the political accommodations, with letters of credit, promissory notes, and his word. And, eventually, if need be, the full financing could be raised by partial liquidation of his massive real estate holdings in Hawaii.

But the near-term expenses—and the necessary payoffs in the LDP—that was different. In Japanese *kosaihi*, the "money politics" of gifts and outright bribes, secrecy was everything. He remembered how he'd had to arrange for the mighty Yoshio Kodama, a powerbroker who had once shared his virtual ownership of the Japanese Diet *and* the Japanese press, to accept responsibility for the CIA-Lockheed bribe affair. It was a close call. That had involved a mere twelve million of American cash to Japanese politicians, but it had changed the rules forever. These days—particularly after the Recruit debacle had disgraced the LDP yet again—money had to be laundered and totally untraceable.

Promises had been made, schedules signed off, the veil of total secrecy kept intact. Everything was arranged. The Soviets, incompetents that they were, had no inkling of the larger plan.

Now it all came down to the funds. He needed the money at once.

He turned in his chair, pressed a gray button on his desk,

and watched the window blinds disappear into their frame. Neko rose from her languorous pose, stretched her spotted white fur, and gazed down. This was the panoramic view she loved almost as much as he did, for her perhaps it was the memory of a snowy Himalayan crest; for him it was the sprawl of Tokyo, the elegant peak of Mount Fuji to the west, the bustling port of Yokohama to the south. From this vantage atop the powerful financial world of Japan, Tanzan Mino wanted two final triumphs to crown his career. He wanted to see Japan become the twenty-first century's leader in space, and he wanted his country finally to realize its historic wartime objective: economic domination of the continent of Asia, from Siberia to Malaysia, with freedom forever from the specter of energy and resource dependence. The plan now in motion would achieve both.

He revolved again in his chair, ignored the subordinate standing before his desk, and studied the model. It was a perfect replica, one-hundredth the actual size, of the spaceplane that would revolutionize the future, the symbol that would soon signify his country's transcendence in the high-tech age to come.

Then his gaze shifted.

"You were 'unsure what action to take'?" He leaned back, touching his fingertips together, and sadness entered his voice. "You know, there was a time when I thought Japan might still one day recapture the spirit we have lost, the spirit of *bushido*. In centuries gone by, a samurai never had to ask himself 'what action to take.' He acted intuitively. Instinctively. Do you understand?"

"Hai, wakarimasu." The man bowed stiffly.

"I am prepared to funnel trillions of yen into this project before it is over. Legitimate, clean funds. So the sum now in question is almost inconsequential. However, it is the bait we need to set the trap, and it must be handled exactly as I have specified."

"Hai, Mino-sama." Again he bowed.

"The next time you stand before me, I want to hear that the laundered Soviet funds have been deposited in the Shokin Gaigoku Bank as agreed. You have one week." He slowly turned back to the window. "Now, must I tell you what you have to do?"

The man bowed low one last time. He knew exactly.

CHAPTER THREE

Wednesday 7:38 P.M.

"Michael! And *Eva*! Again, after so long. *Pós iste*! What a surprise!" The old Greek's sunburned face widened into a smile, his gray mustache opening above his last good teeth. *"Parakaló*, you must come in for a glass of *raki* and some of Adriana's *meze*. She would never forgive me."

They'd dropped by the hotel, then come here. Although Zeno's small taverna was in the center of Iráklion, its facade was still country style, covered with an arbor. A bare electric bulb hung incongruously in the middle of the porch, penetrating the dull glow of dusk now settling over the square called Platia Eleftherias, where the evening's *volta* was just beginning. Once the chaste promenade of eligible young women, it was now a deafening flock of motorscooters, with girls in tight jeans riding on their backs. And the watchful mothers of old were conspicuously absent. Times had indeed changed since his last time here.

"Zeno." Vance shook his hand, then accepted his warm embrace. As he was driving, he'd been wondering what the old Greek would think about the sudden reappearance of Eva. They hadn't been here together since that last trip, well over a decade ago. "Still pouring the meanest *raki* in this town?"

"But of course. Never that tequila you like, Michael." He chuckled with genuine pleasure, recalling that Vance could down his high-potency version of ouzo like a native. "Ah, you know, Michael, your father would never touch it. You, though . . ."

He beckoned them through the *kafeneion*'s doorway, leading the way with a limp. The interior was dark, redolent of Greek cigarettes and retsina wine. Overwhelming it all were the smells of the kitchen—pungent olive oil and onions and garlic and herbs, black pepper and oregano. Although lighting was minimal, around the rickety wooden tables could be seen clusters of aging Greeks drinking coffee and *raki* and gossiping. The white clay walls resounded with the clacks of *komboloi* worry beads and *tavli*, Greek backgammon.

"But then," Zeno continued, "that last trip, your birthday present to him. On his retirement. Do you remember? When we three were sitting at that very table, there in the corner. He called for a bottle of my *raki* and shared a glass with me. We both knew it was our good-bye." His eyes grew misty with emotion. "Yes, coming here finally with his famous son was a kind of benediction, Michael. He was passing the torch to you, to continue his work."

This last was uttered with a slightly censorious tone. But it quickly evaporated as he turned and bowed to Eva, then took her hand in a courtly gesture. The old Greeks in the room would have preferred no women save an obedient mate in their male sanctuary, but traditional hospitality conquered all. "It is so good to see you two back together." He smiled warmly as he glanced up. "Welcome once again to our humble home."

She bowed back, then complimented him in turn, in flawless Greek.

"So beautiful, *and* so accomplished." He beamed. "You still are the treasure I remember. You are a goddess." He kissed her hand. "As I've told Michael before, you could well be from this island. No, even more. You could be Minoan. You bear a fine resemblance to the *'parisiennes'* of the palace. Did he ever tell you?"

"Not often enough." She flashed him her sexiest smile. "But then he never had your eye for women."

"Ah," the old man blushed, "I have more than an eye. If I were thirty years younger, you and I—"

"Zeno, before you drown Eva in that legendary charm, let me bring her up to date," Vance laughed. "She is now in the presence of the man who has probably become the richest tavern owner in all of Crete."

It was true. Zeno Stantopoulos had indeed become a wealthy man, in many ways. His father had once farmed the land on which now stood the unearthed palace at Knossos. The handsome sum Sir Arthur Evans paid for the site was invested in bonds, which he then passed on to Zeno just before the war. Zeno had the foresight to convert them to gold and hide it in Switzerland during the German occupation of Crete. After the war, he used it to purchase miles and miles of impoverished olive groves in the south, which he nursed back to full production. These days oil went up, oil went down, but Zeno always made a profit.

His real wealth, however, was of a different kind. Zeno Stantopoulos knew everything of importance that happened on Crete. His *kafeneion* was the island's clearing-house for gossip and information.

"Don't listen to him, madam." He winked and gestured them toward the wide table in back, near the kitchen. It was known far and wide as the place of honor, the location where Zeno Stantopoulos held court. It had also been the nerve center of the Greek resistance during the Nazi occupation, when Zeno had done his share of killing and dynamiting. The limp, however, came from the fifties, when he was imprisoned and tortured by the right-wing colonels for organizing popular resistance against them.

"Come, let us celebrate with a glass of my *raki*." He turned again to Eva. "I should remind you. You once called it liquid fire."

He clapped for Adriana, who squinted through the kitchen door, her black shawl wrapped tightly about her shoulders. When she finally recognized them, she hobbled forward, her stern Greek eyes softening into a smile.

"Neither of you has changed." Eva gave her a hug. "You both look marvelous."

"Time, my friends, time. That has changed," Zeno went on. "I use a cane now, for long walks. The way Michael's father did his last time here. When I saw him I thought, old age must be God's vengeance on us sinners. And now it has happened to me." He smiled, with a light wink. "But I will tell you a secret. Ask Adriana. I do not yet need a cane for all my exercise." He nodded affectionately in her direction. "I can still make this beauty wake up in the mornings singing a song."

It was true, Vance suspected. Adriana had hinted more than once that every night with him was still a honeymoon.

"Ah, Michael," he sighed, "I still miss seeing your beloved father on his summer trips here. Together you two inspired our soul. The ancient soul of Crete."

At that point Adriana bowed and announced she must return to the kitchen, where she was putting the final touches to her proprietary version of *kalamarakia,* fried squid.

Her peasant face hid well her peasant thoughts. Almost. Vance had known her long enough to read her dark eyes. She didn't quite know what to make of Eva's reappearance yet. Speaking passable Greek, it was true, which counted for much, but she still wore no wedding band. *Adinato!*

"Michael, don't let Adriana stuff you." Zeno watched her disappear, then turned. "To your health." He clicked their small glasses together. *"Eis hygeian."*

"Eis hygeian." Vance took a sip, savoring the moment. Seeing old friends again, real friends, was one of life's most exquisite pleasures.

"And tell me, how long will you two be visiting with us this time?" Zeno's Cretan hospitality flowed unabated. "Perhaps longer than the last? Have you finally decided to come back to stay, maybe make us famous all over again?"

"Can't speak for Eva, but I've been asked to look in on the new German excavation down at Phaistos. A project to try and restore the palace there, the way Evans reconstructed Knossos." He glanced over. She was now sipping the tepid *raki* with the gusto she normally reserved for ice-cold Stolichnaya. "Tonight, though, we're just tourists. Here to see you two again."

At that moment, Adriana reappeared from the kitchen bearing an enormous oak tray. With a flourish she laid before them fried squid and goat cheese and stuffed grape leaves and octopus and wooden bowls of *melidzanosalata,* her baked eggplant puree flavored with garlic, onions and herbs, not forgetting her speciality, pink *taramasalata* made of mullet roe and olive oil.

"Incidentally, we were just out at Knossos, the palace, this afternoon." Vance took a bite of *kalamarakia* while she looked on approvingly.

"Ah, of course, the palace," Zeno smiled. "I love it still. I probably should go more myself, if only to remember the days of my childhood, during the restoration. But with all the tour buses. . . ." He chewed on a sliver of octopus as he glanced out toward the music in the street. "Perhaps it should be better cared for these days. But, alas, we are not as rich now as King Minos was." He shrugged and reached for a roll of *dolmadakia.* "Still, we are not forgotten. Today, perhaps, we count for little in the eyes of the world, but your book brought us fleeting fame once again. Scholars from everywhere came—"

"Hoping to prove me wrong." Vance laughed and took another sip of *raki.*

"What does it matter, my friend. They came." He brightened. "Even today. Just to show you. Today, there was a man here, right here, who was carrying your famous work on the palace. He even—"

"Today?" Vance glanced up. Had he been right?

"Yes, this very day. Outside in the arbor. He even sampled some of Adriana's *meze.*" He nodded at her. "I did not like him, and only our friends are welcome inside, book or no book."

"Was he going out to Knossos?" Eva interjected suddenly, staring. "To the palace?"

"He asked about it. Why else have the book?" He shrugged again, then examined the octopus bowl, searching for a plump piece. "You know, Michael, I could never finish that volume of yours entirely. But your pictures of the frescoes—" He paused to chew his octopus, then smoothed his gray mustache and turned again to Eva, "the frescoes of the women. I love them best of all. And every now and then I see a woman here in life who looks like them. Not often, but I do. And you are one of those rare creatures, my Eva. I swear you are Minoan." He turned back. "Look at her, Michael. Is it not true?"

"Zeno," Eva reached for his gnarled hand. "It's not like you to forget. My people are Russian, remember. From the Steppes."

"Ah, of course. Forgive me. But you see, that only goes to prove it." He nodded conclusively. "The Minoans, we are told, came from central Asia thousands of years ago. The 'brown-haired daughter of Minos' was an oriental beauty, just as you are. I'm sure of it. Look at the frescoes."

"Zeno, tell me." Vance reached to pour more *raki* into their glasses. "The man you mentioned just now. Was he Greek?"

"No, he was a foreigner." He chewed thoughtfully. "I've never seen anyone quite like him. He had a strange way of speaking. In truth, Michael, I did not like him at all. Not a bit."

"What exactly did he say?"

"It wasn't that. It was something else. I don't know."

"And he went? to the palace?"

"I saw him hire a taxi, that was all. But whether he went there or somewhere in the south, only God could know." He looked away. "Perhaps tomorrow I could find out."

"Did this man have a beard?" He pressed.

"No, the thing I remember most was that part of one finger was missing. Curious. I focused on that. But his features, his features were almost Asian I would say." He paused, then turned and asked Adriana to fetch another bottle of *raki*. "Perhaps his accent was from that part of the world." He looked back at Eva. "I suppose you would have known, my marvelous Eva, my Minoan queen."

His eyes lingered on her a moment longer, then he rose. "Enough. Now we must all have something for dinner. I'm sure you do not want to spend the rest of the night trapped here with a crippled old Greek."

He disappeared into the kitchen to select the pick of the day's catch. And that smoky evening they dined on the island's best—*barbounia*, red mullet, which Adriana grilled with the head and served with wedges of Cretan lemon. Afterward came a dessert of grapes and soft, fresh *myzithra* cheese blended with dark honey from the mountains near Sfakiá. Then at the end she brought forth her own *soumada,* a rich nectar made of pressed almonds.

After more *raki,* Zeno was persuaded to get out his ancient *bouzouki,* tune it, and play and sing some traditional songs. The music grew faster and more heated, and then—with only the slightest urging—Eva cleared away the tables and began to dance. Her Russian gypsy movements seemed almost Greek.

When they finally broke away the time was nearly midnight; the *volta* had long-since disbanded; the sky above had changed from a canopy of island stars to a spring torrent. And Michael Vance and Eva Borodin were very, very drunk.

Wednesday 11:34 P.M.

"You know, there was something special about us in the old days," Vance said as they weaved down the rain-washed street toward the hotel. "How we used to be. All we did was eat, drink, and talk. And make love. Tonight it's three down and one to go."

"You're pretty smashed, darling." Eva laughed and looked him over. "A girl learns to watch out for deceptive advertising."

He slipped his arm around her. Eleven years, and in a way, this was like it was all happening over again.

"I never shirk from a challenge."

"I'll drink to that." Her voice indicated the challenge would not be overly daunting. "Do we have any—?"

"There's still that bottle of ouzo in the car."

She stopped dead still, her hair plastered against her upturned face, and ran her hands down her body. "Minoan, that's what Zeno said. What if it's true?" She turned back. "What if I have the same hot blood as the queen who vamped a bull? Imagine what *that* would be like."

"As best I remember, you could probably handle it."

She performed another Russian gypsy whirl in the glistening street. "I want to be Minoan, Michael. I want to soar through time and space. Leap over bulls, maybe even . . ." She twirled again, drunkenly.

"Then why not do it? The queen's bedroom." He stopped and stared at the Galaxy Hotel, ultramodern and garish, now towering upward in the rain. The pool was closed, but the disco still blared. "The hell with everything. I'm taking you back there. Tonight."

Parked next to the lobby entrance was their rented Saab. He paused and looked in at the half bottle of ouzo lying on the seat, then reached and pulled her into his arms. "Come on. And get ready."

"Is that a promise?" She curled around and met his lips.

"Time's a wastin'." He kissed her again and began searching for his keys.

She was unsteadily examining the darkened interior of her purse. "I think I've got an emergency candle in here. We'll use it for light. Just enough."

"I just hope I'm not too wrecked to drive in the rain."

"You'd better not be. I know I am."

"Who cares? Let's just go for it." He was unlocking the car and helping her in, loving the feel of her body, her scent. He'd decided he was ready for anything and anybody, including some mysterious stranger carrying his book.

The night was brisk, with flares of spring lightning over the mountains. As the Saab weaved through the narrow streets leading out of town, Eva climbed up and drunkenly unlatched its sunroof to let in the rain. By the time they reached the winding country road, headlights piercing the downpour, the wind was rushing around them, wild and free.

When they pulled into the parking lot of Knossos it was deserted, and they easily discovered an opening in the guard fence. The palace lay before them.

"Piece of cake." He took her hand and helped her through the wire. "I propose a toast right here. To the past and to the future."

"If I drink much more of this, I may not be around to see the future, but I'll die happy." She reached for the slippery bottle.

As they moved through the abandoned central court, eerie in the rain, he could almost hear the roars of the crowd four thousand years past, see the spotted bulls charging the nubile athletes. A heavy gust flickered her candle, adding mystery to the shadows dancing across the enigmatic women of the frescoes.

"Now I really do feel Minoan." She headed down the grand staircase, brandishing the light. Then she called out, her voice resounding down the maze of windy hallways, "I am the queen. I am Pasiphaë. Where's my white bull?"

"Eva, you're drunk," he yelled after.

"I'm intoxicated. It's different." She laughed, low in her throat. "I'm intoxicated by the palace. The thought of my bull, the eternal male." Her voice echoed more. "Know about eternal males, darling? They're like eternal females, only harder." She grinned at him, then proceeded, tracing the wide marble steps.

As she floated down, carrying the candle, the moist air was scented with jasmine, alive with the music of crickets. They rounded the last curving steps, and the ornate vista of the queen's bedroom spread before them, its blue dolphins cavorting in their pastel sea.

He walked over and patted the alabaster portico. "Hard as this, your eternal male? This is a real test for the eternal female bottom."

She threw herself down, then reached and ran a drunken readiness check across his wet thigh. "I'm ready for something hard inside me." Her voice was strange, detached and ethereal.

"When did you start talking like that?" He loved it. "Not even in the old days—"

"When I became Minoan, darling. When I became the blood relation of Queen Pasiphaë."

She wiggled out of her soaked brown dress and tossed it onto the floor. As he watched her begin to sway before the fresco of the dolphins, he had the definite feeling time was in a warp, that the flow of centuries was in reverse. Maybe Eva *was* none other than Pasiphaë reborn. The room was perfumed and serene, perfect for a queen.

Then she bent down and carefully stationed her candle

on the stone. Looking up she said, "Let me have some more of that ouzo. I love being here. It's shocking and wonderful."

No, this was most assuredly the modern Eva. As she moved against him, her body felt the way he remembered it. Riper now perhaps, with a voluptuousness slightly more toward Rubens than Botticelli, but the skin of her breasts, her thighs, was soft as ever. And the dark triangle was still luxuriant, redolent with her scent.

"Do it. Hard. Like a bull. I want to know what she felt." She drew back across the stone as he drove inside her. "*Yes.*"

While rain slammed against the courtyard above, the ancient, foreboding room began to engulf and rule their senses; the feel of her perfumed nipples against him was hard and urgent. It was an erotic moment outside of time.

Now her head thrashed from side to side as quivering orgasms rippled through her, starting in her groin and welling upward as she arched and flung back her hair. Then she drew up, clinging, as though trying to consume him, herself, in a rite of pure bacchanalian frenzy. Her breath had become labored, not gasps of pleasure, but the need of one seeking air.

Eva, Eva, he suddenly caught himself thinking, you're here for release, escape. I know you too well. You're not really in this room anymore. You want to be but you're not. You're somewhere in a realm of beasts and magic and the bloodthirsty Minotaur.

But yet, yet . . . somehow he'd never felt closer . . .

A final convulsion brought them together and then she fell back, dazed. The candlelight flickered across the alabaster, sending ghostly apparitions against the fresco of the dolphins. Still trying to catch her breath, she reached out and seized the bottle of ouzo, drank from it thirstily, then flung herself once more against the stone. After another long moment, she pulled him to her.

"Michael, hold me." She snuggled into his arms. "Oh, darling, just hold me."

He drew her against him, and the touch of her skin was erotic beyond anything he remembered. . . .

But the palace . . . it was intruding darkly, insinuating its presence. Now it surrounded them like a tomb, ominous as death. Finally he turned her face up and examined her dark eyes. They were flooded with fear.

"Look, you've got to tell me what's going on. I want to know the real reason you're here, and I want to know it now. I'd somehow begun to hope it was for us, but—"

"That's part of it, darling. Truly." She kissed him deeply on the mouth, then reached and began fishing in her purse for the battered pack of Dunhills, trying to regain her bravado. "God, that was hot. I do love being here with you."

"You're stalling. Whenever you don't—"

"You're right." She took out a cigarette, flicked her lighter, and drew a lungful of smoke. "Now I see why Pasiphaë was such a number. This room does something to you."

"Not bad for starters."

She looked down, then smiled. "No, darling, you're just bluffing. I remember that well enough. Plenty of time for a cigarette."

"Some things improve with age." He studied her beautifully disheveled form. Now more than ever he realized she was scared. "Goddammit, enough. Talk to me."

"All right." She sighed, then leaned back on the ledge of the portico. "Well, to begin at the beginning, I've been seeing somebody lately."

"Make you a deal," he interrupted. "You spare me your stories and I'll spare you mine. This doesn't really seem the moment to start swapping indiscretions."

"I'll bet you've got plenty to swap yourself." She looked him over.

"Hold on a minute." Sure, there'd been women in and out of his life. He wasn't a priest. Besides, he *liked* women.

"Darling, relax." She patted his thigh. "We're both adults. You said you wanted to hear this, so for godsake listen. His name was Jerry Ackerman and . . . it started back about nine months ago. Since he was new, he'd drop by my office now and then. You know, to learn the ropes."

"What kind of ropes, exactly?"

"Really, Michael. Anyway, he wasn't exactly world class in the boudoir, if that makes you feel any better. Though needless to say I never told him that. Our little scene tonight would have blown his Brooklyn mind. Now does that preserve your precious male ego? He was just nice, and interesting."

"Was?"

"I'll get to that." She was tracing small circles on the alabaster. "Week before last he dropped off a computer disk at my office. Said he couldn't figure it out. And it was old, maybe two weeks. Which was unusual, especially for satellite intercepts, which this was. Normally we get them the same day. So I ran it through my desk station, figuring it couldn't be that big a deal." She paused nervously, then went on. "Well, the first part was encoded using one of the standard Soviet encryption systems we've had cracked for years, and it had a lot of proper names. But the rest of it was just a string of numbers. No matter what I tried, I got nothing but garbage."

"Really? I thought Fort Meade's football field of Cray supercomputers could crack anything."

"I thought so too. But this encryption was either so clever, or so simple, nothing seemed to click. I couldn't do it. I even began to wonder, maybe it's not a cipher at all. Maybe it's just some obscure foreign language. So I matrixed it against some we have in the data base. And, love, we've got them. A zillion megabytes of memory. Serbo-Croatian, Urdu, Basque . . ." She drew on her cigarette, sending a glow into the dark. Above them the rain continued to pound. "But I still couldn't find anything that would crack it."

"Doesn't sound like you." He drew her around and kissed her. "Half the time you're too smart for your own good."

"Apparently not smart enough." She hugged him back automatically, then continued. "When I told Jerry I couldn't break the encryption, he suddenly got very nervous. Said okay, then he'd just take it and try again himself. So I asked him to sign it out on my log. Just routine. And that's when he started acting strange. At first he refused, but finally he did it when I said, 'It's like this, sweet buns. No tickee, no washee.' By then he'd stopped coming over to my place and things had gotten a little strained at the edges, to put it mildly. So I didn't think too much about it at the time."

"Don't start telling me more about—"

"Michael, that was the last time anybody saw him. He just vanished. That night. There was even something in the paper. 'Mysterious disappearance.' The apartment where he lived had been dismantled. Top to bottom. Somebody must have thought he was holding out."

"And?"

"Well, it just so happened I still had it in computer memory, though that's a blatant violation of security procedures. Anyway, the next day I called Control and said what's with a certain file? Gave them the NSCID number. And they said, 'We have no record of that number.' Quote. They'd never heard of it. So it must have been a free-lance job for somebody outside. Whoever it was must have paid Jerry, or maybe blackmailed him, into getting me to take a crack at it. Which is why it was two weeks old. It wasn't NSA material at all. Somebody else wanted it, and I'm known far and wide as Ms. Give-Her-the-Tough-Ones."

"You always were the best."

"Right." She laughed, then reached into her purse and retrieved a three and a half inch gray computer disk. "And here it is. A complete copy. I've also got it stored on the eighty-meg hard drive of my Zenith Turbo 486 laptop back at the hotel." She tossed it to him. "Jerry's file. That's the good news. The bad news is, it's still encrypted."

He turned it in his fingers. Welcome to the new age, he thought, when thousands of pages can be packed onto a high-density disk the size of a cassette tape.

She took out a compact from her purse and powdered her nose in the light of the candle, then turned and searched the stone for her crumpled dress. He thought he heard a sound from the hallway outside, but then decided it was just more thunder.

"So now what?" She finally found the dress and drew it loosely on, managing not to secure the bustline. "I've tried and tried to crack it, but nothing seems to click. After the preamble, there's nothing on there but a long string of numbers. Whatever it is, it's not any of the standard encryption systems." She reached to take it back. "Why am I telling you all this?"

"Because we've agreed, no more games."

"Darling, there're actually two reasons why I shouldn't. One is I hate to drag you into it, and the other . . . well, there's more."

"I'm waiting."

"Whatever's on here is part of something bigger. I know that because of the preamble, the section I *can* read." She pushed ahead, nervousness in her voice. "Anyway, that's when I decided I had to talk to you. About some of the things you used to work on."

He inhaled. "What are you talking about?"

"There were some proper names."

"I don't get—"

"In the preamble. One was 'Daedalus.' And another was 'Mino.' So I thought, why not talk to Michael? It sounded like something that you'd . . . I don't know . . . maybe you could help me think. Anyway, I finally decided to take a chance and ring you."

"Great. Nice to finally learn exactly where I fit in." He lay silent for a moment, trying to suppress his annoyance. Finally he told himself, Be constructive.

"All right, tell me what *you* think it's all about."

"Well." She paused again, as though unsure. Finally she spoke, her voice faint above the rain. "Did you know the Soviet Union and Japan never actually signed a peace treaty after World War Two?"

"It's because the Soviets kept some Japanese islands, right? Seem to recall they were the Kuriles, and also the southern half of Sakhalin."

"Japan calls those the Northern Territories, and they've refused to sign because of them." She reached over and adjusted the candle, surveying the dark around them. The gloom was almost stygian. "Well, hang on to your diplomatic pouch, because I think they're about to sign. Maybe as the first step toward . . . I'm still not sure what."

He caught his breath. "How did you find out about this?"

"Intelligence. I've been handling our intercepts. But we still haven't put together a briefing package for the president, and State. It just seems so implausible nobody wants to be the one to sign off on it. Besides, nothing's settled. Among other things, the Japanese Diet would eventually have to vote to approve it, and nothing's come through diplomatic channels. It's being closely handled by somebody big and anonymous over there. Anyway, my hunch is a vote in the Diet would be a squeaker. Your average Japanese man on the street still isn't too enthusiastic about the Soviets."

He leaned back to think. Given today's global realities, a deal like that had to be the tip of some gigantic iceberg. In diplomacy, there was always give and take.

"And you believe whatever's on this disk is somehow connected to the treaty?"

"That's precisely what I believe," she sighed. "The treaty has a secret protocol involved. It's hinted at in the intercepts, but never described. And I've got a feeling, somehow, that this is it."

"Doesn't sound like something that would delight Washington." He pondered. "On the other hand, what could the U.S. do anyway? The American military is a hell of a lot more worried about losing its bases in Japan, not to mention NSA's Soviet and Chinese listening posts, than the Japanese are about giving up our so-called protection. There's not a damned thing the U.S. could do about it."

"I'd guess whoever's behind this fully realizes that." She paused, letting a roll of thunder from above die away. "But the protocol . . . nobody has any idea what's in it, not even the KGB. I also know that from our intercepts."

"This is getting more interesting by the minute."

"Well, stay tuned. There's more still. As it happens, I'm also on NSA's oversight panel, the Coordinating Committee. We assemble briefing packages that bring together reports from all the departments, including PHOTOINT, photo intelligence from satellite surveillance."

"The 'spy in the sky' recon? Big Bird, KH-12, radar imaging?"

"Well, we review all of that, sure. But think about it. The Soviets have surveillance satellites too. And p.s., their Cosmos series can now relay down digital imagery in real time." She paused. "It's classified, but put two and two together. If NSA intercepts Soviet voice and data communications . . ."

"Stealing pictures from their spy satellites?" He knew about it. "Why not? All's fair in love and war, I think the saying goes."

"Okay, just pretend you dreamed it up." She sighed. "Now, from here on it gets a little off-the-wall. So off-the-wall everybody at NSA refuses to take it seriously. The committee keeps wanting to study everything, but I think time's running out. Something's going to happen any day now, but—"

"Something bad?" He tried to make out her eyes in the dark, wondering what she was still holding back.

"Michael, I shouldn't . . ." She reached over and took another cigarette out of her purse. "Anyway, the reason I wanted you here was to help me find some answers. Before somebody decides to try and make me disappear too. Like Jerry." She flicked at her lighter three times before it finally flared.

Maybe, he thought, she had good reason to be afraid. He remembered the odd sense that afternoon that they were being watched. And then Zeno mentioning a stranger carrying his book. It was beginning to seem less and less like a coincidence.

"But, Jesus," she went on. "Now they've found me. And I've drawn you into it. I'm really—"

"Just relax." Mainly now he wanted to calm her down. "Nobody's found—"

"Don't you see? Alex. Just happens to call you this morning as you were on your way here to see me. Don't flatter yourself. That call was about *me*. Which means he knows I've got . . ." Her hand quavered as she dropped the lighter back into her purse. "There's already been one murder—"

"Hey, slow down. Take it easy. Novosty's never scared me, even when he's tried. Just—"

"It's not him I'm worried about. Michael, if even a T-Directorate sleaze like Alex knows, then who else . . ." The darkened room fell silent.

"You'd better tell me all of it. Everything." Again he paused, thinking he heard a sound from somewhere in the dark. But it was impossible. Nobody could have followed them here.

"All right." She let the words tumble out, finally. "Yes, we intercept all the Soviet satellite photos. Just the way you thought." She exhaled, then rose and paced the room a moment, its walls now ghostly in the candlelight. "Well, lately for some strange reason their Soyuz series always seems to have a temporary malfunction whenever they pass over one certain spot on the globe. Almost as though somebody were turning off their KFA-1000 high-resolution cameras. I kept noticing it, but nobody else in PHOTOINT thought it was anything but a coincidence. Still, it got me wondering. What if somebody over there is pulling a number on the KGB, or the GRU? Keeping them from seeing something. So I had some of our own photos of that grid sent over, from the new KH-12."

"Where was it?"

"Well, it wasn't necessarily where you'd think. It was the Japanese island of Hokkaido. And the high-resolution grid missing was just the northern tip."

"So?"

"I went back and checked a series of KH-12 recon photos, taken over the last two years. There's something new there now, Michael. Just this last year or so. It's been partly camouflaged, but I think it's a new runway. Or launch facility. Or something. And the radar maps show some funny surface irregularities. At least *I* think they do. Nobody else at NSA . . ." She looked away. "But put it together. Maybe *that's* part of the treaty somehow, their secret protocol. Some joint—"

"A launch facility? Eva, that's impossible. The Japanese space program is all down on Tanegeshima Island, south of Tokyo. The island of Hokkaido is way up north. There's nothing up there but Holsteins and hay fields."

But, he thought suddenly, it's also just across from Sakhalin. The Soviet Far East. The place the party secretary who embezzled . . .

"This isn't hay fields, darling, believe me." Her voice seemed to drift out and blend with the rain. "Something you said this afternoon, that's what made it click. About the first man to leave the earth and soar into space . . ."

"You mean—"

"I didn't ask for this. Oh, Christ, how did I . . ." She paused again, uncertain. "You know, I finally think I've figured out what's happening, why it's so secret—the treaty, the protocol, cutting out their own intelligence. It's partly about space, all right. Has to be. Something's cooking, something they're eventually going to spring on the world like the first Sputnik."

"You still haven't decoded the damned thing."

"Okay, I'm guessing. But how's this? Somebody at the top, in the USSR, has decided to go for a giant gamble. To save their system, they've been forced to turn to some nutcakes in Japan who can loan them billions. And this project is part of it. The Soviets once cut a deal with Nazi Germany to buy time, so why not? The leadership needs time now desperately."

"And you think—?"

"Project Daedalus. That's the code name in the preamble. Think about it. You know what I believe? To get the money and technology they desperately need, the Soviets have had to cave in and do the unthinkable. Form a new alliance. Michael, they're about to start *rearming* Japan."

CHAPTER FOUR

Thursday 7:28 A.M.

"*Hai, so deshoo,*" Taro Ikeda, project director, bowed into the red telephone receiver, using that breathy, clipped speech all Japanese reserve for their superiors.

"*Kore wa honto ni muzakashi desu.* It has been difficult, but they have finally agreed on the revised schedule. In nine days—"

He paused to listen, then continued. "*Hai, so.* There is no other way. *Hai.* The Diet will never approve the treaty unless there is some dramatic symbol of the advantages of the alliance."

He halted. "*Hai,* security has been maintained here. With deepest respect, the problem would seem to be with your—" He paused again.

Now tiny beads of sweat were glistening on his brow. "*Hai,* we are ready. The vehicle is . . . *hai.*" He bowed again. "Of course, there will be no delay. The revised schedule is firm. *Hai,* Mino-sama, we—" He was bowing ever more rapidly into the phone. "*Hai,* we have pushed them as hard as we can." He bowed even deeper. "*Hai,* by tomorrow's report. Of course, Mino-sama. Thank you, *domo arigato gozaimashita. . . .*"

The line, a high-security satellite link connecting the Hokkaido facility to the Mino Industries Building in the Ueno section of Tokyo, had gone dead. Tanzan Mino, CEO of Mino Industries Group, had other matters to concern himself with.

Taro Ikeda repressed a tremble. The technical part, the project here on Hokkaido, was going well; what was happening on the Tokyo end? First the delay of the funds, and now a rumored breach of security. KGB had intercepted the protocol. That was the word from his informant close to the CEO in Tokyo.

Shigata ga nai, he thought; sometimes things can't be helped.

Taro Ikeda was proud he had been personally selected by the CEO to be project director for the top secret Hokkaido operation. He was fifty-four years of age, a graduate of Tokyo University Law School, a twenty-five-year veteran, now retired, of MITI, the Ministry of International Trade and Industry. He was, in short, a mover in the New Japan and he looked it—elegantly graying temples, tailored silk suits, a small mustache to set off his high cheeks. At one time he had been the inside choice for MITI vice minister, before the CEO offered him a chance to fulfill a vision no official source in the ministry could ever admit existed.

Overall, he told himself, the CEO should be pleased. He had carried out his own responsibilities flawlessly. And MITI was providing an unofficial umbrella of technical support, covering any unexpected requirements. Through this project the CEO had set into motion a plan that would soon alter dramatically Japan's place in the equation of world power.

Bushido, the Way of the Warrior. The element of surprise. No one outside Mino Industries knew what was really planned, not even the prime contractors for the project. Security every step of the way. And now the drama was ready, the curtain poised. Only a few more days, and a technological miracle would soar upward from the earth, symbolizing the first step in the realization of Japan's age-old ambition. The world would know the twenty-first century had arrived, the Japanese century. Mino Industries had made it possible.

The CEO's sense of timing was impeccable. Only last week he had approved Taro Ikeda's final briefing to Noboru Takahashi, executive director of the National Space Development Agency. NASDA, through contracts to the Space Systems Division of Mitsubishi Heavy Industries, was in charge of the major hardware of the Japanese rocket program. Takahashi was also an executive of the new Daedalus Corporation, an unofficial "consultant."

Together they had traveled to the agency's space center on Tanegeshima, the island six hundred miles south of Tokyo, to monitor the shakedown launch of Japan's new H-2 rocket series. Although that vehicle was far superior to both the American Titan 34D and the European Ariane 4, it was a technological dinosaur compared to *this* project. This was unlike anything the world had ever seen.

The project had begun over two years earlier, when he was still director of MITI's *Kokuki Buki-ka*, the Aircraft and Ordnance Section. An "anonymous" scenario—conceived by the CEO of Mino Industries Group, Tanzan

Mino—had arrived on his desk, detailing a revolutionary proposal. Every director in MITI had received a copy.

The eventual "consensus" ? It was *too* visionary, would aggravate Japan's already delicate relationship with America. The Liberal Democratic Party could never be seen to embrace such a project publicly.

Accordingly, MITI's parliamentary vice minister turned it down. Officially. But that was merely *tatame,* his "public face." Afterward the classified moves, the real moves, began. Perhaps, it was hinted, if the idea were "explored" outside regular government channels. . . . Top-secret feelers were sent to the Soviets.

With a green light, Tanzan Mino had immediately created the Daedalus Corporation, hiring away Taro Ikeda and forty-seven of his MITI aerospace engineers, the best and brightest, from *Kokuki Buki-ka.* Start-up financing had been provided by the CEO personally, with some matching contributions by the top executives of Japan's major *zaibatsu,* industrial groups. The scenario was an easy sell, since they all realized its payoff would be staggering. The only requirement was that it remain top secret until the appropriate moment, when the Diet would be formally notified. By that time, however, there would be no turning back. Everything would have to go forward as a package.

Under the CEO's direction, Taro Ikeda and his forty-seven MITI engineers had relocated here on Hokkaido to oversee a secret, fast-track project. Forty-seven. Perhaps, he sometimes mused, that number was no coincidence. Perhaps it was an unconscious act of historical resonance. Forty-seven brilliant young technicians, just like the forty-seven *ronin,* the *samurai* of the famous legend. Those *ronin* had bided their time for many years, living in obscurity and ignominy until the moment when they rose up in triumph.

Bushido. You must always make your opponent do battle on your own terms. And today money and technology were Japan's most powerful weapons. Why not use them strategically, the CEO had argued. The time had come to engage other unsuspecting nations with concentrated strength, in a forcible move to achieve Japan's long-term objectives. The Way of the Warrior.

Taro Ikeda surveyed his office, his personal command center. The space was appointed like the headquarters of a field marshall: a deep metallic gray with video screens along one wall permitting him continuously to monitor activities in every sector of the facility. And across the top of his black slate desk was marshalled a line of gray telephones with scramblers, each a secure direct line to the offices of one of the project's prime contractors.

The first was to Nagoya, to the head office of Mitsubishi Heavy Industries. Theirs was the initial contract let by the CEO after the project financing was in place. Indeed, Mitsubishi's Nagoya Aircraft Works was the ideal choice to manufacture the air-breathing turboramjets-scramjets for the vehicle. That conglomerate had produced over fifty thousand aircraft engines during the great Pacific war, and, more recently, their new Komaki North plant was responsible for the powerful oxygen-hydrogen engines that composed the first stage of the giant H-2 booster. The phone on his desk connected him directly to the office of Yoshio Matsunami, Mitsubishi's general manager for space systems. The massive scramjets for this project had been manufactured in Nagoya under a veil of total secrecy, then static-tested at their aeropropulsion test facility and individually shipped here to Hokkaido in unmarked railcars.

Another line connected him to the head office of Nissan's aeronautical and space division in Tokyo, already in charge of all solid rocket boosters for the Japan Institute of Space and Aeronautical Science. The CEO had hired their senior propulsion engineers to resolve problems connected with air-breathing combustion of liquid hydrogen.

The third connection was to Hitachi City, sixty miles from Tokyo. Hitachi, Limited manufactured the booster cases for the new H-2 vehicle, and their extensive experience with composite alloys at high-temperatures made them the obvious choice to create the hypersonic airframe.

There were other lines as well. The vehicle's inertial-guidance system and flight controls—both based on advanced Soviet designs—had been produced at Japan's National Aerospace Laboratory. Preliminary wind-tunnel tests had been assigned to the Kakuda Propulsion Center, whose rocket-engine development facilities were already being used to support NASDA's program in oxygen-hydrogen thruster R&D.

The last high-security line connected him directly to Tsukuba Space Center at Tsukuba Science City, forty miles from Tokyo, the nerve center for all Japanese manned space-flight research. Their clean-rooms and deep-space tracking facilities were comparable to any in the world, and their Fujitsu SX-10 supercomputer—which, with 128 processors for parallel processing, performed nine billion calculations per second—could provide real-time simulation of a complete hypersonic flight profile.

Feeling impatient now to begin the day, Taro Ikeda settled back and reached for the phones. Each contractor would give him a quick morning update, and then he would outline any further component tests or retrofitting as required. In truth, these exchanges had long since become scarcely more than rituals, since the project was all but completed. The major components had already been designed, delivered, and assembled. The contractors had been paid, the reports and evidence of their participation declared top secret and locked away from any possible prying eyes. All traces of the project had been safely secured.

There was, he reminded himself, only one major problem remaining. As part of the initial scenario, the Soviets had agreed to provide a laundered payment of one hundred million American dollars, to be used for Tanzan Mino's "incidental expenses" in the Liberal Democratic Party hierarchy. To avoid another Recruit-bribe fiasco like the one that brought down the prime minister in 1989, the money had to be scrupulously clean and totally untraceable.

But the funds had not arrived.

How the Soviets had secured the hard currency required outside of regular government channels, he could not imagine. There were even reports the money had

been secretly "embezzled" from certain slipshod minis-
tries. That it was, in fact, hot money.

But if those funds didn't come through within eight
days, fully laundered, the project would have to be put on
hold, as a matter of strategy, and precaution. The treaty
could not be placed before the Diet unless passage was
assured. Promises had to be kept.

What had happened to the money? Whatever it was, he
thought with a worried sigh, the CEO had better solve it
and soon. If he didn't, the whole project might have to be
put on hold until next year's session of the Diet, and their
secrecy would probably be impossible to maintain for another whole year. A disaster.

He had just completed the last call when he noticed a
flashing alert on the main computer terminal, advising him
that the morning's hypersonic test in Number One was
scheduled to begin at 0800 hours. He grunted and typed in
an acknowledgment. In his view it was a waste of time,
overkill. The SX-10's simulation had already taken them
further than they needed to go. But, all right, humor the
Soviet team. It would only require a morning.

His contractor briefings now out of the way, he transferred all communication channels to the computer
modems that lined the walls, then rose and walked back to
the small alcove at the rear of his office. He paused a
moment to calm his thoughts, then slid aside the *shoji*
screens to reveal what was, for him, the most important
room in the facility.

Here in the North Quadrant the CEO had constructed a
traditional teahouse, tatami-floored with walls and ceiling
of soft, fresh cedar and pine. In this refuge Taro Ikeda
performed an essential morning ritual, the brief medita-
tion that quieted his spirit. He knew well the famous adage
of swordsmanship, that the true master lives with his mind
in a natural state.

The challenge ahead would require all the discipline of a
samurai warrior, the Way of Zen. And the first rule, the
very first, was your mind must be empty, natural, unat-
tached, in order to succeed.

As he seated himself on the reed surface of the tatami,

zazen-style, he methodically began clearing his mind. The moment was sacred.

But then, drifting through unasked, came an admonition of the great Chinese military strategist Sun Tzu. "Intelligence is everything. You must know your opponent's plan even before he knows it himself."

It was true. The security for this project had been airtight, except for one minor breach. Someone in the Tokyo office had stupidly transmitted the final protocol over an unsecured satellite channel. It had been intercepted by Soviet intelligence.

Fortunately, the Russian blunderers had been unable to decipher the encryption. But someone—either in the KGB or the GRU—had been so desperate he had secretly enlisted the assistance of the U.S. National Security Agency's top cryptographer. It was a brilliant move, because NSA's supercomputers might eventually be able to break the code.

When Tanzan Mino learned of the breach, he had given orders that the NSA expert be neutralized, quickly, and the protocol retrieved. If it became public knowledge prematurely, the entire scenario could be destroyed. Now, happily, the NSA individual had been identified. The rest would be easy. An unfortunate price to pay, but a simple solution.

With that thought to comfort him, he gazed at the polished natural woods of the teahouse and let his mind drift into perfect repose.

Thursday 1:07 A.M.

The first round went wide, nicking the edge of the dolphin fresco. Vance listened, startled, at the explosion, at first thinking it was a sharp crack of thunder from outside. Then he heard the bullet sing into the dark, a high-pitched hiss. For a moment he wondered if he was dreaming, his mind adrift in the bloody myths of the palace. Then a second explosion flared from the direction of the archway, grazing his neck.

"Eva!" He threw his body across hers, slamming her against the alabaster portico. His free hand slapped awkwardly at the candle, crushing out the last sputter of flame. As he swung around, the empty ouzo bottle clattered into the dark, spinning, its revolving sound a beacon. Get it, he thought, and stretched across the stone to grope in the dark. Finally he felt the smoothness of the glass gliding at the edge of his reach. Slowly, carefully, his fingers circled the neck and he pulled it toward him.

The room was black now, its silence deep as a tomb. Then the gun flamed once more, and again, the two rounds ricocheting off the ancient walls somewhere around them. After that, silence returned, no sound except for the heave of breathing, whose he wasn't sure.

As he reached to quiet her, she whispered. "Michael, they want *me*." She tried to struggle up. "You've got to let—"

"No." He forced her back, whispering. "We can't leave when the party's just beginning."

Still grasping the neck of the bottle, he moved silently across the floor. The stone slabs were icy, while the night music of the rain seemed to come from another world.

He pressed against the wall, feeling for the doorway until he sensed a shadow slip past, slowly edging into the room. The muzzle of a pistol glinted against the flare of lightning outside, and he realized it was no more than a couple of feet away.

Now.

He swung the empty bottle with all his might, aiming for the tip of the muzzle.

The impact coursed up his arm as the bottle splintered against the metal. The intruder's startled intake of breath was masked by the clatter of the weapon against the stone floor.

He'll reach for it, Vance told himself. Lots of luck, pal.

He brought the fractured bottle upward with all his strength, aiming for the face. Although the figure was still formless, he let instinct guide his hand. The rough feel of shirt fabric brushed past his fingers and then the softness of flesh. A scream of surprise pierced the dark. Bingo.

Got the neck, he thought, and with a twist he drove the shattered bottle in. A warm wetness gushed against his hand.

I hit an artery. Blind luck.

The figure stumbled backward into the dim passageway. In a flash of lightning Vance saw hands clawing at a neck. Then came the sound of stumbling footsteps, retreating, and again silence.

Still gripping the sticky neck of the bottle, he bent down and began to search the floor. Near his feet he felt a hot muzzle and followed it upward to the still-warm grip. It was, he realized, a 9mm Baretta. He kept an identical chrome-plated model on the *Ulysses*.

All right, chum, now we'll have a rerun.

Grasping it with both hands, in firing position, he turned and peered out the open archway. The glimmers of distant lightning showed nothing but stone walls and an empty passageway. All he could discern was the vertical shaftway connecting the many levels of the palace.

He pressed against the cold stone wall and edged into the hallway leading toward the steps. Then he felt a sharp sensation against the ball of his left foot and reached down. A spent cartridge shell, still warm, lay up-ended on the icy floor.

Pasiphaë, he suddenly found himself thinking. It's as though Eva had lured the killer here, to this very room, like the white bull. And now he, they, who knows how many? want to kill us both. Somebody realized she knows too much.

He tried to control his breathing, straining to hear as the adrenaline continued to pump. From the staircase up above, the crickets had resumed their high-pitched medley. He listened as they chorused, the sounds of centuries past, their hymn to the rain. There was nothing else.

No, faint sounds . . . far above, maybe in the central court. Men were arguing. It was a heated exchange. He heard them grow louder, and with that the metallic click of another automatic weapon being readied. He waited, holding his breath, as the voices became even more animated.

What had happened? There must have been two, maybe even more.

Good time to find a new place to party.

He turned back to the silent room. It was, he suddenly realized, too silent. He felt his way back to the alabaster portico and reached across.

"Eva."

The quiet that followed told him he had been right; she'd panicked, run. No, he thought, she only wants to save you. She thinks she drew them here, and now she's trying to lure them away. Bad time to leave. Just when things were getting interesting.

He reached down and felt for the right-hand pocket of his trousers, still lying crumpled in a pile on the floor. Finally he slid his hand in and searched. The keys were gone. She had taken them, slipped away, left nothing. No trace. Only the smashed candle remained.

Annoyed, he located a box of hotel matches in his shirt and struck one. The room was empty, totally bare, its dolphins frisking alone in their placid sea. Across, on the other side, was the passageway leading through the queen's "bathroom." Beyond it lay the labyrinthine twists of the palace hallways. Perhaps by now Eva had found her way out and escaped. From the maze of Daedalus?

He tried to think as he finished donning his wet clothes in the dark. Eva clearly had gotten too close to somebody's plans. Where would she go?

Cautiously he moved out and began to mount the marble staircase, his rubber soles noiseless against the steps. The automatic was beginning to feel comfortable, even though it had nearly taken his life only minutes before. But he never trusted life to a chunk of metal, no matter how efficient.

Above him the voices still quarreled, and he found himself straining to catch the language. What was it? Greek? no, maybe Russian. Whatever it was, a fierce argument was raging. Again he tried to guess how many there were. He checked the metal clip and decided he had enough rounds to take them all—if he had to.

But that was getting ahead of the game. If she had

eluded them, then why bother? The best thing would be to try to slip past the courtyard, get through the fence, maybe join her at the car. Then they could move the party back to the hotel, keep the momentum. . . .

He moved carefully on through the hall of the procession, edging along the wall. Against his back he could feel the cold frescoes of the cup bearers, locked in their sterile march through time.

Then he heard another voice, this time female.

"Pazdolba! Delaetye vcyo, shto vam yugodno—mnye vcyo . . ."

It was Eva yelling in rapidfire Russian. Arguing, shouting orders? He couldn't make it out.

Now he edged through the final archway, grasping the Baretta. At that moment an eruption of gunfire splintered the silence, a fiery burst in the rainy night, while Eva was yelling for it to stop. It was over as quickly as it had come, but she was still screaming, swearing actually.

Whoever was there, they were no more than thirty feet away. But she was still safe. He could hear her curses, now half muffled in the storm.

Gingerly he edged on out through the entryway and stood at the edge of the courtyard, Baretta cocked and ready. A lighter blossomed in the rain, was brought upward to a cigarette, and momentarily framed a face.

Alex Novosty.

He was holding what appeared to be an Uzi, peering down at the glistening stones. Sprawled across from him were two bodies, both in dark raincoats. Now he was saying something to Eva in Russian, but she was staring past him, toward the entryway where Vance stood. In a flare of lightning their eyes locked, and he saw in hers anger and disbelief.

At that moment the flame of the lighter was cut short, but not before Novosty whirled and followed her gaze.

Instinctively Vance threw himself against the inside wall of the processionway. An instant later, the Uzi blazed again, drowning the sound of Novosty's challenge. He held his own automatic, barely breathing, while the rounds ricocheted against the stone walls. Was Eva part of it? What in *hell* . . .

Then her voice rose again, through the dark, a mixture of Russian and English. She was screaming at Novosty. Finally she called out.

"Michael." A pause, then her voice cracked. "You may as well stop the charade."

Charade? That wasn't the game they'd been playing. He decided to wait. The moment seemed part of a giant contest where none of the players wore team colors.

"Michael, old man, terribly sorry about that." This time the voice was Alex's. "It's been a trying night."

"Novosty," he yelled back. "I've got an automatic too, chum. Touch one hair of her head and you're history. I swear to God. Now let her go, and then we'll talk."

"My friend, my friend, I'm not keeping her." The hesitation in his voice belied his attempt at calm. "You don't understand. We have a problem here, very serious. And I am getting wet. Why don't you come out and let's discuss it somewhere dry."

"No way. You and I have a little catching up to do. Let her go. She's not part of it."

"Ah, but she is very much a part of it. Why do you think I am here tonight, risking everything? I need you now, Michael, more than ever. We are all in deep trouble because of her."

As Vance started to respond, he felt a glancing blow against the side of his neck, powerful, numbing. Awkwardly he stumbled forward, cursing his own stupidity. Of course! The man he'd wounded had merely disappeared into the palace labyrinth. He'd been back there somewhere, waiting. Now they'd guided him here with all the shouting.

He felt the Baretta slip from his grasp as his head slammed against the hard plaster of the fresco. His attacker was reaching for the gun, hands slippery with blood. There was hot breath against his face, the gurgle of labored breathing. It was a dying man with nothing to lose.

Now Alex was shouting at Eva through the rain, telling her to run for it.

Good, he thought, and turned to shove his fist into the face of the figure struggling to turn the pistol on him. The weapon fired, a lethal blast next to his ear, but the muzzle was still directed away. The round glanced off the stone archway and ricocheted down the hallway. As their struggle continued, he heard the sound of the Saab, its engine coughing to life.

Too bad. I'll miss the ride back.

With that he brought his knee against the assailant's groin, shoving him against the wall. Even then, though, he still could not see the face; it was darkened or swathed in a black cloth, he couldn't tell which.

Suddenly the passageway flared, and he looked up to see Novosty, rain-soaked, holding his small Italian lighter. In his left hand. In his right was the black metallic shape of the Uzi. Just then the attacker, drenched in blood, finally wrenched away the Baretta and was turning, trying to speak. Vance noticed, absently, that blood streamed from a gash across the side of his neck.

"I am sorry, my friend." Alex was lifting his weapon, calmly and with perfect precision. "Things have become complicated, but do not worry. I have handled it." And the Uzi erupted.

The dying man actually managed to squeeze off a round, a shot that went wild, as the impact of the Uzi slammed him against the wall. Then he fired again, almost a death tremor, and pitched forward.

Vance started to stretch for the pistol as it clattered across the floor toward him, but Novosty's voice sounded through the storm.

"Michael, do us both a favor, just leave it. I've killed enough men tonight. Three. And I knew them all. I am very weary of it, so please . . ." He was walking over, still holding the Uzi. "Let's have a drink and talk. This is very unsettling to my nerves."

"You and your friends screwed up a perfectly fine evening. You'd better have a good excuse." Vance watched him, very much wanting the pistol in his hands. Should he make a grab for it and take his chances?

"As I tried to tell you just now, it is very complicated."

Novosty was picking up the Baretta, grasping it carefully with a piece of wet cloth he'd ripped from the dead man's shirt. Then he looked up. "Are your prints on this?"

"Sort of figures, doesn't it? I borrowed it from *him*." He pointed down at the blood-soaked corpse between them.

"So we must clean it," he sighed. "What happened here tonight was a terrible accident, my friend. Obviously. How else can it be explained? There will be an international inquiry. We must now try and simplify the work of whoever has that unpleasant duty."

"You've got some explaining of your own to do. What about Eva?"

"Ah yes, Eva. She should have known better than to come here." He looked up. "Tonight simply need not have happened. It has always distressed me, the imprudence of some women." He sighed again. "I do not know if I can cover up this affair. It may well be the end for me."

"No kidding. Killing those two men out there may dampen your welcome in these parts."

"I regret to say it was necessary. They wanted to take her. But when I reasoned against it, they became suspicious. Which is why I had no choice."

Was Novosty here protecting Eva, he suddenly wondered? After all, there *was* age-old blood connecting them; Eva Borodin and Alex Novosty went back centuries together, centuries of Russian history. Aristocrats both, they shared family, pain, and glory from an age long before the October Revolution. But would she turn to him for refuge? No, not likely. She'd never be *that* desperate.

"Like you said this morning, Alex, it's unhealthy in this business to know too much. Tends to spoil all the interesting surprises."

"Yes, I agree. Ignorance is often bliss, I think that's the expression. But having solved one problem, I then faced another. What to do about them? Happily our friend here was available to help. I honestly think he would have died anyway from his neck wound." He glanced up. "Did you do this?"

"Spur of the moment."

"You are still good, Michael." He bent over and examined the severed artery again. "My compliments. You haven't lost it. An excellent job. I believe this incision would have been fatal." He turned back and smiled. "You have a surgeon's touch."

"Are you going to tell me who the hell he is, or do we play twenty questions?"

"He was . . . a professional acquaintance. This was most regrettable. For everyone. Mine was a distasteful task, I assure you." He sighed once more as he laid both weapons against the wall. "I will trust you, Michael. In turn you must trust me. And help me. We need to move this poor unfortunate to a more plausible location."

Vance now realized what Novosty was planning. He was about to pin the murder of the two outside on a dead man, this one. But who were they? Whoever this one was, one of his hands only had three fingers; the little finger had been cut away just below the knuckle.

"Forget it. I'm not going to help you do anything. I'm going to walk out of here, try and find Eva, and get the hell away from all this. You're a negative influence, Alex."

"My friend, be reasonable." He pointed toward the weapons. "We have work to do. We must remove all the prints from those, yours and mine, then create an accident."

"Look, you broke up a small party I had going here tonight. But now that you've ruined my evening, I damned sure don't plan to help you clean up."

"Michael, neither of us had anything to do with this unfortunate business. You or me. I wasn't even in Greece. It must have been some terrible misunderstanding among men of questionable livelihood. Tempers obviously flared. Who knows? Everybody is dead, so there can be no explanation beyond what appearances suggest." He shrugged and slipped his arms underneath the body. "Incidentally, they told me that Volodin was captured this morning. But he didn't talk. Instead he killed himself. So our situation is still secure."

"You must have a hearing problem. Maybe you ought to get it checked. I just told you it's Eva I'm going to help, not you. You can take the money and—"

"My friend, my friend, you are impetuous. Please. Everything is going as planned. But now we must move quickly." He smiled. "By the way, did you leave anything down below?"

"Just a broken bottle." Vance stared out into the rain.

"Then you might wish to make it disappear." He began dragging the body into the courtyard. "It will have prints. Glass preserves them perfectly."

He's right for once, Vance thought. Rubbing at his neck, a glimmer of pain intruding, he turned and retraced his steps into the dark, into the labyrinth.

As he descended, the chill of the palace enveloped him. He was bored with the place now, its ancient horrors and its modern ones. When the dark became too depressing, he extracted a folder of hotel matches and struck one. Its puny light flared and then expired, almost helpless against the blackness engulfing him.

The sound of crickets followed as he entered the bedroom of the queen once more. He paused a moment in the dark, then struck another match and walked over to the stone bed. There was the neck of the splintered bottle, covered with bloody fingerprints. Novosty was right about one thing: It would have opened a whole new area of inquiry. Nobody at Interpol had his prints on file, at least as far as he knew. But that wasn't good enough. Leave nothing to chance.

Carrying the fractured bottle, he began remounting the steps. This time he wanted the dark, needed it, to clear his mind, to mask the horrors of the palace. The confusion of the shootout swirled in his mind. Alex Novosty had killed three men as calmly as lighting a cigarette. Why? Was it just for the money?

When he emerged, distant lightning glinted on the ancient stones of the courtyard, contrasting brightly with the darkness below. For an instant the palace seemed magical all over again.

And there, perfectly choreographed on the wet pavement, was evidence of a lethal duel. Three bodies lay across from each other, two together and one opposite, gripping a weapon, his neck slashed. Perhaps it looked too pat, but who would know? Things happened that way.

The only participant missing was Aleksei Ilyich Novosty.

He gazed around, but he knew he would see nothing. Yes, Alex had gotten out quickly and cleanly. He'd always been hit and run.

All right, Vance told himself, now it's time to answer a few questions. Who the hell is looking for Eva, and who wants to silence her? Are they the same people?

Carefully, methodically he began to search the pockets of the two men Novosty had killed outside. He knew what he was looking for. The first appeared to be in his fifties, pockmarked cheeks, looked very Russian in spite of it all. He had a small Spanish Llama 9mm compact in a shoulder holster.

The other man was younger, though already balding. His cheeks were drawn, and blood was already staining around the two holes in his cheap polyester suit. His last expression was one of disbelief frozen in time. He's the back-up, Vance told himself, number two. That's always how they work. He should have stayed back home, maybe digging potatoes.

The passports were Bulgarian, a forgery, stamped with a Greek entry visa one week old. Port of entry: Athens. But they had to be KGB. No wonder Novosty was in trouble now. He was playing both sides of the game.

Finally he pulled around the head of the other man, the one swathed in black, the one who had almost killed him twice. This was the one he'd been saving till last, trying to guess.

A bloody, brutal face stared back at him, and through the torn shirt he could see a garish tatoo covering the back and chest. At first he couldn't believe it, so he lit a match and cupped it against the rain while he ripped open the rest of the cloth to be sure. History swirled around him.

Irezumi. The rose-colored dragon-and-phoenix tattoo was regulation issue—insignia of a *kobun* of the right-wing ultranationalist Mino-gumi, the foremost Yakuza crime syndicate of Japan. He knew it well.

CHAPTER FIVE

Thursday 7:30 A.M.

Andrei Petrovich Androv, director of propulsion systems, gazed out across the windy strait, feeling the chill of the sea air cut through his fur-lined trench coat.

Physically, he was almost mythic, a giant from Grimms' fairy tales. He had a heavy face nature should wish on no man, tousled gray hair, bushy eyebrows eternally cocked in skepticism, and a powerful taste for Beethoven's string quartets, which he played incessantly in the instrument room. He bore, in fact, more than a passing resemblance to that aging, half-mad genius. Now seventy-one, he, too, possessed a monumental mind and was acknowledged worldwide as the founding intellect behind the Soviet space program.

Yes, he was thinking, this location had been ideal. Here in remote Hokkaido they had constructed a high-security facility surrounded by wind-swept wilderness—virgin forests and snow-covered volcanos. Even for him, a man long used to the harsh winters of Baikonur, the almost Siberian weather along this coast was intimidating. This was the most isolated, austere, and yes, lonely spot he'd ever known.

But it was the perfect site. Mino Industries had insisted, rightly, on this northernmost point of Japan for the facility, here in a national park on Cape Soya, fifty kilometers west of Wakkanai. The facility itself had been constructed entirely underground, excavated beneath this rocky northern coast in order to be secure and invisible to satellite reconnaisance, both Soviet and American. Such excessive precautions, hardly a problem in the New Mexico desert when the first atomic bomb was tested, were the order of the day in this new era of space photography. Nowadays you even had to find ways to mask telltale waste heat expulsion, which always betrayed an unmistakable infra-red signature.

In that respect, too, their choice of this spot was strategic, with the freezing currents of the La Perouse Strait between northern Hokkaido and Sakhalin providing a continuous and thermally stable 12 degrees Celsius feed for the heat exchangers. Only the ten-thousand-meter test runway could not be concealed full-time, but it had been carefully camouflaged and was used only at night.

A massive breaker crashed against the rocks at the north end of the shore, sending ice-flecked spray upward into the morning mist. As he watched the freezing cloud and felt its ice collecting on his cheeks, he glanced at his watch. It was seven-forty. He took one last survey of the choppy gray sea and turned back. His daily morning walk down to the shore had achieved its purpose: His mind was as sharp as the icy wind whistling through the rocks. He needed to be at Number One by 0800 hours, when the final test run was scheduled to begin.

As he did every morning, he retraced the concrete steps that led down to the stainless steel entry door leading into the West Quadrant. When he reached it, he inserted a coded plastic card into the slot, pronounced his name into the black microphone flush with the metal doorframe, and signaled the TV eye. Two seconds later a simulated voice from the computer granted him access, the door sliding aside.

He nodded to the guards, then moved on down the long neon-lit, gray hallway. When he reached the unmarked door of Number One, he paused to listen. The whine of the fans was still a high growl as the engineers ran through the warm-up preparatory to bringing its six 25,000-horse-power motors to full power. Contenting himself that vibration in the fan housings remained at acceptable levels, he flashed his ID to the guard, inserted his magnetic card, and shoved open the door.

Without a word, he marched to his desk by the main video panel and slipped a scratched old Melodiya disk onto his ancient turntable. Moments later, the first movement of Beethoven's Quartet in A Minor boomed from the speakers.

"We are ready to switch on the laser field, Comrade Doktor Androv." A young Soviet technician approached gingerly. "If you wish, we can direct the holograms here to the master terminal."

"More of your pretty pictures?" He was examining the data on the video screens. Then he nodded. *"Da. Ya gotov.* When you will."

As he stared at the screens, he again found himself growing pensive. The project was all but finished now. His lifelong dream.

He silently counted their breakthroughs. The new material being used for the leading edges and scramjet struts, a proprietary titanium alloy coated with a ceramic skin, had turned out to be much lighter than aluminum and eight times as strong. Full-scale sections of the leading edges of the wings and the engine struts had been subjected to ten-minute blasts of 3,500 degrees Fahrenheit air at Mach 7 in the high-temperature tunnel with no deformation or structural failure.

Then the turboramjet-scramjets, four meters in diameter and nine meters long, had all been given full-scale static tests at the aeropropulsion facility in the south, where they were operated to Mach 8 at temperatures ranging from minus 100 to over 1900 degrees Fahrenheit. Massive refrigeration units and gas heaters had been used to achieve the temperature range, while liquified air was pumped into the intakes to duplicate a complete hypersonic duty cycle.

Maybe, he thought, they *were* ready for a full-scale test flight. Only one problem remained: a hint of supersonic wave drag the low-temperature helium wind tunnel had shown could develop behind the leading edges. He had ordered the project director to run a computer simulation examining the performance of two new ceramic spoilers, modified canard foreplanes, and the preliminary results indicated the drag would be effectively damped. Still, he was determined to test that design modification with a full run-up here in Number One, the massive hypersonic tunnel that contained a ten-meter scale model of the vehicle.

As he sat thinking, he neglected to acknowledge the arrival of the project director, now advancing down the concrete steps that led from the steel entry door.

"Dobriy utro, Doktor Androv." Taro Ikeda's good-morning greeting was heavily accented. *"Kak pashaviatye?"*

"Khoroshau." Andrei Petrovich Androv nodded absently, still engaged in his thoughts. *"Dobriy utro."*

"Today I have more good news," Ikeda continued as he headed for the coffee urn. "My 0730 briefing included a report that during the night our Tsukuba team completed a simulation of the aerodynamic performance of your suggested modification all the way to Mach 25. Just as you envisioned, leading-edge deformation and vortex bursts were reduced to values well within the acceptable envelope." He looked back. "Which makes me question whether we really need to proceed with this morning's run."

"Your SX-10 only tells us how a fuselage performs if airflows are ideal," Androv replied. "At hypersonic temperatures and velocities air doesn't behave predictably, like a perfect gas. Fluid dynamics models can only give us approximations of actual characteristics." He glanced up from the video control panel, his face determined. "It is my son, Yuri, who will be in the cockpit of these vehicles, and my experience is you never put your faith in simulations. In the hypersonic regime, computer simulations are just guesswork, a shortcut not worth a *drozhky* driver's fart."

"As you wish," Ikeda replied evenly, taking his first sip of coffee.

In truth, Andrei Androv did not dismiss simulations out of hand. He knew their Fujitsu supercomputer was truly a marvel, capable of replicating the aerodynamic characteristics of a given fuselage component, modifying it, testing it, over and over millions of times, iterating to the optimum design in almost the twinkling of an eye.

In every respect the high technology available here was astonishing. Take their hypersonic wind tunnel. Its laser probes shone thin slices of coherent light through the swirling air currents, revealing complexities otherwise hidden amid whorls of turbulence. These data were then enhanced through holography, which used the laser light to create colored 3-D representations of the flow around the model. Finally those holograms were fed into the supercomputer and analyzed from all angles.

This project would have been impossible anywhere else on earth. But here, the foreign team had created a feather-light hypersonic airframe that used turbo-ramjets for horizontal takeoff and then changed their geometry into fuel-injected supersonic combustion ramjets, or scramjets, which combusted fuel and atmospheric oxygen using an internal shock wave instead of conventional compressors to achieve orbital velocity, Mach 25. It was his dream come true.

"Brief me again on the simulation." Androv turned back to Ikeda. "You say you went all the way to our maximum design objective?"

"We ran through the entire flight profile in real time," the other man replied. "There were no stability problems whatsoever. Either during the power-up or during the switch-over to scramjet engine geometry at Mach 4.8."

"Encouraging, encouraging." Androv turned back to his video panel as the fans continued to accelerate. The violins of the A Minor quartet, his favorite of all Beethoven's late works, washed over the room. "All the same, we must run a complete sequence here for any design alterations."

He then fell silent, studying the screens. *Mach 25.* That was—yes—almost seventeen thousand miles per hour. A velocity greater than any existing missile. And it was air-breathing!

Their supercomputer's revolutionary aerodynamic design had made it possible. Problem: at velocities higher than Mach 5 unprecedented airflows were required, due to heat buildup in the fuel-injection struts and the shortage of oxygen at rarified altitudes. Solution: the entire under-side of the vehicle had been shaped to serve as an exten-sion of the intakes for the twelve massive scramjets. The fuselage of the plane itself was going to act as a giant funnel, scooping in air. And it had appeared to work, at least in the computer. Then finally the Japanese engineers had perfected the liquid-air-cycle process, permitting the cryogenic hydrogen fuel to be used to liquify a portion of the incoming air and inject it under high pressure into the engine. The final, essential breakthrough.

Andrei Androv was both an idealist and a pragmatist. In Russia you had to be. That education began almost half a century earlier when, as a student, he had been on hand to assist in the first free flight of a Russian-made liquid fuel rocket, at an army base just outside Moscow. He had experienced the exhilaration of a new frontier, and plunging himself into the new science of rocketry, he had become a self-taught expert who published theoretical works read and praised by men three times his age.

Ironically, therefore, Andrei Petrovich Androv had not enjoyed the luxury of being ignored, as the American rocket pioneer Goddard had been. Joseph Stalin, always paranoid, decided that the rocket researchers' "fireworks" were "dangerous to the country." Consequently, Andrei Petrovich Androv was arrested, interrogated at Butyrskaya Prison in Moscow, and dispatched on the Trans-Siberian Railroad to a convict coal mine on the Pacific coast.

Eventually the political winds shifted. As a recognized rocket expert, he was part of the 1946 Soviet team that shipped German scientists and V-2 launchers back to Russia. Finally, under Khrushchev, he rose to genuine prominence, since that general secretary believed that only rockets, not manned aircraft, had the range to drop bombs on the U.S. Nikita S. Khrushchev put Andrei Androv in charge of all Soviet rocketry, and Andrei Androv put Russia in space.

He'd been in charge of constructing the sprawling Baikonur Cosmodrome, near Tyuratram in Kazakhstan, central Asia, still the world's largest space center. From it he orbited the world's first satellite, Sputnik, and the world's first astronaut, Yuri Gagarin. He knew the byways of that top secret facility almost better than he knew his own living room—the gantry systems, the fueling apparatus, the clean rooms, the rocket assembly areas, the sectors where satellites were readied. Most recently, in 1987, he had been in charge of the successful first test launch of the most powerful vehicle the world had ever seen—the Energia, propelled by liquid hydrogen engines capable of lifting a hundred-ton space platform into orbit.

Also during that time his only son, Yuri Andreevich, had become the Soviet Union's leading test pilot. Yuri was rarely home, and then, nine years ago, Andrei Androv's wife had died of pneumonia. Isolated in the long, snowy nights at Baikonur, he'd consoled himself with string quartets, his studies of classical Greek, and his designs, his dreams of the ultimate space vehicle.

But he knew Russia would never be able to build it alone. Soviet computer and materials technology already was slipping behind those of the West.

He grimaced to think how his country had been brought to today's humiliating state of affairs, reduced to bargaining with foreigners like Arabs in a *medina*. Eventually, though, pragmatism had overruled all. Underlying this bizarre new alliance was one simple reality: the USSR needed Japanese high technology desperately. And it needed that technology *now*.

It had begun two years earlier, when the president himself had paid a surprise secret visit to the space complex at Baikonur, supposedly to review the Energia launch schedule. That, however, was merely the official excuse. He actually had an entirely different agenda.

Without saying why, he had invited his old friend Andrei Petrovich Androv to join him at the secluded hunting lodge where he was staying—to talk, one-on-one, about the future of Soviet science. As that long snowy evening wore on, wind whistling through the log walls and pine smoke clouding the air, their conversation had turned to hard truths and blunt language.

In vino, veritas. By midnight, the uniformed bodyguards outside were stamping their heavy boots to keep warm, and Andrei Petrovich and Mikhail Sergeevich were both drinking vodka directly from the bottle, had flung its tinfoil cap onto the rough-hewn boards of the cabin's floor. By then, too, the revered Andrei Petrovich Androv was boldly speaking his mind.

"Mikhail Sergeevich, time has run out for Russia. There is nothing to buy, almost nothing to eat, and prices are soaring. There is so much corruption you will not leave a Soviet hospital alive unless you've bribed everyone, right down to the drunken orderlies. And those bribes can't be money. Who wants rubles? They are worthless. These days you have to bribe with vodka." He'd laughed sadly, then picked up an old copy of *Pravda* there by the fireplace, waved it in the air, and tossed it into the crackling flames. "When we start cooperatives, they are immediately taken over by our new mafia, Russia's ruble millionares. Everything—"

"Perestroika will succeed in time, Andrei Petrovich," the president had insisted perfunctorily, still not having explained why they were meeting. "We are moving as rapidly as circumstances will permit. The bureaucracy—"

"Perestroika!" Androv had roared back. "Have you heard the latest joke from Moscow? Perestroika is like a country where everyone is switching from driving on the left side to the right side—gradually. Our half-measure concessions to a market economy have produced the worst of both systems. We now have a land with socialist initiative and capitalist conscience." He paused to laugh again, then sobered. "And soon, very soon, we're going to find ourselves in the technological Third World. We need a vision. Even more, we need hard currency, and Western technology *now*. And we need massive amounts. Nothing less can save us."

That was when the president had nodded silently, then lifted a top secret document from his black leather briefcase. He explained that it was a proposal from a consortium of foreigners. He wanted Andrei Androv's honest assessment.

"Read this, Andrei Petrovich," he said, passing it over, "and tell me what you think. It may well be a terrible thing even to consider, but I must know your view. You, my old friend, are one of the few men I know I can trust. This proposal, can it work?"

As he squinted by the flickering light of the fire, Andrei Petrovich Androv almost couldn't believe what he was reading. Among other things, the dream he had dreamed so long was there, his for the taking. The dream of a bold venture in space achieved with a whole new level of technology.

Along with it, the Soviet Union would receive everything it needed. The foreigners would provide billions and billions in long-term, low-interest loans and a flood of subsidized consumer goods to erase the pain of perestroika, providing the president with the badly needed financing, not to mention popular support, he needed to bring it off. But there were price tags, several of them. The first would be total access to all Soviet space and propulsion technology. That component would actually make sense technically, but the others were higher, much higher. Could it be done? Should it be done?

"What do you think, Andrei Petrovich?" the president had finally spoken, his voice a whisper above the snap of embers and the howl of wind. "Do we dare?"

The room had fallen silent for a long moment. Was this some kind of trap? he almost wondered, like the old days. No, he'd quickly concluded, this time Russia was different. He would have to trust Mikhail Sergeevich. Most of all, though, he was holding his life-long ambition in his hand. At last he replied, hope mingled with apprehension.

"I think we have no choice." He had looked up at the president's troubled eyes. *"You* have no choice."

"Unfortunately, I think you are right." He had sighed and turned his gaze to the blackness outside the snow-banked window. *"Ve tyomnuyu noch, ya znayu.* Yes, Andrei Petrovich. On this dark night, I finally know what we must do."

After one final vodka, they had set about devising the scenario that would change the world forever. . . .

The airflow around the model continued to accelerate, while laser holograms of its complex aerodynamics were now being converted by the computer into multi-colored graphic art. Androv watched the wall-size liquid crystal display screen in the control room begin generating a vivid depiction of the streams whirling past the model, simulating the incremental stages of hypersonic climb. It was like watching a hallucination, he thought, as colors swirled around the fuselage of an object seemingly composed of 3-D lines and curves.

"We are now at Mach 6, Comrade Doktor Androv." The voice of a Soviet technician interrupted his thoughts. "The laser data show that the supersonic wave drag peaks at Mach 3.8, then subsides. Your new canard foreplanes appear to be working, at least for this portion of the flight envelope."

Androv studied the screen, noncommittal. "Thus far it would appear to be so. Perhaps the SX-10 was correct. All the same, at Mach 7, I want to switch on the enhancer, then capture those data and analyze them to be doubly sure."

The hypersonic enhancer permitted wind-tunnel burst tests at far higher velocities than a conventional facility could achieve. More high tech.

"There could still be a problem," Androv continued, "when the vortex of air currents shed from the nose of the fuselage encounters the shock waves from the wings, particularly around Mach 11." He turned to Ikeda. "Those vortexes have been responsible for significant damage to several American space shuttles during reentry phase. I need to see the data."

"As you wish." The director walked to the thick glass window that looked out onto the model suspended in the airstream. The crew of technicians hovered over the controls, watching for any signs of vibration. He studied the screens for a few moments, then spoke quietly to the head of the technical team, an intense young man in spectacles. This lieutenant turned and passed the order to his colleagues, who nodded gravely and stationed themselves at the switches.

Above the roar, a brilliant arc of electricity suddenly exploded just in front of the nose of the model, adding an additional burst of pressure at Mach 6 to the velocity already passing across. It was a blinding, microsecond pulse that momentarily boosted simulated vehicle velocity to

Mach 13. The lasers registered the data, then passed it directly, via microwave link, into the memory banks of the powerful SX-10 operating hundreds of miles away.

Seconds later the turbulence data appeared in visual form on the liquid crystal screen above them. As the colored numbers flashed, a cheer went up from the normally somber technicians.

"Still no sign of any wave drag outside the theoretical envelope, not even at Mach 13," the young head-technician beamed.

"Just as we simulated," Ikeda noted quietly.

This time even the grave Androv smiled. "I must congratulate all of you." He was rising from his chair, the central one facing the main controls.

"Then I will order the modification installed," Ikeda nodded, "if you formally authorize it."

"Authorized. I think you are right. Perhaps we *are* ready for a hypersonic test flight." Androv reached to switch off his turntable. "I would like to go down to the hangar now myself, in fact. Perhaps celebrate this moment with a glass of tea."

"Of course." Ikeda spoke quickly to his Japanese technicians, then followed the Russian out the door.

The hallways were a connected maze of brilliantly lighted and scrupulously clean tunnels. They moved down the main corridor to the central checkpoint, then turned and entered the South Quadrant, passing the various assembly sections. Those sectors were mostly quiet now, since the final work had been completed several weeks earlier.

Androv said nothing as they walked toward the doorways connecting the South Quadrant with the underground hangar. He merely whistled a portion of the third movement of the A Minor quartet, Beethoven's hymn of thanksgiving in the Greek, Lydian mode. He recalled that the English writer Aldous Huxley had once suggested that particular movement was proof of God's existence.

Was there a God? He wasn't sure. The only miracles he knew of on this earth were performed by men. He was on the verge of performing one himself.

The history of space exploration had been played out entirely in his lifetime. He himself had been the architect of much of that progress. But putting a man into space remained an expensive and dangerous proposition. Launch vehicles still exploded with alarming regularity. Man was trapped on this planet. God was still in the heavens.

Man's hope of reaching God at will required a special creation, one that could taxi off a runway just like a normal aircraft, then accelerate to hypersonic speeds, reaching low-earth orbit. An air-breathing space vehicle. Its potential for the peaceful exploration of near-earth space defied imagination.

Peace. All his life, Andrei Petrovich Androv had worked in the shadow of war. Now, at last, he had created the ultimate symbol of peace.

The entry to the hangar was secured, but when the guards saw Dr. Androv and the project director approaching, they saluted and punched in the codes on the locks. Moments later the heavy steel doors slid aside, revealing the brilliant lights of the hangar. It was cavernous, over a hundred feet high, with gantries now standing idle along the walls. White-coated technicians swarmed over the two prototypes, checking the final seals, while others were on twenty-foot-high trucks servicing the engines.

Looming above them were what appeared to be two giant prehistoric birds, streaks of gleaming silver over three hundred feet in length, with pen-sharp noses that dipped rakishly downward. Androv paused to admire them a moment, marveling in spite of himself. The long, sleek lines swept back in a clean curve, without the interruption of a windshield. The "cockpit," in fact, was deep inside the nose, where shock waves would not impact the computer guidance system. From the nose its lines burgeoned into a sharp, clean fan, and beneath the two abbreviated wings were suspended twelve massive turboramjet-scramjets. They had already been certified at Mach 4.5. In ten days one of these vehicles would achieve the ultimate. Mach 25, seventeen thousand miles per hour.

The Americans had code-named their fledgling design

for a hypersonic space plane—still at least a decade away—the X-30. But no such mundane designation would satisfy Andrei Petrovich Androv, devoted disciple of the ancients. He had long believed the Americans were high-tech vulgarians with no poetry in their soul, no sense of history.

Across the towering tail assembly of both aircraft was an insignia that symbolized the joining of two of the world's great superpowers, a double ax. And along their titanium-composite fuselage was lettered a single word, in Cyrillic characters. Andrei Androv had insisted on that name, in celebration of the first human ever to soar above the earth, the dream of ancient man. Now, he had declared, four thousand years later, there was another dream, his dream, a hypersonic vehicle that could loft man directly into space from anywhere on the planet.

He had dreamed that dream. And the Mino Industries Group had permitted him to pick the name for the creation that would realize it, for the miracle that would master time and space, the earth itself . . .

DAEDALUS

Thursday 9:16 A.M.

Yuri Androv stood at the far end of the flood-lit hangar, staring up at the underbelly of *Daedalus I* and thinking. This morning's run-up in the centrifuge had gone well. At last he was convinced there was no physiological barrier to hypersonic flight, at least none he couldn't handle. The scramjets had all been put through their paces at the aero-propulsion facility. On the test stand, at least, they met their specifications.

Yes, he was thinking, this plane just might do it. He would ease through the Mach 4.8 barrier slowly, then convert to scramjet geometry, switch to liquid hydrogen, and go full throttle. It was scary, sure, but you only lived once. Fuck the danger.

The prospect was exhilarating and chilling. He looked up, again awed. Even for someone who'd seen and flown them all, this was an inspiring creation. Not only was it easily the most technologically advanced flight vehicle in the world, it also was stunningly beautiful.

Right now, however, there were two simple problems: first, without a hypersonic test flight nobody could really be sure it would do what it was supposed to; second, as of now both prototypes still belonged to Mino Industries and would continue to belong to Mino Industries until the final treaty and agreement were signed.

Actually, taking the *Daedalus* hypersonic might be the least of the project's worries. That was the part he knew how to handle. The unknowns lay in another direction entirely, the strategic direction.

Strategically, he still didn't trust Russia's new partner. From what he'd heard, the conditions demanded in return for all their high technology had been heavy, and that was just the short-term price. The long-term cost might be even greater. Was the Soviet Union about to become the financial and technological captive of a shadowy group of foreigners, men whose identities remained, even now, shrouded in secrecy? Was this a Faustian bargain?

Just then he noticed the doors at the far end of the hangar slide open and two men in white lab coats enter. Perfect timing, he thought. Even at that distance he knew immediately who they were: the joint venture's two top technical officers: his father, Andrei Petrovich Androv, and Taro Ikeda, the project director for the Japanese team. The men held equal authority. Supposedly. But in fact all the real decisions on this project were being made by somebody else entirely. The shots were actually being called from a skyscraper in Tokyo, by a mysterious CEO known as Tanzan Mino.

Now Ikeda and the elder Androv were headed his way. As he watched Ikeda, he felt himself involuntarily stiffen. Perhaps his unease about the man was his intuitive, right brain working, trying to tell him something. But what? All communications with the CEO were channeled through Ikeda. Fair enough, he told himself, he was accustomed to secrecy. Maybe Japanese industrialists were as careful about protecting their asses as the Soviet *nomenklatura* were. Maybe it was just part of the landscape here too. But still . . .

"*Strastvitya,* Yuri Andreevich." Ikeda smiled, extending his pale hand as he simultanously bowed. "*Kak pashaviatye?*"

"*Khoroshau. Spahcebo.*" He shook Ikeda's hand, then nodded toward his father. "If this is a good time, I'd like to discuss the scramjet power-up sequence with Dr. Androv for a few moments."

"If it's anything serious, then perhaps we should all confer with the prime contractors," Ikeda responded smoothly. "Right now, in my office. In fact, I was just on the phone with—"

"No need to bring them in. Just a few technical items, nothing more."

"Yuri Andreevich." Ikeda smiled and bowed again, his eyes trying to display a warmth they clearly did not possess. "Every issue here is of importance to us all. If—"

"Not every nut and bolt," he interrupted. "I just have some sequencing questions, that's all."

Ikeda bowed once more, quickly. "You know we are all depending on you. No one in Japan has the experience to take up a plane like this. At least not at this stage of the project. So be aware that any matter weighing upon the success of your test flight, or your safety—" he flashed another quick, concerned smile "—is naturally of gravest concern to me, and to the CEO."

"Then you should be glad to hear the power-up simulation in the centrifuge this morning took me right through Mach 9.8 with no problems. Which means the scramjet ignition sequence looks like a go."

"Congratulations." Ikeda nodded.

"One last thing. I'll be sending a memo to Engineering about a modification of the cockpit, to permit more latitude in the seat. Nothing major. I think we could still reduce vascular stress in the high-G regime."

Andrei Androv noticed the look of concern on his son's face. "Yuri, you seem troubled. This morning, did anything—?"

"Of course, send Engineering your memo by all means,"

Ikeda interjected. "I'll personally see it's taken care of. We want nothing to go wrong. Not even the smallest—"

"Good. That's all I want." Yuri turned and wrapped his arm around his father's aging shoulders, gently urging him in the direction of the trucks stationed beneath the silver nose of *Daedalus I.* He wanted to get rid of Ikeda so he could talk. After they moved a few feet, he yelled back over his shoulder. "But wait on the decision till you read my memo."

"As you wish." Ikeda nodded farewell. "I'll be in my office until 1300 hours if we need contractor input."

Which meant, Yuri knew, that no further communication with him was permissible after that time. Technical consultations were only held during mornings. Afternoons he seemed to have other pressing matters to attend to.

"Yuri, the run-up in Number One went well this morning. I think we've finally eliminated the supersonic wave drag." The elder Androv was heading over to check the hydraulic lifts supporting the landing gear and its heavy 22-ply retractable tires. Then he glanced back and smiled. "I'm beginning to believe in miracles. We might just succeed."

"*If* those damned scramjets up there," he pointed skyward, "actually achieve ignition when they're supposed to."

"I've studied the static-test data carefully. At the propulsion facility they routinely achieved ignition at Mach 4.8. The numbers were there and they looked all right. Temperature regime, pounds thrust, all the rest."

What's really happening, Yuri thought suddenly, is they've taken *our* engineering design and built it. But what if we're just being used somehow, having our brains picked, our expertise stolen? Then what?

He said nothing, though, just listened quietly as the older man continued.

"Also, the new ceramic composite they've come up with for the fuel injection struts was heated to thirty-five hundred degrees Fahrenheit and repeatedly stress-tested. Those data were particularly impressive. You know, the struts have always been the Achilles heel for a scramjet, since the fuel has to be injected directly through them into the combustion chamber. They have to withstand shock waves, and thermal stresses, far beyond anything ever encountered in a conventional engine. Nobody else has ever come up with a material that can do it. Not us, not the Americans, not anybody. But now, their high-temperature materials and liquid air cycle have finally made the scramjet concept a reality. The last roadblock is gone." He looked up, still marveling. "All we or the Americans can do is make engineering drawings of those engines, just pictures."

"I hope you're right. But when we switch over from JP-7 to liquid hydrogen, nobody knows what can happen. It's never been done before."

"Are you really worried?" The old man studied him.

"Damned right I am. Who wouldn't be?" He looked around at the milling Japanese technicians, then lowered his voice. "And I'll tell you something else. There're other things around here worrying me too, maybe even more. Something about this project is starting to feel wrong."

"What do you mean?" Andrei stared.

"I'm beginning to suspect . . . I don't know. So far it's just a sense, but—"

"Yuri, let me tell you a hard fact," the elder Androv interjected. "Like it or not, this project is the only chance the Soviet Union has to ever own a vehicle like this."

"That may be true, but if we—"

"Remember the sad fate of the TU-144," he went on, "the supersonic passenger plane we built based on some engineering drawings for the Concorde we managed to get hold of. We copied it, but we got it wrong, and in 1973 we had that horrible tragedy at the Paris Air Show, when it crashed in a ball of fire. That was the end of it. We failed, and it was humiliating. The Soviet Union couldn't even build a supersonic passenger jet. The real truth is, we didn't have the computers we needed to design it." He looked up, smiling. "But now, all that humiliation will be undone."

Yuri suddenly realized his father was being swept up in his dreams. The same way he sometimes got lost in those damned string quartets, or reading Euripides in the original Greek. He was going off in his fantasy world again. He couldn't see that maybe he was being used.

"Have you ever wondered where this project is going to lead? Where it has to lead?"

"It will lead the way to peace. It will be a symbol of cooperation between two great nations, demonstrating that the human spirit can triumph."

"*Moi otyets*, it could just as well 'lead the way' to something else entirely. Don't you realize what's happening here? We're giving away our thruster engineering, Russia's leading technology. It's the one area where we still lead the world. We've just handed it over . . . for the price of one fucking airplane. And even if we eventually get our hands on these prototypes, we can't build more without begging the materials from them. We can't fabricate these composite alloys in the Soviet Union."

"But this is a joint venture. Everything will be shared." He smiled again, his face gnomelike beneath his mane of white hair. "It will also give us both a chance to overcome the lead of Europe and America in commercial passenger transport in the next century. That's what this is all about. The future of nonmilitary aviation, it's right here."

"Do you really believe that?" He stifled a snort of incredulity. "Don't you see what this vehicle really is? Let me tell you. It's the most deadly weapons delivery system the world has ever seen. And we're showing them how to build it, even testing it for them to make sure it'll perform."

"The *Daedalus* will never be a military plane. I would never have participated if I thought—"

"Exactly. That's what they want us to believe. But it sure as hell could be. And Mino Industries will be the only company on earth that can actually build more of them." He sensed it was useless to argue further. Nothing mattered to Andrei Petrovich Androv except what he wanted to believe. At this point, nothing could be done to expose the dangers, because nobody on the Soviet team would listen.

Or maybe there *was* something. Why not make a small revision in the test flight? Once he was aloft, what was anybody going to do? He would be up there, alone. If he could get around their flight computer, he might just show the world a thing or two. He'd been thinking about it for weeks now.

"All right." He turned back. "If this thing is supposedly ready to fly, then I'll fly it. But get ready for some surprises."

"Yuri, what are you planning?"

"Just a small unscheduled maneuver." The hell with it, he thought. "They've got seven days, and then I take it up . . . and power-in the scramjets. I'm ready to go. Tell Ikeda to prepare to have liquid hydrogen pumped into the tanks."

"But that's not how we've structured the test schedule." Andrei examined him, startled. Yuri had always been fiery, but never irrational. "We need ten—"

"Fuck the schedule. I'm going to take this vehicle hypersonic in a week, or they can get themselves another test pilot." He turned away. "Reschedule, or forget it. We don't have much time left. Once all the agreements are signed—"

"Yuri, I don't like this." His eyes were grave. "It's not—"

"Just tell them to get *Daedalus I* prepped. I think these bastards that call themselves Mino Industries have a whole agenda they're not telling us about. But I'm about to rearrange their timetable."

CHAPTER SIX

Thursday 2:51 A.M.

A very wet, very annoyed Michael Vance rapped on the door of Zeno Stantopoulos's darkened *kafeneion*. He'd walked the lonely back road into Iráklion in the dark, guiding himself by the rain-battered groves of plane trees, olive, and wild pear, trying to figure out what in hell was happening.

To begin with, members of the intelligence services of major nations didn't go around knocking each other off; that was an unwritten rule among spooks. Very bad taste. Maybe you tried to get somebody to talk with sodium pentathol or scopolamine, but guns were stupid and everybody knew it. You could get killed with one of those things, for godsake.

So this operation, whatever it was, was outside the system. Good. That was the way he had long since learned to work.

There was a lot on his mind, and the walk, the isolation, gave him a chance to think over some of the past. In particular, the austere Cretan countryside brought to mind an evening five years ago when he'd traveled this little-used route with his father, Michael Vance, Sr. That occasion, autumn brisk with a first glimmering of starlight, they'd laughed and joked for much of the way, the old man occasionally tapping the packed earth sharply with his cane, almost as though he wanted to establish final authority over the island and make it his, once and for all. Finally, the conversation turned serious.

"Michael, don't tell me you never miss academic life," his father had finally brought himself to say, masking the remark by casually brushing aside yet another pale stone with his cane. "More and more, your theory about the palace is gaining credence. You may find yourself famous all over again. It's an enviable position."

"Maybe one turn in the snake pit was enough," he smiled. "Academia and I form a sort of mutual disrespect society."

"Well," his father had gone on, "the choice is yours, but you know I'll be retiring from Penn at the end of this term. Naturally there'll be some vicious in-house jockeying to fill my shoes, but if you'd like, I could probably arrange things with the search committee."

Vindicated at last, he'd realized. It seemed the only sin in academia greater than being wrong was being right too soon. But the small-minded universe of departmental politics was the last thing he wanted in his life. These days he played in the big time.

"I'm afraid I'll have to pass."

"I suppose university life is too limiting for you now," the old man had finally said, grudgingly but admiringly.

He'd said that, and nothing more. Two months later he'd had a second stroke and retired permanently. These days he grew orchids in Darien, Connecticut, and penned impassioned longhand letters to the *Times* every day or so, just to keep his capacity for moral outrage honed.

Vance had definitely gone his own way. First he'd published a book that rocked the scholarly world; then he'd compounded that offense by walking out on the brouhaha that followed and going free-lance, starting his own business. Next he'd become involved with the Washington intelligence community, and finally he'd begun working with the Association of Retired Mercenaries. It was a universe so alien to his father it might as well have been on Mars. But if the old man was disappointed that Michael Vance, Jr., hadn't turned out the way he'd planned, he still took pride in his son.

Now, though, Stuttgart and the restoration of Phaistos would have to be put on hold till the latest game with Novosty was sorted out. The protocol. It was still running through his mind. Could there be some sort of alliance cooking between the Soviets and the Japanese mob? What in hell . . . ?

"Michael, she is here." A hoarse whisper emerged as the rickety wooden door of the *kafeneion* edged open. Zeno tugged down his nightshirt and carefully edged it wider, squinting out at the street. "Come in. Quickly. Before you are seen."

So his guess had been right: she was avoiding the hotel. Good move. Smart and typical of Eva. She was handling this one exactly right.

He stepped through the door. "Where is she now?"

"She's in back. Adriana gave her something to make her sleep." Zeno was pulling out a chair from one of the empty tables. The room was shrouded in darkness, and the stale odor of the kitchen permeated the air. "She was not herself, Michael. What happened? She claimed someone was trying to murder her. At the palace. Did you two—?"

"We tried throwing a party, but it started getting crowded." He looked around. "I could use some of that *raki* of yours. I just had a close encounter with a guy you wouldn't sit down next to on a bus. He refused to leave politely so . . . I had to make him disappear. Bad scene."

"You killed him?"

"He was shooting, at Eva and me. Very unsociable." He glanced toward the back of the darkened room. "Zeno, our party guest tonight was—you're not going to believe this— a Japanese hood. Tell me something. Is the Yakuza trying to get a foothold in Crete? You know, maybe buying up property? That's their usual style. It's more or less how they first moved in on Hawaii."

"Michael, this country is so poor, there's nothing here for gangsters to steal." He laughed. "Let me tell you a secret. If a stranger came around here and tried to muscle me, or any of my friends, he would not live to see the sun tomorrow. Even the Sicilian Cosa Nostra is afraid of us. Crete is still a small village in many ways, in spite of the crazy tourists. We tolerate strangers, even open our homes to them if they are well behaved, but we know each other's secrets like a family. So, to answer your question, the idea of a Japanese syndicate coming here is impossible to imagine. You know that as well as I do."

"That's what I thought. But I saw a *kobun* from the biggest Yakuza organization in Japan tonight. I know because I had a little tango with their godfather a few years back. Anyway, what's one of his street men doing here, shooting at Eva and me?" He paused as the implications of the night began to sink in. "This scene could start to get rough."

"You did nothing more than anybody here would have done." He looked pensive in the dim light. "Years ago, when the colonels and their junta seized Greece, I once had to—" He hesitated. "Sometimes we do things we don't like to talk about afterwards. But you always remember the eyes of a man you must kill. You dream about them."

"Our party lighting was pretty minimal. It was too dark to make out his eyes."

"Then you are luckier than you know." He glanced away. "This was not somebody you knew from another job, Michael? Perhaps the mercenary group you sometimes—"

"Never saw the guy before in my life, swear to God. Anyway, I think it was Eva he really wanted. But whatever's going on, I have to get her out of Crete now, before whoever it is finds her again."

"I agree." He was turning toward the living quarters in the rear. "You should stay here tonight, and then tomorrow we can get you both passage on the car ferry to Athens, off the island. I will take care of everything. Tickets, all of it." He returned carrying two tumblers of *raki*. After setting them on the table, he continued. "I am very worried for her, Michael. And for you. We all make enemies, but—" He took a sip from his glass. "By the way, do you have a pistol?"

"Not with me." He reached for the glass, wishing it was tequila—straight, with a twist of lime—and he was back on the *Ulysses*, trimming the genoa. "That's a mistake I may not make again soon."

"Then I will arrange for one. Like I said, everything. I have many friends. Do not worry." He drank again. "By the way, she asked me go to the hotel and get something for you. She seemed to think it was important. One of your modern American inventions. She had it locked in the safe at the desk. And she gave me money to pay for her room." He sighed. "Why would she waste money on a hotel when she could have stayed here with us?"

"What is it?"

"I think it's a computer, though it's barely the size of a briefcase. Part of the new age that mercifully has passed us by. I have it in back, with the rest of her things." His voice disappeared into the darkened kitchen. Moments later he reappeared carrying Eva's laptop. With a worried look he settled it gingerly on the table. "Do you have any idea why she had this with her?"

"I think she may have something stored in here." He settled it on the table and flipped up the top. Then he felt along the side for the switch, and a second later the screen glowed blue. After the operating system was in place, he punched up the files.

A long line of names filled the screen, arranged alphabetically. But nothing seemed right. It was a stream of unclassified NSA memos, and then a lot of personal letters. He resisted the temptation to call them up and delve into her private life. How many men . . . ?

Stick to business. Save the fun for later. Where's the file?

Then he noticed the very first alphanumeric.

"Ackerman."

Hold on, he thought, wasn't that the name of the NSA guy she said gave her the disk? He highlighted the file on the screen and hit Retrieve. An instant later it appeared.

Yep, this one had to be it. Clearly an NSA document, very carefully stored.

(NSCID No. 37896)   Page 1 of 28
Dept: R1/SIGINT
Classification: TOP SECRET
Authorization: Dept/H/O/D only
Analyst: Eva Borodin
Init: EKB
Encryption: DES/UNKNOWN
Reference: Classified

DAEDALUS PROTOCOL

The Union of Soviet Socialist Republics (USSR) and Mino Industries Group, hereinafter referred to as the Parties;

MINDFUL of their obligation to strive for technological progress in both nations,

CONVINCED that the technical and financial agreements specified in this Protocol will serve the long-range strategic interests of both Parties,

CONSCIOUS that the success of Project Daedalus will lead to increased cooperation and mutual understanding between the peoples of the USSR and Japan,

HAVE HEREBY AGREED AS FOLLOWS:

Article I

4659830481867394210786980498673261559798093
0291870980798578367251426478966596983748586
7030945896970980549381738405401290487571092
3836142543495019294766477810298378578576924
8598504821273850956070971070901613386089274
765608021834860 . . .

That was it. The stream of numbers filled three pages, and then came Article II. Thus it went, for ten articles. As he scrolled up page after page, he realized that the numbers continued for the rest of the document:

She was right. Outside of occasional repetitions, there seemed to be no real pattern. He'd seen a lot of encryptions in the old days, but this one didn't look like anything standard.

He sat staring at the screen. Mino Industries Group. *That* explained the Mino-gumi goon. The godfather was planning his biggest play yet, global.

But what was it? What was in the deal? This was something he had to see.

Eva had said she tried the Data Encryption Standard, the DES system, and got nowhere. Which meant NSA had been foiled. How had he done it?

DES was a procedure whereby data were passed through a series of eight S-boxes, actually mathematical operations, that when combined with a unique user key converted it into what appeared to be alphanumeric garbage. The receiver also had a copy of the key, which could be used in combination with the same set of mathematical operations to convert it back.

He knew that back when DES was being invented by IBM, the National Security Agency had purposely sabo-

taged Big Blue's original plan to make it uncrackable. NSA
had insisted that the key, a string of zeroes and ones, be
limited to 56 bits, rather than the proposed 128 bits, which
would have made the system so complex it would have
been safe forever. The reason, of course, was that NSA
didn't want an unbreakable cipher loose on the planet;
after all, their primary business was reading other people's
mail. IBM didn't know it at the time, but the smaller key
was already a pushover for NSA's Cray supercomputers,
which could try a trillion random keys per second and
routinely crack any 56-bit DES encryption in the world in
half a day.

Anybody familiar with the intelligence business was well
aware of that. Which was, obviously, why somebody had
turned to NSA.

But Eva said she'd tried the usual random-key procedure and got nowhere. So what was the answer?

His head was buzzing from the *raki* now, but he kept
turning over in his mind the possibility that she'd been
looking in the wrong place. Trying to find the DES key
when in fact this encryption used some entirely different
scheme.

He rubbed at his temples and tried to run the scenario
backward.

Project Daedalus. The more he thought about it, the
more . . .

"Zeno." He looked up from the screen. "Do you still
have that copy of *Realm of the Spirit*?" He'd sent the old
Greek an autographed first edition the week it came out.

"Your book, Michael? Of course I have it. I treasure it.
It's in the bedroom, in back."

"Mind getting it for me? I feel like a little light reading."

"At four in the morning? Michael, I think—"

"You know how it is when your mind gets filled up with
garbage at bedtime."

"You should be getting some sleep, like Eva. Tomorrow
we have to—"

"I need to relax a little first. And I need that book.
There's a chart in the appendix guaranteed to put anybody
to sleep."

"Very well." He sighed, drank off the last of his *raki*, and pulled himself erect. "Sometimes you can be as headstrong as your father."

As quiet settled over the room, Vance continued to stare at the screen. Why did he have a hunch he was right on this one? Could he really crack a cypher with a 486 portable when NSA's Cray supercomputers had bombed?

Maybe. Stranger things had happened. The samurai swordsmen said you needed to know your opponent's mind. Here, in the waning hours before dawn in the middle of Crete, he was feeling a curious oneness with whoever had devised this random-looking string of numbers. He'd created number strings just like this himself, back before the CIA had come into his life.

"Here it is, Michael. Adriana said Eva is still asleep. I don't know what she gave her, perhaps one of her old wives potions." He chuckled quietly. "That's one of the reasons I love her so much. When you get ancient like I am, it's good to be married to a nurse."

Vance took the book and, in spite of himself, weighed it in his hand. What was it? maybe two pounds? The glistening dust jacket, unusual for a university book back in those days, was still pristine. He smiled, realizing it was unread.

"Thanks." He finally remembered Zeno. "This should do the trick. Now why don't you go on to bed? I'll just stretch out here on a table when I get sleepy."

"Michael, sometimes I think you are a madman." He shrugged, then turned to hobble back toward the bedroom. "Just don't answer the door, whatever you do."

"Get some sleep. I'll be doing the same."

"Then good night. May God give you rest." He was gone.

Vance barely nodded, since he was already turning to the appendix of the book and switching on the dim overhead light. The volume brought back a world long lost for him. Now he wanted it back, if only for a moment.

He flipped to Appendix C. There he'd reproduced, as a dutiful scholar should, the standard numerical correlates for the syllabary of Linear B.

Mycenaen Syllabary (after *Ventris*, 1953)

da	qa	sa	je	o	ra
01	16	31	46	61	76

ro	za	qo	pu	pte	ka
02	17	32	47	62	77

pa	zo	ti	du	ta	qe
03	18	33	48	63	78

. . .

The numbers continued on to ninety. He checked the files and, sure enough, she had a Lotus data management system on the hard disk. He quickly structured a format for his matrix, then began coding in the sounds. The setup was simple, but the next part would need some programming. The numbers in the protocol had to be converted to sounds. It looked easy, but what if they'd been deliberately garbled somehow? He'd be no better off than before.

Think positive.

As he finished coding in the grid, he could hear the tentative stirrings of early morning Iráklion outside. Trucks were starting up, birds coming alive. He began noticing the lack of sleep, but he pushed it aside and took another sip of *raki*. Just keep going, he told himself. You're about to find out if great minds really do think alike.

"Darling, what in the world are you doing with my 486?" The voice was like a whisper over his shoulder.

"How about checking to see if you've got any video games?" He turned around, startled in spite of himself. What had woken her? She was probably wired. "Eva, why did you take off tonight? And what was that nonsense you were yelling at me?"

"Maybe it wasn't nonsense. Alex said you were working for him. He said you two were partners. It's not really true, is it?" She slumped into a chair. She was wearing a light dressing gown, her hair tousled. With a groan she rubbed at her eyes. "I don't need this."

"You can forget about Alex. He's playing way over his

head. It's always bad judgment to underestimate the other team's strengths." He reached for her. "You've just got to decide who you trust. You might start with Zeno. He's offered to help me get you out of Crete."

"And go where?" She moved against him. "Michael, they found me here. They'll find me anywhere."

"Not if we turn this scene around and take the action to *them.* But that's the next move. Right now, you just have to be out of Crete while I do a little checking. How about flying to Miami, grabbing a plane down to Nassau, then—"

"You're going to get me on the *Ulysses* or die trying, aren't you."

He decided to let the crack pass. It was true, however. If she ever saw it, he was sure she'd start to understand.

"You know," she went on, "this afternoon I was merely worried. Now I'm actually frightened. Guess I'm not as brave as I thought. I'm sorry about tonight, running off like that."

"Not the first time I've had a woman give me the gate." He laughed, then reached out and stroked her hair, missing the long tresses of the old days. "Now, you can help me out with something. Does the name Yakuza mean anything to you?"

"What are you talking about?" She studied him, puzzled.

"I probably shouldn't tell you this, maybe it'll just upset your morning, but that wiseguy who broke up our party last night was a Japanese hood. From the Mino-gumi syndicate. Back home they're Numero Uno. They run Tokyo and Osaka and they've got half the Liberal Democratic Party in their pocket. Then there's the old CIA connection, from days gone by."

"How do you know?"

"After you took off, our friend dropped in again. Uninvited as usual. That's when Novosty finished him off with his Uzi and I got a closer look."

"Alex killed—! My God, that makes three."

"By actual count. He's gone a little trigger happy in his old age. That or he's very, very scared." He rubbed at the scratch on his neck, remembering. "What if it's the Japanese mob that's behind this? They have the funding, that's for sure. Among other things, they run consumer loans in Japan, legalized loan sharking. They've got more money than God."

"This is too much. I don't know anything about . . ." She rose, trembling. "I'll go with you to Nassau, Michael. Let's take the *Ulysses* and just disappear in the middle of the Atlantic."

"It's a deal." He beamed. "But first we've got to answer some questions. You say the Yakuza are not part of anything you know about?"

"I'm only vaguely aware they exist."

"And you don't know who runs Mino Industries?"

"Never heard of it before."

"It's a bunch of nice, clean-cut mobsters. Problem is, one of the owner's *kobun*, street men, tried to kill us tonight. Maybe we're finally getting a little light at the end of the tunnel." He looked her over. Eva was always beautiful in the mornings. There was something wanton about her this time of day. "Come here a minute."

He took her and cradled her in his arms, then brushed his lips against her brow. "You okay?"

"I think so." She took a deep breath.

"Never knew you to quit just because things got tough." He drew her around. "You're the cryptography expert. Why don't we try to find out what kind of phonetics Ventris's numerical correlates for Linear B would produce from these numbers?"

"What are you talking about?" She rubbed at her eyes.

"You know, in my travels I've discovered something. A great mind often has a touch of poetry. Sometimes, in order to think like the other guy, you need to be a little artistic. So, I wonder . . . about that cipher."

"You mean—?"

"Just a crazy, early morning idea." He patted the keyboard of the laptop. "What if the mind behind it is using a system no computer in the world would ever have heard of?"

"There's no such thing, believe me."

"Maybe yes, maybe no." He flipped open his book to the

central section, a glossy portfolio of photos. He'd shot them himself with an old Nikon. "Take a look at this and refresh your memory."

She looked down at the photo of a large Minoan clay jar from the palace, a giant *pithoi*, once a container for oil or ungents or water for the bath. Along the sides were inscribed rows of wavy lines and symbols. It was the Minoan written language, which, along with cuneiform and hieroglyphics, was among the oldest in the world. "You mean Linear B."

"Language of King Minos. As you undoubtedly remember, it's actually a syllabary, and a damned good one. Each of these little pictures is a syllable, a consonant followed by a vowel. Come on, this was your thing, way back when. Look, this wavy flag here reads *mi*, and here, this little pitchfork with a tail reads *no*." He glanced up. "Anyway, surely you recall that Linear B has almost a hundred of these syllable signs. But Ventris assigned them numbers since they're so hard to reproduce in typeface. For example, this series here, *mi-no-ta-ro* reads numerically as—" he checked the appendix, "13-52-59-02. Run them together and *minotaro* reads 13525902. And just like the early Greeks, the Minoans didn't insert a space between words. If somebody was using Linear B, via Ventris's system, the thing would come out looking like an unintelligible string of numbers."

"You don't really—"

"You say you've tried everything else. NSA's Crays drew a blank. Maybe you were looking for some fancy new encryption system when it was actually one so old nobody would ever think of it. Almost four thousand years old, to be exact."

"Darling, that's very romantic. You're improving in the romance department." She gazed at him a second, then flashed a wry smile. "But I can't say the same for the good-sense arena. No offense, but that's like the kind of thing kids write to us suggesting. Nobody employs anything remotely that simple these days."

"I knew you'd think I was crazy. You're not the first." He rose. "But humor me. Just slice those number sequences into pairs and see what they look like phonetically. Something to take your mind off all the madness around here."

"Well, all right." She sighed, then settled unsteadily into the rickety chair he'd just vacated. "Make you a proposition, sweetie. Get me some coffee, nice and strong, and I'll forget I have good sense and play with this a little."

"You're a trooper." He turned and headed for the kitchen. "I remember that about you. Not to mention great in bed."

"We strive for excellence in all things."

Just as he reached the doorway, the kitchen light flicked on. It was Adriana, in blue robe and furry slippers, now reaching up to retrieve her coffee pan.

While Eva was typing away behind him, he leaned against the doorframe in his still-wet clothes to watch a Greek grandmother shuffle about her private domain preparing a traditional breakfast. He suspected no male hand had ever touched those sparkling utensils. The Old World had its ways, yesterday and forever.

While he drowsed against the doorjamb, the aroma of fresh Greek coffee began filling the room. *Sarakin*. That was the Japanese name for their homegrown loan sharks, the so-called salary-men financiers. He knew that the Yakuza's four largest *sarakin* operations gave out more consumer loans than all of Japan's banks combined. If you added to that the profits in illegal amphetamines, prostitution, bars, shakedowns of businesses, protection rackets . . . the usual list, and you were talking multi multibillions. The major problem was washing all that dirty money. They routinely invested in respectable but losing propositions abroad, on the sound theory that one dollar cleaned was worth two unlaundered.

Was that what the Soviet scam was all about? Money from the Japanese mob being laundered through loans to the USSR? What better way to wash it? Nobody would ever bother asking where it came from.

But there was one major problem with that neat scenario. Politically the Yakuza were ultrarightist hardliners. So why would they expose their money with the Soviets, laundered or not? Particularly now, with so much political instability there—hardliners, reformers, nationalists. Somehow it didn't compute.

"Michael, come here a second." The voice had an edge of triumph.

"What?" He glanced around groggily.

"Just come here and take a look at this." She was staring at the screen.

He turned and walked over, still entranced by the heady, pungent essence of fresh Greek coffee now flooding the room. "Is it anything—?"

"Just look at it and tell me what you think." She leaned back from the screen and shifted the Zenith toward him. The ice-blue letters cast an eerie glow through the dull morning light. The color reflected off his eyes, matching them.

"You did it already?"

"I started with a one-to-one replacement of numbers with letters. But it's sequence-inverted, which means I had to . . . anyway, what do think so far? Am I a genius or what?"

He drew a chair next to the screen and started to examine it. But at that moment Adriana set a tray of coffee down beside the computer, steaming and fresh, together with dark figs and two bowls of yogurt.

"Kafé evropaiko," she commanded, then thrust a cup into his hand.

"Malista, efcharistó." He absently nodded his thanks, took a sip of the steaming brew, then returned his attention to the screen.

At first he thought he was just groggy, his vision playing tricks, but then the string of letters began to come into focus. Incredible!

"Okay, what about this part here," he asked, pointing to the fourth line, where the letters turned to nonsensical garbage, "and then down here again?"

"That's what I was talking about. The interlacing switches there. It happens every hundred numbers. They started by taking the second fifty digits and interlacing them back into the first fifty. Then they switched the algorithm and interlaced the third fifty digits ahead, into the fourth fifty, but backwards. Then it repeats again."

"You figured all that out just fooling around with it?"

"Darling, I do this for a living, for godsake. After a while you have good instincts." She tapped her fingers nervously on the wooden table, then remembered the coffee and reached for a cup. "Nice little trick. Standard but nice. Every so often you fold the data back into themselves somehow. That way there are no repetitions of number sequences—for words that are used a lot—to give you away. But once you've played with this stuff as much as I have . . . anyway, it's always the first thing I check for."

"Congratulations."

"Tell me the truth." She looked at him, sipping her coffee. "Can you really still read this? It's been years."

"Memory like an elephant. Though you may have to help me along now and then." He pointed. "Look. I think that word's modern Greek. They've mixed it in where there's not an old word for something." He pushed around the computer. "Want to run the whole data file through your system? Clean it up?"

"My pleasure." She was clearing the screen. "I can't believe it just fell apart like this. The reason our Crays didn't crack it was it's too simple by half."

He reached for his coffee, feeling a surge of satisfaction. His hunch had been dead on. Whoever came up with this idea for an encryption must have been a fan of ancient Greek history, and a knowledgeable one. What better cipher for Project Daedalus communiqués than the language Daedalus himself used? They'd taken that four-thousand-year-old tongue, an archaic forerunner of ancient Greek, and then scrambled it using a mathematical algorithm. Mino Industries was communicating with the Soviets using an encoded version of Minoan Linear B.

It was absolutely poetic. It also appeared, upon first examination, to be very naive. Yet upon reflection it turned out to be brilliant. You convert a totally unheard-of language to numbers, throw in a few encryption tricks, and the result is something that would drive all the hotdog DES-oriented supercomputers crazy. All those chips would be trying trillions of keys when there actually was no key. Yes, you had to admit it was inspired.

Except the Daedalus crowd was about to experience a problem, a small headache. Make that a major headache. Because their secret protocol was about to become headlines. He figured that ought to go a long way toward stopping any more shooting.

"Okay. It's humming." She reached for her yogurt. "This time around all the garbage will be gone." She took a bite, then burst out laughing. "You know, this is wonderful, working with you. Darling, I've just decided. Let's do something together, maybe live on the *Ulysses* for a while. I might even get to like it. It sounds romantic."

"I'm still looking for the romance in life."

"Well, love, you've found it. It's me." She leaned over and kissed him on the lips. "End of quest."

"Thought I'd never hear you say that. But first you have to help me translate this. I'm over a decade out of date. My modern Greek's a little rusty too, and a lot of the technical terms in this look to be transliterated—"

"No, sweetie, that's not the first thing we have to do. The first thing is to make sure you've got a separate copy of anything you're working with. *Not in the computer.* I'll spare you my horror stories about erased files, hard disks going down, all the rest." She was rising, energized. "Cardinal computer rule number one. *Always* dupe anything you're working on, no matter how sure you are nothing can go wrong. Believe me."

"Sounds good." He looked up. "What are you doing?"

"I need that disk I showed you tonight. We can use it for the backup. It's in my purse, which I now realize I left in the car when I came in. I was slightly crazy at the time." She was turning. "God, it seems like ages."

"Look, why don't you let me—?"

"You don't know where I parked it. My secret hiding place."

"Maybe we ought to send Zeno, or Adriana—"

"Just sit tight. Only be a minute." She wrapped her coat about her and, before he could protest, disappeared out the door, humming.

She was a marvel. Everything he'd remembered.

"Are you still awake?" Zeno was trudging into the room, still wearing his frayed nightshirt.

"We just solved the riddle of the sphinx, old friend. Except now we have to translate it."

"You should be sleeping, Michael. Go now, catch an hour or so. I will start making arrangements. Get tickets for you both on the car ferry to Athens, a pistol, maybe new passports if you want. We have work to do." He reached and took the cup of coffee Adriana was urging on him.

"All right. As soon as she gets back."

"What?" He froze, then looked toward the back. "What do you mean? I thought she was still asleep."

"She went out to the car, wherever it is."

"I wish she had asked me. I would have been happy—"

"You know how she is. There's no stopping her when she gets rolling."

"This is not good." He turned and called to Adriana to bring his trousers and shoes. "We must find her."

"You're right. It was stupid. Damned stupid." He was getting up. "Let's do it together."

CHAPTER SEVEN

Thursday 6:28 A.M.

The morning air was sharp and she wished she'd grabbed one of Adriana's black knit shawls before going out. Could she pass for one of those stooped Greek peasant women? she wondered. Not likely. She shivered and pulled her thin coat around her.

The rain was over now, leaving the air moist and fragrant, but the early morning gloom had an ominous undertone. They'd found the key to open the first box, but the message inside still had to be translated. What was it? What could possibly be in the protocol that would make somebody want to kill her?

She stared down the vacant street leading away from the square, a mosaic of predawn shadows, and tried to think.

Alex Novosty was the classic middleman, that much was a given. But then she'd known that for years. Yes, she'd known about Alex Novosty all her life—his work for the KGB, his laundering of Techmashimport funds. She knew about it because they were second cousins. Fortunately their family tie was distant enough not to have made its way into NSA's security file, but around the Russian expatriate dinner tables of Brighton Beach and Oyster Bay, Alex was very well known indeed. He was the Romanov descendant who'd sold out to the Soviets, an unforgivable lapse of breeding.

But for all that, he wasn't an assassin. For him to do what he'd done tonight could only mean one thing: he was terrified. Very out of character. But why?

The answer to that wasn't hard: He must be mixed up in Project Daedalus, whatever it was, right up to his shifty eyeballs. But what about Michael? What did Alex want from *him*?

The answer to that could go a lot of ways. When she first met Michael Vance, Jr., she'd been smitten by the fact he was so different. Always kidding around, yet tough as steel when anybody crossed him. A WASP street fighter. She liked that a lot. He was somebody she felt she could depend on, no matter what.

She still remembered her first sight of Mike as though it were yesterday. She was taking notes on Etruscan pottery in a black notebook, standing in a corner of the Yale art gallery on Chapel Street, when she looked up and—no, it couldn't be. She felt herself just gawking.

He'd caught her look and strolled over with a puzzled smile. "Is my tie crooked, or—" Then he laughed. "Name's Mike Vance. I used to be part of this place. How about you?"

"Vance?" She'd just kept on staring, still not quite believing her eyes. "My thesis adviser at Penn was . . . you look just like him."

And he did. The same sharp chin, the same twinkle in the blue eyes. Even when he was angry, as Mike certainly had been that day, he seemed to be having fun.

Thus it began.

At first they were so right for each other it seemed as though she'd known Michael Vance for approximately a hundred years, give or take. She'd been one of his father's many ardent disciples, and after finishing her master's at Penn, she'd gone on to become a doctoral candidate at Yale, where she'd specialized in the linguistics of the ancient Aegean languages. She'd known but forgotten that Michael Vance, Sr., had a son who was finishing his own doctorate at Yale, writing a dissertation about Minoan Crete.

That day in the museum he was steaming, declaring he'd dropped by one last time as part of a ritualistic, formal farewell to archaeology. The decision was connected with the hostile reception being given a book he'd just published, a commercial version of his dissertation. As of that day he'd decided to tell academia to stuff it. He'd be doing something else for a living. There'd been feelers from some agency in D.C. about helping trace hot money.

In the brief weeks that followed they grew inseparable, the perfect couple. One weekend they'd scout the New England countryside for old-fashioned inns, the next they'd drive up to Boston to spend a day in the Museum of Fine Arts, then come back and argue and make love till dawn in her New Haven apartment. During all those days and nights, she came very close to talking him out of quitting university life. Close, but she didn't.

He had put off everything for a couple of months, and they had traveled the world—London, Greece, Morocco, Moscow. Once their parents even met, at Count Sergei Borodin's sprawling Oyster Bay home. It was a convocation of the Russian Nobility Association, with three hundred guests in attendance, and the air rang with Russian songs and balalaikas. Michael Vance, Sr., who arrived in his natty bowler, scarcely knew what to make of all the Slavic exuberance.

Shortly after that, the intensity of Michael became too

much for her. She felt herself being drawn into his orbit, and she wanted an orbit of her own. The next thing she knew, he'd departed for the Caribbean; her father had died; and she'd gone back to work on her own doctorate.

Michael. He was driven, obsessive, always determined to do what he wanted, just as she was. But the tension that likeness brought to their relationship those many years ago now made everything seem to click. Why? she wondered.

Maybe it was merely as simple as life cycles. Maybe back then they were just out of synch. He'd already survived his first midlife crisis, even though he was hardly thirty. When they split up, she'd been twenty-five and at the beginning of a campaign to test herself, find out what she could do.

Well, she thought, she'd found out. She was good, very good. So now what?

She was relieved to see the car was still parked on the side street, actually a little alley, where she'd left it. Thinking more clearly now, she realized she'd been a trifle careless, stashing the car in the first location she could find and then running for Zeno's.

As she headed down the alley in between the white plaster houses, she suddenly felt her heart stop. Someone was standing next to the Saab, a dark figure waiting. She watched as it suddenly moved briskly toward her.

Alex Novosty.

"What?" She couldn't believe her eyes.

"Budetya ostorozhyi!" He whispered the warning as he raised his hand and furtively tried to urge her back.

"Kak! Shto—?" She froze. "How did you find the car?"

"The hotel. They directed us to a *kafeneion* near here, but then I noticed your car. I thought . . ." He moved out of the shadows, quickly, still speaking in Russian. "Just tell me where you have the copies of the protocol, quickly. Maybe I can still handle it."

"Handle what?" That's when she saw the two other men, in dark overcoats, against the shadow of the building.

"The . . . situation." His eyes were intense. "They want it back, all copies. I've tried to tell them that killing you won't solve anything, but—" He glanced back with a small shiver. "You must tell them Michael has a copy, stall them."

"It's true. He does."

"No! Then say there's a copy back in your office. Just let me try and—"

"Alex, I'm not going to play any more of your games."

"Please," he continued in a whisper, "don't contradict anything I say. Let me do the talking. I'll—"

"You're in it with them, aren't you?" She tried to push past. "Well, you can tell your friends we're onto their 'project.' If anything happens to me, Michael will track them down and personally take them apart. Tell them that."

"You don't understand." He caught her arm. "One of their people was killed tonight."

"The one trying to shoot Michael and me, you mean?" She was trying to calm the quaver in her voice.

"He was killed by the KGB. I had nothing to do with—"

"Is that what you told them?"

"That's the way it happened. There was an argument."

"Over what?"

"Everybody wants you. It's the protocol." His look darkened. "Eva, they are in no mood for niceties."

"Neither am I." She noticed the two men were now moving toward them. One was taller and seemed to be in charge, but they both were carrying what looked like small-caliber automatic weapons.

The protocol, whatever it was, was still in code. She didn't know what she didn't know. How could she bargain?

It was too late to think about it now. Their faces were hard and smooth, with the cold eyes of men who killed on command. My God, she thought, what had Michael said about the Mino-gumi?

The Japanese mob.

The taller man, she was soon to learn, was Kazuo Inagawa, who had been a London-based *kobun* for the Mino-gumi for the past decade. He had a thin, pasty face and had once been first *kobun* for their entire Osaka organization, in charge of gambling and nightclub shakedowns. Even in the early dawn light, he wore sunglasses, masking his eyes.

The shorter one was Takahashi Takenaka, whose pock-marked face was distinguished by a thin moustache, an aquiline nose, and the same sunglasses.

Alex, she realized, must have lied to them, covering up what really happened out at the palace. Now he was bluffing for his life.

"You can just tell them I don't know anything about it." She felt the cold air closing in.

"Eva, that's impossible. They know you were given the protocol. Now where is it?"

He clearly wanted her to say it was somewhere else. But why bother?

"It's in the car. In my purse." She pointed. "Why don't they just go ahead and take it? By the way, it's still encrypted."

She fumbled in her pockets. "Here's . . ."

Then she realized she'd left the key in the car. There it dangled, inside the locked door. Her purse rested on the seat across from the driver's side.

"Get it," Inagawa commanded his lieutenant. Takenaka bowed obediently, then turned and tried the doorhandle, without success.

"*So.*" He frowned.

Inagawa muttered a curse and brutally slammed the butt of his automatic against the curved window. The sound of splintering glass rent the morning air.

Quickly Novosty stepped forward and reached through to unlock the door. Then he pulled it open and leaned in.

Why is *he* doing it? she wondered. Easy answer: He's trying to keep control of the situation.

Whose side is he really on?

Then he backed out and handed her the brown leather purse while he tried to catch her eye.

She took it, snapped it open, and lifted out the gray computer disk. "There," she said as she handed it to Inagawa, "whatever's on it, you'll have to figure it out for yourself."

"That can't be the only one," Novosty sputtered. "Surely there are other copies."

"That's it, sweetheart."

Inagawa turned it in his hand, then passed it to Takenaka and said something in Japanese. The other man took it, then barked *"Hai"* and bowed lightly.

"Are you sure this is the only copy?" Inagawa asked.

"The only one."

He nodded to his lieutenant, who began screwing a dark silencer onto the barrel of his automatic.

Oh my God, she thought. They're going to finish the job.

"Wait." Novosty reached for his arm. "She's lying. This is a disk from a computer. There *must* be other copies."

"Yes." She was finally coming to her senses. "There are plenty of other copies. In my computer. In—"

"Where is it?" Inagawa looked at her.

"It's—it's at the hotel. The Galaxy." She was trying desperately to think. "And then I left another—"

"You're lying. We have been there. They said a tavern keeper came and took all your luggage." He was staring down the street, toward Zeno's place. "They also told us where he could be found. We will go there now."

"My friends," Novosty interrupted again, "it would be most unwise to attempt any violence on a Greek national here. The consequences could be extremely awkward, for all of us."

"We must retrieve it."

"But why not do it the easy way?" He tried to smile. "There's another man here, traveling with her. We should work through him. I know he will deal. He's a professional."

"Who is he?"

"An American. If we hold her, keep her alive, we can use her to make him bring it to us. We can offer a trade."

"No. We will just find him and take it." Inagawa started to move. "Now."

"He's armed, my friends," Novosty continued evenly. "He's also experienced. There would be gunfire, I promise you. If that happened, you could have the entire street here filled with rifles in a minute. You do not know these people as I do. They still remember World War Two and the Resistance. Killing unfriendly foreigners became a way of life some of them have yet to forget."

Alex is bluffing, she thought. Again. Michael doesn't have a gun. Does Zeno? Who knows?

"Let me try and talk to him," Novosty continued. "Surely something can be worked out."

"You will stay here, with us." Inagawa seized his arm, then turned and began a heated exchange with his partner. Again Takenaka bowed repeatedly, sucking in his breath and muttering *hai*. At last they seemed to arrive at a consensus, though it was the taller man who'd actually made the decision, whatever it was.

"She comes with us."

"Oh, no I don't." She looked at Novosty, who seemed defeated, then back at the Japanese. She suddenly realized she was on her own. Novosty had played all his cards. "If I don't reappear in Washington day after tomorrow, you'll have the entire U.S. National Security Agency looking for me. People know I'm here. So think about that."

"That is not our concern." Inagawa reached for her. "We do not work for the American government." Then he turned to Novosty. "Tell your friend that this woman will be released when we have all copies of the protocol. All. Do you understand?"

"But how can I tell him if you won't let me—?"

"That is your problem."

"Perhaps . . . perhaps we should just leave a message here," Novosty sputtered. "I'm sure he'll find the car."

"Alex, I'm not going anywhere with these animals." She drew back.

"Don't worry. I'll take care of everything."

"*No*, I'm not—"

That was all she could say before a hand was roughly clapped against her mouth, her body shoved against the broken window.

Mike Vance and Zeno Stantopoulos searched for over half an hour before they found the Saab. When they did, the left-hand window was broken, and Eva's purse was missing. She was missing too. The only thing remaining was a hastily scrawled note from Alex Novosty.

CHAPTER EIGHT

Saturday 6:13 P.M.

"Vance?" The portly, balding desk clerk studied his computer screen at the Athenaeum Inter-Continental. Here in this teeming marble lobby the new world met the old. "Dr. M. Vance. Yes, we have your reservation."

Good. Novosty had done exactly what he said. The play was going down.

"Welcome back." The man looked up and smiled, his eyes mirroring the green numbers on the screen as he looked over Vance's shoulder. "Our records show you were just with us, four days ago. We still have your old room, if you like."

"That would be fine."

He was back in a city renowned as much for its hospitality as for its mind-numbing brown haze of smog. It was also said to be the safest city in Europe, with a miniscule crime rate. However, Michael Vance did not feel safe as he stood in the lobby of Athens's most luxurious hotel.

"Were you on a bus tour of the Peloponnisos, perhaps?" the clerk continued with a pale smile, his voice trying for perfunctory brightness. "The Mycenean ruins in the south are always—"

"Business." Vance tossed his passport onto the counter. They both knew he didn't look anything like a candidate for a four-day CHAT package tour on a bus. But the man seemed nervous, anxious to make conversation.

"I'll be needing a car in the morning. Early. Is that in your reservation file too?"

"No problem." The clerk ignored, or missed, his impatient tone. "We have a Hertz outlet now, just over there," he pointed, "next to the travel desk. I'm sure they will be happy to arrange for it."

Vance tossed his Amex card onto the counter, then reached for the slate clipboard holding the registration slip. Dusk was falling outside, but here in the warm glow of chandeliers the moment felt like sleepwalking. His mental bearings kept shifting. Nothing was real. He wanted to think it was merely routine, like checking into a thousand other streamlined international hotels, something he'd done more times than he cared to count. But that was wrong; danger lurked somewhere nearby. His senses were warning him.

He kept thinking about Eva. Was she serious about getting back together, sailing on the *Ulysses?* Maybe he didn't know her as well as he thought, which was troubling for a lot of reasons, not the least being that right now he needed to be able to think *exactly* the way she did. They'd have to work as a perfectly coordinated team tomorrow, with no rehearsals.

"May I have someone take your bag?" The clerk glanced down at the new leather suitcase sitting on the floor, then reached to ring for a bellhop.

"No." Vance lunged to stop his hand.

Whoa, he lectured himself, chill out. Keep the lid on. Why not just let it happen? Here. Maybe you *want* them to do it here. Why wait?

The clerk tried to hold his composure. "As you wish. Of course you know your room."

"I can find it." He tried to smile, then thumbed over his shoulder. "You're busy anyway. The tour coming in . . ."

"Yes." The clerk was shoving across the heavy brass key. "You remember our schedule. Breakfast is served until ten over there in the dining room, eleven in your room."

"Thanks." He picked up the bag, heavy, and turned.

The rental car desk was across the lobby, past the tour group now pouring through the revolving doors. They clearly were just off a Paris flight, chattering in French, brandishing tour badges, and quarreling about luggage with Gallic impatience.

"I need a car for tomorrow. Early."

The dark-haired woman at the desk looked up as he began fishing for his credit card and driver's license. Her Hertz uniform was unbuttoned down the front to display as much of her bosom as Greek propriety, perhaps even the law, would permit. A heavy silver chain nestled between her ample breasts.

"Our pleasure." She swept back her hair as she mechanically shoved forward a typed sheet encased in smudged cellophane. "We have some new Austin subcompacts, or if you want a full-size—"

"What's the best car you've got?" It would be a long drive, over uncertain Greek roads. He wanted to take no chances.

"We do have an Alfa, sir. Only one. A Milano." She absently adjusted the V-neck of her uniform. "For VIPs. I should warn you it's expensive." She bent forward to whisper. "To tell you the truth, *ine poli akrivo*. It's a rip-off." She leaned back, proud of her new American slang. "Take my advice and—"

"Can you have it here, out front, at six in the morning?"

"I can check." She sniffed, then reached for the battered phone. A quick exchange in Greek followed, then she hung up. "They say it just came in. There should be no problem."

He glanced around the lobby once more as she picked up the charge card and license to begin filling out the form. There was still no sign, no indication. And yet the whole scene felt *wrong*. Something, something was warning him.

That's what it was. The man standing across the lobby, at the far side next to the elevators. He had a newspaper folded in his hand, but he wasn't reading. He was speaking *into* it.

Hotel security? Not a chance. For one thing, he wasn't Greek. Although he was too far away to see his face, something about the way he stood gave him away.

Where the hell was Novosty? This wasn't supposed to be the drill.

He suddenly found himself wondering how much clout Alex had left. Maybe Novosty was out of the play. Maybe the rules had changed.

"Could you please hurry that along." He turned back to the dark-haired girl.

"You said you wouldn't be needing the car until tomorrow, sir." Formal now, abrupt.

"I just changed my mind. I'd like it tonight. Right now, as a matter of fact."

"Do you want the insurance? It will be an extra—"

"No. Yes. Look, I don't *care*. Just let me sign that damned thing and give me the keys."

"Well, give me a chance." She petulantly turned the form toward him and shoved it across the desk. "If you'll just initial here and here," she was pointing with her pen, "and sign there. And did you say you wanted the car now?"

"Immediately."

"I'm afraid that's not possible." She retrieved the form.

"*What*?"

"It's just—"

"Then give me something else." He glanced toward the man, still speaking into his newspaper, then back. They would make their move any second now. "What's the problem with the car?"

"I'm trying to tell you it just came in. Our people will need at least half an hour to clean it, go over the checklist. So if you'd like to have a cup of coffee in the dining room, I'll call you when—"

"Where is it now?"

"They said it's just been returned. It's probably parked somewhere outside." She gestured toward the glass revolving door. "Across the street. That's where they usually—"

"An Alfa?"

"That's right. Dark blue. But like I said, it's not—"

"Give me the keys."

"They're probably still in it. Our people—"

"Thanks." He reached down for the suitcase.

"Your card, sir, and your license." She pushed the items across with a tight smile, clearly happy to be rid of him.

As he reached for them, out of the corner of his eye he saw the first movement. The man had stuffed the newspaper, and walkie-talkie, into his trench coat and was approaching across the marble lobby. Just as Vance expected, the garb was polyester, the hair a slicked-up punch-perm, but he still couldn't make out the face.

He didn't need to. He knew who they were. The encounter at Knossos flashed through his mind.

They know I've got a copy of their protocol. And until that gets iced, there's always a chance their secret is no longer a secret. But they can't know we've cracked the encryption. Unless she told them. Which she never would.

No, they couldn't know that yet, which meant he still had the bargaining chip he'd need.

Except for one problem. They were about to try and break the rules. Just like the old days. Maybe they'd forgot he knew how to break rules too.

As he pushed through the milling crowd of French tourists, suitcases and knapsacks piling up near the entrance, he sensed the man was gaining. But only a few feet more and he'd be at the revolving door. Halfway home.

This wasn't going to be easy. There'd be a backup. Probably just outside, at the entrance.

As he reached for the rubber flange of the revolving door, he knew the man was just behind him, maybe two steps. Just right. He turned to see a hand emerge from the polyester suit jacket, grasping a Heckler & Koch KA1 machine pistol, a cut-down version of the MP5.

The barrel was rising, the hard face closing in. But it was the suitcase he wanted.

So why not give it to him?

"Here." He jammed his foot into the revolving door, leaving a small opening, then wheeled around, hoisting the case. The quick turn brought just enough surprise to break his attacker's momentum. As the man involuntarily raised his left hand, Vance caught his right wrist, just back of the pistol's grip, and shoved it forward, into the door. Then he brought up his elbow and smashed it into the attacker's jaw. As the man groaned, he caught his other wrist and shoved him around.

Now.

He rammed his shoulder against the revolving door, closing it and wedging the gun inside.

"Let's keep this simple, okay? No muss, no fuss."

He threw his full weight against the man's body, bending him back around the curved metal and glass of the door. There was a snap and a muted groan as the wrist bones shattered. The machine pistol clattered to the marble floor inside the circular enclosure.

"Sorry about that." Before the attacker could regain his balance, he kneed him into the next revolving partition and rammed it closed. Only one foot remained outside, kicking at an awkward angle across the floor.

Now where's the other one? He glanced around as he drew away. There's sure to be two. Somebody was on the other end of that radio. Novosty? Did *he* set this up?

He swept up the suitcase and shouldered his way through the auxiliary door on the side. Odd, but the scuffle had gone unnoticed amid the din of the arriving tour. Or maybe Parisians weren't ruffled by anything so everyday as an attempted murder.

Now what?

As he emerged onto the street, he saw what he was looking for. The other assailant was waiting just across the wide entryway, past the jumble of bellboys, taxi drivers, and the last straggle of tourists coming off the bus.

Their eyes met, and the man's right hand darted inside his dark suit jacket.

Use the crowd, Vance thought. Enough hand-to-hand heroics. These guys mean business.

Since the pile of luggage coming off the bus separated them, he had an advantage now, if only for a second or so. Without thinking he seized the straps of a canvas knapsack sitting on the sidewalk with his free hand and flung it with all his strength.

It caught his attacker squarely in the chest, breaking his rhythm and knocking him back half a step. It was only a moment's reprieve, but it was all Vance needed to disappear around the rear of the bus, which was pouring black exhaust into the evening air, blocking all view of the avenue. Maybe he could move fast enough to just disappear.

As he dashed into the honking traffic, headlights half

blinding him, he surveyed the street opposite looking for the Alfa.

There? No. There?

A pair of headlights swerved by, inches away, accompanied by honking and a cursing Greek driver. Only a few feet more now and he'd be across.

There. A blue Alfa. It had to be the one.

But it was already moving, its front wheels turning inward as the Hertz attendant backed it around to begin pulling out.

He wrenched open the door and seized a brown sleeve. The arm inside belonged to a young Greek, barely twenty, his uniform grease-covered and wrinkled. He looked up, surprise in his eyes, and grabbed for the door handle.

"Change of plans." Vance heard the Alfa's bumper slam against the car parked behind as the startled attendant's foot brushed against the accelerator.

"Den katalaveno!"

"Out." Vance yanked him around and shoved him toward the asphalt pavement. "And stay down."

Now the bus had begun pulling out from the entryway across the street. Although traffic still clogged the avenue, he was a clear target.

He threw the suitcase onto the seat, then slid in and reached to secure the door. As he pulled it shut, he heard the ping of a bullet ricochetting off metal somewhere. Next came a burst of automatic fire that seemed to splatter all around him.

The young Greek pulled himself up off the pavement and reached . . .

"Down." Vance waved him away as he shifted the transmission into drive.

At that moment a slug caught the young attendant in the shoulder, spinning him around. He gave a yelp of surprise, then stumbled backward. But now he was out of the way, clear, with what was probably only a flesh wound.

Vance shoved his foot against the accelerator, ramming the rear fender of the car in front, then again, knocking it clear. Another spray of bullets spattered through the back window as he pulled into the flow of traffic.

Your time will come, friend, he told himself. Tomorrow, by God, we finish this little dance.

He finally became aware of the pumping of his own heart as he made his way north up Syngrou Avenue, trying to urge the traffic forward by sheer will.

The thing now was to get out of Athens, take Leoforos Athinon west, then head up the new Highway 1 toward the mountains, lose them in the country, find some place to spend the night. His final destination was only about two hundred kilometers away. He just had to be fresh and ready tomorrow, with everything in place.

But at least he now knew the game had no rules. Maybe knowing that gave him an edge. And so far his timing was still intact. He'd handled it. Maybe not too well, maybe with too much risk, but he'd handled it.

Novosty's note had said there would be a straight swap. But the other team clearly had no intention of bothering with niceties. Fine. That cut both ways.

Sunday 11:45 A.M.

The place was Delphi, the location Novosty had specified. Heading warily up the Sacred Way, Vance paused for a moment to take in the view. From where he stood, the vista was majestic, overwhelming humanity's puny scale. He'd always loved it. Toward the north the sheer granite cliffs of the Phaedriades Mountains towered almost two thousand feet skyward to form a semicircular barrier, while down below the river Pleistos meandered through mile after mile of dark olive groves. It was an eyeful of rugged grandeur, craggy peaks encircling a harsh plain that stretched as far as the eye could see. Greece in the midday sun: austere, timeless.

His destination, the ancient temple of the Delphic oracle farther up the hill, overlooked this panorama, row center in a magnificient natural amphitheater. The Greek legends told that the great god Zeus had once dispatched two eagles, one flying east and one flying west, to find out where they would meet. They came together at the center of the earth, Delphi, whose main temple, the Sanctuary of Apollo, contained the domelike boulder Omphalos, thereafter named the "navel of the world." Here east and west met.

He'd parked the Alfa on the roadway down below, and now as he stared up the mountainside, past the conical cypress trees, he could just make out the remains of the stone temple where almost three thousand years ago the priestess, the Delphic oracle, screamed her prophesies. She was a Pythia, an ancient woman innocent of mind who lived in the depths of the temple next to a fiery altar whose flame was attended night and day. There, perched on a high tripod poised over a vaporous fissure in the earth, she inhaled intoxicating gases, chewed laurel leaves, and issued wild, frenzied utterances. Those incoherent sounds were translated by priests into answers appropriate to the queries set before her.

Delphi. He loved its remote setting, its sacred legends. Those stories, in fact, told that the god Apollo had once summoned priests from Crete, the ancient font of culture, to come here to create this Holy of Holies.

Was he about to become a priest too? After sending off a telegram to the Stuttgart team, notifying them of a delay in his schedule, he'd journeyed from that island back to Athens via the ANEK Lines overnight car ferry from Iráklion. Not at all godlike. But it had a well-worn forward section it called first class, and it was a low-profile mode of travel, requiring no identity questions. He'd ended up in the bar of the tourist section for much of the trip, stretched out on a stained couch and napping intermittently during the twelve-hour voyage. It had cleared his mind. Then from Piraeus, the port of Athens, he'd taken a cab into the city. After that the hotel and the car.

As he stared up the hill, he had in his possession a wallet with nine hundred American dollars and eighty thousand Greek drachmas, the suitcase, and a Spanish 9mm automatic from Zeno. He also had a translated version of the opening section of the protocol.

His anger still simmering, he continued up the cobbled

path of the Sacred Way, toward the exposed remains of the oracle's temple situated halfway up the hill. Nothing was left of the structure now except its stone floor and a few columns that had been reerected, standing bare and wistful in the sunshine. In fact, the only building at Delphi that had been rebuilt to anything resembling its original glory was the small marble "treasure house" of the Athenians, a showplace of that city's wealth dating from 480 B.C. Today its simple white blocks glistened in the harsh midday glare, while tourists milled around speaking German, French, English, or Dutch. Even in the simmering heat of noon, Delphi still attracted visitors who revered the ancient Greeks as devoutly as those Greeks had once worshipped their own adulterous gods and goddesses.

So where the hell was Novosty? Noon at the Temple of Apollo, his note had said.

He searched the hillside looking for telltale signs of another ambush—movement, color, anything. But there was nothing. Although tourists wandered about, the temple ruins seemed abandoned for thousands of years, their silence almost palpable. Even the sky was empty save for a few swooping hawks.

If Alex is here waiting, he asked himself, where would he be?

Then he looked again at the treasure house. Of course. Probably in there, taking a little respite from the blistering sun. It figured. The front, its columns, and porch were open, and the interior would be protected. Conveniently, the wide steps of the stone pathway led directly past. A natural rendezvous.

In his belt, under his suede jacket, was Zeno's 9mm Llama. It was fully loaded, with fifteen rounds in the magazine plus one up the tube. He reached into his belt and eased off the safety.

Holding it beneath his coat, he continued on up the cobbled pathway toward the front of the treasure house. As he moved into the shade of the portico, he thought for a moment he heard sounds from inside. He stopped, gripping the Llama, and listened.

No, nothing.

Slowly, carefully, he walked up the steps. When he reached the top, he paused, then gingerly stepped in through the open doorway. It was cool and dank inside. And empty. His footsteps rang hollow on the stone floor. Maybe Novosty's dead by now, he thought fleetingly. Maybe his luck finally ran out.

He turned and walked back out to the porch, then settled himself on the steps. In the valley below, beyond the milling tourists, the dark green olive groves spread out toward the horizon.

The protocol. The mind-boggling protocol. Something was afoot that would change the balance of world power. He'd translated the first page of Article I, but it had raised more questions than it answered. All the same, he'd taken action. Today he was ready.

Novosty had to know the score. Had to. But now Vance knew at least part of the story too.

He glanced down at the suitcase. It contained Eva's Zenith Turbo 486, of course, which undoubtedly was why it was such a popular item. But it also had a hard copy of the scrambled text of the protocol, courtesy of a printer Zeno had borrowed from a newspaper office in Iráklion, as well as a photocopy of Vance's partial translation.

They didn't know it yet, but there was another full copy, which he'd transmitted by DataNet to his "office" computer in Nassau. It was waiting there in the silicon memory.

Quite a document. Twenty-eight pages in length, it was the final version of a legally binding agreement that had been hammered out over a long period of time. From the page he'd translated, he could recognize the style. The text referred to the rights and obligations of two distinct entities—the Union of Soviet Socialist Republics and Mino Industries Group.

As he seated himself beneath a lone almond tree and took a last look at the olive groves down below, he was tempted to pull out the translation and reread it one more time. But that was unnecessary; he'd memorized it, right down to the last comma.

Article I

1. For the full and complete compensation of one hundred million American dollars ($100,000,000.), to be deposited in the Shokin Gaigoku Bank of Tokyo on or before May 1, Mino Industries Group will legally transfer to the USSR full ownership of one operational prototype, this transfer to be executed on the agreed date, May 1, Mayday. At the time of this transfer the prototype will satisfy all technical performance criteria enumerated in Document 327-A, "Specifications." The USSR may thereafter, at its discretion, contract for production models at the price specified in Document 508-J.

2. Upon the USSR having satisfied the terms stipulated in Article II, Mino Industries Group will extend the USSR financial credits in the amount of five hundred billion American dollars ($500,000,000,000.), such credits to be provided in increments of one hundred billion dollars ($100,000,000,000.) annually for a period of five years. These credits will be arranged through Vneshekonombank, the Bank for Foreign Economic Affairs (Article IV).

3. Within one year of the satisfaction of all formalities pursuant to the above-designated credits, the USSR will. . . .

That's as far as he'd translated. The rest was still in Minoan Linear B. He took a deep breath, again trying to digest what it meant in the grand scheme of global strategic alliances.

Most importantly, what was the "prototype"? *Something* was about to appear on the planet that would make its owner unassailable. But what?

Eva's stumbled onto dynamite. Mayday. That means it explodes in less than a fortnight. No wonder Mino Industries wants her out of the way.

Among the clusters of tourists on the road below, a white limousine was pulling to a stop, followed by a gray Saab.

He watched as Novosty emerged from the Saab and glanced up the hill, then started the climb. Nobody got out of the limo.

Vance watched as he slowly made his way along the cobbled path leading up the hill, puffing. He was almost out of breath by the time he reached the top.

"Michael, I'm so glad you could manage to make it." He heaved a sigh as he trudged up the last remaining steps.

"It was the lure of your scintillating company."

"I'm sure." He looked around.

"Is Eva down there? She'd damned well better be."

"She is safe." Novosty sighed again. "It was most unwise for her to have gotten involved in all this, Michael. She is making matters difficult for us all."

"Too bad." He removed the Llama from beneath his coat. "By the way, congratulations on your new clients. Mino Industries. That's a Yakuza front, partner. Guess you know. The CEO was a Class A war criminal. These days he owns the LDP and runs Japan. Alex, you asshole, you're way over your head here. Mino Industries is owned lock, stock, and hardware by *the* Japanese godfather. His *kobun* make your KGB look like a Boy Scout troop."

"Michael, please."

"And here I was thinking you'd finished consorting with the criminal element, decided to live clean. Then the next thing I know, your client's gorillas are trying to kill Eva and me. Me, your new partner. Things like that tend to inspire mistrust, and just when we were starting to hit it off so well." He finally stood up, holding the Llama. Novosty was lounging nervously in the sunshine, fishing for a cigarette. "Where's your Uzi? You just may need it."

"Michael, all this has nothing to do with me." His eyes were weary. "I'm operating independently this time."

"Cash and carry. Maybe you should just post your prices, like a cheap cathouse."

"I prefer to think of myself as an expediter. But this time I encountered more difficulties than reasonably could be anticipated. Which is why I need your help now to straighten it out."

"What? The whole shoddy scene? Looks like the KGB's

hot on the trail, say maybe about two feet in back of your ass. Or is it your client, who you're about to try and screw out of a hundred million dollars? Incidentally, that's probably a serious miscalculation, health-wise."

"The situation *has* grown awkward."

"Of course that touching fable about returning the hundred million to Moscow was just the usual 'disinformation.'"

"You are perfectly correct. It will not be returned. But any thought I might have had of keeping it now also seems out of the question." He sighed. "Instead I'm afraid we must—"

"*We?* Now that's what I call balls of brass." He laughed. "Surely even a fevered imagination like yours can't suppose—"

"Michael, I told you I would split the commission I took for cleaning it. That offer still holds. Fifty-fifty. I might even go sixty-forty. What more can you want? But those funds *must* be delivered. Given the new situation—"

"Not by me."

"Be a realist, my friend. I no longer have freedom of movement, so now you are my only hope. If those funds aren't transferred within the week, I'd prefer not to reflect on the consequences."

"The consequences to your own neck, you mean." Vance stared at him. "By the way, just out of curiosity, what's the 'prototype'?"

"That's the one thing I cannot possibly discuss, Michael." Novosty caught his breath. "But what if the contract for it is abrogated because of those funds not being delivered, what then? What if the USSR just makes a move to seize it? I fear there could be war, my friend. Bang, the apocalypse." He flicked his lighter. "Even worse though, as you say, both parties to the agreement would probably spend a week devising the most interesting way possible for me to depart this earth."

"If the KGB somehow locates and freezes the embezzled funds before you can finish transferring them, it could scuttle the whole deal. Mino Industries would probably be very annoyed. Not to mention certain parties back home."

"Precisely. You can see we are on a knife edge here. But first things first. You must return Eva's pirate copy of the protocol, please. I beg you. It must disappear. I have promised them that, as an act of good faith. I'm afraid the participants in Tokyo are near to losing patience with me."

"And what about her?"

"She's with them now." He pointed down the hill, to the long white limousine. "Unfortunately, they have taken over the situation."

"Better buckle your seat belt, pal. It's about to be a bumpy afternoon."

"She is safe, don't worry. They have assured me. It is only the protocol they care about. The matter of security. They know you have her only other copy, in the computer. Now please let me just give whatever you have to them. Then let's all try and forget she ever had it."

"You know, those hoods down there tried a little number on me last night in Athens." He hadn't moved. "It took the edge off my evening."

"Michael, I tried to tell them that was imprudent. But they are very concerned about time. Just be reasonable, my friend, and I'm sure everything can be straightened out." He sighed again. "You know, these tactics of kidnapping and such are very distasteful to me as well. But when she told them she didn't have all the material, that you still had a copy, they decided that taking her into their custody was the best way to ensure your cooperation."

"They don't know me very well." He looked down the hill. "Tell your buddies they can go take a jump. Nobody blackmails me. Nobody. I plan to hang on to this little suitcase till she's out of danger. That's how we're going to work things. Tell them it's her insurance. They release her right now, or I'll personally blow their whole deal sky high."

"Tell them yourself, Michael. I'm just here as an observer." He gestured toward the white limo parked below, nestled in among the line of tourist automobiles and busses. "And while you're doing that, perhaps you should ask her if that's her wish as well. They refuse to release her until they recover the materials she had. They are calling it 'protection.'"

He stared down. "You've got a hell of a nerve. All of you. Alex, when this is over—"

"Please. Let's just get this ghastly protocol affair sorted out." He rubbed at his beard. "Then we can all concern ourselves with what's really important. The money."

"Right. I almost forgot."

He scanned the hillside. Was everything set? He'd seen no sign. But then that's how it was supposed to be. The other problem was the tourists, everywhere, complicating the play.

But maybe the tourists would be a help, would make it start out slow. Think. How can you use them? Clearly the other side had hoped for an abandoned place in the middle of nowhere. They had to be off balance now too.

He hesitated a moment, then decided. Go for it. He had the Llama. Just settle it here and now.

He took one last look at the temple as he rose. The Delphic oracle. That's what Eva had been all along. She'd somehow divined the outlines of the story, but after the disappearance of her old lover at the NSA she didn't dare speak it directly. Everything was coded language. So what better place than here on this mountain to finally have a little plain talk?

As they passed down the last stone steps leading to the roadway, he found himself thinking about Mino Industries. Did they really have half a trillion dollars lying around? Not likely. To come up with that kind of money, even in Japan, you'd have to be deeply plugged into legitimate financial circles—pension funds, insurance companies, brokerage houses, banks, all the rest. But still, the Mino-gumi had connections that went wide and deep, everywhere. Their *oyabun*, Tanzan Mino, had been in the game for a long, long time.

Now, as he approached the limousine, one of its white doors slowly began to open. Then a Japanese emerged, dressed in a black polyester suit. He wore dark sunglasses, and his right wrist was in a cast. The eyes were very familiar. Also, one of his little fingers was missing.

But Vance's gaze didn't linger long on the hands. His attention was riveted on what was in them. Yep, he'd seen it right last night. It was a Heckler & Koch machine pistol. One of those could lay down all thirty rounds in an eight-inch group at thirty yards. World-class hardware.

It figured. The Mino-gumi was known everywhere as the best-run Yakuza syndicate of them all. Hardened criminals, they considered themselves modern-day samurai, upholding some centuries-old code of honor. It was a contradiction only the Japanese mind could fully accommodate.

Heavy-duty connections, Vance told himself, the very best. Which meant Novosty was in even bigger trouble than he probably imagined. The latest rumor in the world of hot money was that Tanzan Mino and his Yakuza had, through dummy fronts, just bought up half of Hawaii. If that were true, it meant he laundered *real* money these days. Who the hell needed a small-time operator like Alex?

Then the man reached in and caught Eva's arm, pulling her into the midday glare.

Thank God, he thought, she still looks vaguely okay. Will she be able to stay on top of this once it gets moving?

He noticed she was wearing a new brown dress, but her short hair was tangled, her face streaked with pain.

The bastards. They must have worked her over, trying to find out everything she knew.

There were two "representatives," Novosty had said. So the other man was still in the limo, in the driver's seat, covering in case there was trouble.

Good move. Because there was definitely going to be trouble. A lot of it. Tanzan Mino's goons were about to have all the trouble they could handle.

"Michael, oh, *Christ.*" She finally recognized him. "Thank God. Just give them—"

"Can you understand what's going on here?" He raised his hand. "These guys are *kobun,* professional hit men. They have a very sick sense of humor. They also have no intention of—"

"Please, they have given me their word." Novosty interrupted him, then glanced back. "You can see she is well."

She didn't look well at all. She seemed drugged, standing shakily in the brilliant sunshine, a glazed stare from her eyes, hands twisting at her skirt.

Eva, Eva, he thought, what did they do to you? Whatever it was, it worked. You look defeated, helpless.

"Michael, just let them have the computer." She spoke again, her voice quivering. "They say it's all they want. Then they'll—"

"Eva, it's all a lie. The big lie. So just lighten up and enjoy this. We're not giving them so much as the time of day until they let you go. First tell me, how badly did they rough you up? I want to know."

"Michael, *please.*"

"You will be happy to learn that Dr. Michael Vance is a specialist in international finance," Novosty interrupted, addressing the tall Japanese. "He has kindly offered to serve as my agent in completing the final arrangements for the transfer of funds from London. He will resolve any remaining difficulties. As I said, he is my agent, and it is important that he not be harmed."

"Alex, back off. I haven't agreed to anything." Vance turned to the Japanese. "How's the arm? Hope the damage wasn't permanent."

"Where are the NSA materials." The man ignored Vance's question. His voice was sharp and his English almost perfect. "That is our first order of business."

"Right here." He lifted the suitcase. "I assume we're all going to deal honorably for a change. Eva first, then we talk about this."

"I'm sure Dr. Vance has brought everything you want," Novosty added quickly, glancing over. "Perhaps if he gave the materials to you now, the woman could be released. Then he and I can proceed immediately with the matter of the funds."

"You are not involved," the Japanese snapped back. "We have been authorized to personally handle this breach of security." He stared at Novosty. "The funds, in fact, were your sole responsibility. They were to have been transferred to Shokin Gaigoku Bank in Tokyo over a week ago. You demanded an exorbitant commission, and you did not deliver. Consequently you will return that commission and our London *oyabun* will handle it himself."

The Mino-gumi probably should have handled it in the first place, Vance thought fleetingly. Alex was definitely out of his depth.

"Just a couple of days more . . ." Novosty went pale. "I thought I had explained—"

"Your 'explanations' are not adequate." The man cut him off, then pointed to the suitcase in Vance's hand. "Now give us that."

"Why not." He settled the brown leather case onto the asphalt. "It's good business always to check out the merchandise, make sure it's what you're paying for."

"She said it was a portable computer." The man walked over, then cradled the H&K automatic in his bandaged arm while he reached down to loosen the straps. Next he pulled the zipper around and laid open the case.

"What is this?" He lifted out the pile of printed paper.

"Guess she forgot to tell you. We cracked the encryption. I thought maybe you'd like to have a printed version, so I threw one in for free."

He stared at it a second, almost disbelieving, then looked up. "This is a photocopy. Where is the original?"

"Original? You mean that's not—?" Vanced looked at it. "Gee, my mistake. Guess I must have left it somewhere. Sorry you had to drive all the way out here from Athens for nothing."

"*Jesus*, Michael," Eva blurted. "Don't start playing games with them. They'll—"

"I need all the copies." The man's voice hardened, menacingly. "Where are they?"

"I don't remember precisely. Tell you what, though. You put her on a plane back to the States and maybe my recollection might start improving."

"We are wasting time." The door by the steering wheel opened and the second *kobun* emerged, also carrying an automatic. He was shorter, but the punch-perm hair and polyester suit appeared to have come from standard issue, just like the sunglasses. He gestured his weapon toward

Vance. "There is a simple way to improve your memory. You have exactly ten seconds—"

"My friend, be reasonable," Novosty interrupted, his voice still trying for calm. "There are people here." He motioned toward the crowd of gathering tourists. From their puzzled stares, they seemed to be thinking they were witnessing a rehearsal for some Greek gangster film.

The first man motioned his partner back, then turned to Vance. "You realize we will be forced to kill her right now if you don't produce all originals and copies."

"Don't really think you want to do that." Vance stared at him. "Because if anything happens to her, you're going to be reading about your 'prototype' all over the American newspapers. I can probably even swing some prime-time TV time for you. I'll take care of it personally."

"No one will believe you."

"Don't think so? My guess is the *Washington Post* will run your entire protocol on page one. I'll see they get a very literal translation into English. Then you won't need this. You can just buy all the copies you want." He picked up the laptop and walked over to where Eva was standing.

"Here, take this, and get back in the car, now. I think these guys have got an attitude problem. So screw them."

"*Michael.*" She reached for the computer.

"Get in that one." He pointed toward Alex's gray Saab. "And take the next plane out of Greece. That place we talked about. Anywhere. Just go."

"We're getting nowhere," the second man barked again. Then he leveled his automatic at Vance's right knee and clicked off the safety. There was a gasp from the gawking tourists, and the crowd began stumbling backward for cover. "We have ways of extracting information."

Oh, shit, he thought, whoa.

The man's voice suddenly trailed off, while a quizzical expression spread through his eyes and a red spot appeared on his cheek. Next his head jerked back and his automatic slammed against the car door, then clattered across the asphalt.

Not a second too soon, Vance thought.

"*No,*" Eva screamed, "what's happening?" She lurched

backward, then turned and stumbled for the Saab, carrying the computer.

The first *kobun* glanced around, then raised the H&K in his left hand, trying to get a grip.

He'll hit the ground and roll, Vance thought, like any pro under fire.

And he did exactly that, with a quick motion over onto his back and then to his feet again, clicking off the safety as he came up.

"You want to kill us both?" Vance was holding his Llama now, trained on the sunglasses that had been crushed by the roll, momentarily distorting the man's line of fire. "Then go for it." He squeezed the trigger.

The walnut stock kicked slightly, but he just kept gripping the satin chrome trigger. Now the gunman's automatic came around, its muzzle erupting in flame. The crowd scattered, shouting in half a dozen languages, terrified.

Vance just kept firing, dull thunks into the figure stumbling backward as the H&K machine pistol erupted spasmodically into the hot, dry air.

"Kill him, Michael. Oh, God! Yes. The bastards." Eva was still yelling as she slammed shut the door of the Saab. Yelling, cursing, screaming. Less than a second later the motor roared to life.

Now Novosty was diving across the pavement, toward the open front door of the limousine.

"Michael, we've got to split up. Get out." He yelled over his shoulder. "I'll have to go to London now. There's nowhere left. They're going to come for the money."

Vance scarcely heard him as he held the Llama steady and kept on squeezing until the magazine was empty and only vacant clicks coursed through his hand.

The screech of tires brought him back. He looked up to see the white limousine careening along the edge of the road, barely avoiding the ditch, its door still open, Novosty at the wheel. Eva was already gone.

He noticed that they'd removed the plates from the limousine, just as he'd done on his rented Alfa. There would be nothing but terrified tourists and two illegally armed, very dead Japanese hoods here when the Greek police finally arrived. The story would come out in a babel of languages and be totally inconsistent.

Christ! he thought. It was supposed to be over by now, and instead it's just beginning. When word of this gets back to Tokyo, life's going to get very interesting, very fast. The Mino-gumi knows how to play for keeps. We've got to blow this thing.

Across, on the hot asphalt, the two Japanese were sprawled askew, sunglasses crumpled. One body was bleeding profusely from the chest, the other from a single, perfect hole in the cheek. The *kobun* who had come within moments of removing his kneecaps now lay with a small hole in front of one ear and the opposite side of the face half missing.

What a shot!

But why did he wait so long? We had them in the clear. I see now why the Resistance scared hell out of . . .

"Never look at the eyes, Michael." The voice sounded from the boulders of the hillside above, where the muzzle of a World War II German carbine, oiled and perfect, glinted. "Remember I told you. It gives you very bad dreams."

BOOK TWO

CHAPTER NINE

Monday 12:08 A.M.

The massive hulk of *Daedalus I* was being towed slowly through the hangar doors, now open to their full 250-foot span. As it rolled out, the titanium-composite skin glistened in the fluorescent lights of the hangar, then acquired a ghostly glow under the pale moonlight. First came the pen-sharp nose containing the navigational gear, radar, and video cameras for visible light and infrared; next the massive ramjet-scramjets, six beneath each swept-back, blunt wing; and finally the towering tail assembly, twin vertical stabilizers positioned high and outboard to avoid blanketing from the fuselage. The tow-truck drivers and watching technicians all thought it was the most beautiful creation they had ever seen.

This would be Yuri Androv's last scheduled test flight before he took the vehicle hypersonic. In four more days. He wore a full pressure suit and an astronaut-style life-support unit rested next to him. As he finished adjusting the cockpit seat, he monitored the roll-out on his liquid crystal helmet screens, calling up the visual display that provided pretakeoff and line-up checks of the instruments. Not surprisingly, the numbers were nominal—all hydraulic pressures stable, all temperatures ambient. As usual, the

Japanese technicians had meticulously executed their own preflight prep, poring over the vehicle with their computerized checklists. Everything was in the green.

All the same, this moment always brought a gut-tightening blend of anticipation and fear. This was the part he dreaded most in any test flight—when he was strapped in the cockpit but without operational control. He lived by control, and this was one of the few times when he knew he had none. It fed all the adrenaline surging through him, pressed his nerves to the limit.

He flipped a switch under his hand and displayed the infrared cameras on his helmet screens, then absently monitored the massive white trucks towing him onto the darkened tarmac. The landing lights along the runway were off; they would be switched on only for final approach, when, guided by the radar installation, their focused beams would be invisible outside a hundred-yard perimeter of the nose cameras.

The asphalt beneath him, swept by the freezing winds of Hokkaido, was a special synthetic, carefully camouflaged. He knew it well. Two nights earlier he'd come out here to have a talk with the project *kurirovat*, Ivan Semenovich Lemontov, the lean and wily Soviet officer-in-charge. Formerly that post had belonged to the CPSU's official spy, but now party control was supposed to be a thing of the past. So what was he doing here?

Whatever it was, the isolated landing strip had seemed the most secure place for some straight answers. As they strolled in the moonlight, the harsh gale off the straits cutting into their skin, he'd demanded Lemontov tell him what was *really* going on.

By the time they were finished, he'd almost wished he hadn't asked.

"Yuri Andreevich, on this project you are merely the test pilot. Your job is to follow orders." Lemontov had paused to light a Russian cigarette, cupping his hands against the wind to reveal his thin, foxlike face. He was a hardliner left over from the old days, and occasionally it still showed. "Strategic matters should not concern you."

"I was brought in late, only four months ago, after the

prototypes were ready for initial flight testing. But if I'm flying the *Daedalus,* then I want to know its ultimate purpose. The truth. Nobody's told me anything. The only thing I'm sure of is that all the talk about near-space research is bullshit. Which means I'm being used." He had caught Lemontov's arm and drew him around. The officer's eyes were half hidden in the dark. "Now, dammit, I want to know what in hell is the real purpose of this vehicle."

Lemontov had grunted, then pulled away and drew on his cigarette. Finally he spoke: "Yuri Andreevich, sometimes it's wiser to leave strategy to the professionals. You do your job and I'll do mine."

Yuri remembered how he'd felt his anger boil. He'd begun to suspect that certain CPSU hardliners like Lemontov, together with the military or the KGB, had their own plans for the vehicle. But what were they up to?

"Look, I'm doing my job. So how about a little openness, a little glasnost? This is not supposed to be like the old days."

Lemontov had drawn a few paces ahead on the tarmac, walking briskly, with the quick energy that had brought him to his powerful party post. Finally he'd slowed and waited for Yuri to catch up. He had made a decision and he had made it quickly. That was characteristic.

"Yuri Andreevich, in a way you represent part of our 'technology exchange' with Mino Industries. You have an indispensible role to play here. This whole program depends on you."

"I'm well aware of that." However, it hadn't answered his questions.

"Then you should also be aware of something else. This undertaking is a small, but highly crucial, part of something much larger. Nothing less than the fate of the Soviet Union in the next century rests on whether Project Daedalus succeeds."

"What do you mean?" Yuri had watched him walk on, feeling his own impatience growing.

Lemontov had turned back again, brusquely. "This hypersonic spacecraft is the symbol, the flagship, of a new

Soviet alliance with the most technologically advanced nation on earth. Even a 'flyboy' like you should be able to grasp that. Through this alliance we eventually will find a way to tap all of Japan's new technology. The world of the future—advanced semiconductors, robots, biotechnology, superconductivity, all of it—is going to be controlled by Japan, and we must have access to it."

Yuri had listened in silence, once more feeling he was being fed half-truths. Then Lemontov lowered his voice.

"Yuri Andreevich, by forming what amounts to a strategic alliance with Mino Industries, we will achieve two objectives. We will gain access to Japanese technology and capital, to rejuvenate Soviet industry and placate our people. And we will strike a preemptive blow against the peril of a new China on our borders in the next century."

"China?" Yuri had studied him, startled.

"My friend, don't be fooled by summits and talks of reconciliation. Neither we nor China care a kopeck about the other. Think about it. In the long run, China can only be our nightmare. If America had to look across its Canadian border and see China, they too would be terrified. China has the numbers and, soon, the technology to threaten us. It's the worst nightmare you or I could ever have." Lemontov had paused to crush out his cigarette, grinding it savagely into the asphalt. "We must prepare for it now."

The hardliners have just found a new enemy, Yuri had realized. The Cold War lives!

"Like it or not," Lemontov had continued, "and just between us I'm not sure I *do* like it, we have no choice but to turn to Japan in order to have an ally in Asia to counter the new, frightening specter of a hostile China rising up on our flank."

"So how does Daedalus figure into all this?"

"As I said, it is the first step in our new alliance. From now on our space programs will be united as one." He had sighed into the icy wind. "It will be our mutual platform for near-earth space exploration."

"With only peaceful intent?" Yuri had tried to study his eyes, but the dark obscured them.

"I've told you all you need to know." A match had flared again as he lit another cigarette. In the tiny blaze of light he gave a small wink. "Even though the *Daedalus* could easily be converted to a . . . first-strike platform, we naturally have no intention of outfitting these prototypes, or later production models, for any such purpose. The Japanese would never agree."

What had he been saying? That the hardliners were planning to seize the vehicles and retrofit them as first-strike bombers? Maybe even make a preemptive strike against China? Were they planning to doublecross the Japanese?

What they didn't seem to realize was that these vehicles didn't *need* to be retrofitted. *Daedalus* was already faster and more deadly than any existing missile. It couldn't be shot down, not by America's yet-to-be-built SDI, not by anything. And speed was only part of the story. What about the vehicle's other capabilities?

He switched his helmet screens momentarily to the infrared cameras in the nose and studied the runway. Infrared. Pure military. And that was just the beginning. There also was phased-array radar and slit-scan radar, both equipped for frequency hopping and "squirt" emissions to evade detection. And how about the radar altimeter, which allowed subsonic maneuvering at low altitudes, "on the deck"? Or the auxiliary fuel capacity in the forward bay, which permitted long-distance sustained operation?

No "space platform" needed all this radar-evasive, weapons-systems management capability. Or a hyper-accurate inertial navigation system. Kick in the scramjets and *Daedalus* could climb a hundred thousand miles straight up in seven minutes, reenter the lower atmosphere at will, loiter over an area, kick ass, then return to the untouchable safety of space. There was enough cruise missile capacity to take out fifty hardened sites. It could perform troop surveillance, deploy commandos to any firefight on the globe in two hours . . . you name it. He also suspected there was yet another feature, even more ominous, which he planned to check out tonight.

While the Soviet military was secretly drooling to get its

hands on this new bomber, sending the cream of Soviet propulsion engineers here to make sure it worked, they already had been outflanked. Typical idiocy. What they'd overlooked was that these two planes still belonged to Mino Industries, and only Mino Industries had access to the high-temperature ceramics and titanium composites required to build more. Tanzan Mino held all the cards. *He* surely knew the capabilities of this plane. Everything was already in place. Mino Industries now owned the ultimate weapon: they had built or subcontracted every component. Was Lemontov such a dumb party hack he couldn't see that?

All the more reason to get the cards on the table. And soon.

So far the plan was on track. He had demanded that the schedule be moved up, and Ikeda had reluctantly agreed. In four days Yuri Androv would take *Daedalus* into the region of near space using liquid hydrogen, the first full hypersonic test flight. And that's when he intended to blow everybody's neat scenario wide open.

He felt the fuselage shudder as the trucks disengaged from the eyelets on the landing gear. Then the radio crackled.

"This is control, *Daedalus I.* Do you read?"

"*Daedalus I.* Preflight nominal."

"Verified. Engine oil now heated to thirty degrees Celsius. Begin ignition sequence."

"Check. *Daedalus I* starting engines." He scanned through the instrument readings on his helmet screens, then slipped his hand down the throttle quadrant and pushed the button on the left. He could almost feel the special low-flashpoint JP-7—originally developed for the high-altitude American SR-71 Blackbird—begin to flow from the wing tanks into the twelve turboramjets, priming them. Then the ground crew engaged the engines with their huge trolley-mounted starters. As the rpm began to surge, he reminded himself he was carrying only 2,100,000 pounds of fuel and it would burn fast.

He switched his helmet screens to the priority-one display and scanned the master instrument panel: white bars showing engine rpm, fuel flow, turbine inlet temperature, exhaust temperature, oil pressure, hydraulics. Then he cut back to the infrared cameras and glanced over the tarmac stretching out in front of him. Since the American KH-12 satellite had passed twenty minutes earlier, flight conditions should now be totally secure.

For tonight's program he was scheduled to take the vehicle to Mach 4, then terminate the JP-7 feeds in the portside outboard trident and let those three engines "unstart," after which he would manually switch them to scramjet geometry, all the while controlling pitch and yaw with the stability augmentation equipment. That would be the easy part. The next step required him to manually switch them back to turboramjet geometry and initiate restart. At sixty-three thousand feet. Forty minutes later he was scheduled to have her back safely in the hangar chocks, skin cooling.

Nothing to it.

He flipped his helmet screens back and looked over the readouts one final time. Fuel pressure was stable, engine nozzle control switches locked in Auto Alpha configuration, flaps and slats set to fifteen degrees for max performance takeoff. He ran through the checklist on the screen: "Fuel panel, check. Radar altimeter index, set. Throttle quadrant, auto lock."

The thrust required to take *Daedalus I* airborne was less than that needed for a vertically launched space shuttle, since lift was gained from the wings, but still he was always amazed by the G-forces the vehicle developed on takeoff. The awesome power at his fingertips inspired a very deceptive sense of security.

"Chase cars in place, Yuri. You're cleared for taxi. *Ne puzha, ne pera!*"

He started to respond, thinking it was the computer. But this time there *was* no computer. He'd deliberately shut it down. If he couldn't get this damned *samolyot* off a runway manually, he had no hopes for the next step. The voice was merely Sergei, in flight control.

"Power to military thrust." He paused, toes on the brakes, and relished the splendid isolation, the pure energy at his command as *Daedalus* began to quiver. Multibillions at his fingertips, the most advanced . . .

Fuck it. This was the *fun* part.

"Brake release."

In full unstick, he rammed the heavy handles on the throttle quadrant to lock, commanding engines to max afterburner, and grinned ear to ear as the twelve turboramjets screamed instantly to a million pounds of thrust, slamming him against the cockpit supports.

Sunday 7:29 P.M.

"We are now cruising at twenty-nine thousand feet. However, the captain has requested all passengers to please remain seated, with their seat belts fastened." The female voice faltered as the plane dropped through another air pocket. "We may possibly be experiencing mild turbulence for the next hour."

Michael Vance wanted a drink, for a lot of reasons. However, the service in first class was temporarily suspended, since attendants on the British Airways flight to London were themselves strapped into the flip-down seats adjacent to the 757's galley. The turbulence was more than "mild." What lay ahead, in the skies and on the sea below, was nothing less than a major storm.

Why not, he sighed? Everything else in the last four days had gone wrong. He'd been shot at, he'd killed a mobster, and Eva had been kidnapped.

Furthermore, the drive back to Athens, then down to the port of Piraeus to put Zeno onto the overnight ferry to Crete, had been a rain-swept nightmare. Yet another storm had blown up from the Aegean, engulfing the coast and even the mountains. When they finally reached the docks at Piraeus, the old Greek had just managed to slip onto the boat as it was pulling out, his German rifle wrapped in a soggy bundle of clothing.

"Michael, I must hurry." He kissed Vance on both cheeks. "Be safe."

"You too." He took his hand, then passed him the Llama,

half glad to be rid of it and half wondering whether he might need it again. "Here, take this. And lose it."

"It's final resting place will be in the depths of our wine dark sea, my friend." Zeno pocketed it without a glance. "No one will ever know what we had to do, not even Adriana. But we failed. She is still gone."

"Don't worry. I'll find her. And thank you again, for saving my life."

"You would have done the same for me. Now hurry. The airport. Perhaps there's still time to catch her." With a final embrace he disappeared into the milling throng of rain-soaked travelers.

The downpour was letting up, but the trip still took almost an hour. When he finally pulled in at the aging Eastern terminal, he'd left the car in the first space he could find and raced in. It was bedlam now, with flights backed up by the storm, but he saw no sign of Eva. Where was she? Had she even come here?

Planes had just started flying again. According to the huge schedule board over the center of the floor, the first departure was a British Air to Heathrow, leaving in five minutes.

There was no chance of getting through passport control without a ticket, so he'd elbowed his way to the front of the British Airways desk.

"That flight boarding. Three-seventy-one. I want a seat."

"I'm sorry, sir, but you'll have to wait—"

"Just sell me a ticket, dammit."

The harried agent barely looked up. "I'm afraid that's out of the question. Now if you'll just take—"

"There's a woman who may be on it," he lifted up the empty leather suitcase, "and she left this at the hotel."

"The equipment is already preparing to leave the gate." He glanced at the screen, then turned to a pile of tickets he was methodically sorting. "So if you'd *please*—"

"Let me check the manifest." He'd stepped over the baggage scale, nudging the agent aside. "To make double sure she's aboard. Maybe I can try and locate her in London."

"Sir!" The young Englishman paled. "You're not allowed to—"

"Just take a second." Vance ignored his protest and punched up the flight on the computer.

It was a 757, completely full. And there she was, in seat 18A, second cabin.

Thank God she'd made it.

While the outraged British Airways agent was frantically calling for airport security, he scanned more of the file.

Alex Novosty was aboard too. In the very last row. Christ! He'd even used his own name. His mind must be totally blown.

Did she know? Did *he* know? What now?

With the ticket agent still yelling, he'd quickly disappeared into the crowd, having no choice but to pace a departure lounge for an hour and a half, then take the only remaining London flight of the evening. All right, he'd thought after cooling down, Novosty wants to use you; maybe you can use him.

But now he suspected things weren't going to be that simple.

He remembered the two KGB operatives Alex had shot and killed at Knossos. They'd been there to find Eva, which meant they knew she had something. Now he realized that wasn't all they knew.

Across the aisle in first class sat a tall, willowy woman who radiated all the self-confidence of a seasoned European traveler. She was also elegantly beautiful—with dark eyes, auburn hair, and pursed red lips—and she carried a large brown leather purse, Florentine. She could have been a French fashion model, a high-paid American cosmetics executive, a Spanish diplomat's mistress.

The problem was, Vance knew, she was none of those things. The French passport he'd seen her brandish at the Greek behind the glass windows at emigration control was a forgery. She was neither French, nor American, nor Spanish. She was an executive vice president with Techmashimport, the importing cover for T-Directorate. KGB.

Vera Karanova was always a prominent presence at

Western trade shows. But there was no trade show in London now, no new high-tech toys to be dangled before the wondering eyes of Techmashimport, which routinely arranged to try and obtain restricted computers, surveillance gear, weapons-systems blueprints.

So why's Comrade Karanova on this flight? Off to buy a designer dress at a Sloane Street boutique? Catch the latest West End musical?

How about the simplest answer of all: She's going to help them track Alex Novosty to earth. Or grab Eva. Or both. They're about to tighten the noose.

So the nightmare was still on. The KGB must have had the airport under surveillance, and somebody spotted Novosty—or was it Eva?—getting on the British Air flight to London. Now they were closing in.

Does she know *me*? Vance wondered. My photo's in their files somewhere, surely.

But she'd betrayed no hint of recognition. So maybe not. He'd always worked away from the limelight as much as possible. Once more it had paid off.

As the plane dipped and shuddered from the turbulence, he watched out of the corner of his eye as she lifted the fake French passport out of her open leather handbag, now nestled in the empty seat by the window, and began copying the number onto her landing card.

Very unprofessional, he thought. You always memorize the numbers on a forgery. First rule. T-Directorate's getting sloppy these days.

He waited till she'd finished, then leaned over and ran his hand roughly down the arm of her blue silk blouse.

"*Êtes-vous aller à Londres pour du commerce?*" He deliberately made his French as American-accented as possible.

"*Comment?*" She glanced up, annoyed, and removed his hand. "*Excusez moi, que dites-vous?*"

"*D'affaires?*" He grinned and craned to look at the front of her open neckline. "Business?"

"*Oui* . . . yes." She switched quickly to English, her relief almost too obvious.

"Get over there often?" He pushed.

"From time to time."

No fooling, lady. You've been in London four times since '88, by actual count, setting up phony third-party pass-through deals.

"Just business, huh?" He grinned again, then looked up at the liquor service being unveiled in the galley. The turbulence had subsided slightly and the attendants were trying to restore normality, at least in first class. "What do you say to a drink?"

She beckoned the approaching steward, hoping to out-flank this obnoxious American across the aisle. "Vodka and tonic, please."

"Same as the lady's having, pal." He gave the young Englishman a wink and a thumbs-up sign, then turned back. "By the way, I'm booked in at the Holiday Inn over by Marble Arch. Great room service. Almost like home. You staying around there?"

"No." She watched the steward pour her drink.

"Sorry to hear that. I was wondering, maybe we . . . Do these 'business' trips of yours include taking some time off? Let you in on a secret, just between you and me. I know this little club in Soho where they have live—" he winked, "I got a membership. Tell you one thing, there's nothing like it in Chicago."

"I'm afraid I'll be busy."

"Too bad." He drew on his drink, then continued. "Long stay this trip?"

"If you'll excuse me, Mr. —"

"Warner. William J. Warner. Friends call me Bill."

"Mr. Warner, I've had a very trying day. So, if you don't mind, I'd like to *attempt* to get some rest."

"Sure. You make yourself comfortable, now."

He watched as she shifted to the window seat, as far as possible from him, and stationed her leather handbag onto the aisle side. Just then the plane hit another air pocket, rattling the liquor bottles in the galley.

"Maybe we'll catch up with each other in London," he yelled.

"Most unlikely." She glared as she gulped the last of her

drink, then carefully rotated to the window and adjusted her seat to full recline. Her face disappeared.

Good riddance.

After that the flight went smoothly for a few minutes, and Michael Vance began to worry. But then the turbulence resumed, shutting down drink service as their puny airplane again became a toy rattle in the hands of the gods, thirty thousand feet over the Mediterranean, buffeted by the powerful, unseen gusts of a spring storm. For a moment he found himself envying Zeno, who had only the churning sea to face.

Almost hesitantly he unbuckled his seat belt and pulled himself up, balancing with one hand as he reached in the air to grapple drunkenly with the overhead baggage compartment.

"Sir," the steward yelled down the aisle, "I'm sorry, but you really must remain—"

"Take it easy, chum. I just need to—"

Another burst of turbulence slammed the wings, tossing the cabin in a sickening lurch to the left.

Now.

He lunged backward, flinging his hand around to catch the leather purse and sweep it, upended, onto the floor. With a clatter the contents sprayed down the aisle. Comrade Karanova popped alert, reaching out too late to try and grab it. Her eyes were shooting daggers.

"Ho, sorry about that. Damned thing just . . . Here, let me try and . . ." He bent over, blocking her view as he began sweeping up the contents off the carpeted aisle—cosmetics, keys, and documents.

The name in the passport was Helena Alsace. Inside the boarding packet was a hotel reservation slip issued by an Athens travel agent. The Savoy.

Well, well, well. Looks like T-Directorate travels first class everywhere these days. Learning the ways of the capitalist West.

"Here you go. Never understood why women carry so much junk in their purse." He was settling the bag back onto the seat. "Sure am sorry about that. Maybe I can buy you dinner to make amends. Or how about trying out that room service I told you about?"

"That will *not* be necessary, Mr. Warner." She reached for the bag.

"Well, just in case I'm in the neighborhood, what hotel you staying at?"

"The Connaught," she answered without a blink.

"Great. I'll try and make an excuse to catch you there."

"Please, just let me . . ." She leaned back again, arms wrapped around her purse, and firmly closed her eyes.

The Savoy, he thought again. Just my luck. That's where *I* always stay.

Monday 9:43 A.M.

"Michael, I can't tell you how happy I am to hear from you, old man. We must have lunch today." The voice emerged from the receiver in the crisp diction of London's financial district, the City, even though the speaker had been born on the opposite side of the globe. Vance noticed it betrayed a hint of unease. "Are you by any chance free around noon? We could do with a chat."

"I think I can make it." He took a sip of coffee from the Strand Palace's cheap porcelain cup on the breakfast cart and leaned back. He'd known the London financial scene long enough to understand what the invitation meant. Lunch, in the private upstairs dining rooms of the City's ruling merchant banks, was the deepest gesture of personal confidence. It was a ritual believed to have the magical power to engender trust and cooperation—cementing a deal, stroking an overly inquisitive journalist, soothing a recalcitrant Labor politician. "We had him to lunch" often substituted for a character reference in the City, a confirmation that the individual in question had passed muster.

"Superb." Kenji Nogami was trying hard to sound British. "What say you pop round about one-ish? I'll make sure my table is ready."

"Ken, can we meet somewhere outside today? Anywhere but at the bank."

"Pleasure not business, Michael? But that's how business works in this town, remember? It masquerades as pleasure. We 'new boys' have to have our perks these days, just like the 'old boys.'" He laughed. "Well then, how about that ghastly pub full of public-school jobbers down by the new Leadenhall Market. Know it? We could pop in for a pint. Nobody you or I know would be caught dead drinking there."

"Across from that brokers club, right?"

"That's the one. It's bloody loud at lunch, but we can still talk." Another laugh. "Matter of fact, I might even be asking a trifling favor of you, old man. So you'd best be warned."

"What's a small favor between enemies. See you at one."

"On the dot."

As he cradled the receiver and poured the last dregs of caffeine into his cup, he listened to the blare of horns on the Strand and wondered what was wrong with the conversation that had just ended. Simple: Kenji Nogami was too quick and chipper. Which meant he was worried. Why? These days he should be on top of the world. He'd just acquired a controlling interest in the Westminster Union Bank, one of the top ten merchant banks in the City, after an unprecedented hostile takeover. Was the new venture suddenly in trouble?

Not likely. Nogami had brought in a crackerjack Japanese team and dragged the bank kicking and screaming into the lucrative Eurobond business, the issuing of corporate debentures in currencies other than that of a company's home country. Eurocurrencies and Eurobonds now moved in wholesale amounts between governments, central banks, and large multinational firms. The trading of Eurobonds was centered in London, global leader in foreign exchange dealing, and they represented the world's largest debt market. In addition, Nogami had aggressively stepped up Westminster Union's traditional merchant bank operations by financing foreign trade, structuring corporate finance deals, and underwriting new issues of shares and bonds. He also excelled in the new game of corporate takeovers. None of the major London merchant bankers—the Rothschilds, Schroders, Hambros, Barings—had originally been British, so maybe Kenji was merely following in the footsteps of the greats. Vance did know he was a first-class manager, a paragon of Japanese prudence here in the new booming, go-go London financial scene.

This town used to be one of Michael Vance's sentimental favorites, a living monument to British dignity, reserve, fair play. But today it was changing fast. After the Big Bang, London had become a prisoner of the paper prosperity of its money changers, who'd been loosed in the Temple. Thanks to them the City, that square mile comprising London's old financial center, would never again be the same. After the Big Bang, the City had become a bustling beehive of brash, ambitious young men and women whose emblem, fittingly, seemed to be the outrageous new headquarters Lloyds had built for itself, a monsterous spaceship dropped remorselessly into the middle of Greek Revival facades and Victorian respectability. It was, to his mind, like watching the new money give the finger to the old. The staid headquarters of the Bank of England up the way, that grand Old Lady of Threadneedle Street, now seemed a doddering dowager at a rock concert.

All the same, he liked to stay near the City, close to the action. The Savoy, a brisk ten-minute walk from the financial district, was his usual spot, but since that was out of the question this time, he'd checked into the refurbished Strand Palace, just across the street.

Today he had work to do. He had to get word to the Mino-gumi to back off. And he was tired of dealing with lieutenants and enforcers, *kobun.* The time had come to go to the top, the Tokyo *oyabun.* The game of cat and mouse had to stop. Tokyo knew how to make deals. It was time to make one.

Kenji Nogami, he figured, was just the man. Nogami, a wiry executive with appropriately graying hair and a smile of granite, was a consummate tactician who'd survived in the global financial jungle for almost three decades. When the Japanese finally got tired of the British financial club playing school tie and bowler hats and "old boy" with them, shutting them out, they'd picked Nogami to handle the hostile takeover of one of the pillars of London's merchant banking community. Japan might still be afraid to go that route with the Americans, who loved to rattle protectionist sabers, but England didn't scare them a whit.

In years gone by, such attempts to violate British class privilege were squelched by a few of the Eton grads of the City chipping in to undermine the hostile bid. These days, however, nobody had the money to scare off Japan. The game was up. And after the deregulation of Big Bang, wholesale pursuit of profit had become the City's guiding principle. Unfortunately, that turned out to be a game Kenji Nogami and his Shokin Gaigoku Bank could play better than anybody in the world. Nogami saw himself as an advance man for the eventual Japanese domination of the globe's financial landscape. Maybe he was.

Michael Vance knew him from a wholly different direction, now almost another life. In years gone by, Nogami had traveled with equal ease in two worlds—that of straight money and that of "hot" money. He'd always maintained the cover of a legitimate banker, but insiders knew he'd made his real fortune laundering Yakuza amphetamine receipts and importing small-caliber weapons. It was that second career that now made him the perfect pipeline for a message that needed to be delivered fast.

Vance finished off the last of the coffee in his cup, then rose and strolled to the window to gaze down on the bustling Strand. The weather looked murky, typical for London.

Where was Eva now? he wondered. What was she doing? Maybe she'd managed to lose Novosty and get back to thinking about the protocol.

Well, he had some pressing business of his own, but the first thing was to try and find her.

Maybe she was wondering right now how to get in touch with *him*. What places here had they been together, back in the old days? Maybe there was some location . . . the V&A? St. Pauls? or how about a restaurant? What was that one she'd loved so much? The place the IRA shot up a few years back?

At that moment the white phone beside his bed interrupted his thoughts with its insistent British double chirp. He whirled around, startled.

Who knew he was here? If it was the KGB, or the Japanese mob, they wouldn't bother ringing for an appointment.

Finally, after the fifth burst, he decided to reach for it. Probably just the desk, calling about the breakfast things.

The voice was the last one he expected.

"Hello, darling."

"Eva!" He almost shouted. "Where the hell are you?"

"You really must stop shooting people, you know," she lectured. "You're getting to be a horrible menace to society."

"What—?"

"Michael." The voice hardened. "Christ, what a mess."

"Are you okay?"

"Yes, I think so." She paused to inhale. "But I'm literally afraid to move. I think KGB got Alex, there in Terminal Four at Heathrow. He was trying to bluff them, though, so maybe he pulled it off. Anyway, they were so tied up I just slipped past."

"The hell with him. Where are—?"

"I don't dare take a step outside this room now. Let's meet tonight. Besides, I want to work on translating . . . you know. I rang a scholarly bookshop I used to order from and they're delivering one of Ventris's books. Maybe I can make some headway."

"I already did a bit of it."

"I saw that in the files. A whole page." She laughed. "Congratulations."

"Give me a break. It's been ten years."

"Well, it looks like you're still able to fake the scholar bit. But just barely."

"Thanks. What do you think of it so far?"

"Scary. Very scary. But we have to do more. Enough so we can go public."

"Exactly. Look, I've got to do a couple of things today. Can you—?"

"That's fine, because I want to work on this." She

sounded businesslike again, her old self. "Something to while away the empty hours. The saga inside my little Zenith 486 has got to be the ticket out of this madness."

"Maybe, but we need to put some more spin on the scenario. Just to be safe."

"What?"

"Not on the phone. Can you just sit tight? Play your game and let me take a shot at mine?"

"It better be good."

"That remains to be seen." Who knew how it would go? But if it proceeded as planned, the whole thing could be turned around. "Now where the hell are you?"

"The place *we* always stayed, of course. Figuring you'd come here. But you stood me up, naturally. Same old Michael. So this morning I started calling around."

"You mean you're—?"

"At the Savoy, sweetie, our love nest of happy times past. Right across the street."

CHAPTER TEN

Monday 6:32 P.M.

Tanzan Mino was dressed in a black three-quarter sleeved kimono, staring straight ahead as he knelt before the sword resting in front of him. His hands were settled lightly on his thighs, his face expressionless. Then he reached out and touched the scabbard, bowing low to it. Inside was a twelfth-century *katana*, a five-foot-long razor created by swordsmiths of the Mino School, from the town of Seki, near Gifu in the heart of old Honshu. It was, he believed, a perfect metaphor for Japanese excellence and discipline.

The sword had now been reverenced; next he would use it to test his own centering. At this moment his mind was empty, knowing nothing, feeling nothing.

As his torso drew erect, he grasped the upper portion of the scabbard with his right hand, its tip with his left, and pulled it around to insert it into the black sash at his waist. He sat rigid for a moment, poised, then thrust his right foot forward as he simultaneously grasped the hilt of the sword with his right hand, the upper portion of the scabbard with his left. In a lightning move he twisted the hilt a half-turn and drew the blade out and across, his right foot moving into the attack stance. The whip of steel fairly sang through the empty air as the sword and his body moved together. It was the *chudan no kamae* stroke, the tip of the blade thrust directly at an opponent's face, an exercise in precision, balance.

Rising to a half kneel, he next lifted the sword above his head, his left hand moving up to seize the hilt in a powerful two-handed grip. An instant later he slashed downward with fierce yet controlled intensity, still holding the hilt at arm's length. It was the powerful *jodan no kamae* stroke, known to sever iron.

Finally, holding the hilt straight in front of him, he rotated the blade ninety degrees, then pulled his left hand back and grasped the mouth of the scabbard. As he rose to both feet, he raised the sword with his right hand and touched its *tsuba* handguard to his forehead in silent reverence, even as he shifted the scabbard forward. Then in a single motion he brought the blade around and caught it with his left hand just in front of the guard, still holding the scabbard. With ritual precision he guided the blade up its full length, until the tip met the opening of the sheath, and then he slowly slipped it in.

This weapon, he reflected with pride, was crafted of the finest steel the world had ever seen, created by folding and hammering heated layers again and again until it consisted of hundreds of thousands of paper-thin sheets. The metallurgy of Japan had been unsurpassed for eight hundred years, and now the *Daedalus* spaceplane had once again reaffirmed that superiority. Building on centuries of expertise, he had succeeded in fashioning the heretofore-unknown materials necessary to withstand the intense heat of scramjet operation.

The remaining problems now lay in another direction entirely. The difficulty was not technology; it was human blundering. Lack of discipline.

Discipline. The news he had just received had only served to assure him once again that discipline was essential in all of life.

As he turned and stationed the sword across his desk, he surveyed his penthouse domain and understood why heads of state must feel such isolation, such impotence. You could have the best planning, the best organization, the tightest coordination, and yet your fate still rode on luck and chance. And on others.

Overall, however, the scenario possessed an inescapable inevitability. A lifetime of experience told him he was right. He glanced at the sword one last time, again inspired by it, and settled himself at the desk.

Tanzan Mino was known throughout Japan as a *kuromaku,* a man who made things happen. Named after the unseen stagehand who pulled the wires in Japanese theater, manipulating the stage and those on it from behind a black curtain, the *kuromaku* had been a fixture in Japanese politics since the late nineteenth century. He fit the classic profile perfectly: He was an ultranationalist who coordinated the interests of the right-wing underworld with the on-stage players in industry and politics. In this role, he had risen from the ruins of World War II to become the most powerful man in Asia.

It had been a long and difficult road. He'd begun as an Osaka street operator in the late thirties, a fervent nationalist and open admirer of Mussolini who made his followers wear black shirts in imitation of the Italian fascists. When the Pacific War began, he had followed the Japanese army into Shanghai where, under the guise of procuring "strategic materials" for the imperial Navy, he trafficked in booty looted from Chinese warehouses and operated an intelligence network for the Kempei Tai, the Japanese secret police. After Japan lost China, and the war, the occupying supreme commander for the allied powers (SCAP) labeled him a Class A war criminal and handed him a three-year term in Sugamo prison.

The stone floors and hunger and rats gave him the incentive to plan for better things. The ruins of Japan, he concluded, offered enormous opportunity for men of determination. The country would be rebuilt, and those builders would rule.

Thus it was that while still in Sugamo he set about devising the realization of his foremost ambition: to make himself *oyabun* of the Tokyo Yakuza. His first step, he had decided, would be to become Japan's gambling czar, and upon his release—he was thirty years old at the time—he had made a deal with various local governments to organize speedboat races and split the take on the accompanying wagering. It was an offer none chose to refuse, and over the next forty years he and his Mino-gumi Yakuza amassed a fortune from the receipts.

While still in Sugamo prison he had yet another insight: That to succeed in the New Japan it would be necessary to align himself temporarily with the globe's powerful new player, America. Accordingly he began cultivating connections with American intelligence, and upon his release, he landed a job as an undercover agent for the occupation's G-2 section, Intelligence. He'd specialized in black-bag operations for the Kempei Tai in Shanghai during the war, so he had the requisite skills.

When SCAP's era of reconstruction wound down, he thoughtfully offered his services to the CIA, volunteering to help them crush any new Japanese political movements that smacked of leftism. It was love at first sight, and soon Tanzan Mino was fronting for the Company, putting to good use his Mino-gumi Yakuza as strikebreakers. With Tanzan Mino as *kuromaku,* the Yakuza and the American CIA had run postwar Japan during the early years, keeping it safe for capitalism.

Then as prosperity returned, new areas of expansion beckoned. When goods could again be bought openly, the black market, long a Yakuza mainstay, began to wither away. But he had converted this into an opportunity, stepping in to fill the new Japanese consumer's need for cash by opening storefront loan services known as *sarakin.* Although his Yakuza charged interest rates as high as 70 percent, the average Japanese could walk into a side-street office and minutes later walk out with several thousand dollars, no questions asked.

Unlike banks, he didn't bother with credit checks—he had well-proven collection techniques—and before long his *sarakin* were handling more consumer loans than all Japan's banks combined. His success was such that foreign bankers wanting to gain a foothold in Japan soon started coming to him. Bank of America, Bankers Trust, Chase Manhattan, American Express Bank—all began placing capital wholesale through the Yakuza's *sarakin*.

When the CIA bankrolled the Corsican mob as strike-breakers in Marseilles in the fifties, they were merely financing heroin labs for the French Connection, but when they and America's leading banks hired on with Tanzan Mino's Yakuza, they were furthering the career of the man destined to become the world's richest right-winger. The CIA arrangement had lasted until a midlevel field consultant blew the whistle.

The score for *that* had yet to be settled.

He shrugged away the thought with a glimmer of anger and turned to study the column of green figures on the computer screen atop his desk, mentally running a total. The numbers, at least, pleased him. Capitalization for the first year was ready to be issued; the dummy corporations were in place, their paperwork impeccable. None of the financing packages was likely to raise eyebrows. The plan was as flawless as human ability could make it.

As the pale light of dusk crept through the blinds, laying faint shadows across his silver hair, he reached over with a smile and touched the white stingray-skin binding on the sword's hilt. Yes, the plan was brilliant. A third world war, one of economics, had begun, but none of the other combatants fully realized it.

The European trading nations of 1992 were banding together, also bringing in the new capitalists of Eastern Europe, to create a trade monolith. At the same time Japan had, through strategic planning, achieved its own Pacific trade bloc, finally realizing its aim during the war, a Greater East Asia Coprosperity Sphere. Now only one final target remained: the new consumers of the Soviet Union, who represented the world's largest untapped market for goods, technology, investment. The Europeans, the Americans, all the capitalists, were fighting for that prize, but Tanzan Mino was within a whisker of seizing it for Japan and Mino Industries. The Soviets would have no choice.

He reached down to stroke Neko, the snow leopard who slept beside his desk, and reflected on the scenario. The Soviets had bought into it with eyes open. The plan was turning out to be absurdly easy.

At the moment all he needed was the cleanly laundered payoff money. The political risks, the financial risks, everything had to be covered. The powers in the Liberal Democratic Party feared going out on a limb for such a risky strategic objective. They required encouragement. And certain prominent Japanese bankers, who would have to assist in the scenario, also needed inducement. But the money had to be cash and totally untraceable. No more Recruit-style fiascos.

Where was it?

He pushed that worry aside momentarily as he studied the gleaming model of the *Daedalus*, poised like a Greek statue in the center of his office. To think that the Soviets would agree not only to the hard financial and territorial terms he had demanded, but actually were willing to help Mino Industries develop the most advanced airplane the world had ever seen. Their plight was fully as desperate as he'd assumed. It was a game where he won everything.

Yes, the *Daedalus* was as important as all the rest combined. It would leapfrog Japan to the undisputed ranks of the major powers, erasing forever the distinction between civilian and military technology.

Still, though, there were problems. Always problems. First, the news he had just received: The laundered funds still had not been delivered. Then there was the matter of the NSA cryptographer who had been given an intercepted copy of the protocol. Three men had been lost attempting to retrieve it, but she remained at large. That was unacceptable. It had to be reclaimed, no matter the cost, lest there be a premature exposure of the plan. Timing was everything.

Added to that was the puzzling matter of the Soviet test pilot, on whom the fate of the entire project hinged. He'd begun making outrageous demands, insisting on moving up the first hypersonic flight to Friday. Why? He'd once spent time in the United States as an exchange pilot. Could he be fully trusted?

Tanzan Mino had finally, reluctantly, approved the schedule change, though his instincts told him to beware. His instincts rarely failed, but it was better not to appear too inflexible too soon. At this stage the test pilot had become the crucial component of the project. Sometimes you had to bend to get what you wanted, and instincts be damned.

As if all that were not enough, he'd just heard an unsettling rumble out of London concerning Kenji Nogami, a Mino-gumi *kobun* for thirty years, a man he'd made rich.

He turned his attention back to the computer screen and studied the numbers once more. However, he could not concentrate.

The problems. He felt his anger rise, unbidden. He was too old for problems. Surmounting human incompetence was a young man's game. He had, he told himself, struggled enough for a dozen men. And now, having dedicated himself to fashioning Japan's twenty-first century ascendancy, he no longer really cared about money. No, what mattered now was the triumph of the Japanese people, the emperor, the Yamato spirit.

His countrymen, he had always believed, shared a noble heritage with another race, one distant in time and place but brothers still. Both the modern Japanese and the ancient Greeks had pursued a mission to refine the civilizations around them, offering a powerful vision of human possibilities. They both were unique peoples chosen by the gods. He wanted, more than anything, for the entire world to at last understand that.

With a sigh he turned and gave Neko a loving pat on her spotted muzzle, then touched the buzzer on his desk. Time to start solving the problems.

Monday 1:03 P.M.

"Michael, I'm terribly glad you could make it." Kenji Nogami smiled and reached for his pint of amber-colored lager. His tailoring was Savile Row via Bond Street, his accent Cambridge, his background well concealed. In a business where appearances counted for much, he had all the careful touches that separated the players from the pretenders—cheeks sleek from a daily workout at his club, eyes penetrating and always alert, hair graying at the temples. Today he stood out like a beacon in the mob of chatting brokers and jobbers in the paneled gloom of the pub, his aloof bearing and dark pinstripe suit proclaiming IN-SIDER as clearly as neon. A Japanese to the core, he still looked as though he had belonged there for a hundred years.

"By the way, congratulations on the takeover." Vance caught the pint of ale sliding across the beer-soaked mahogany, then lifted it. "I hear you scared hell out of the big players here in the City. Here's to going straight. Hope it doesn't take all the fun out of life."

"It had to happen eventually, Michael." He nodded with innocent guile and raised his glass tankard in return. "Cheers."

"To your health and wealth." Vance joined him in a sip. It was warm and bitter, the way he liked it. "No more intrigue."

"Well . . ." He winked and drank again, blowing back the foam. "We bankers still thrive on intrigue, old man. And secrecy. Otherwise somebody else would start making the money."

The young brokers laughing, smoking, and drinking in the pub all looked as though they made buckets of money. Outside, the ocher-trimmed Doric columns of the refurbished Leadenhall Market looked down on the lunchtime crowds of the financial district, almost all men in white shirts and dark suits, the modern uniform of the money changer.

"Trouble with secrets, though"—Vance settled his mug

onto the wet bar and looked up—"is that eventually the word gets out."

Nogami studied him. "Are you hinting at something? Something I should know?"

"Maybe I'm just thinking out loud. But what if a guy like me came across some proprietary information, sort of by accident, and consequently an old friend of ours back home in Tokyo was very unhappy?"

"If that 'friend' is who I think you mean, he's not someone either of us wants to see unhappy, do we?" He sipped solemnly at his beer.

"Speak for yourself," Vance replied, and drank again. "But to continue, what if this hypothetical guy had decided to try and simplify the situation, get news back to Tokyo about a way to solve everybody's problem? Then he'd need an information conduit. One that's tried and true."

Nogami reached for a tray of peanuts, took a small handful and shook them in his fist before popping one into his mouth. He chewed for a second, then smiled. "One way might be to have a drink with an old, shall we say, acquaintance, in hopes he might be able to help with some communication."

"Sounds like we're making headway here." He paused. "Say this hypothetical guy wants to talk a deal."

"What sort of deal?" Nogami chewed on more peanuts, his eyes noncommittal.

"For instance, if Tokyo'll lay off, he'll see what he can do about some laundered funds our friend's been waiting for. He's in a position to make it happen. But if they keep on with the muscle, the deal's off. In other words, no play, no pay."

"Supposing I know the individual in Tokyo you mean, as things stand now you've quite possibly come to the wrong man." He sighed. "This isn't the old days, my friend. I'm not wired in like I used to be. Times have changed, thank God. I'm out. I run an honest merchant bank, at least as honest as you can in this new day and age. And I like it that way."

"Ken, don't start the runaround." Vance tried to keep

his tone easy. "You're not talking to some bank examiner now. In Japan connections last forever. We both know that."

"You were never more correct." Nogami examined his lager. "Obligations remain, even though influence wanes. Which is, in fact, one of the reasons I wanted to see you today. Michael, if I do you this favor, could you perhaps do one for me in return?"

"Is it legit?"

"I suppose that depends," he laughed. "Look, of course I'd be more than happy to send a secure telex, if that's all you want. Heaven knows I owe you that much." He paused to sip from his mug. "But I'll sound rather a fool if I don't know the first thing about the situation. Can't you at least give me some idea?"

"Tokyo'll understand. And the less you know, the better for everybody."

"All right. But my position right now is . . . well, I may not be able to help as much as I'd like."

"I don't like the sound of that."

"It's the problem I mentioned to you. That 'individual' is calling in favors with *me* now, not the other way around. So this could be a trifle awkward, if you see what I mean."

"Ken, have you forgot I took care of you once? Remember the Toshiba milling-machine sale to the Soviets? All the posturing back in the U.S.? It could have been a lot worse for your team politically. Afterwards you said you owed me one."

"Yes, and I still appreciate what you did, tipping me off about the French, the fact they'd already sold such machines to the Soviets years ago. It helped us dampen the fires of moral indignation on Capitol Hill." He took another sip. "I got a lot of points with the right people in the LDP."

"I just got fed up with all the bullshit. No harm done." He leaned back. "But now it's your turn."

"Fair enough." He gazed around the crowded, smoke-filled pub. "Michael, I don't know if we really should be talking here. Care to take a walk, down to the Thames? Get a bit of air. Maybe hope for some sunshine?"

"All right." Vance tossed down a five-pound note and reached for his overcoat, draped across the stool next to them. "Weather's nice. At least for London."

Nogami nodded as they pushed through the crowded doorway and into the street. "Don't say what you're thinking. Don't say you can't imagine why I moved here."

"Never crossed my mind." Vance took a breath of the fresh air, expelling the residual smoke from his lungs. The lunchtime mob elbowed them from every side.

"You know the reason as well as I do. It's all part of our overall strategy. Japan is a world player now, Michael. I'm part of the vanguard that's going to do to financial services worldwide what we did to semiconductors and electronics. You just watch and see."

"I already believe it." He did. Japan's dominance of the world money scene was just a matter of time.

They navigated their way through the midday throng. On every side lunchtime shoppers were munching sandwiches, lining up for knick-knacks to take back to the office. They strolled past the rear of the tubular-steel Lloyds building, then headed down a cobblestone side street toward the river.

"But we had to come here and buy our base in order to be part of the financial game in Europe," Nogami continued, not missing a beat. "We expect to be major players before long."

"I'd say you're already one. When the Plaza Accord sliced the greenback in half, it doubled the value of Japan's bankroll. Every yen you had was suddenly worth twice as many dollars, as if by magic."

"We can't complain." He paused to inhale the gray, heavy air. "Of course the locals here in London are constantly enlisting their 'old boy' regulators to make up new rules to hamper us, but Tokyo invented that little ploy. It almost makes this place feel like home."

"Word is you play all the games. I hear Westminster Union now handles more Eurodollar deals than anybody."

"We pull our weight." He smiled and dodged a red double-decker bus as they crossed Lower Thames Street.

"You name a major currency, we'll underwrite the debt offering."

"Lots of action."

"There is indeed. Sometimes perhaps too much. Which is why I wanted to talk down here, by the river. Shall we stroll out onto London Bridge?"

"Sounds good."

Spread before them now was the muddy, gray expanse of London's timeless waterway. Shakespeare had gazed on it. Handel had written music to accompany fireworks shot over it. Today a few tugs were moving slowly up the center channel, and a sightseeing boat was headed down to Greenwich. Cranes of the new Docklands development loomed over the horizon downriver.

"So what's the problem?" Vance turned to study his face. There was worry there, and pain.

"Michael, that 'individual' you spoke of. He has, in the famous phrase, 'made me an offer I can't refuse.' He wants me to handle a debt issue, corporate debentures, bigger than anything this town has ever seen. Anything Europe has ever seen."

"You should be ordering champagne."

"Not this time." He turned back to study the river. "The whole thing stinks."

"Who're the players."

"It's supposedly to raise capital for the Mino Industries Group. I've been 'asked' to underwrite the bonds, then unload them with minimal fanfare and keep a low profile." He looked back. "But it's almost fraud, Michael. I don't think there's anything behind them at all. Nothing. The beneficiaries are just phony Mino Industries shadow corporations. Only nobody will know it. You see, the bonds are zero-coupons, paying no interest till they mature ten years from now. So it will be a full decade before the buyers find out they've acquired paper with no backing."

"Won't be the first time the sheep got sheared by a hustler."

"Michael, I'm not a hustler," he snapped. "And there's more. They're so-called bearer bonds. Which means there's no record of who holds them. Just one more trick to keep this thing below the radar."

"Typical. 'Bearer bonds' always sell like hotcakes in high-tax locales like the Benelux countries. That mythical Belgian dentist can buy them anonymously and screw the tax man."

"Yes, that's part of what makes Eurocurrency ideal for this, all that homeless money floating around over here. No government is really responsible for keeping track of it. In fact, every effort has been made to ensure that these debentures appeal to greed. Their yield will float, pegged at two full points above the thirty-year British government bond, the gilt. As lead underwriter I'll have the main responsibility, but I'm also supposed to form a syndicate of Japanese brokerage houses here—Nomura, Daiwa, Sumitomo, the others—to make sure the offering goes off without a hitch. But that precaution will hardly be necessary. At those interest rates, they should practically fly out the door." He sighed. "Which is a good thing, because . . . because, Michael, the amount I'm being asked to underwrite is a hundred billion dollars."

"And that's just for the first year, right?"

Nogami looked up, startled. "How did you know?"

"Call it a lucky guess." He took a deep breath. So *that's* where the funding stipulated in the protocol was going to come from. European suckers. My God, he thought, the play is superb.

"Michael, nobody could float an offering like that and have it covered with real assets. Nobody. Taken all together that's enough money to capitalize a dozen world-class corporations." He paused. "Of course, I won't be offering it all at once. The debentures will dribble out over the period of a year, and then the next year, it starts all over again. For five years."

"So you're supposed to raise five hundred billion dollars in the Eurobond market over five years. Not impossible, but it's a tall order."

"Especially since the ratings will be smoke and mirrors. It is, in effect, an unsecured loan." He looked away, down at the swirling brown surface of the Thames. "You know what it really means? He wants me to sell *junk bonds*. And I can't refuse." His voice came close to a quaver. "Just when I was well into earning the esteem of the European banking community, I'm suddenly about to become the Drexel Burnham of Eurobonds. I'll be operating the investment equivalent of a shell game."

"Ken, why are you telling me all this?" Vance had never seen him this upset.

"Because I have to find out what this is all about. What the money's going to be used for."

"I take it the Tokyo *oyabun*'s not talking."

"Michael, no one dares question him. You know that." His voice grew formal. "It's the Yakuza way."

"Well, you're in London now. A free man."

"It's not that simple. You may not know—it's a very well-kept secret—that he capitalized my takeover of the Westminster Union Bank here. He put together a consortium of private financiers for me. A lot of the money was actually his. The whole thing had to be low profile, since none of our banks dared have its name associated with a hostile takeover in London. Our institutions are still squeamish about such things. They all cheered me on in private, but in public they didn't know anything about it."

"Maybe he had this little return favor in mind all along."

"To tell you the truth, I've since wondered that myself. Anyway, now he's calling in my obligation. We Japanese call it *giri*. I have to play. But either way I'm ruined. If I do it, I'll become a pariah in the European banking community. If I don't . . . well, the consequences are almost unthinkable."

"Ken, I don't know how to say this, but there's a chance this whole scenario is bigger than anything you can imagine."

Nogami turned to stare. "What do you know?"

"Let's just say I hear things. But first we need to strike our deal."

"Of course. As I said, I'll send a telex, from my secure trading room, for what good it may do. But you've got to help me too. Please." He turned back to the river. "You know, Michael, I like my life here. More and more. Even given all that's going on here these days, the pace is still much more civilized than Tokyo. For all our prosperity back home, I think we've traded something very valuable. Call it our soul perhaps. Here I feel almost free from the old days, part of a real, legitimate world. I hated all the money laundering, the shady deals. These days I can look myself in the face."

"I was temporarily changing professions myself, until about a week ago. Then this problem came up." He waved to a pleasure boat slowly motoring up the river. It was only a thirty footer, but the lines reminded him of the *Ulysses*. It made him suddenly homesick for real sunshine and real air.

"Michael, what's going on? We need to work together."

"I'll just say this. I think the godfather's got a big surprise cooking. Maybe we're both caught in the middle."

He smiled. "If that's true, we can help each other out. Though I can't push too hard." He took a deep breath and gazed at the murky London sky. "But still . . . I'll tell you the truth. I'm very seriously thinking I may just refuse to touch the whole thing. Tanzan Mino—yes, why not name names? He's even made vague threats against my family. The man has pushed me too far this time. Somewhere it has to end."

"You're a brave man. He still runs some very persuasive muscle. Better have your life insurance paid up."

"I'm well aware. But I don't want to jeopardize everything I've built here. My whole new life. So that's why I need you. If you could find out what's behind all this, I could decide whether I should risk everything and go ahead with the offering. Or just stand up to him at last. Otherwise . . ."

"What's the timing?"

"I have to list the first offering with the Issuing House Association day after tomorrow. We've already put together the paperwork, just in case."

"Pretty tight."

"Michael, I'll see what I can do about your problem. And if there's anything else, you know I'll try my best."

"Depending on whether my message gets through, I

could be needing somebody to handle some cash. A reasonably substantial sum. Maybe as part of our little quid pro quo you could arrange it."

"Is this money . . . ?" He paused awkwardly. "Well, you understand my question."

"It's laundered. Clean as a hound's tooth."

"Where is it now?"

"Don't worry," Vance smiled. "It's liquid."

"And the sum?"

"Hang on to your bowler hat. It's around a hundred million U.S."

"Is that all?" he laughed. "That figure is barely a blip on the screen these days. For a minute there I thought you were talking real money."

"Seems a reasonably substantial sum."

"It's scarcely more than walking-around money in our business, as you well know. Over two hundred *billion* passes through the foreign exchange markets every day, a large amount of it right here in London."

"Well, there could be a small complication, if the KGB gets into the action."

"KGB?" He pulled up sharply. "What in bloody hell do they—?"

"It's a long story."

"But why would Soviet intelligence be involved? They're supposed to be keeping a lower profile these days."

"Rumor has it they let this one get past them. The money left home without a passport and now they look like fools for letting it happen."

"I see." He grew silent, then glanced at his watch and pulled his overcoat tighter. "Well, perhaps I should send that cable now. Before Tokyo tucks in for the night."

"The sooner the better."

"And the matter of concern to me?"

"Let me think it over." Vance spoke slowly. "But in the meantime, I'd strongly advise you to hold off with the offering."

"You're not telling me what you know. Is that fair?"

"No. But who said the world's got to be fair? There's a

play about to go down. I know about part of it, not all. But before I'm through, well, let's just say that when somebody starts using muscle on me, I sort of lose my sense of proportion."

"Is it that bad?" His stare carried alarm. "What am I supposed to do?"

"Sit tight on the offering. Don't say yes or no, just find a way to postpone it. And send that telex. I'll dictate it for you. After that, you can reach me at my hotel. Strand Palace."

"The Strand Palace? Michael, you?" He smiled. "Hardly up to your usual standards."

"I don't do as much free lance these days as I used to. So I have to learn to live closer to my means."

"I'll believe that when I see it," he said with a laugh. "You're not telling me the truth. About anything."

"You're right. And it's for your own good. You just stall on the offering and let me play this my way. If things aren't straightened out in a day, two tops, we're both in a lot of trouble."

"Two days?"

"It has to happen by then. Too much is going on."

"Now you're really starting to make me alarmed."

"You should be."

Because if this isn't settled in two days, he thought, somebody's probably going to be dead.

CHAPTER ELEVEN

Monday 8:05 P.M.

She checked her watch, then took a last look around the spacious room. It was time. Her bag lay on the bed, packed and waiting to be sent later. The part of her luggage that mattered was the vinyl flight bag by the door, containing the Zenith Turbo 486.

With a sigh she rose, threw on her light tan raincoat, and grabbed the bag. This was the part she'd been dreading, and she'd done her best to try and look inconspicuous—a dressy beige outfit and a few silver accessories. She'd also washed her hair, which always made her feel better.

The carpeted hallway was clear as she closed the door, tugged to be certain it was secure, then took a deep breath, turned, and headed toward the elevator. She hadn't been outside the room for almost twenty-four hours. This, she told herself, must be what house arrest feels like.

It was about to be over. All she had to do now was make her way through the Savoy lobby, walk diagonally across the Strand, then through another lobby, another elevator, and she'd be with Michael.

The more she allowed herself to think about the whole situation, the angrier she got, at all the bean-counters at NSA who wouldn't listen to her, at the entire American intelligence establishment. How could everybody have missed what was happening?

Maybe, she thought, the air outside would help cool her off. She definitely needed to get out of the Savoy, if only to counter the claustrophobia. Stretch your legs, sweetheart, and think.

The elevator chimed and the doors slid open. The crisp, shiny, expensive fashions greeted her, the iridescence of diamonds; the night people of London were headed out for dinner and the clubs. A cross section of the jet set and the bored rich. Nobody seemed to be having fun.

She looked at them as she stepped in, wondering what they would think if they knew what was in her vinyl bag. Michael used to say the only thing people like these were interested in was impressing headwaiters. He was probably dead right.

The LOBBY light flashed above the doors, and they slid open to reveal muted wood paneling, English antiques, and sparkling mirrors. Gray-suited bellboys carrying baggage and opening elevator doors mingled with the bustling evening throng. It was a world unto itself.

Not pausing, she strode past the pink marble columns and glowing chandeliers, then headed for the glassed en-

trance. Outside, the traffic on the Strand, the glitter of
London at night, all of it beckoned.

Being in Crete again had really made her think, about a
lot of things. Mostly though, she'd thought about Michael
Vance, Jr. Ex-archaeologist, ex-spook, ex- . . . God knew
what. Still, she'd seen plenty worse . . . the paunchy as-
sistant-this and vice-that, all divorced and paying alimony
and whining. But in this man-short time, with hungry
divorcées flocking the bars, they didn't have to bother
keeping up appearances. Middle-aged decay was their in-
alienable right. Mike, whatever else you said about him,
still looked as good as he had a decade ago. He was showing
some mileage, sure, but on him it didn't look half bad.
Maybe it was the tequila.

Could they start over again, that new beginning he'd
hinted about? Maybe it was at least worth a try.

She moved on through the milling mob in the lobby,
trying to be casual, to blend. He'd said she should get out of
the Savoy as soon as possible, just send her things and move
in with him. But why didn't he come over and stay with
her? she'd asked. The Savoy was more romantic, more like
the old days. That's when he'd abruptly switched the subject, saying they couldn't discuss it on the phone.

Probably he had something working. Well, she had a few
surprises too. She'd spent the day hacking away at the
protocol, and she'd learned a lot more. It was even worse
than she'd imagined.

As she pushed through the revolving doors and into the
driveway, the *clack-clack* of London taxi motors and the
rush of cold air brought back all the adrenaline of that
moment in Iráklion when she had first seen Alex.

She grasped the flight bag more firmly and moved on
down the left-hand sidewalk, past the National Westminster Bank at the corner and toward the street. Almost
there. Just across waited the Strand Palace and safety.

In her rush, she'd missed an important event. Mingled in
among the lobby crowd was a couple she'd failed to notice.
They'd been over on her left, by the desk. The man, in a
rumpled brown jacket, was haggard, with bloodshot eyes.
His beard was untrimmed, but it did disguise the bruises

on his face. Unseen by Eva he'd suddenly raised his hand and pointed at her. Nor did she see the woman with him—dark coiffure, elegant makeup, Oscar de la Renta cocktail dress—though she wouldn't have recognized her in any case.

Only moments after Eva Borodin walked up the Savoy driveway, the woman was speaking into the radio she'd had in her shiny evening purse.

Monday 8:08 P.M.

He glanced at his watch, then looked out his smudgy hotel window and down at the Strand. Two more minutes and there should be a knock on the door.

Would she believe him? That he'd set up the play? Maybe he couldn't quite believe it himself, but still, they had the biggest share of poker chips now. They were about to take control of the game.

It was almost, almost time to relax.

Then he saw her, moving briskly across the Strand while furtively looking left and right. Good. After he watched her disappear into the lobby down below, he turned back from the window and walked to the bar. Time to crack open the Sauza Tres Generaciones, Tequila Añejo—Mexico's well-aged contribution to the well-being of all humankind. Hard enough to come by anywhere, it was virtually unobtainable here in London, but his search had succeeded. He lifted it out of its tan box, admiring the coal black bottle, then gave the cork a twist and sniffed the fragrance, fresh as nectar, before settling it back on the bar. Next he removed a bottle of rare Stolichnaya Starka vodka from the freezer and stationed it beside the Sauza. This, he knew, was Eva's favorite, made with water from the Niva River and flavored with pear leaves and Crimean apples as well as a touch of brandy and a dash of port.

A few moments later he heard a light knock on the door, and with a feeling of relief he stepped over.

"Michael," the voice was a muted whisper, "hurry."

He swung it inward and there she was. Without a word she moved into his arms.

"Are you okay?" He touched her face, then lifted her lips to his. They were cold, tight.

"Yes. I . . . I think so. God, what a day. I kept wanting to call you, darling."

"I was out."

"I assumed that. I can't wait to show you my translation."

"Hey, slow down." He kissed her again. "Let's have a celebration drink first. Just you and me."

"Michael, don't talk nonsense. We've got to *think*."

"I got a bottle of your native wine, a little Tequila Añejo for me. Never hurt the mental processes. Come on, what do you say?" He turned and headed for the bar.

She was unzipping the vinyl flight bag. "How can you . . . ?" Then she caught herself and laughed. "It better be frozen. Like ice-cold syrup."

"Cold as Siberia. It should go down well with the latest news item. We've now got a deal on the table with Tokyo."

"What kind of deal?" She glanced over.

"I told them if they'll call off the gorillas, I'll see about lightening up their money problems. The Alex Novosty imbroglio."

"You're not really going to do it?"

He laughed. "What do you think?"

"Darling, whatever you're planning, it's not going to stop them."

"Why don't we wait and see?"

"I've seen enough already."

"Stay mellow." He was handing her a tall, thin glass of clear liquid, already frosting on the sides. "Make any progress on the protocol?"

"Nobody in the world is going to believe it. This is just *too* big. I almost wonder if a newspaper would touch it, at least until we have more than we have now." She'd set down her drink and was opening the flight bag. Out came the Zenith, and moments later a text was on the screen.

"How much farther did you get?"

"Only another page or so. This is tougher going than I

thought. But here, look. This section picks up from where you left off. Mother Russia's practically giving away the store."

. . . 3. Within one year of the satisfaction of all formalities pursuant to the above-designated credits, the USSR will renounce sole proprietorship of the Kurile Islands and the Soviet *oblast* of Sakhalin. Those territories will thereafter be administered as a free-trade zone and joint protectorate of the USSR and Japan, with exclusive economic development rights extended to all designated corporations comprised in Mino Industries Group (MIG).

4. MIG is hereby granted full rights to engage in capital investment and manufacturing development in the USSR, which capital investment may comprise all or part of the financial credits specified in Item 1. MIG will be permitted to hold 51% or greater interest in all joint industrial facilities, and the operation and control of those facilities will rest solely with managers designated by MIG unless otherwise mutually agreed.

5. Within two years of the date of this agreement, the Soviet ruble will be declared a free-market currency, convertible to yen and other Western currencies at rates governed solely by the established world currency exchanges. Furthermore, from that time forward, Japanese-manufactured durables and consumer goods may be purchased directly in rubles, at prevailing rates of exchange.

6. Upon ratification of this Protocol by the Japanese Diet and the Supreme Soviet of the USSR, the Japanese Self-Defense Forces will have full access, for purposes not hostile to the sovereign security of the USSR, to all military installations on Sakhalin and the Kurile Islands including facilities now used exclusively by the Soviet Navy and Soviet Air Force. The security of the Far Eastern *oblast* of the USSR will henceforth be a joint obligation of the USSR and the Japanese Self-Defense Forces. . . .

He looked up, his eyes narrowing. "So it's just what we thought. A global horsetrade. Tokyo supplies Moscow with half a trillion in loans and financing over the next five years, the money they need for 'restructuring,' and the Soviets cede back the territory they took after the war, the Kurile Islands and Sakhalin, that perennial thorn in the side of the Japanese right."

"Not to mention which, Japan also gets a whole new target for all that excess capital burning a hole in its pocket. As well as first crack at Sakhalin's oil reserves. Michael, put it together and you realize Japan's about to wrap up what she's been angling for ever since the war—total economic dominance of the Far East, Russia and all."

Right, he thought, but which Russians are making this secret deal? Could it be the hardliners, who're lining up a new military alliance? Is that what the "prototype" is all about.

"By the way, did you look closely at the early part, the bit I translated?" He walked over and checked the traffic on the Strand below. "There's some kind of surprise package under the tree. I don't think it's Christmas chocolates."

"You mean the prototype? Bothers me too." She took another sip of her freezing Stoly. "What do you think it is?"

"My wild guess would be some kind of advanced weapons system. If the Soviets are planning to give back territory, they'd better be getting some goodies."

"Well, any way you look at it, this whole thing is brilliant, synergistic. Everybody comes out with something they want."

"World geopolitics is about to become a whole new ball game. But that other bit, the prototype, seems to be a really important part of it. There're specifications, a hard delivery date, the works. That's where the quid pro quo starts getting kinky."

"It does sound like some entirely new kind of weapon," she agreed.

"Who knows? Whatever it turns out to be, though, it's something they had to develop together. Which probably means high-tech. But we're going to find out, you and me." He studied the street below, where traffic was a blaze of headlights, then turned back. "Tell me again about those satellite photos you mentioned out at the palace."

"You mean the ones of Hokkaido, the Japanese island up north?"

"Right. What exactly was in them? You said it looked like a runway?"

"I said that's what I thought it was. But nobody at NSA is authorized to be interested officially in what goes on in Japan, so the oversight committee wouldn't spring for a real analysis, an infrared overlay or anything. The budget cuts, et cetera."

"Which is exactly what whoever planned this figured on, right? If you had some military surprise cooking, what better place to hide it than in the wilds of northern Japan, where nobody would bother to pay attention?"

"Well, the location couldn't be more perfect for a joint project. Hokkaido is right across the straits from Sakhalin. All nice and convenient." She stared at her vodka as the room fell silent. "Maybe if we finished the translation."

"Somehow I doubt it's going to spell out the details. The so-called prototype hasn't been described so far, at least as far as we've got. Probably a deliberate omission."

"Our problem is, without the full text nobody's going to take our word for all this." She finished off her Stoly with a gulp, then got up to pour another.

"Maybe there's a way." He caught her and pulled her into his arms. "But first things first. Why don't we forget about everything just for tonight?"

She stared at him incredulously. "Darling, get serious. Right now there are people out there wanting to make us disappear because we know too much. They've already tried. That's *very* real."

"Look, that's being handled. Why can't you trust me?" He hugged her again. "I think it's time we had an evening just for us. So how about a small intimate reunion tonight, right here, dinner for two? While we wait for the fish to bite."

"I don't believe I'm hearing this."

"We'll both slip into something comfortable, have the greatest meal in the world sent up, along with about a case of wine, then retire to that plush bed over there and spend the rest of the evening getting reacquainted?"

"You're serious, aren't you?" She studied his eyes. They had a lascivious twinkle.

"Of course."

She hesitated, then thought, Why not call his bluff?

"All right. If you can be insane, then I can too. But if we're going to do it, then let's go all the way. I'm sick of living off room service." She slapped down her glass. "Know what I really want? I want to go out somewhere expensive and splashy. With you. I want to *do* London."

"Great!" He was beaming.

Whoops. He hadn't been bluffing.

"I dare you." She rose and threw her arms around him. Suddenly it was all too wonderful to forgo. "We'll put this Zenith in the hotel safe and act like real people for an evening. Then we'll come back here and you'll get totally ravished. That's a promise, sweetheart."

"I sort of had it figured for the other way around."

"Oh, yeah. We'll see, and may the best ravisher win." She clicked off the computer and shoved it into the flight bag, then turned back. "How about that wonderful restaurant we went to way back when? You know. That night we both got so drunk and you almost offered to make an honest woman of me."

"An offer you saw fit to refuse in advance." He looked her over. "But I assume you mean that place up in Islington? What was it? The Wellington or something?"

"Right. It was sort of out of the way. Down a little alley." She threw her arms around him. "That night was so wonderfully romantic, like a honeymoon."

"It almost was," he smiled, remembering. "Let's call for a reservation and just go."

"Darling, are we acting insane?" She looked up, eyes uncertain. "I'm half afraid."

"Don't be." He touseled her hair before thinking. "Nobody's going to touch you, believe me. I've nailed the bastards. All of them."

Monday 11:28 P.M.

It was flawless. They dined in a Gothic, ivy-covered greenhouse in the garden of a maître nineteenth-century inn where waiters scurried, the maitre d' hovered, and the wine steward nodded obsequiously every time he passed their table. It was even better than their first visit. After a roulade of red caviar, Eva had the ragoût au gratin, Vance the boeuf à la ficelle, his favorite. For dessert they shared the house specialty, tulipe glacée aux fruits, after which they lingered over Stilton cheese and a World War I bottle of Lisbon port.

And they talked and laughed and talked. They both tried to focus on the good times: trips they'd taken, places they'd shared, what they'd do next—together. She even agreed to spend August helping him sail the *Ulysses* over to Crete, his latest plan. The gap in time began slowly to drop away. It was as though they'd been reborn; everything felt new, fresh, and full of delight. Who said you couldn't start over?

Neither wanted it to end, but finally, reluctantly, he signaled for the check. After a round of farewells from the staff, they staggered out into the brisk evening air.

"Where to now?" He was helping her into a black London taxicab, after drunkenly handing the uniformed doorman a fiver.

"God, I'm so giddy I can't think." She crashed into the seat and leaned her head against his shoulder.

"Yanks?" The driver glanced back with a genuine smile. He wore a dark cap and sported a handlebar mustache of Dickensian proportions. "Been to New York myself, you know, with the missus. Two years back. Don't know how you lot can stand the bleedin' crime, though."

"Worse every year," Vance nodded.

"So, where'll it be, my lords and ladies?" He hit the ignition.

"How about heading down to the Thames, say Victoria Embankment Gardens, around in there."

"Lovely spot for a stroll. Private like, if you know what I

mean." He winked, then revved the engine and started working the vehicle down the narrow street, headed toward the avenue. "Thing about the States, you'd be daft to walk in a park *there* after dark." He glanced back. "So how was it?"

"What?"

"The Wellington, mate. You know, I take plenty of Arabs there, bleedin' wogs, them and their fine Soho hookers."

"We made do."

"If you've got the quid, why not. That's what I always say." He smiled above his mustache. "Guess you know IRA bombed the front room about ten years back, bloody bastards. Lobbed one right through the big window."

"We were hoping they'd never hit the same place twice."

"With those bloodthirsty micks you never know, mate, you never know. Only good thing about the States, no bleedin' IRA." He made a right turn off Goswell Road onto Clerkenwell Road. Even at this late hour, the traffic was brisk, black taxis side by side.

"Michael, I love Victoria Gardens." Eva reached up and bit his ear. "Can we dance in the moonlight?"

"Why not. I think it's romantic as hell." He drew her closer. "Probably shouldn't tell you this, but back in my youth, when I was living in London one summer, I used to take a plump little Irish hotel maid down there. I confess to a series of failed assaults on her well-guarded Catholic virtue."

"Maybe this time your luck will change," she giggled. And she bit him again.

"I'll never be seventeen again, but I'm willing to give it one more try." He turned to study the traffic behind them. Had the play started already?

Yep, there it was. A dark car was following them, had pulled out right behind as they left the restaurant's side street. It was trailing discreetly, but it was in place.

Pretty much on schedule, he told himself. They must have found out by now.

"Darling, I want to make you feel seventeen all over again." She snuggled closer. "I'm starting to feel good again. I'd almost forgot you could do that for me. Thank you."

He kissed her, then leaned forward and spoke through the partition. "See those headlights behind us?"

"I think they were waiting outside, at the restaurant. Noticed them there. Now they look to be going wherever you're going." The burly cabbie glanced into his side mirror. "Friends of yours?"

"In a manner of speaking. I think we've just revised our destination. Make it the Savoy instead. The main entrance there on the Strand."

"Whatever you say. Forget the park?"

"You've got it. And try not to lose them. Just make sure they don't know that you know. Figure it out."

"Having some sport with your friends, eh?"

"Work on it."

"Oh, Christ." Eva revolved to look. "Michael, what is it?"

"My guess is somebody found out something, and they're very upset."

She grasped his hand. "Why not try and lose them in the traffic?"

"They probably know where we're staying. What's the point?"

"I do hope you know what you're doing."

"Trust me. The Savoy's a nice friendly place for a drink. We'll ask them in, maybe drop by the American bar, there on the mezzanine."

"Why did we go out?" She threw her arms around him. "I knew it was a risk and still—"

"Relax." He kissed her. "We're just headed home after a lovely dinner. And when we get there, maybe we'll ask them in for a nightcap."

"Who do you think it is?"

"This is a friendly town. Why don't we just wait and find out?"

"Right. I'm dying to know who wants to kill us now." She turned to stare again at the headlights. "After all, it's been almost a day and a half since somebody's—"

"Hey, we've had a great evening. Nobody's going to

spoil that. This will just top it off." He looked back again, then leaned forward as the driver turned onto the Strand. "Be sure and take us all the way down the driveway."

"Whatever you say." He flipped on his blinker, then checked the mirror. "Seems your friends are coming along."

"That's the idea." Vance passed him a ten-pound note as they rolled to a halt. "Nice job, by the way."

"Anything for a Yank." He checked the bill, then tipped his hat. "Many thanks, gov'nor."

"Michael." Eva froze. "I'm not getting out."

"Come on." He reached for her hand. "This is going to be the most fun we've had all night." He looked up at the gray-uniformed Savoy doorman approaching. "Trust me."

The other car, a black Mercedes, had stopped just behind them, and now its doors swung out on both sides. The first to emerge were two surly men in heavy, bulging suits; next came an expensively dressed, dark-haired woman; and the last was a bearded man who had to be helped. He seemed weak and shaky.

Vance waved to him and beckoned him forward. "Alex, what a surprise. Glad you brought your friends. I was starting to worry we might miss each other this time."

"Michael." His voice faltered as he walked past the others, limping. "We must talk. Now."

"Great idea. Let's ask everybody in for a drink."

The woman was staring, cold as ice, while the two men flanked her on either side, waiting. Vance smiled and greeted her.

"Vera, talk about luck. And I'll bet you were worried we wouldn't manage to meet up in London. Small world."

The woman was trying to ignore him as she addressed Eva. "You have in your possession classified Soviet materials."

"If I do, that's your problem." She glared back.

"No, Ms. Borodin." The woman moved forward, carrying a leather purse. "It is your problem."

"Well, now. Looks like we're all ready for a nightcap." Vance took Eva's hand, nodded at the doorman, and led her through the lobby doors. Over his shoulder he yelled back. "I honestly recommend the American bar upstairs. Terrific view."

"Michael, please wait." Novosty limped after him, through the doorway, then grasped his arm. "We need to talk first."

"About what?"

"You know very well. The money. Michael, the game is up, can't you see? I've got to return it, all of it, and face the consequences, God help me. I have no choice. They—"

"You know, Alex, that's probably a good idea. Things were getting too rough. This was a hustle you should have left to the big boys. I tried to tell you that back in Athens, the other morning. Just give it back."

"What are you saying?" He went pale.

"Just return the money. Try and make them see it was a misunderstanding. How were you supposed to know it was embezzled? You were just following orders, right? They can probably cover the whole thing over as just some kind of paperwork shuffle."

"Michael, don't play games with me." He was clenching Vance's sleeve, his voice pleading.

"Hey, we're partners, remember? I'll back you all the way." He urged Eva on past the gaggle of bellmen and into the marbled lobby. The chandeliers sparkled and the room still bustled with bejeweled evening people. "Now we're all just going to have a very civilized drink."

The possibility of that seemed to be diminishing, however. The two men, clearly KGB "chauffeurs," had now moved alongside menacingly.

"You will come with us." Vera Karanova was approaching Eva. "Both of you. A car is waiting, at the entrance on the river side."

"Down by the park?" Vance kept urging Eva across the lobby, toward the staircase leading up to the bar. "Funny thing. We were just talking about the Embankment Gardens."

Vera nodded toward the empty tearoom and the steps beyond, which led down toward the river side, then spoke quietly in Russian to the two men. They shouldered against Vance, the one on the right reaching for Eva's arm.

"Easy with the muscle, hero." He caught the man's paisley tie and yanked him around, spinning him off balance, then kneed him onto the floor.

"Michael, wait." Novosty stepped between them, then took Vance's arm and drew him farther ahead. "About the money. You've—"

"What about it?" He looked puzzled. "Just return it, like I told you."

Novosty's eyes twitched above his beard. "Michael, the entire sum was withdrawn from the Moscow Narodny Bank at eleven o'clock this morning. The whole hundred million. It's vanished."

"Sounds like a problem. Now how do you suppose a thing like that could have happened?"

"You know very well." His voice was almost a sob. "It was authorized right after the bank opened. Someone requested that the funds be converted into Eurodollar bearer bonds and open cashiers checks, all small denominations. Which were then picked up by a bonded courier service." His voice cracked again. "I don't know what to do. The bank claims they have no more responsibility."

"Legally, I guess that's right. They're probably in the clear."

"Michael, you must have arranged it. Using the account numbers and identification I gave you—"

"Prove it."

"But how? I have to return the funds, or they'll kill me. I told them only you could have done it, but they don't believe me."

"Interesting thing about bearer bonds and open cashiers checks. They're same as cash. Everybody's favorite form of hot money. Very liquid and totally untraceable. For all we know your hundred million could be in Geneva by now, taking in the view of the lake." He turned and pecked Eva on the cheek. "Ready for that nightcap?"

Novosty caught his arm and tried to pull him back. "You won't get away with this. I'm warning you. You're a dead man."

"You know, I sort of look at it the other way around. I figure whoever copped that cash this morning got a hundred-million-dollar insurance policy. Because you see, if T-Directorate wants to kiss their hundred million *do svedania,* the best way possible would be to keep up with the muscle here tonight. That could make it just disappear forever. There'd be a lot of explaining to do. Probably make a very negative impression on certain people back at Dzerzhinsky Square. Vera here might even have to turn in all her gold cards."

"What are you saying?" Now Comrade Karanova had moved closer. "Is it really true *you* have the embezzled funds?" She examined Vance with a startled look, then glanced at Novosty, as though to confirm. His eyes were defeated as he nodded.

"You should check the desk here more often." Vance pointed toward the mahogany reception. "Photocopies of the open cashiers checks were dropped off for you at nine o'clock tonight. So maybe it's time everybody talked to me." He thumbed back at her two bodyguards. "For starters how about losing those two apes. Send them down to the park for a stroll. Then maybe we can talk. Over a drink. The vanguard of the proletariat sits down with the decadent capitalists. Could be there's a deal here yet. East meets West."

"Tell me what you want," Vera Karanova said, without noticeable enthusiasm.

"For starters, how about some protection. If these incompetents of yours can manage it."

"From whom?"

"Look, Comrade, there's a deal cooking, and I think there's more to it than meets the eye. I do know there's a very smart individual, on the other side of the globe, who's got some very definite plans for Eva and me. As well as for Mother Russia. I would suggest it might be in your interest to help us stop him while we still can. He's never played straight, and I don't think he's about to start now."

"I have my responsibilities too. Just return the money and we will handle the situation after that."

"The best thing you can do right now is stay out of the way. I've seen too many screwups out of Dzerzhinsky Square to turn this thing over to Moscow."

"Dr. Vance, you are playing a dangerous game."

"If you want to see the money again, it's the only game going. Now do we play or what?"

CHAPTER TWELVE

Monday 11:32 P.M.

"When did you receive this?" Tanzan Mino glanced over the cable message once again, then looked up. Although the time was near midnight, the aide had found him still behind his black slate desk. The lights in his penthouse office were turned low, muting the already dull earth tones of the walls. Neko paced across the expanse fronting the wide picture window, flicking her tail and anticipating her evening dinner of water buffalo *tartare*.

"Fifteen minutes ago, Mino-sama." He eyed the leopard nervously. "It was logged in on the eleventh floor, over the secure telex. I was reluctant to bother you at this late hour."

"When you live to my age, you no longer have the patience for sleep. There is so much to do and so little time. Two or three hours are all I allow myself now." He tossed the paper onto his desk, then rose, strolled to the darkened window and, gently pushing Neko aside, gazed down. Below, the neon-lighted streets of Tokyo's Ueno district blazed. "In a way this news is welcome. Perhaps the money is no longer in the hands of an incompetent. I have always preferred doing business with a professional."

"You would consider dealing with him?" The subordinate, in dark suit and crisp white shirt, tried to mask the surprise in his voice. The *oyabun* had never let himself be blackmailed.

"You seem startled." He smiled, then walked over and extracted a raw steak from the cooler in the corner. Neko dropped to her haunches as he tossed it to her. "Don't be. I've spent a lifetime in negotiation."

That much, his subordinate knew, was true. Tanzan Mino had seen more deals than most men would in a hundred lifetimes. The most important ones had been the back-room kind. For thirty-five years, he'd funneled vast chunks of laundered cash to the ruling Liberal Democratic Party's leading politicians, and as a result, he enjoyed final say over all its major decisions, dictating the choice of cabinet ministers, even prime ministers. He was the undisputed godfather of Japan's *kuroi kiri*, "black mist," the unseen world of political dealmaking.

The subordinate also admired Tanzan Mino's discretion. After his ascension to kingpin of the LDP, U.S. interests had funneled over $12 million in cash bribes through him to Japan's most powerful political figures, much of it handled by the Lockheed Corporation. In return, that corporation received over $1 billion in sales to Japan's government and civilian airlines, while the CIA got to sleep easy, knowing America's interests were receiving the close attention of Japan's decision makers. But then, when newspapers finally broke the story that Lockheed's American money had reached the highest levels of the LDP, Tanzan Mino arranged for a rival *kuromaku*, Yoshio Kodama, to take the fall. As befitted a true professional, he escaped without a hint of scandal.

It was a deft move that brought him much prestige among those in the circles of power. Besides, with a Yakuza income in the billions, he certainly needed none of the Lockheed money himself. His perennial concern, as everyone also knew, was what to do with all his cash. By the late fifties, Mino Industries Group already owned real estate, shipping lines, construction companies, trucking concerns, newspapers, baseball teams, film companies, even banks. Eventually, when Japan couldn't absorb any more investment, he'd expanded abroad, opening luxurious offices in other Southeast Asian cities, including new digs in Manila's Makati, the Wall Street of Asia, in Hong Kong, in Singapore (a favorite Yakuza town for recruiting prostitutes), in

Taipei, and on and on. But still, there was the money. And more money . . .

Kenji Nogami's predecessor had finally suggested the perfect solution to Tanzan Mino's cash dilemma. The safest, most welcome haven for Mino Industries' excess money was just across the Pacific, on the island of Hawaii, where his investments could be protected by the American fleet at Pearl Harbor. In the early sixties he opened a branch of his shadow investment company, Shoshu Kagai, in Honolulu, and today he was, through dummy corporations, the largest landowner in the state.

Having long since solidified his ties with former militarists and prominent rightists in the Japanese business community, Tanzan Mino turned abroad in the early seventies, offering deals and support to Pacific Rim strongmen such as Chiang Kai-shek, Syngman Rhee, Ferdinand Marcos.

All of it, however, had merely been preparation for this, his final objective. He was about to reclaim Japanese territory lost in the war, open Soviet Asia for Japan, and pillage the world's leading space program—all in one synergistic strike. Best of all, he was going to do it using foreign, *gaijin* money.

Any Yakuza understood well the truth of that classic banking precept: If a man owes you a hundred dollars, you have power over him; if he owes you a million dollars, he has power over *you*. Tanzan Mino, his subordinate knew, had no intention of handing over half a trillion dollars of Yakuza capital to the Soviet Union, Japan's long-time military adversary. Only a fool would risk that kind of financial exposure, and Tanzan Mino was no fool.

Which was why he had arranged to tap into the most free-wheeling capital pool of them all: Eurodollars. The money would be raised in London from thousands of anonymous investors through a standard bait-and-switch, then passed through Tokyo banks. No one, least of all the stupid Soviets, would have the slightest idea what was going on. The scenario was brilliant: Japanese financial, industrial, and technological muscle used in concert to realize the ultimate strategic global coup. His lieutenants were unanimous in their admiration.

"The man's name is Vance?" Tanzan Mino asked.

"*Hai*, Mino-sama. Michael Vance. We ran his name through the computer on the eleventh floor, and the printout showed that he once was with the CIA. The open file ended almost exactly eight years ago, however, and all information subsequent to that—"

"Vance? CIA?" He felt a sharp pain in his chest, a wrench.

"*Hai*, Mino-sama. The file says he was involved in some difficulties that arose over a clandestine funding arrangement, but the rest of our data here are restricted, to be accessed only by your—"

"Opening his file will not be necessary." Tanzan Mino's voice boomed from the shadows.

"As you wish." The *kobun* bowed to the silhouette of his back, still puzzled. "In any case, we have reason to believe he is connected to the NSA cryptographer," he continued nervously, disturbed by the *oyabun*'s change of mood, "the woman we have—"

"What?" He snapped back from his reverie, his voice still part of the shadows from the window.

"We suspect that the terms he wants to discuss, in exchange for the funds, may involve her in some way. When our people questioned her in Greece, she claimed that a man named Vance had a duplicate copy of the protocol. At the time we had no idea—"

"And now you think this is the same man?" His steely eyes narrowed again.

"*Hai, so deshoo*. It does lend credibility to his claim he has access to the funds. If he is involved in both our problems—"

"He has been involved in my 'problems' before." At last, he thought. This was going to be more poetic than he'd realized.

"If he knows where the protocol is, then—"

"Then he thinks he is dealing from a position of strength," Tanzan Mino allowed himself a tiny smile. "I would like to contact him directly, through the secure facilities at Westminster Union."

"*Hai*, Mino-sama," the man bowed again. "I can so inform Nogami-san in London."

Below, in the blazing streets of Ueno, the traffic continued to flow. Time. Time was slipping away.

"Authorize it." He turned back, his silver hair backlighted from the window. "Once we have him . . . perhaps both problems can be solved at once." And, he told himself, I can finally settle an account that has been outstanding far too long. "But I want this solved. Now. No more delays and bungling."

The sharpness in his voice momentarily startled Neko, who growled her readiness for another steak, then dropped into a defensive crouch.

"*Hai*, Mino-sama." A sharp, crisp bow. "I will transmit your wishes to Nogami-san immediately."

"What news do we have of the woman?"

"We know she is in London. Our people there have located the hotel where she is staying."

"Then don't waste any more time. Already two attempts by my London *oyabun* to recover the protocol have been mishandled. He sacrificed three men; two of them were like sons to me. Now I'm beginning to think Vance was responsible."

"We still do not know what happened in Greece." The dark-eyed *kobun* watched with relief as Neko returned her attention to the window, tail switching. "Authorities there advise that all our men were found shot, one in Crete and two at Delphi. They have an investigation underway, but they only will say that different weapons were used in each case."

"They will be avenged." Tanzan Mino flexed his knuckles together thoughtfully, feeling his resolve strengthen. "I am sending four *kobun* to London tonight. My personal Boeing is being fueled and readied as we speak. Tell them I will radio initial instructions after they are in flight. Further orders will be channeled through the Docklands office."

"But the man . . . Vance? If the woman is part of the 'deal' he wants in order to forward the funds, then—"

"That is all." His dark eyes had grown strangely opaque.

"As soon as I've completed my 'arrangement' with him, they will kill her."

Tuesday 2:00 P.M.

The meeting was in the North Quadrant of the Hokkaido facility, in the senior staff briefing room. The project *kurirovat,* Ivan Semenovich Lemontov, was at the head of the table as comoderator. Flanked on his left was Petr Ivanovich Gladkov, the youthful director of aeronautics; Felix Vasilevich Budnikov, robust director of flight control systems; and Andrei Petrovich Androv, director of propulsion systems. On Lemontov's right was the other comoderator, the Japanese project director, Taro Ikeda.

Seated across the metal table, facing them all, was Yuri Andreevich Androv.

"We will begin today's agenda by reviewing Monday morning's test flight," Ikeda began, speaking in Russian. He was chairing the meeting as though by mutual consent. Soviet booster technology and aerodynamic know-how might be what made the project go, but when all was said and done, it was the money that talked. And the project financing was Japanese. "The pilot's report will be our first item."

Yuri nodded and glanced at the notes on the table before him. Make this quick, he told himself.

"I'm happy to report that, once again, the handling characteristics of the vehicle correlated closely with our up-and-away simulation in the Fujitsu SX-10. On takeoff the vehicle rotated very nicely into a lift-off attitude of six point five degrees. My target attitude was seven point five degrees, and once I'd captured that I accelerated out to seven hundred knots, then climbed to forty-nine thousand feet for the first series of maneuver blocks—the roll maneuvers, pitch maneuvers, and yaw maneuvers—intended to verify handling characteristics and control activity at high altitude. As on all other flights, the directional stability was excellent, with a very large restoring moment. In the yaw maneuvers, one rudder kick gave me an overshoot but the vehicle immediately steadied. And the pitch maneuvers again showed that her actuating system enhances stability very fast. In fact, all maneuvers matched our simulations within acceptable limits. I also did some banks up to fifty degrees to get the stick force as I pulled back. The turn performance matched specifications, with very little control activity required. I also carried out some bank-to-bank maneuvers, to get the roll rates; the block included quarter stick, half stick, and three-quarter stick. Very stable. The augmented controls did not move out, that is, move around a lot."

He paused for breath, stealing a glance at the room. Just bury them in data overload, he thought. Don't give them time to ask questions.

Before anyone could speak, he pressed on. "I also took the vehicle through the prescribed block of throttle maneuvers. Remember that in ramjet mode the engines are fan-controlled, with all controls in the initial stage. As scheduled, I pulled all the throttles to idle and then took them all the way up to rated thrust. And as always, they were very responsive and didn't have to hunt for their setting."

"Good," Ikeda said, "but the main reason—"

"Exactly. As scheduled, at 0210 hours I terminated JP-7 feed to the portside outboard trident, causing an unstart. With asymmetric thrust, I expected adverse yaw, as in the roll maneuver, but the control system stabilized it immediately. I also assumed there'd be some sideslip, so I put rudder in, but then I realized handling was going to be feet on the floor. This vehicle is a dream." He paused to smile. "Anyway, I then initiated restart at 0219 hours." He shoved forward the documents piled by his side. "These charts indicate that rpm achieved ninety percent nominal within eleven seconds. All the—"

"I've already reviewed those," Ikeda interrupted, not looking down. "We are pleased with the results of your maneuver blocks, Major Androv, and also the vehicle's turboramjet restart characteristics." He cleared his throat. "However, there was another maneuver last night that does not please us."

Here it comes, Yuri thought. The fucker wants to know what happened. Get your story ready.

"As you are undoubtedly aware," Ikeda continued, "the Japanese space program has an advanced spacecraft tracking center at Tsukuba Science City, with two Facom M-380-R primary computers. The center is linked to a tracking antenna at Katsura, near Tokyo, as well as to one at the Masuda station, near our spacecraft launch pads on Tanegeshima." He glared at the younger Androv. "You *are* cognizant of that, are you not?"

"I am." He met Ikeda's gaze.

"We engage those tracking stations for your test flights because of the altitudes involved. When *Daedalus* is airborne, all their other assignments are temporarily shunted to our deep-space tracking facility on Okinawa, in the south." He paused again, as though to control his anger. "In other words, we have arranged it so that the stations at Katsura and Masuda are dedicated to your flights whenever you take her aloft. You are aware of that as well?"

"Of course." Yuri started to smile, but stopped himself.

"Then we are puzzled, Major Androv. How do you explain the following events? At 0230 hours you shut down your air-traffic-control transponder. That was proper, since you were scheduled to switch to classified frequencies. But you did not report immediately on those frequencies, as specified in the mission flight plan. For approximately twelve minutes we had no navigational information from you whatsoever. Also, radio and computer linkages were interrupted."

"An inadvertent mistake," Yuri said, shifting.

"We thought so at first. In fact, both our tracking stations automatically performed a computerized frequency scan, thinking you'd switched to the wrong channels by accident, but you had not. You deliberately terminated all communications. We want to know why."

"I was pretty busy in the cockpit just then. I guess—"

"Yes, we assumed you would be, since you insisted on shutting down the navigational computers," Ikeda continued, his voice like the icy wind whistling across the island. "We find your next action particularly troubling. At that time we still had you on tracking radar, and we observed that as soon as the transponder was turned off, you altered your heading one hundred forty degrees . . . south, over the Japan Sea. Then you performed some unscheduled maneuver, perhaps a snap-roll, and immediately began a rapid descent. At that moment we lost you on the radar. With no radio contact, we feared it was a flame-out, that you'd crashed the vehicle. But then, at exactly 0242 hours you reappeared on the Katsura radar, ascending at thirty-eight thousand feet. At that time radio contact also was resumed." Ikeda paused, trying to maintain his composure. "What explanation do you have for this occurrence, and for what appeared to be an explicit radar-evasion maneuver?"

"I don't know anything about the radar. I just wanted to check out handling characteristics under different conditions. It was only a minor add-on to the scheduled maneuvers, which is why I didn't—"

"Which is why you didn't include it in your flight report." Ikeda's dark eyes bored into him. "Is that what you expect us to assume?"

The Soviet team was exchanging nervous glances. They all knew Yuri Androv was sometimes what the Americans called a cowboy, but this unauthorized hotdogging sounded very irresponsible. None of them had heard about it until now.

"An oversight. There was so much—"

"Major Androv," Ikeda interrupted him, "you are on official leave from the Soviet Air Force. No one in this room has the military rank to discipline you. But I would like you to know that we view this infraction as a very grave circumstance."

"You're right. It was stupid." Time to knuckle under, he thought. "Let me formally apologize to the project management, here and now. It was a grave lapse of judgment on my part."

"Yuri Andreevich, I must say I'm astonished," the elder Androv finally spoke up. "I had no idea you would ever take it into your head to do something like this, to violate a formal test sequence."

He smiled weakly. "I just . . . well, I always like to try and expand the envelope a little, see what a new bird's got in her."

And, he told himself, I did. Just now. I found out two things. First, I can evade the bastards' tracking stations by switching off the transponder, then going "on the deck." I can defeat their network and disappear. I needed to find out if it could be done and now I have. Great! Ikeda's other little slip merely confirms what I'd begun to suspect. This fucking plane is designed to—

"Major Androv, this unacceptable behavior must not be repeated." Ikeda's eyes were filled with anger and his tone carried an unmistakable edge of threat. "Do you understand? _Never_. This project has far too much at stake to jeopardize it by going outside stipulated procedure."

"I understand." Yuri bowed his head.

"Do you?" The project director's voice rose, uncharacteristically. "If any such reckless action is ever repeated, I warn you now that there will be consequences. Very grave consequences."

Bet your ass there'll be consequences, Yuri thought. Because the next time I do it, I'm going to smoke out Mino Industries' whole game plan. There'll be consequences like you never dreamed of, you smooth-talking, scheming son of a bitch.

Tuesday 8:46 P.M.

"What does it tell you?" Yuri shaded his eyes from the glare of the hangar fluorescents and pointed, directing his father's gaze toward the dark gray of the fuselage above them. The old man squinted and looked up. "Can you see it? The underside is darker, and it's honeycombed. The air scoops, even the engine housings, everywhere. Very faint, but it's there."

Andrei Androv stared a moment before he spoke. "Interesting. Odd I hadn't noticed it before. But I assume that's just part of the skin undersupport."

"Wrong. Just beneath the titanium-composite exterior is

some kind of carbon-ferrite material, deliberately extruded into honeycombing. But you almost can't see it in direct light." He placed his hand on his father's shoulder. "Now come on and let me show you something else."

He led the elder Androv toward the truck-mounted stair, gleaming steel, that led up into the open hatch just aft of the wide wings.

"Let's go up into the aft cargo bay. That's where it's exposed."

The Japanese technicians and mechanics were scurrying about, paying them virtually no heed as they mounted the steel steps and then disappeared into the cavernous underbelly of the *Daedalus*. The interior of the bay was lighted along the perimeter with high-voltage sodium lamps.

"Have you ever been inside here?" Yuri's voice echoed slightly as he asked the question, then waited. He already suspected the answer.

"Of course. The propulsion staff all had a quick tour, several months ago. Back before—"

"Just what I suspected. A quick walk-through. Now I want you to see something else. I'm going to perform an experiment on this 'aluminum' strut." He extracted a pocket knife and quickly opened it.

"This frame looks like metal, right? But watch."

He rammed the blade into the supporting I-beam that ran along the side of the cargo bay.

"Yuri, what—"

It had passed through almost as though the beam were made of Styrofoam.

"It's not metal. It's a layered carbon-carbon composite. Just like the flaps. A damned expensive material, even for them. For the leading edges, maybe even all the exterior, it makes sense, because of the skin temperature in the hypersonic regime. But why in here? Inside? Why use it for these interior structural components?"

"Perhaps it was to economize on weight, I don't know." The old man wrinkled his already-wrinkled brow.

"Wrong again. Now look up there." He directed his father's gaze to the ceiling of the bay. "Notice how the lining is sawtooth-shaped. I've seen this kind of design before. Weight's not the reason."

"So what are you saying?" The old man's confusion was genuine.

"You're out of touch with the real world." He smiled grimly. "Maybe you've been buried at Baikonur too long, with your head in string quartets and classical Greek. This carbon-carbon composite is used for all the structural elements. There's virtually no metal in this plane at all. And the shape of the fuselage, all those sweeping curves and streamlining. It's probably smart aerodynamic design, sure, but it serves another purpose too. This vehicle has been well thought out."

"What do you mean?"

"Don't you get it? Radar. The shape of the fuselage is deliberately designed to diffuse and deflect *radar*. And all that honeycombing on the underside is radar-absorbing. Then this in here. The carbon-carbon composites used for this airframe, and that saw-toothing up there, will just absorb what radar energy does get through." He turned back. "This vehicle is as radar-defeating as the U.S. Stealth bomber. Maybe more so. Some of our experimental planes use the same techniques."

"But why? I don't understand. There's no reason."

"You're right about that. There's no need for all this radar-evasive design, all these special materials. *Unless . . .*" He paused, then checked below to make sure that no technicians were within earshot. "Last night, when I took her down, I maintained the yaw at ninety degrees, making sure their tracking antenna at Katsura could only see the underside of the fuselage. And guess what. The real story slipped out there at the meeting. This plane just vanished off their radar screens. Disappeared. But now Ikeda knows I know."

The elder Androv stared at him. For years people had told him his son was too smart to be a jet jockey. They were right. All these years he'd never given him enough credit. "I think I'm beginning to understand what you're saying. For a space platform to have—"

"Exactly. The underside of this vehicle has an almost

nonexistent radar signature. Probably about like a medium-sized bird. All you'd have to do is darken it some more and it's gone. Now what the hell's the purpose?"

The elder Androv didn't respond immediately. He was still puzzling over the staff meeting. He'd never seen the project director so upset. Admittedly Yuri had violated procedures and violated them egregiously, but still . . . Ikeda's flare of anger was a side of the man not previously witnessed by anybody on the Soviet team.

Also, he continued to wonder at their sudden rush to a hypersonic test flight. Pushing it ahead by months had created a lot of fast-track problems. Why was Mino Industries suddenly in such a hurry? And now, this mystery. Yuri was right. An air-breathing orbital platform for near-space research didn't need to evade radar. The world would be cheering it, not shooting at it. Very puzzling. And troubling.

"Yuri, you've got a point. None of this makes any sense."

"Damned right it doesn't. And there's more. You should see the ECM equipment on this thing, the electronic countermeasures for defeating hostile surveillance and defense systems. It's all state of the art."

Andrei Androv's dark eyes clouded. "Why wasn't I informed of any of this?"

"Your propulsion team, your aeronautics specialists, all your technical people have been given green eyeshades and assigned neat little compartments. Nobody's getting the whole picture. Besides, I don't know anybody here who's really on top of the latest classified Stealth technology."

"Well, the truth is none of us has had time to think about it." The old man had never seemed older.

"Let me tell you a secret." Yuri lowered his voice to something approaching a whisper. "Lemontov has thought about it. Our little project *kurirovat*, that CPSU hack, thinks he's going to take this plane back home and copy the design to build a fleet of hypersonic—whatever you want to call these—invisible death machines, maybe. He hinted as much to me about four nights ago."

"I absolutely won't hear of it." Andrei Androv's eyes were grim with determination.

"My dear father," Yuri used the affectionate Russian diminutive, "you may not have a damned thing to say about it. I'm convinced Lemontov or whoever gives him his orders has every intention of trying to convert this vehicle into a weapons delivery system, and Mino Industries, I also now believe, has already built one. Right here. It's ready to go. But whichever way, space research is way down everybody's list. So the real question is, who's going to try and fuck who first?"

"I guess the last person able to answer that question is me." The old man's eyes were despondent as he ran his fingers through his long mane of white hair.

Yuri laughed and draped his arm around his father once again. "Well, nobody else around here seems to know either. Or care."

"But what are we going to do?"

"I've got a little plan cooking. I don't want to talk about it now, but let's just say I'm going to screw them all, count on it."

CHAPTER THIRTEEN

Tuesday 9:31 A.M.

When Michael Vance walked into the third-floor trading room of Kenji Nogami's Westminster Union Bank, it had just opened for morning business. Computer screens were scrolling green numbers; traders in shirtsleeves were making their first calls to Paris and Zurich; the pounds and dollars and deutsche marks and yen were starting to flow.

Nogami, in a conservative charcoal black suit, nervously led the way. His glassed-in office was situated on the corner, close to the floor action, with only a low partition to separate him from the yells of traders and the clack of computers. It was his Japanese style of hands-on management, a oneness with the troops. England, the land that virtually invented class privilege, had never seen anything remotely comparable with this.

But there was something ominous about his mood as he rang for morning tea. Vance noticed it. The openness of the previous afternoon was gone, replaced by a transparent unease.

A uniformed Japanese "office lady" brought their brew, dark and strong, on a silver service with thin Wedgewood cups.

Vance needed it. His nightcap with Eva at the Savoy had lasted almost two hours, but when it was finished, part of the play was in place. First thing this morning, still recovering from last night's encounter, they had shared a pot of English Breakfast, and then she'd gone back to work on the translation of the protocol. He was still waking up.

"Michael, I received a reply." All Nogami's synthetic British bonhomie had evaporated. "I think he is willing to talk. However, there are terms. And his people want to see you. He also mentioned 'all parties.' I take it others are involved."

"There is someone else." His hangover was dissipating rapidly now, thanks to the tea. "But I think she's had all the contact she's going to have with his 'people.'"

Nogami glanced up sharply. "I don't know what this is about, but the meeting could be held on neutral ground. I assure you there would be nothing to fear."

"Tell him he can forget it."

"You're free to telex back your own conditions." He shrugged, then tried to smile. "I'm merely the messenger here. I have no idea what this is about and I don't think I really want to know."

"I'll try my best to keep you out of it, but that may not be entirely possible."

"Michael, I've handled my part of our bargain. I've set up the dialogue." Nogami's voice was barely audible above the din of traders. "What about yours?"

"I'm still working on it."

"There isn't much time." His brow wrinkled. "Some kind of preliminary offering has to be scheduled tomorrow, the day after at the latest."

"Well, why not get rolling? Doing that should help smoke out an answer for you. For everybody."

"What do you mean?"

"If the bonds are really—but first let's see what Tokyo's got to say. Is there a deal or not?"

"Perhaps his reply will give you some idea." He removed a shiny sheet of paper from a manila envelope and passed it over. "It's why I rang you so early. It was telexed here, using our secure lines, during the night. See what you make of it. I must admit I find it a trifle cryptic."

As Vance took the sheet, it reminded him fleetingly of the 'paper' Alex Novosty had given him that morning atop the Acropolis. The heading was exactly the same. Yep, he thought, we've hit paydirt. Across the top was one line of type, bold and assertive.

THE DAEDALUS CORPORATION

Advisory received 2315 hours. CEO has reviewed and requests direct contact with all parties immediately. The money must be received by Shokin Gaigoku no later than close of business tomorrow, Tokyo time. Authorize reply through secure facilities at Westminster Union. No other communication channel acceptable.

"Looks like he went for it." Vance handed back the sheet.

"If you want to reply, you can use our telex here, just as he asks."

"Ken, how good is his word? If he agrees to lay off, will he stick to it? Or should I be expecting a double cross?"

"You know his style of operation pretty well. What do you think? For my own part, I've always been able to trust him. He has a reputation for doing what he says."

"Maybe that's all about to change. He's always played for

big stakes, but this time it's a whole new level. It's global, and I've got a feeling he's not going to let niceties stand in the way. It could be his last big score."

"And the Eurodollar debentures he wants me to under-write?" Nogami studied him. "You already know what they're for, don't you?"

"I think I might have a rough idea."

"I suspected as much," he sighed. "All right then, how do you want to handle this?"

"To begin with, no direct contact. Everything goes through third parties. You can send the reply. I'm not going to start out using his rules. Bad precedent. And I want him to know that if anything happens to either of us, he gets nailed. The protocol goes to the newspapers."

"The protocol?" Nogami's brow furrowed again.

"He'll know what I mean. We just need to use the word."

"As you wish. And the message?"

"That if he'll keep his end of the bargain and lay off, then he can access the money. But part of the deal is, I plan to keep a line on it, at least for the time being."

"What do you mean?"

"To start out, it's going to be handled in the tried-and-true hot-money way. The hundred million will be used to purchase British gilts, which will then be held here at the bank and used as collateral for a loan."

"The standard laundry cycle," Nogami smiled. "Almost makes me nostalgic for the old days."

"It's only going to be standard up to a point. After that the setup gets a twist. The loan will then be used to acquire a special hundred-million first issue of those Mino Industries corporate debentures you're supposed to float, to be bought entirely by me."

"And thus he gets his funds, all freshly laundered and clean and untraceable," Nogami nodded approvingly. "Style, Michael, style. You always—"

"Yes and no. You see, I never really let go. Instead of ten-year zero-coupons, those debentures are going to be a little unique—they'll be redeemable at *any time* by the holder, on twenty-four hours' notice."

"And you'll be the holder?" Nogami suddenly seemed considerably less pleased.

"Only indirectly. I'll assign power-of-attorney to a third party. If any unfortunate 'accidents' happen to me or to another individual I'll specify, the bonds will be redeemed immediately. And if he defaults, doesn't pony up the full hundred million on the spot, he can kiss the rest of his big scheme good-bye, because a default by Mino Industries would make the front page of the *Financial Times*. He won't be able to give away the rest of that bogus paper. He's instant history in this town."

"Michael." Nogami's frown deepened. "I've never heard of—"

"He gets his money, all right, but I retain a firm grip on his *cojones*."

"Those are pretty rugged terms. I doubt he'll agree."

"It's the only way we play. He gets his money, cleaned, but I come away with a hundred-million-dollar insurance policy. I hope we can do business, because otherwise he'll never see those funds, period. Guaranteed."

"Then if you'll word the language the way you want it, I'll transmit it." He paused. "But I can tell you right now he will not be happy. This is very irregular. Also, I'm not sure I want to start issuing those Mino Industries debentures, no matter what their maturities. Once on that road, how will I ever turn back? You're putting me on the spot here."

"You'll be taken care of. Look, Ken, we can't stop the man from selling phony Mino Industries paper to European suckers. Nobody can. If you back away, he'll just make an end run around you and arrange it some other way. We both know that."

"So what am I supposed to do?"

"Set up what I want, to get me some leverage. I'll take it from there. It's not just the hundred million he'll have hanging over his head. There's also the protocol I mentioned. I want him to know I'm in a position to go public with it if he doesn't lay off. That, together with the threat of exposing his plan to defraud Eurodollar tax dodgers, should be enough to keep him in line."

"Whatever you say." He looked dubious. "But I'm convinced nothing is going to go forward without a meeting. There'll be no getting around it."

"Let's just send that telex and find out."

Tuesday 12:54 P.M.

"And we'll be doing it using Mino Industries debentures?" Novosty listened, startled. "Corporate bonds?"

The black Mercedes—heavily tinted, bullet-proof windows—was parked on the side street behind the Savoy, just above Victoria Embankment Gardens. Vance and Alex Novosty were in the front seat. Vance had the keys; it was part of the deal.

"That's going to be our collateral. We're going to put them up as surety with one of the go-go Japanese banks here and borrow back the hundred million."

"If I understand this right, the money's going to be in two places at once. Michael, it's smoke and mirrors."

"What do you care? If the Japanese banks here won't lend on bearer bonds from Mino Industries, what the hell will they do? You'll have your cash, clean, and be over the hill before the whole thing goes down the drain."

"I have to do this, don't I?" he sighed. "I have to front the street action. Both this and the other part."

"It's give and take, Alex. Nobody in this car's a virgin. You've done worse. Besides, think of it this way. In a couple of days, you'll have your hundred million back and maybe you can go home again in one piece. I'm saving your two-timing Russian ass, for chrissake, so I expect a little gratitude."

"I suppose I should be thankful, but somehow . . ." He was lighting a cigarette. After the black lighter clicked shut, he peered through the cloud of smoke. "But what about you? Where can you go when this house of cards collapses? You know it will. It has to."

"Eva and I'll both be out of here too, God willing." He paused, his mind racing. "Okay, now tell me what else you know about this prototype."

Novosty's voice was weary. "You guessed correctly. I've

been afraid to talk about it to anybody, but now . . . you're right, it's an advanced airplane. That's all I know for sure. The word I hear is that it's faster than anything the world has ever seen. Much faster. A marvel of high technology."

"We suspected that, from the runway." He glanced out the tinted windows. The late morning above the Thames was still only a glimmer through the misty haze. "Exactly how fast is it supposed to be?"

"Many, many times the speed of sound. Ten, maybe even twenty, who knows. I think the project is at least a decade ahead of the U.S. or Europe. It's almost ready for a first full test flight, or so I understand. Needless to say, it's supposedly intended for peaceful uses, space research, but—"

"Get serious. Tanzan Mino plays for keeps, all the way. And you were laundering the seed money for the deal."

"When I got involved I had no idea." Novosty drew on his cigarette. "I swear it. When Viktor Fedorovich Volodin asked me to help, he said it was merely part of a secret trade agreement. The hardliners were being kept out of it. Now I realize he probably didn't know the real story either."

"Right."

"It was only later that I pieced together the rest. About the prototype and its capabilities."

"Figure it out. Mino Industries is about to become the ultimate arms supplier to the world, sole retailer of the newest must-have weapon, and the Soviets and the Americans get to join each other neck-and-neck in a 'debt race,' buying them up. Your military is just like ours; they never saw a new weapons system they didn't like."

"Inevitably." He was trying to keep his composure. "But I don't see how you can stop it."

"We're going to start by nailing the godfather in his tracks, and you're part of the team. So you've got to keep yourself together. Remember our agreement last night, what you have to do."

"Michael, Tanzan Mino is running out of time. I hear that the prototype can't be unveiled, or the protocol brought before the Diet for a vote, until the powers in the Liberal Democratic Party are well placated. This time it's not just insider stock trading info he's giving out, it's laundered cash. Since the money's still here in London, he's very upset."

"You say you think the whole thing is scheduled to go forward in less than a week." Vance studied him. "But it's possible only if the hundred million is there, in hand."

"Bribes, my friend. Or as they call it, *kosaihi*. All the way up and down the line." He smiled wryly and rubbed at his beard. "Michael, you of all people should know how things work over there. Very little has changed, really, from the old days when the CIA was running half of Japan's politicians. It's an honorable tradition to take care of the right people. But the timing is crucial."

"No *kosaihi* payoffs, no deal."

"That's what I hear. Everybody knows the Diet is a rubber stamp. Everything is decided at the top, a 'consensus' among the leaders of the Liberal Democratic Party. But the behind-the-scenes powers in the LDP refuse to endorse such a controversial prospect, a partnership with Russia, unless it's worth their while. At least that's what I hear. So the payoff money must be distributed, in tidy untraceable bundles with fancy gift-wrappings and bows. It's the traditional way, Michael. The dictates of proper etiquette. You know the system."

"Then it shouldn't be too hard to deal with the man at the top. He's in a bind."

"I seriously doubt he will be in a mood for compromise this time. He's used to getting what he wants, no questions asked." Novosty's dark eyes were knowing. "I shouldn't think that would be news to you, considering how you—"

"It has a familiar ring. But this time maybe it'll be different."

"Michael, I'm in a hopeless position. You know that. If the funds aren't delivered to Tokyo, and soon, God only knows what will happen. But if I don't return the money to Moscow, I am also a dead man. I don't see any realistic way out of this. Either way I'm finished. There is no way a hundred million dollars can be in two places at once."

"Smoke and mirrors, like you said, smoke and mirrors."
He shoved the key into the ignition and the engine roared
to life. "Look, we're dealing with perceptions now. And a
tight schedule. When this thing explodes, the money's going to be the least of anybody's problems."

"You're right. There's also the matter of the protocol. If
it's leaked before the treaty is formally announced, I'll be
blamed. *We'll* be blamed. He will track us to the ends of
the earth. You know it and I know it."

"It's a poker game. To win you just have to keep up the
bluff."

"The problem, Michael, is that he's not bluffing."

Tuesday 1:23 P.M.

"As you can see, it's all just numbers." Eva was speaking
in Russian as she pointed to the screen. "That's how I
received it, and the NSA Cray supercomputer I ran it
through couldn't find the DES key."

"Interesting." Vera Karanova studied the lines of ice-
blue numbers, then turned and gazed out the hotel room
window. The late morning traffic blared on the Strand.
"But I know what must be in it. It is a sellout. Otherwise
our intelligence service would have been informed."

"You're free to make any assumptions you like. I'm still
trying to find something that will crack it."

Vera studied her with dark, unbelieving eyes. "We know
you are the best there is. I find it hard to believe that—"

"Well, take it or leave it." Eva switched off the computer
and turned around. "I'm still working on it. I haven't given
up yet."

With a sigh Comrade Karanova eased herself gracefully
onto the plush couch in the sitting area. Then she exhaled
impatiently. "We know something will happen any day
now. Are you sure you did not break any part of the encryption?" She looked up. "No dates, no deadlines?"

"Nothing." Eva poured more cold tea into her china
cup. She did not bother offering seconds to her Russian
guest. The time was approaching noon, and she'd only

gotten two hours of translating done. The day was slipping away, and her head still hurt from the dregs of alcohol.

"Then you have nothing to tell me. We are all wasting time," Vera declared finally, rising.

"Michael will keep his end of the bargain, don't worry. Moving money is his specialty."

"So I'm told. But if he does not return the embezzled funds by the end of the week . . ."

"If he said he'll handle it, he'll handle it." Eva handed her the fur coat that had been tossed across their rumpled bed. It was real sable, the genuine article. She used to have one too. "Now if you don't mind . . ."

"As we agreed, I have arranged for an . . . individual from our embassy to be here outside your door around the clock. The first shift came this morning with me and is here now."

"Inconspicuous?"

"He is wearing a tradesman's uniform."

"How about the lobby?"

"I have also arranged for one of our people to be there as well. We haven't informed the hotel staff, for obvious reasons, so we will rotate our people downstairs to avoid suspicion."

"Is that the best you can do?"

"It's the best I intend to do." Her voice was cold. "Getting even this much for you was not easy. None of this is happening officially. I had to pull strings."

"It's appreciated."

"I'll know the extent of your appreciation when the embezzled funds are returned."

"Naturally," Eva said, and opened the door. As promised, there was indeed an overweight Russian security man standing there, wearing an ill-fitting telephone repairman's coveralls. His looks wouldn't have deceived anybody, but maybe that was the point.

She waited till Vera Karanova disappeared into the elevator and then she turned back, flashing a thin smile at her new bodyguard. He didn't look very competent, but he was probably better than nothing.

Probably. Unless he wasn't there to protect them, unless

he was there to make sure they didn't check out and disappear.

Okay, back to work.

She closed the door and locked it. Then she took a deep breath, clicked on the Turbo 486, and called up the active file.

The part of the protocol she'd translated this morning had begun expanding on the elements of the pending deal. The Soviets were agreeing to open their space program completely to the Japanese, effectively making it a joint venture. In return, Mino Industries and the Japanese government would join with the USSR to create a new trade bloc comprising all the Asian economic dynamos that currently were allies of the United States.

Russia shared some islands, along with its space expertise, and in return it got bottomless financing—and a trading axis with Japan that would, eventually, totally undermine America's hegemony in the Pacific. The new economic alliance, an Orwellian Eastasia, would have the USSR as one superpower cornerstone, Japan the other.

> . . . 7. Within sixty days of the formal delivery of the prototype, the USSR will provide representatives of Mino Industries Group with full and unrestricted access to all facilities at the Baikonur Cosmodrome. The space program of the USSR will be integrated with that of Japan—all personnel, equipment, and launch facilities being operated thereafter as a single, unified entity. Future costs of the combined space program will be borne equally by Japan and the USSR. Japanese satellites and Japanese astronauts subsequently will be launched from either the Baikonur Cosmodrome or the Tanegeshima Space Center as schedules mandate.
>
> 8. Although the level of Japanese-Soviet trade is currently twice that between the United States and the Soviet Union, it accounts for only 1.5 percent of total Japanese overseas trade. Through joint ventures arranged by Mino Industries Group, this amount will be increased over the ensuing five-year period to a sum

representing not less than ten percent of all Japanese foreign trade. All tariff barriers between the USSR and Japan will be phased out over the same five-year period.

9. As part of an Asian trade and diplomatic initiative, the USSR will join with Mino Industries Group to begin governmental and private steps toward establishing a Pacific Basin tariff-free trade zone encompassing the USSR, Japan, South Korea, North Korea, Taiwan, Vietnam, Hong Kong, Singapore, and Indonesia. All offices, contracts, and trade agreements currently held by Mino Industries Group will henceforth be reopened to encompass the representatives and interests of the USSR. . . .

It boggled Eva's mind. The alliance might be partly military, but the Japanese and the Soviets were no fools. They realized full well that the real battleground of the next century would be an economic struggle, with the ultimate aim of every country being to surpass the United States.

She stared at the blue screen, mesmerized. This secret protocol was a detailed battle plan whereby the Soviets and the Japanese provided each other exactly what they'd need to emerge as the dominant superpowers of the twenty-first century. Synergism in high-tech, control of space, a trade bloc, a defense alliance—all of it was there.

But governments weren't that smart. They usually had to be dragged into doing what was sensible strategically. Which meant that this whole scenario had to be the brainchild of some private genius. Only one man in Japan, according to Michael, had the money and clout to put a deal like this together. His name was Tanzan Mino. A Yakuza godfather.

Incredible!

What other bombshells did the protocol hold? she wondered. What was left?

The answer to that last remaining question was the prototype. It had to be the weapon to end all weapons.

Great. But did the Soviets really know what they were getting into?

The euphoria of the night before was rapidly dissipating. There were too many chances for the plan to slip up. Mike always figured he could play these things close on the wind, tempt fate, but he hadn't always been lucky. Sometimes his luck ran out, and somehow she had a feeling this was about to be one of those times.

Tuesday 1:28 P.M.

"Sato-sama, *ohayo gozaimasu*." Kenji Nogami rose, then bowed low as Jiro Sato and his dark-suited bodyguard were ushered into the Westminster Union Bank's upstairs dining room. The walls were ice gray, with a gold-leafed Momoyama screen depicting a fierce eagle perched on a pine branch mounted on one side. On the other was a modern oil painting, an impressionistic rendering of the rising sun of the Japanese flag. Both were symbols intended to impress Nogami's City guests with Japan's new financial power.

"*Ohayo*." Jiro Sato nodded lightly in return, signifying his superior rank. In the floor-to-ceiling mirror at the far end of the room his light-grey hair had turned to blue steel in the subdued lighting. It now matched the hardness of his eyes.

Jiro Sato, born in Osaka sixty years ago, was the Minogumi's London *oyabun*, the man in charge. He had lean cheeks and wore a pin-striped suit and dark sunglasses that further camouflaged his already expressionless eyes. His dark felt hat almost looked like a bowler. Although that traditional City headwear was no longer *de rigueur* in London's financial district, had it been, he most certainly would have worn one. Blending in was what he was all about.

Nogami waited until his guest had settled into one of the molded birch chairs at the end of the long oak table, then he seated himself and clapped for sake. The banker's personal chef, a licensed artisan he had stolen from Tokyo's exclusive Edo Club, was already preparing raw *fugu*, the sometimes-lethal blowfish, to be served with scorching *wasabi* on rare Shino ware. It was a Japanese power lunch.

Jiro Sato's career and that of Kenji Nogami had been entwined for thirty years. They had always been in charge of Tanzan Mino's financial matters, had never worked at street level. No tattoos, no missing finger digits. They were part of the brains, not the brawn, of the Mino-gumi.

Although they both knew that a certain bond issue of a hundred billion Eurodollars was the purpose of the luncheon, they gave no hint as their traditional small talk began with saucers of sake and a learned discussion of the Momoyama screen on the wall, thought to have been commissioned by the shogun Toyotomi Hideyoshi at the end of the sixteenth century. From there their chat expanded to the glories of Momoyama art, then the "nightingale" floors of Shogun Hideyoshi's Kyoto palace—beveled boards designed to announce silent intruders—and finally to Hideyoshi's betrayal at the hands of Ieyasu Tokugawa. The oblique topics were standard, the Japanese way of beginning a business meeting.

Jiro Sato's official position was CEO of the London-based Nippon Shipbuilding Company. In that role he supervised the Mino-gumi's London interests with an iron hand, as was expected by those who served him, and by his superiors in Tokyo. Nippon Shipbuilding built no ships, nor had it for twenty years. Instead it laundered Tanzan Mino's hot money. Funds flashed daily over the satellite link from Tokyo, and investments ranged from real estate to British gilts to the most arcane products of the financial markets.

Money laundering was but the latest enterprise of the Yakuza, an ancient brotherhood rooted in over three hundred years of Japanese history. The *kana* symbols for the syllables Ya-Ku-Za were the same as those for the numbers eight, nine, and three—a total of twenty, which was a losing number in Japanese gaming. The losers: that was what the Japanese underworld, with ironic humility, had chosen to call itself. In earlier centuries the Yakuza were carnival operators, gamblers, fast-moving purveyors of questionable wares. They also took it upon themselves to be a kind of private militia, protecting a defenseless citizenry from the predations of aristocratic warlords. They were, in their own minds at least, Robin Hoods who championed the common man, while also, not incidentally, catering to his penchant for entertainment, excitement, and sin.

These days the Yakuza considered themselves the last heirs of the samurai, but they still supplied escapism, be it in the form of nightclubs, gambling, or amphetamines. And in so doing they had grown fabulously rich. Jiro Sato's job in London was to reinvest and clean a portion of that wealth.

Nippon Shipbuilding was headquartered in an eight-story building in the new Docklands redevelopment, yet another expensive architectural nonentity in that multibillion dollar new city on the banks of the Thames downriver from the financial district. It was, in many ways, the perfect location for a Yakuza beachhead. Unlike the older parts of London, Docklands was ready-made for the parvenu, since everything there was new and anonymous, yet it stood only minutes away from the City—the best of both worlds. The London operation was going well, and with the recent construction of their new Docklands financial complex, at a cost of fifty million pounds sterling, matters were on a solid footing.

Jiro Sato's relations with Kenji Nogami had, until today, been conducted within the strict social dictates of Yakuza etiquette. As the London *oyabun*, he had, in fact, bent the rules in journeying into the City for their meeting today. Convention required that Nogami should have come to him. However, a recent turn of events necessitated a new concern with discretion. A muckraking series in the *Telegraph* two months before had accused the Nippon Shipbuilding Company of being an organized-crime front. Consequently he now had to take pains not to connect his own operations with the workings of Westminster Union. It was better all around if Kenji Nogami were not seen entering the Docklands office by some snooping newspaper hack. Nogami was a useful asset who needed to be kept above press speculation.

Also, Jiro Sato was beginning to wonder if the banker

would actually have come. Kenji Nogami was rapidly losing touch with the old ways.

None of this would ever have been known from the light talk at lunch. It was only when the meal was over, and the staffers had discreetly absented themselves with deep bows, that things finally got down to matters at hand. But even then, as tradition required, the opening was Japanese and indirect.

"Nogami-san," Sato Jiro said as he leaned back and reached for his fifth *go* of sake, "do you recall the famous story comparing the three great shoguns who ruled during that unsettled period surrounding the Momoyama? The tale says they each were once asked what they would do if they had a nightingale who refused to sing."

Nogami nodded and sipped from his sake saucer. Of course he knew the story. Every Japanese did.

"You doubtless recall that Ieyasu Tokugawa replied, 'I will merely wait until it does sing.' He was a patient man. Toyotomi Hideyoshi, by contrast, said he would prefer to try and reason with the bird, hoping to convince it to sing." He paused and smiled. "Sometimes gentle persuasion does work. But the great warlord Oda Nobunaga declared he would just ring the wretched creature's neck. He had no patience with disobedience."

"Perhaps Ieyasu Tokugawa's answer was the wisest, Sato-sama." The banker's eyes were defiant.

"He also enjoyed the luxury of time, Nogami-san. I suppose the pace of affairs was more leisurely back then." Sato set down his black raku sake saucer and lit a Peace cigarette, the unfiltered Japanese brand. "These days events do not always allow us such luxuries, no matter how much we might wish it. Sometimes it is necessary to proceed forcefully."

"There is always a problem when the bird finds the song is . . . unsuitable." Nogami again sipped from his own saucer, meeting Sato's gaze. "When the notes are discordant."

Jiro Sato listened thoughtfully, appreciating Nogami's indirect and poetic answer. Then the banker went on.

"*Ninjo*, Sato-sama. For over three centuries *ninjo* has

been what made our brotherhood unique. Are we to forget that now?"

They both knew what he meant. *Ninjo* was uniquely Japanese, because no other people in the world had Japan's sense of tribal unity. The Western terms *chivalry* or *compassion* carried only a superficial sense of *ninjo*. It was the inborn golden rule of Japanese culture that surfaced daily in expressions of racial togetherness, support and cooperation. It also was a deep-seated part of the Yakuza tradition. Great *oyabun* of the past liked to point out that the Yakuza's honoring of *ninjo* was what set their brotherhood apart from the American Mafia.

"The Yakuza have historically served the people," Nogami went on. "Yakuza do not run dishonest gambling tables, even if the victims are to be *gaijin*. It is not the Yakuza way to perpetrate fraud, which is what the CEO's Eurobond issue amounts to."

Jiro Sato did not offer to refute the assertion. Instead he replied from a different direction, his voice soft.

"There is *ninjo*, Nogami-san. And there is *giri*. Which do you respect more?"

He knew he had just presented Nogami with a hopeless dilemma. *Giri*. It was a word no *gaijin* could ever entirely comprehend. The closest a foreign language, or a foreign mind, could manage was "duty." But that pale concept missed entirely the reverberations of moral obligation in *giri*. One could never fully repay such indebtedness, even with one's life. A Japanese called it "the burden hardest to bear."

A Yakuza's foremost expression of *giri* was to honor and obey his *oyabun*. The great *oyabun* of Japan's leading Yakuza syndicates were more than merely godfathers. They were Confucian elders, patriarchs, wisdom figures who embodied all the traditions of the clan. Their authority was absolute and unquestioned.

Kenji Nogami owed as much *giri* to Tanzan Mino as any man could. The Tokyo *oyabun* had made him everything he was; it was an obligation he could never fully discharge. One look at his face told how his heart was torn.

But as Jiro Sato studied Nogami's pained eyes, he was

torn as well. Tokyo was near to losing confidence in him. The CEO had just announced by telex that a team of *kobun* had been posted to London to "assist." But if the *oyabun*'s Tokyo people had to step in and solve the problem, a lot more would be lost than finger digits.

Finally Nogami spoke, his voice firm. "Perhaps you will be pleased to learn, Sato-sama, that I am prepared to make certain preliminary accommodations. An initial offering of Eurobonds will be formally issued tomorrow."

"That is a wise decision." Jiro Sato tried to disguise his surge of relief beneath a mask of unconcern. Nogami was going to go along after all!

"It will be for one hundred million Eurodollars," the banker continued. "And it is already fully subscribed, in advance."

"Only one hundred million?" Sato felt his iron facade crack. "What purpose—?"

"It will provide the immediate funds I understand are now needed. After that, we can discuss further steps."

Further steps? Sato thought. Yes, the Tokyo *oyabun* would definitely see to it that there were further steps. His bird would sing. Or else. Kenji Nogami was acting as though obligation, *giri*, had ceased to exist. But such things were not possible. *Giri* lasted forever. Did Nogami think the old ways no longer counted for anything?

"The debentures will be purchased by an American investor," Nogami went on, his voice cutting through the silence. "His name is Vance."

"I have heard of him already." Sato felt his anger boil. Vance, he knew, had the *oyabun*'s hundred million and was trying to hold the entire scenario ransom. What he hadn't known until this instant was that Kenji Nogami was helping him.

Well, he thought, perhaps the two problems can be solved simultaneously. An example is going to be made of Vance, an example that will also serve to provide a certain recalcitrant bird a needed refresher course in *giri*.

Yes, Jiro Sato thought, the CEO's *kobun* from Tokyo are going to arrive to find their work has been done. Enough face has been lost, not to mention three men. The situation is intolerable. The only way to regain the London office's tattered honor, to avenge its disgrace, is to resolve the Vance situation immediately.

CHAPTER FOURTEEN

Tuesday 5:31 P.M.

"It's the best I can manage, Michael." Nogami's voice was apologetic. "Nobody knows I keep this place, not even my wife."

"Afternoon business conferences."

"You catch my meaning." He smiled and walked on up the sandstone steps.

The townhouse was in the quiet residential South Kensington section of London. From the outside, it looked to be the perfect safe house.

"So that's how the situation stands now," the banker continued. "Tanzan Mino has agreed to your terms. He even seemed to like the idea of laundering the hundred million one last time through a purchase of Mino Industries debentures."

"Now we'll see if he sticks to his word."

"You've got leverage at the moment." He was fishing for his keys. "Incidentally, I should tell you I broke the news to his London *oyabun* here this afternoon. About postponing the rest of the issue. He was not pleased. It's been a bad week for him."

"Are you planning to make this break with the organization permanent?" Vance knew it was not something a Yakuza would do lightly.

"I'm still not sure." His voice was pained. "I don't even know if I can."

"The long arm of the Tokyo *oyabun*. Plenty of reach."

"It's not just that." Nogami was inserting a large key into the front door, white with Georgian decorations and a leaded glass transom above. "You understand the kind of obligation we Japanese must bear for past favors. It's onerous, but all the same it's very real. We can't just say thanks for the memories."

"*Giri.*" Vance nodded. "The 'burden.'"

"Ah, you know. Yes, it's called *giri* and there's nothing we can do about it." He was switching on the hall light. "*Giri* rules our lives."

Vance noticed the floor had a pristine carpet in conservative gray. A polished mahogany staircase led to the upper floors.

"Nice, Ken, very nice. The quintessential banker's pad."

"I have the entire building, my little indulgence. I keep a few antiques here, some of my art. You know, special things. Unfortunately I don't have a chance to use it much these days. The . . . friend I used to meet here . . . well, her husband was transferred back to Osaka. And I haven't had time to come up with a replacement."

"First things first, Ken. You should always make time for living. One of my few rules in life. You never get another shot."

He laughed and opened the door leading from the hallway into the parlor suite. It smelled slightly musty from disuse. "I'm better at giving advice than taking it too, old man."

"Touché." Vance shrugged, then looked around the spacious drawing room. It was furnished in standard English style, with overstuffed chairs, a Victorian fireplace, an oak tea caddy and bar. But the nineteenth-century appointments weren't what concerned him. Was it safe?

"Michael, we both may need this place if your plan doesn't work. I don't know where else I can go." He walked to the bar, a collection of bottles on the bottom tray of the caddy, and selected a flask of cognac. "Now could you repeat that story again? About the protocol. I must confess I'm dazzled."

In the limousine driving up from Westminster Union, Vance had finally told him the real purpose of the bond issue, what the money was going to be used for. The banker had listened in silence, stunned.

"Well, to make a long story short, you're being used, in what's probably going to be the biggest shell game in history. Tanzan Mino steals unsecured billions from European tax evaders and uses it to finance the opening of Russia's markets for Mino Industries. You're right to bail out now. If he pulls it off, he'll look like a genius. But if it backfires and the truth comes out, you'll get full credit. Not exactly a terrific downside."

"I didn't get this far exposing myself unnecessarily, and I don't intend to start now. Not for him or anybody."

"Then we'll proceed with Plan A."

"This reminds me a lot of the old days." He laughed and poured a snifter for each of them. "Here's to the end of *giri*."

"And the beginning of a new life." Vance clicked their glasses, then took a sip. "Now, we need to get our coordination synchronized."

"Everything is ready at my end. Tomorrow morning I'll issue the zero-coupon debentures you're going to purchase, and you'll make the trade. After that I'll wire your hundred million to Tokyo, and Tanzan Mino is taken care of. I've simultaneously arranged with Sumitomo Bank to accept that paper as collateral for a loan. You'll get the money from them on the spot. By the way, how do you want it?"

"Just park it in gilts, through the trading desk at Moscow Narodny Bank, the new branch on Saint Swithins Lane."

"Done," Nogami nodded.

"Now how about the debentures that are Sumitomo's security? And mine. Who's holding them?"

"We Japanese still act like gentlemen, Michael. At least up to a point. They've agreed to let me hold them until we close our books at the end of the month. I did them a similar favor last year." He sipped at his brandy with satisfaction. "So you can still call them anytime if, God help us, it comes to that. You'll have your leverage, and Tanzan Mino will know it. If you should have to call them and he defaults, he'll then have to answer to Sumitomo. And he wouldn't dare. I happen to know they hold a forty-million-dollar mortgage on his new office building down in the

Docklands. They'd eat him and not even blink. There's some bad blood between them, though I don't know exactly what it is."

"Okay, so far, so good." Vance looked around the room. "You're absolutely positive nobody knows about this place?"

"It's been my little secret for four years now. I paid cash and I don't even report the expenses on my tax forms, which gives you some idea how I value my privacy. So there's absolutely no way anybody could know about it."

"You never came here in your limo?"

"Only if I came without a driver, the way we did today."

"Then it sounds clean."

"This place is the least of your worries, Michael." He settled into a chair. "After my meeting this afternoon, I have an idea that the London *oyabun*, Jiro Sato, has every intention of taking things into his own hands . . . to try and break me. He's going to push the pace—in swordsmanship it's called *mukatsu kasuru to iu koto*. He's lost too much face. He can't let you get away with this and still control the organization. After the debacle in Greece, he's near to becoming a laughing stock among his own *kobun*."

"Can't Tokyo manage him?"

"Theoretically. But the organization is getting a little far-flung these days. I don't know. My instincts tell me he's going to undertake some face-saving on his own. Just temporarily overlook any agreement you may have with the front office." He rose and splashed some more brandy into his glass. "It's going to get rough, that's all I know for sure. So the sooner you proceed with the rest of your plan, the better."

"Everything's ready."

"Then I suppose it's time we wished each other well and got going." Nogami finished off his brandy and dug the keys from his pocket. He jangled them a moment in his hand, then tossed them over. "Take them now. You might as well secure the place as we leave and start getting used to that tricky front door lock. There won't be any time to practice."

"Here's to you, Ken." Vance saluted him with the snifter,

then drained it. "And many thanks. If you ever owed me any *giri*, consider it paid."

"That works both ways. I'm doing myself a favor too. I had to make a break. If this financing double cross of his backfires, it could turn into a worldwide scandal. I'd be ruined. Not to mention Westminster Union, which the regulators here would probably padlock. With scarcely concealed glee. It would merely confirm what everybody here wants to think about those 'win-at-any-cost' Japanese these days."

"Well, I appreciate it. I mean that. I'm sorry we didn't get to know each other better over the years." Vance tried locking the front door. It was difficult, as Nogami had warned, but finally it clicked securely. Outside the evening air was brisk, with a few of Nogami's neighbors stoically walking large dogs and pretending to enjoy the ambience of London's chilly dusk.

"If we both live long enough, maybe we can try. You're one of the few Westerners I've known who ever really understood Japan."

"I had a crash course several years back."

"So I understand." He smiled as he opened the limo door. Vance would drive. "Which is one of the reasons I wonder if this arrangement is going to be as simple as we'd hoped. Tanzan Mino has a long memory, Michael. He doesn't forgive or forget. I'm sure he still remembers you were responsible for shutting down his cozy CIA arrangement."

"I thought it was time the Company cleaned up its act. But hell, that was almost eight years ago."

"That's a mere snap of the fingers in Japanese time, as you well know."

"Well, fuck him if he can't take a joke."

"A joke is the one thing he can't take, my friend. He never smiles unless there's a camera around."

"Look, you say he's agreed to deal. Let's assume for now he means it, but in the meantime we proceed as planned. You trust your mother, but you cut the cards."

Nogami settled into the seat and shut the door. Then he looked down quizzically. "What's this? I didn't notice it before." He reached down and picked up a black leather sachel off the floor, testing its weight. "Somehow I've got a feeling it's not a new tie from Harrods."

"As it happens, that's a little housewarming gift from the Soviet embassy. Part of my deal, along with the car. It's registered and legal, or so they tell me."

"My God." He settled it back on the floor. "I must be getting old. Hardware terrifies me these days. I'm not used to working this close to the street anymore."

"It's only till we take care of business. You handle your end tomorrow and we're both clear. At least for now."

"If it was really that simple, you wouldn't need this."

"The point is *not* to need this."

"My friend, if Jiro Sato breaks rank and moves on us, we're going to need twenty of these. And more."

Tuesday 9:28 P.M.

"A KGB security squad was posted at the hotel, around ten o'clock this morning, Sato-sama. They are armed."

"*Saaa,*" he hissed an exhale of displeasure and leaned forward, an unlit cigarette in his mouth. One of the black-suited *kobun* immediately stepped up and flicked a lighter. He inhaled, then leaned back. "I'd hoped this could be handled without any fuss. But we still must proceed."

"Your decisions are always correct, Sato-sama." The second *kobun* bowed. "But perhaps it might be wise to discuss the possibility of waiting for the backup team from Tokyo, if only to convince ourselves they are not needed."

"This office lost much face because of our problems in Greece. There's only one way to regain it. We have to act now."

Worst of all, *I've* lost face too, Jiro Sato reminded himself, among my own *kobun.* An *oyabun* has to lead. The minute he shows weakness, he's through. Buddha only knows what would happen if I lost control here. There's no turning back. An example has to be made of the American meddlers, if only to make Nogami-san understand the organization still means business.

The Tokyo *oyabun*'s daring project is going to succeed. In the long run it's inevitable. The problems now are short-term. But if anything else goes wrong with this office's responsibilities . . .

The *kobun*, five in all, bowed respectfully. They understood his thoughts as clearly as if they had been projected in neon across the back wall. The office had already lost three men. Face was at stake. This problem could not be solved from Tokyo. It was time to draw together.

The operation was scheduled to begin at 11:00 P.M. sharp. The five *kobun* had already synchronized their digital watches and stashed their H&K automatics in the two gray Fords now waiting in the building's underground garage. No flashy limousines tonight; the operation would be lowest of low profiles.

Three more of their team were already at the hotel, with walkie-talkies, monitoring the entrances. The KGB security in the lobby would be quietly diverted and then neutralized. The guard upstairs would simply be overpowered, or taken out with a silencer if the situation got out of hand. Since they were professionals, however, matters rarely went that far.

The time had come to move. All five lined up in front of Jiro Sato's massive oak desk and bowed to the waist; then one by one they filed out.

Tuesday 10:27 P.M.

It was going to be a simple operation, that much he was sure of. No violence, no bloodshed. The bottle should take care of the situation. All the same, he had a 9mm automatic in a shoulder holster. Life had taught him that when something could go wrong, chances were good that it would.

After this one last job, he was going to disappear. The situation had deteriorated far past where any reasonable man would want to touch it. The time had come to bail out and let the chips fall. One more day, that was all.

Standing now at the side entrance of the Strand Palace, the small alleyway named Burleigh that curved around the rear of the hotel and met the main avenue, he pulled his overcoat tighter and glanced down at his Piaget.

It read 10:28. Time to get started. Everything was synchronized down to seconds.

He'd already made sure the service entrance was unlocked. He'd taped the latch on the metal door during the comings and goings of the staff during the evening shift change. Now all he had to do was slip through and the rest should go like clockwork.

In he went. The neon-lit hallway was empty, again according to plan. This was a slow time for all the staff except room service and the kitchen.

He slipped off his overcoat and threw it into a large laundry hamper parked halfway down the hall. Underneath he was wearing the uniform of a Strand Palace security man.

He checked his watch. Sixty-five seconds . . .

At that moment the door of the service elevator opened and a tall Irishman stepped off. He was wearing the same uniform.

It was a Strand Palace security guard, a *real* one. The worst possible luck.

The moment seemed frozen in time. However, one thing was certain: the security guard wasn't fooled for an instant by the intruder. He automatically grabbed one of his trouser legs and knelt with a practiced move, reaching for the holster strapped to his ankle.

The intruder was quicker. As the guard dropped down, his knee came up, slamming against the man's square jaw. The Irishman toppled back against the side of the elevator with a groan, but not before his fist lashed out, aimed for the groin.

It was a glancing blow, and it was too late. The intruder chopped down against his neck, disabling his left arm, then slammed his head against the steel strut running down the center of the elevator wall. He groaned and twitched backward.

Should I just break his neck? he wondered. Just kill him now? One twist would do it.

No, he lectured himself, be a professional.

Instead he rammed the Irishman's head against the steel strut a second time, and a third, till he felt the body go fully limp.

Not good enough, he told himself, and reached into his pocket for the bottle. The ether was going to get more use than he'd planned.

He doused the heavy cloth he'd brought along and shoved it against the fallen figure's nostrils. He continued to hold it on the ruddy face as he closed the elevator door and pushed the button that would take him up.

As the lift rose, he checked his watch and smiled to see that his timing was perfect. Ten seconds to go.

Tuesday 10:29 P.M.

"You bastard," Eva screamed as she slapped Vance with all her might, knocking him against the door of their room. The thin walls shook.

"Don't *ever* do that again." He drew up and swung for her, missing and crashing against a chair.

"Get away from me. You're drunk." She shoved him farther into the room, her voice trembling with anger. Then she wrenched open the hotel room door and stumbled into the hallway. *"Pomogethya mnye!"*

Their KGB guard, Igor Borisovich, was already running down the hall, *"Shto . . . ?"*

"Help me." She seized his arm and pulled him in.

Mike Vance was standing in the middle of the room, weaving shakily, now grasping a letter opener in his right hand.

"Get the hell out of here." He started moving on the Russian, brandishing the weapon, but stumbled and had to pause to collect his balance.

"He drank half a bottle of tequila and went crazy." She was shouting in Russian. "Do something!"

Igor nodded knowingly. He came from a land where alcoholism easily edged out soccer as the national pastime.

"What is problem?" The hulking Soviet moved forward, gingerly trying to retrieve the letter opener from Vance's hand.

"Get away from me." Vance shoved him off, then stumbled back.

"No, you must give me knife," the Russian demanded. "We want no trouble."

Nobody noticed, but the time was 10:30. Exactly.

The room was brought up sharp by the sound of the door slamming and a click of the lock. They turned to see a figure wearing a black ski mask and the uniform of a Strand Palace security guard. In his right hand was a 9mm automatic.

"Who the hell . . . ?" Vance yelled drunkenly.

Igor whirled to stare. His hand started for his shoulder holster, but then he thought better of it and instead he backed slowly against the wall, silently glaring.

"Where is it?" the hooded figure demanded as he brandished his pistol toward Eva.

"Fuck you, whoever you are." Vance tried to move toward him, still grasping the letter opener.

"Shut up." The intruder shoved him backward, sending him sprawling onto the couch. Then he turned to Eva. "Where's the computer?"

Almost at that moment he saw it, on the writing table by the window. Without waiting for an answer, he moved quickly and seized it by the handle. After he'd stationed it next to the door, he waved the weapon at Eva again and barked. "Get your things. And all copies of the protocol."

"Listen, you son of a bitch," Vance sputtered as he drew himself up and moved again on the intruder. "She's not going anywhere. Now get out of here before I ram that goddam—"

The intruder slammed the pistol across his face, sending him crumpling to the floor. But now his back was turned to Igor Borisovich, who lunged.

The intruder saw the movement, reflected in the tall mirror above the dressing table. He easily sidestepped the lumbering Russian, then brought the pistol hard against his skull. Igor Borisovich groaned and staggered sideways flailing for balance.

The hooded figure seemed prepared. His hand plunged into a pocket and out came a bottle whose stopper had been replaced by a wadded rag. He flung the contents of the bottle across the Russian's face, then shoved the soaking rag against his mouth and nostrils.

Igor Borisovich struggled and clawed limply at his face for a few moments before lapsing unconscious.

"You fucker." Vance pulled himself up off the floor, muttering.

"Problem?" The intruder glanced at him.

"One small one, yeah. You damned near broke my jaw."

"This is the theater of the real, my friend," Alex Novosty laughed as he pulled off the ski mask. "If you're going to be kidnapped, it has to look authentic. I'm a professional. I never do these things by halves."

"Any problem downstairs?" Eva was already collecting her scant belongings.

"Yes, one very big problem. I had a small misunderstanding with one of the hotel's security people. The natives here are not friendly. He's on the service elevator now, sound asleep like this one."

"Where did you park it?" She opened the room door and looked up and down the hall.

"It should still be on this floor. I put it on Emergency Stop. But he's going to wake up any time now and sound the alarm."

"Then we've got to finish here and get out fast." She slammed the door and turned back.

They went to work, quickly turning over chairs, ripping curtains, leaving evidence of a violent struggle. Belongings were strewn across the bed and floor, as though there'd been a hasty search. It was done quietly and efficiently and took about a minute. Novosty thoughtfully positioned his black ski mask in the middle of the floor, just one more clue in what they hoped would be signs of an abrupt, forced departure.

Then they grabbed what they needed, including the

Zenith Turbo, locked the door, and made their way down the hallway. The Strand Palace security guard was still on the service elevator, unconscious but beginning to stir.

"What do you propose we do with him?" Novosty gave the Irishman a shake.

"How about a little more ether," Eva suggested. She was clasping the Zenith next to her. "And then let's get out of here."

He obligingly gave the man a final dose from the almost-empty bottle, leaving the rag across his face. By the time he finished, the elevator had reached the service area in the basement. Their Soviet limousine was parked in the alley, ready. In seconds they were in it and gone.

Tuesday 10:43 P.M.

Michael Vance, Eva Borodin, and Aleksei Novosty were luckier than they knew. When they emerged, the Japanese guard Jiro Sato had stationed at the Burleigh entrance had momentarily been called away by radio to confer at the Strand corner. Since the alleyway was curved slightly, as London alleys invariably are, the huddled Yakuza team saw nothing but the tinted windows of a limousine with diplomatic license plates speeding past. They paid it no heed.

Watches were checked one more time, and then the dark-suited men fanned out. The guard stationed down Burleigh returned to his post, while the five who had been in the Docklands office made their way into the teeming lobby on the Strand. While two started up the fire stairs, the other three converged on the KGB guard, disarmed him discreetly, and then informed him that he had pressing business outside. He was shoved into one of the waiting Fords, gagged, and handcuffed to the steering column. It took less than a minute to neutralize him.

Then the three returned to the lobby and got on the elevator. On the eighth floor they met the other two, who had come in from the stairway at the opposite end of the hall. Together they swept the corridors.

The KGB guard was nowhere to be seen.

"Perhaps they pulled the security on this floor," one of them said.

"Or he has gone into the room, to piss out some vodka," another suggested.

"This will be easier than we thought," a third was heard to observe.

Together they converged on the room registered in the name of Michael Vance, and then they stood aside as one knocked.

When there was no answer, they elected to shoulder it in.

As they rushed the room, they were met by a fusillade of automatic pistol fire from a boiling mad KGB security agent, nursing a headache and crouched just inside the bathroom door.

CHAPTER FIFTEEN

Wednesday 1:09 A.M.

"Darling, do you think they'll figure out it was a ruse?"

"Who knows." He looked up from stoking the fireplace, where nothing but embers remained. "Tanzan Mino may be a genius, but the rest of his Yakuza hoods are not exactly rocket scientists. Ditto T-Directorate's flunkies. With any luck both sides will think the other one's kidnapped us and they'll go after each other. That's the idea at least."

"Well, we're pretty vulnerable." She kicked off her shoes and leaned back on the couch.

"Look, after tomorrow Tanzan Mino won't dare send his goons after us . . . unless he's got something up his sleeve we don't know about."

"That's just it," she sighed. "If he manages to find us . . . why mince words, if he decides to try and kill us again, what then? Will this Japanese banker friend of yours stick with us? Whose side is he on, I mean really?"

"Well, we're here, aren't we? Nobody knows about this place, not even Alex."

They had ditched Novosty three blocks down the Strand. Trust had its limits.

"Except, of course, your Japanese banker friend. He knows."

"The only player we can rely on now is Ken. And he's the only one—particularly after Novosty gets his money—who's got the slightest incentive to hang tough."

"I'm wondering what's the best way to break the story. We've got to make sure it doesn't get away from us, get lost."

He looked up from the fireplace. "I've already told you what I think. I say we just go see an editor friend of mine at the *Financial Times*, give him a big scoop concerning a forthcoming Mino Industries Eurobond offering. We point out there's no collateral at all behind the debentures, and we'll also hint there's more to it, but that angle we save for *The Times* of London, which will get a nicely translated copy of the protocol. We hit the godfather with a one-two press exposé, then make ourselves scarce and let investigative journalism do its thing. Believe me, nobody's going to ignore what could be the biggest story of the decade. After that starts snowballing, Tanzan Mino'll have too much on his plate to bother eating us. We'll be out of it."

"Michael," she sighed, "you're a dreamer. You don't really think it's going to be that easy."

He rose and joined her on the couch, slipping his arm around her shoulders. "Maybe not, but we won't be a sitting target. We'll keep on the move. Why don't you come and join me on the boat. I may have to postpone visiting with the Stuttgart team down at Phaistos, but we'll find something. It'll be simple."

"Sounds really simple."

"All great ideas are basically that way."

"Well, if life's as simple as you make out, then why did you insist on Alex's friends at the Soviet embassy lending you that thing?" She pointed to the black leather satchel stationed next to the fireplace.

"Guess I'm nervous." He grinned weakly.

"You mean you're scared. Cut the bull. I'm scared too." She got up, walked over and picked up the leather bag. "Now, I want you to show me how to work this."

"What?" He didn't like the idea. "You sure?"

"Absolutely. We're in this together." She settled the bag down on the carpet, unzipped the top, and drew out an object whose black matte-satin finish glistened in the soft glow of the coals. "This is an Uzi, right?"

"The tried and true. Major Uziel Gal's contribution to the mayhem of the world." He reached over and took it. "You know, this is an instrument of sudden death. Do you really want your finger on the trigger?"

"Sweetheart, just tell me what I need to know." She met his gaze.

"Okay, here goes." He still hated the thought, for a lot of reasons. The mere sight of an Uzi reminded him of things in the past he preferred to forget. But there clearly was no stopping her. "A quick run-through of the care and feeding of your classic assault machine."

"Good." She reached and took it, tugging at the collapsed metal stock a second before turning back to him. "By the way, is it loaded?"

"No, but it probably should be. You can take care of that yourself in just a second. But first things first." He pointed down. "See this thumb button right here, on the left top of the grip? Notice there're three positions—all the way back is the safety, next is semiautomatic fire, and all the way forward is full-auto. There's also a backup safety here, at the top rear of the pistol grip. The action stays locked unless it's depressed, which happens when you squeeze down to deliver a round."

"Two safeties?"

"Don't knock it. This baby fires ten rounds a second on full-auto. We've only got five magazines."

"How many rounds in a magazine?"

"I insisted on the enlarged thirty-two-round version instead of the usual twenty-five. But still, with that little button forward on full-auto you can empty a magazine in about three seconds. It's a good way to get the attention of everybody in the room."

"Can you actually hold your aim in full-auto?"

"Well enough. The recoil's surprisingly minimal. Remember to fire in short bursts and you'll do okay." He pointed down. "Now, the cocking handle is this knurled knob here on the top. Notice it's got a slot cut in it so it doesn't block the sights. You yank it back to ready it. And don't forget, always use your left hand to cock the action and change magazines, and your right to operate the safety-selector switch."

"Got it."

"Okay, now you're ready to load." He picked one of the black rectangular metal cases out of the leather satchel on the floor. "This is a charged magazine. *Always* cock the action and set the thumb switch to safety before you insert one."

She pulled the knob back firmly, then pushed her thumb against the switch.

"Now feed the magazine into the bottom of the pistol grip."

She shoved it in with a click and it was secured.

"You're ready to party. Thumb off the safety and it's a go project."

"How do you take the magazine out when it's empty?" She aimed into the fireplace. For a second he thought she was going to take out a few half-burnt logs.

"There's a release catch on the bottom left side of the pistol grip. Just depress it."

"And what about the stock? Should I bother?"

He reached and took it back. "You push the butt downward to release it, and then you pull it back like this till it's fully extended and locks." He clicked it into place, a hard sound in the silence of the London night. "To retract it you just depress this locking button here on the left front and fold it back under again."

"Okay, let me try," she said, taking it back. She folded and unfolded it twice. "Think I've got the hang of it. But do I need it?"

"Use it if you want to. I've always thought that when they switched over from the original wooden stock to this metal contraption they positioned the damned thing too high. You have to bend your head down low to align the sights. My guess is, God forbid you should ever have to use this, you won't have time to bother with it."

"Speaking of aiming, is this what I think it is?" She retrieved a small boxlike object from the bag.

"LS-45 compact laser sight. Probably useless for our purposes, but I figured, what the hell." He reached out for her hand. "For now let's just think of all this hardware as life insurance. Something you'd as soon never use." He took the gun and laid it on the tea trolley. "In the meantime why don't we have one last nightcap and go on up to bed?"

"Thought you'd never ask." She kissed him, deeply.

The four-poster upstairs was canopied, the mattress downy as a cloud. They were both hungry for each other, exhausted but deliriously free. Perhaps it was the same relish with which a condemned prisoner consumes his last meal, the delight in every taste, every nuance. If tomorrow brings the prospect of death, then how much sweeter is life in the short hours before dawn.

Wednesday 2:00 A.M.

Kenji Nogami wandered alone through the bond trading floor of Westminster Union Bank, staring at the blank computer screens. His bank was a member of Globex, a twenty-four-hour world-wide trading network for currency futures, but tonight he'd ordered all his traders to square their positions—neither short nor long—and take the night off. Then he had dismissed the cleaning crew. He wanted to have the space entirely to himself, to think and to reflect. Time was growing short.

He settled in one of the traders' empty chairs, withdrew a stubby Cuban Montecristo, a thick No. 2, from the breast pocket of his coat, clipped the pointed end with a monogrammed implement, and swept a wooden match against the floor and up to the tip with a single gesture. If we're going to have a showdown, he thought, I might as well die with a good cigar in hand.

Then from another pocket he took out the telex from Tokyo that had come through just after midnight. The Tokyo *oyabun* was in a rare frenzy. Tanzan Mino had never been thwarted like this—well, only once before, when a certain Michael Vance, Jr., had blown the whistle on his CIA connections.

Tanzan Mino was demanding compliance. Somebody had to give in. The obvious question: Who'd be the first to blink?

The worst he can do is kill me, Nogami thought. And he can't do that yet. If something happens to me tonight, he won't get his hundred million tomorrow.

But then what?

You've gone this far knowing full well the consequences, he told himself, so don't back down now. You're spitting on *giri*, and yet . . . and yet it's the first thing you've ever done in your life that's made you feel free. It's exhilarating.

Did Michael arrive safely at the South Kensington flat? He'd toyed with the idea of calling but had decided against it. They wouldn't answer the phone. In fact, he never answered it himself when he was there. Thinking about it now, he wondered why he'd ever bothered to have one installed in the first place.

He drew on the Montecristo, then studied its perfect ash. Waiting. Waiting.

"Nogami-san, *sumimasen*," the voice sounded down the empty room, almost an echo.

They'd arrived. Finally. Why had it taken so long?

"*Kombanwa*," he replied without moving. The cigar remained poised above his head as he continued to examine it. "It is an honor to see you."

There was no reply, only the sound of footsteps approaching.

He revolved in his chair to see Jiro Sato, flanked by two of his *kobun*.

"I see you are working late," Jiro Sato said, examining the cigar as he nodded a stiff, formal greeting. "I deeply apologize for this inconvenience."

"I was expecting you," Nogami replied, nodding back. "Please allow me to make tea."

"Thank you but it is not required." Jiro Sato stood before him, gray sunglasses glistening in the fluorescents. "One of my *kobun* was shot and killed tonight, Nogami-san, and two more wounded. I want to know where to find Vance and the woman. Now."

"Were they responsible?"

"With deepest apologies, that need not trouble you." He stood ramrod straight.

"With deepest apologies, Sato-sama, it troubles me very much." Nogami examined his cigar. "This entire affair is very troublesome. In times past I remember a certain prejudice in favor of civility on the part of Tokyo. Have things really changed that much?"

"The moment for soft words is past. Tonight ended that."

Nogami drew on his cigar. "Assuming you locate Vance, what action do you propose taking?"

"We have one last chance here to deal with this problem. Tomorrow the *oyabun's* people arrive, and then they will be in control. The decisions will no longer be ours. Tonight I attempted to salvage the situation and failed. Surely you know what that means, for us both. But if you will give me Vance, perhaps we can both still be saved. If you refuse to cooperate, the *oyabun* will destroy you as well as Vance. We both know that. I am offering you a way out."

"With deepest gratitude, I must tell you it is too late, Sato-sama, which I am sure you realize," Nogami said, drawing on his cigar and taking care not to disturb the ash. "So with due respect I must inquire concerning the purpose of this meeting."

"I need to locate this man Vance. Before the *kobun* from Tokyo arrive. If you care about his well-being, then you should remember that his treatment at my hands will be more understanding than—"

"When do they arrive?"

"As I said, we received word that they will be here tomorrow, Nogami-san. With respect, you have befriended a man who is attempting to blackmail the Tokyo *oyabun*. That is a career decision which, I assure you, is most unwise."

"It is made. And I am aware of the consequences. So it would appear we both know all there is to know about the future."

"Perhaps not entirely. Someone has attempted to make us think Vance and the woman were kidnapped, that they are being held somewhere beyond our reach. Perhaps it is true, perhaps it is not. But if the transaction for the hundred million is to take place tomorrow, then he must appear here. The *oyabun*'s people may be here by then. If they are not, *we* will be."

"But if he *has* been kidnapped," Nogami's brow furrowed as he studied his cigar, its ash still growing, "then there could be a problem with the transaction. Who do you suppose would want him, besides the Tokyo *oyabun*?"

"That I could not speculate upon. The KGB seems to have a great interest in his activities. Perhaps they are guarding him in some more secure place. Or perhaps something else has happened." He bowed. "Again you must forgive me for this rude intrusion. It is important for you to be aware that the situation is not resolved. That you still have a chance to save yourself."

"The CEO will receive his hundred million, *if* there is no interference. That much I have already arranged for. When that is completed, I will consider my responsibilities discharged."

"Your responsibilities will never be discharged, Nogami-san. *Giri* lasts forever." His voice was cutting. "The sooner you realize that, the better."

"After tomorrow, it will be over, Sato-sama." He stretched out his arm and tapped the inch-long ash into a trash basket beside the desk.

"Tomorrow," Jiro Sato bowed, "it only begins."

Wednesday 2:25 A.M.

Yuri Andreevich Androv stood facing the bulkhead that sealed the forward avionics bays, feeling almost as though he were looking at a bank vault. As in all high-security facilities, the access doors were controlled electronically.

Since the final retrofits were now completed, the Japanese maintenance crews were only working two shifts; nobody was around at this hour except the security guards. He'd told them he'd thought of something and wanted to go up and take a look at the heavy-duty EN-15 turbo pumps, which transferred hydrogen to the scramjets after it was converted from liquid to gaseous phase for combustion. He'd been worrying about their pulse rating and couldn't sleep.

He'd gone on to explain that although static testing had shown they would achieve operating pressure in twenty milliseconds if they were fully primed in advance, that was static testing, not flight testing, and he'd been unable to sleep wondering about the adhesive around the seals.

It was just technical mumbo-jumbo, although maybe he *should* be checking them, he thought grimly. But he trusted the engineering team. He had to. Besides, the pumps had been developed specially for the massive *Energia* booster, and they'd functioned flawlessly in routine launchings of those vehicles at the Baikonur Cosmodrome.

Of course, at Baikonur they always were initiated while the *Energia* was on the launch pad, at full atmospheric pressure. On the *Daedalus* they'd have to be powered in during flight, at sixty thousand feet and 2,700 miles per hour. But still . . .

The late-night security team had listened sympathetically. They had no objection if Androv wanted to roll a stair-truck under the fuselage of *Daedalus I*, then climb into the underbay and inspect turbo pumps in the dead of night. Everybody knew he was eccentric. No, make that insane. You'd have to be to want to ride a rocket. They'd just waved him in. After all, the classified avionics in the forward bays were secured.

He smiled grimly to think that he'd been absolutely right. Hangar Control was getting lax about security in these waning days before the big test. It always happened after a few months of mechanics trooping in and out.

That also explained why he now had a full set of magnetic access cards for all the sealed forward bays. Just as he'd figured, the mechanics were now leaving them stuffed in the pockets of the coveralls they kept in their lockers in the changing room.

Time to get started.

There was, naturally, double security, with a massive airlock port opening onto a pressure bay, where three more secure ports sealed the avionics bays themselves. The airlock port was like an airplane door, double reinforced to withstand the near vacuum of space, and in the center was a green metallic slot for a magnetic card.

He began trying cards, slipping them into the slot. The first, the second, the third, the fourth, and then, payoff. The three green diodes above the lock handle flashed.

He quickly shoved down the grip and pushed. The door eased inward, then rotated to the side, opening onto the pressure bay.

The temperature inside was a constant 5 degrees Celsius, kept just above freezing to extend the life of the sensitive electronic gear in the next three bays. The high-voltage sodium lamps along the sides of the fuselage now switched on automatically as the door swung inward. He fleetingly thought about turning them off, then realized they weren't manually operated.

Through the clouds of his condensing breath he could see that the interior of the entry bay was a pale, military green. The color definitely seemed appropriate, given what he now knew about this vehicle.

He quickly turned and, after making sure the outer door could be reopened from the inside, closed it behind him. When it clicked secure, the sodium lights automatically shut off with a faint hum.

Just like a damned refrigerator, he thought.

But the dark was what he wanted. He withdrew a small penlight from his pocket and scanned the three bulkhead hatches leading to the forward bays. The portside bay, on the left, contained electronics for the multimode phased array radar scanner in the nose, radar processors, radar power supply, radar transmitters and receivers, Doppler processor, shrouded scanner tracking mechanism, and an RF oscillator. He knew; he'd checked the engineering diagrams.

He also knew the starboard equipment bay, the one on the right, contained signal processors for the inertial navigation system (INS), the instrument landing system (ILS), the foreplane hydraulic actuator, the structural mode control system (SMCS), station controller, and the pilot's liquid-oxygen tanks and evaporator.

The third forward bay, located beneath the other two and down a set of steel stairs, was the one he needed to penetrate. It contained all the computer gear: flight control, navigation, and most importantly, the artificial intelligence (AI) system for pilot interface and backup.

He suddenly found himself thinking a strange thought. Since no air-breathing vehicle had ever flown hypersonic, every component in this plane was, in a sense, untested. To his mind, though, that was merely one more argument for shutting down the damned AI system's override functions before he went hypersonic. If something did go wrong, he wanted this baby on manual. He only needed the computer to alert him to potential problems. The solutions he'd have to work out with his own brain. And balls. After all, that's why he was there.

As he walked down the steel steps, he thumbed through the magnetic cards, praying he had the one needed to open the lower bay and access the computers. Then he began inserting them one by one into the green metallic slot, trying to keep his hand steady in the freezing cold.

Finally one worked. The three encoded diodes blinked, and a hydraulic arm automatically slid the port open. Next the interior lights came on, an orange high-voltage sodium glow illuminating the gray walls.

This third bay, like the two above it, was big enough to stand in. As he stepped in, he glanced back up the stairs, then quickly resealed the door. Off went the lights again, so he withdrew his penlight and turned to start searching for what he wanted.

Directly in front of him was a steel monolith with banks of toggle switches: electrical power controls, communications controls, propulsion system controls, reaction-control systems. Okay, that's the command console, which was preset for each flight and then monitored from the cockpit.

Now where's the damned on-board AI module?

He scanned the bay. The AI system was the key to his plan. He had to make certain the computer's artificial intelligence functions could be completely shut down, disengaged, when the crucial moment came. He couldn't afford for the on-board system-override to abort his planned revision in the hypersonic flight plan. His job tonight was to make sure all the surprises were his, not somebody else's. There wouldn't be any margin for screwups. Everything had to go like clockwork.

He edged his way on through the freezing bay, searching the banks of equipment for a clue, and then he saw what he was looking for. There, along the portside bulkhead. It was a white, rectangular console, and everything about it told him immediately it was what he wanted.

He studied it a second, trying to decide where to begin.

At that moment he also caught himself wondering fleetingly how he'd ever gotten into this crazy situation. Maybe he should have quit the Air Force years ago and gone to engineering school like his father had wanted. Right now, he had to admit, a little electrical engineering would definitely come in handy.

He took out a pocket screwdriver and began carefully removing the AI console's faceplate, a bronzed rectangle. Eight screws later, he lifted it off and settled it on the floor.

The penlight revealed a line of chips connected by neat sections of plastic-coated wires. Somewhere in this electronic ganglia there had to be a crucial node where he could attach the device he'd brought.

It had taken some doing, but he'd managed to assemble an item that should take care of his problem beautifully when the moment came. It was a radio-controlled, electrically operated blade that, when clamped onto a strand of wires, could sever them in an instant. The radio range was fifty meters, which would be adequate; the transmitter, no larger than a small tape recorder, was going to be with him in his flight suit. The instant he switched the turboramjets over to the scramjet mode, he was going to activate it and blow their fucking AI module out of the system. Permanently.

He figured he had ten minutes before one of the security team came looking to see what he was doing; he'd timed this moment to coincide with their regular tea break. Even the Japanese didn't work around the clock.

Now, holding the penlight and shivering from the cold, he began carefully checking the wires. Carefully, so very carefully. He didn't have a diagram of their computer linkages, and he had to make sure he didn't accidentally interrupt the main power source, since the one thing he didn't want to do was disconnect any of the other flight control systems. He wanted to cut in somewhere between the AI module's power supply and its central processor. The power source led in here . . . and then up the side over to there, a high-voltage transformer . . . and then out from . . .

There. Just after the step-up transformer and before the motherboard with the dedicated CPU and I/O. That should avoid any shorting in the main power system and keep the interruption nice and localized.

The line was almost half an inch thick, double-stranded, copper grounded with a coaxial sheath. But there was a clear section that led directly down to the CPU. That's where he'd place the blade, and hope it'd at least short-circuit the power feed even if it didn't sever the wires completely.

He tested the radio transmitter one last time, making sure it would activate the blade, then reached down and clamped the mechanism onto the wire, tightening it with thumb screws. When it was as secure as he could make it, he stood back and examined his handiwork. If somebody decided to remove the faceplate, they'd spot it in a second, but otherwise . . .

Quickly, hands trembling from the cold, he fitted the cover back on the module and began replacing the screws with the tiny screwdriver. It wasn't magnetized, a deliberate choice, so the small screws kept slipping between his bulky fingers, a problem made more acute by the numbing cold.

Three screws to go . . . then he heard the noise. Footsteps on the aluminum catwalk in the pressure bay above. Shit.

He kept working as fast as he could, grimly holding the screws secure and fighting back the numbness and pain in his freezing fingers.

Only one more. Above, he could hear the sounds of someone checking each of the equipment bays, methodically opening and then resecuring them. First the starboard side bay was opened and closed, then the portside bay. Now he heard footsteps advancing down the metal stairs leading to the computer bay. They were five seconds away from discovering him.

The last screw was in.

He tried to stand, and realized his knees were numb. He staggered backward, grabbing for something to steady himself . . . and the light came on.

"Yuri Andreevich, so this is where you are. What are you doing here?"

It was the gravel voice of his father. He felt like a child again, caught with his hand in his pants. What should he do? tell the truth?

"I'm—I'm checking over the consoles, passing the time. I couldn't sleep."

"Don't lie to me." Andrei Androv's ancient eyebrows gathered into the skeptical furrow Yuri knew so well. "You're up to something, another of your tricks."

Yuri stared at him a moment. How had he known? a sixth sense?

"Moi otyets, why are you here? You should be getting your sleep."

"I'm an old man. An old man worries. I had a feeling you might be in here tonight, tinkering with the vehicle. You told me you were planning something. I think the time has come to tell me what it is."

Yuri took a deep breath and looked him over.

No, it was too risky. For them both. His secret had to be ironclad.

"It's better if you don't know."

"As you wish," the old man sighed. "But if you do something foolish . . ."

"I damned sure intend to try." He met his father's steely gaze.

"So did you do it?" Andrei Androv examined him, his ancient face ashen beneath his mane of white hair. "Did you manage to sabotage the AI module?"

He caught himself laughing out loud. Whatever else, his father was no fool. He'd been a Russian too long to believe anything he heard or half of what he saw. Intrigue was a way of life for him.

"Let's go. They'll come looking for us soon. This is the wrong place to be found."

"You're right."

"Go back to the West Quadrant. Listen to a string quartet." He opened the port and waited for his father to step out. Then he followed, closing it behind them. "There's no reason for you to be involved. Heads are going to roll, but why should yours be one of them?"

Andrei Petrovich Androv moved lightly up the metal stair, the spring in his step belying his age. At the top he paused and turned back.

"You're acting out of principle, aren't you Yuri? For once in your life."

"I guess you could say that." He smiled, then moved on up the steps.

"Someday, the Russian people will thank you."

"Someday. Though I may not live to see it."

Andrei Androv stopped, his ancient eyes tearing as his voice dropped to a whisper. "Of all the things you've ever done, my son, nothing could make me more proud of you than what you just said. I've thought it over, about the military uses for this vehicle, and I think the future of the world is about to be rewritten here. You must stop them. You're the only chance we have left."

CHAPTER SIXTEEN

Wednesday 10:05 A.M.

The limousine had already left the Savoy and was headed down the Strand when Alex Novosty broke the silence. He leaned forward, pushed the button on the two-way microphone linking the passenger compartment to the driver, and spoke in Russian.

"Igor Borisovich, there's been an alteration in our plans. We will not be going to Westminster Union. Take us to Moscow Narodny Bank. The trading branch on Saint Swithins Lane."

"Shto ve skazale?" Igor, still nursing his head from the kidnapping, glanced into his rearview mirror. "The bank's main office is on King William Street. We always—"

"Just do as you're told." Novosty cut him off, then killed the mike.

Vera Karanova stared at him, her dark eyes flooding with concern. "But you said the transaction was scheduled for Westminster Union Bank, this morning at ten-thirty."

"That was merely a diversion." Novosty leaned back. "The actual arrangement is turned around. For security reasons."

"I don't like this." Her displeasure was obvious, and mounting. "There is no reason—"

"It's better, I assure you." He withdrew a white tin of Balkan Sobranie cigarettes from his coat, snapped it open, and withdrew one. Made of fine Turkish Yenidje tobacco, they were what he always smoked on important days. This was an important day.

As he flicked his lighter and drew in the first lungful of rich smoke, he thought about how much he hated the dark-haired woman seated beside him, dressed in a gray Armani business suit, sable coat, Cartier jewelry. The bad blood between them traced back over five years, beginning with a T-Directorate reshuffle in which she'd moved up to the number three slot, cutting him out of a well-deserved promotion. The rumor going around Dzerzhinsky Square was that she'd done it by making the right connections, so to speak. It was the kind of in-house screw-job Alex Novosty didn't soon forget, or forgive.

Their black limo was now passing the Royal Courts of Justice, on the left, headed onto Fleet Street. Ahead was Cannon Street, which intersected the end of Saint Swithins Lane. Just a few blocks more. After today, he fully intended never to see her again.

"We've arranged for the transaction to take place through MNB's bond trading desk," Novosty continued, almost as though to nobody in particular. "Michael and I have taken care of everything."

"Who approved this change?" She angrily gripped the handrest.

"I did," Novosty replied sharply. "We're in charge." He masked a smile, pleased to see her upset. The morning traffic was now almost at a standstill, but they would be on time. "After all, he still has the money."

"And for all you know he may be in Brazil by now. Perhaps that's the reason he and the woman disappeared last night, with the help of an accomplice who assaulted Igor Borisovich."

"Michael will be there," Novosty said. "Have no fear. He's not going anywhere till this is finished."

"After this is completed," she said matter-of-factly, "*he* will be finished. I hope you have planned for that."

Novosty glanced over, wondering what she meant. Had all the surprises been covered? He hoped so, because this deal was his gateway to freedom. The two million commission would mean a new beginning for him.

Wednesday 10:18 A.M.

Kenji Nogami sat upright at his wide oak desk, waiting for the phone to ring. How would Michael play it? Admittedly it was smart to keep everything close to the chest, but still. He would have felt better if Michael Vance, Jr., had favored him with a little more trust.

On the other hand, keeping the details of the operation under wraps as long as possible was probably wise. It minimized the chance for some inadvertent slip-up.

Yes, it was definitely best. Because he was staring across his desk at four of Tanzan Mino's Tokyo *kobun,* all dressed in shiny black leather jackets. They'd arrived at the Docklands office just after dawn, announcing they were there to hand-deliver the money to Tokyo. Jiro Sato had directed them to Westminster Union.

The four all carried black briefcases, which did not contain business papers. They intended to accomplish their mission by whatever means necessary. Jiro Sato, the London *oyabun,* had not been invited to send his people along with them this morning. He was now humiliated and disgraced, officially removed from the operation, on Tokyo's orders. The regional office had failed, so Tokyo had sent in a Mino-gumi version of the Delta Force. They clearly had orders concerning what to do with Michael Vance.

He didn't like this new twist. For everything to go according to plan, violence had to be kept out of it. There was no way he and Michael could go head to head with street enforcers. If Michael was thinking of doing that, the man was crazy.

He glanced at his gold Omega, noting that it read ten-nineteen. In eleven more minutes he'd know how Michael intended to run the scenario.

But whatever happened, he wasn't going to be intimidated by these *kobun* hoods, dark sunglasses and automatics notwithstanding. Those days were over. Michael had given him a perfect opportunity to start building a new life. He didn't care if all hell was about to break loose.

Wednesday 10:23 A.M.

"Polovena decyat?" She examined him with her dark eyes.

"Da." Novosty nodded. "They will be here at ten-thirty. That is the schedule."

He was feeling nervous, which was unusual and he didn't like it. Whenever he got that way, things always started going off the track.

They were now in the paneled elevator, heading up to the sixth floor of the Moscow Narodny Bank. The hundred million had been held overnight in the vault of Victoria Courier Service Limited, which was scheduled to deliver the satchels this morning at ten-thirty sharp. The location for the delivery, however, was known only to him and to Michael Vance. He wanted to be sure and arrive there ahead of the money. He also would have much preferred being without the company of Vera Karanova.

One thing you had to say for Michael: He'd arranged the deal with great finesse. He didn't trust anybody. Until he notified Victoria Courier this morning, nobody knew where the money would be taken, not even the Japanese banker Nogami. Still, the instruments were negotiable, leaving the possibility of trouble if the timing went sour.

He intended to make sure it didn't. The planning had been split-second up until now; this was no moment to relax his guard.

Yes, it was good he was here. As he studied Comrade Karanova, he realized that something about her was still making him uneasy. So far it was merely a hunch, but his hunches had been right more often than he liked to think.

He tried to push the feeling aside. Probably just paranoia. She obviously was here today for the same reason he was, to make sure the Soviet money was returned safely. She probably was also still worried about the protocol, but that problem was hers, not his. From today on, the KGB would have to work out their in-fighting back home the best way they could. The ground rules were changing fast in Moscow.

Besides, Dzerzhinsky Square was about to become part of a previous life for him. If he could just clear this up, get his commission, he'd be set. Forever. Enough was enough. Maybe he'd end up in the Caribbean like Michael, drinking margaritas and counting string bikinis.

The elevator door opened. Facing them were Michael Vance and Eva Borodin.

"Glad you could make it." Vance glanced coldly at Vera. "Right on time. The money arrives in exactly seven minutes."

She nodded a silent greeting, pulling her sable coat tighter as she strode past. The bank officials lined up along the corridor watched her with nervous awe. Even in London, T-Directorate brass had clout.

They moved as a group down the long carpeted hallway leading to the counting room. On this floor everything was high-security, with uniformed guards at all the doorways. Negotiable instruments weren't handled casually.

Wednesday 10:30 A.M.

An armoured van with V.C.S., Ltd. lettered on its side pulled up to the black marble front of Moscow Narodny Bank's financial trading branch on Saint Swithins Lane. Everything was on schedule.

"They're here." Eva was watching from the narrow window. Saint Swithins Lane down below, virtually an alley, was so narrow it could accommodate only one vehicle at a time. Across was Banque Worms, its unicorn insignia staring out, its lobby chandeliers glowing. Nobody there even bothered to notice. Just another armored truck interrupting the view.

Then three blue-uniformed guards emerged from the cab and approached the rear doors from both sides, .38's in unsnapped holsters.

"Mr. Vance, they had better have the money, all of it." Vera stepped over to the window and followed Eva's gaze down.

"It'll be there."

"For your sake I hope so," she replied as she turned back.

"Just hang around and watch," Vance said.

Just one more day, he told himself. One more lousy day. We'll have enough of the protocol translated by tomorrow, the press package ready. Then we drop it on the papers and blow town.

From the hallway outside a bell chimed faintly as the elevator opened, a private lift that came directly up from the lobby. When he heard the heavy footsteps of the couriers, accompanied by MNB guards, he stepped over and quickly glanced out. The two blue-suits were each carrying a large satchel handcuffed to the left wrist. Obviously the third had stayed downstairs, guarding the van.

"This way." The heavy-jowled director of the MNB bond trading desk stepped out and motioned them in. The play was on.

Kenji Nogami's issue of Mino Industries debentures had been registered with the Issuing House Association the previous day. This morning they would be acquired by Vance, using a wire transfer between the Moscow Narodny Bank on Saint Swithins Lane and Westminster Union Bank's bond desk. After that there would be a second transaction, whereby Sumitomo Bank, Limited would accept the debentures as security for a loan of one hundred million dollars, to be wire-transferred back to Westminster Union and from there to Moscow Narodny Bank. Everything had been prearranged. The whole transaction would require only minutes.

Unless there was a glitch.

Vance had fully expected that Tanzan Mino would send a welcoming committee to Nogami's premises, which was why he'd arranged for the money to be delivered here at Moscow Narodny's side-street branch. He figured the Soviets, at least, would play it straight. KGB wanted its file closed.

Then too, Eva still had the protocol. Their back-up insurance policy.

"Mr. Vance." Vera Karanova watched as the two security men unlatched their satchels and began withdrawing the bundles of open cashiers checks and bearer bonds. "I want to recount these securities, now."

"There're double-counted tallys already prepared"—he pointed toward the bundles—"yesterday by the main branch of Moscow Narodny. The printouts are attached."

"That was their count," she replied. "I intend to make my own, before we go any further."

Which means time lost, he thought. Doesn't she realize we've got to get this cash recycled, those bonds purchased and in place, before Tanzan Mino's *kobun* have a chance to move on us? If the deal to acquire Ken's new Mino Industries debentures doesn't go through, giving us something to hold over the godfather's head . . .

She's literally playing into his hands.

"The instruments are all here, all negotiable, and all ready to go," he said, stealing a quick glance toward Eva. One look at her eyes told him she also sensed trouble brewing. "Now, we're damn well going to move and move fast. We credit the funds here, then wire them to Westminster Union. And by God we do it immediately."

"Mr. Vance, you are no longer giving the orders," she replied sharply. "I'm in charge here now. As a matter of fact, I have no intention of wiring the money anywhere. There will be no purchase of debentures. As far as I'm concerned, it has now been returned." She paused for emphasis. "But first we will count it."

"Vera, my love," Eva said, cutting her off, "if you try and double-cross us, you're making a very big mistake. You seem to forget we've got that protocol. What we didn't get around to telling you is that we've deciphered it."

"You—?"

"That's right. As it happens, I don't think you're going to like what it's got to say, but you might at least want to know the story before you read about it in *The Times* day after tomorrow."

Alex Novosty's face had turned ashen. "Michael, Tanzan Mino's people are probably headed here by now. Unless they go to the main office on King William Street first." He was nervously glancing out the window. "We're running out of time."

The game's about to get rough, Vance thought. Better take charge.

But before he could move, Novosty was gripping a Ruger P-85, a lightweight 9mm automatic, pulled from a holster under the back of his jacket. He'd worn it where the MNB guards would miss it.

The two Victoria couriers were caught flat-footed. Bankers weren't supposed to start drawing weapons. They stared in astonishment as he gestured for them to turn and face the wall.

"Michael," he said as he glanced over, "would you kindly give me a hand and take those two .38's? We really must get this party moving."

Vera Karanova was smiling a thin smile. "I don't know how far you think you will get with this."

"We seem to be working toward different objectives," Novosty answered. "Michael has a solution to everybody's problem. I regret very much you've chosen not to help facilitate it."

"The only problem he solved was yours," she shot back. "Mr. Vance devised what amounts to an enormous check kiting scheme. You two planned to perpetrate fraud. You're nothing better than criminals, both of you, and I intend to make sure you haven't also given us a short count."

"Comrade, fraud is a harsh word," Vance interjected.

"You are not as amusing as you think," she replied.

"Humor makes the world go round."

"This is not a joke. The negotiable instruments in this room are Soviet funds. I intend to make sure those funds are intact. There will be a full and complete count. Now."

She's gone over the edge, he told himself. She's definitely going to try and screw us, either wittingly or unwittingly. But who in the room is going to help her? That huddled group of Russian bankers now staring terrified at Novosty's 9mm? Not damned likely. She's improvising, on her own. But her little stunt could well end up sinking the ship.

The two couriers were now spread against the brown textured fabric of the wall, legs apart. He walked over and reached into the leather holsters at their hips, drawing out their revolvers. They were snub-nosed Smith & Wesson Bodyguards, .38 caliber. He looked them over, cocked them, and handed one to Eva.

"How about covering the door? I think it's time we got down to business and traded some bonds."

"With pleasure." She stepped over and glanced out. It was clear.

"What do you think, Alex?" Vance turned back. "Word's going around there's a hot new issue of Mino Industries zero-coupons coming out today. What do you say we go long? In for a hundred. Just take the lot."

"I heard the same rumor, this very morning," he smiled. "You're right. My instincts say it's a definite buy."

"Fine." Vance turned to MNB's jowled branch chief. "We'd like to do a little trading here this morning. Mind getting the bond desk at Westminster Union on the line? Tell Nogami we're good for a hundred in Mino Industries debentures, the new issue. At par."

"Michael." It was Eva's voice, suddenly alarmed.

"What?"

"We've got company. They look like field reps."

"Good God." Novosty strode to the door and looked out. A group of four leather-jacketed Japanese were headed down the hallway, two disarmed MNB guards in front. Also with them was Kenji Nogami.

Turning back, he looked imploringly at Vance. "What do we do?"

"Figure they came prepared." He waved toward Eva. "Better lose that .38. Put it on the table for now. Maybe we can still talk this thing through."

She nodded, then stepped over and laid her weapon beside the bundles of securities. Vance took one last look at the Smith & Wesson in his own hand and did the same. Even ex-archaeologists could do arithmetic.

All this time Vera Karanova had said nothing. She merely stood watching the proceedings with a detached smile. Finally she spoke. "Now we can proceed with the counting," she said calmly.

"Maybe you don't fully grasp the situation here, comrade." Vance stared at her. "Those gorillas aren't dropping in for tea. We've got to stand together."

She burst out laughing. "Mr. Vance, you are truly naive. No, you're worse. You actually thought you could sabotage the most powerful new global alliance of the twentieth century." Her dark eyes were gradually turning glacial. "It will not be allowed to happen, believe me."

My God, he realized, that's why she wanted to get her hands on the protocol. To deep-six it. She's been biding her time, stringing us along. And today she managed to stall us long enough for Mino's boys to figure out the switch. She's no longer working for T-Directorate; she's part of Tanzan Mino's operation. All this time she's been working with *them*.

"The negotiable certificates in this room will be delivered to their rightful recipient by his personal jet," she continued. "Today."

"Over my dead body." He found himself thinking it might well be true.

"No, Mr. Vance, not exactly. Your contribution will be more substantial than that."

He was speechless, for the first time.

The Russian bankers in the room were taken totally by surprise. Double-dealing KGB games had always been part of the landscape, but this was confusing in the extreme. Whose money was it anyway?

"Michael." Novosty's voice was trembling. "This cannot be allowed to happen."

"I agree. We've definitely got a situation here."

He glanced around to see the four Mino-gumi *kobun* poised in the doorway, all with H&K automatics now out of their briefcases. Kenji Nogami was standing behind them, his eyes defeated.

Novosty still looked stunned. The range of options was rapidly narrowing to none.

Vera indicated his Ruger. "You would be wise to put that away. Now."

"If they take these securities, my life's not worth a kopeck." Novosty seemed to be thinking out loud. "What does it matter."

It wasn't a question. It was a statement.

Remembering it all later, Vance could barely recall the precise sequence of events. He did remember shoving Eva back against the wall as the fireworks began.

Novosty's first round caught the lead Mino-gumi *kobun* squarely between the eyes. As he pitched backward, arms flailing, he tumbled against the others, giving Novosty time to fire again. With deadly accuracy he caught another in the chest.

Kenji Nogami had already thrown himself on the thick hallway carpet, safely avoiding the fusillade. The Russian bankers, too, had all hit the floor, along with the MNB guards and the two couriers.

Then came a shot with a different sound—the dull thunk of a silencer. Novosty jerked in surprise, pain spreading through his eyes. The silencer thunked again, and again.

It was Vera Karanova. She was holding a small .22 caliber Walther PP, with a specially equipped silencer. And her aim was flawless. Novosty had three slugs arranged neatly down the side of his head before he even realized what was happening. He collapsed forward, never knowing whose hand had been on the gun.

She's probably wanted to get rid of him for years, Vance thought fleetingly. She finally got her golden opportunity, the double-crossing bitch.

He briefly considered grabbing back one of the .38's and avenging Alex then and there, but he knew it would be suicidal.

"Alex, no!" Eva's voice sobbed.

"Both of you, hands on the wall." Comrade Karanova was definitely in charge.

"Michael," Eva said, turning to comply, "what happened to our well-laid plans?"

"Looks like too little, too late." He stretched beside her. "What did she mean just now? About our 'contribution'?"

"Probably the protocol. My guess is she wants to see it destroyed. Let's hope that'll be the end of it. The godfather's got his money. And Alex's problem is solved permanently."

Now Kenji Nogami was entering the room, an island of Zen-like calm amidst all the bedlam.

"Michael, I'm so sorry." He stepped over. "When the money didn't show up as scheduled, they called Jiro Sato and he suggested they try here. There was nothing I could do."

Vance nodded. "That's how I figured it'd be played. We didn't move fast enough on this end. It was my fault."

"Too bad. We came close." He sighed. "But I'm not going to underwrite the rest of those bogus debentures. He'll have to kill me."

"And he'll probably do just that. The hell with it. You tried, we all tried. Now it looks like Tanzan Mino's scam is going to go through whether we play or not. You might as well save your own skin. With any luck, we can still sort out our end, but you—you're going to have to be dealing with that bastard for years to come. Think about it."

"I'm still deciding," he said finally. "Let's wait and see how things go."

"Alex opted for suicide. You shouldn't follow his lead."

"I'm not suicidal." He stepped back as Vera proceeded to pat them down. "I think very carefully about my options."

"Get the money." She was directing the two remaining Mino-gumi *kobun* toward the table.

"Gonna just rob the bank now, Comrade?" Vance turned and looked at her, then at the three bodies strewn on the floor. The *kobun* seemed to consider their late colleagues merely casualties of war. The dead men received almost no notice. "Pretty costly little enterprise, wouldn't you say. Not a very propitious start for your new era of world serenity."

"You would be advised to shut up," she responded sharply.

"I feel personally violated by all this." Nogami had turned to her and his voice was like steel. "As of this moment, you can put out of your mind any illusion I might cooperate further. This outrage is beyond acceptability."

"We did what had to be done," Vera said. "We still expect your cooperation and I do not think we will be disappointed."

"Then your expectation is sadly misplaced," he replied icily. His eyes signified he meant every word.

"We will see." She dismissed him as she turned her attention to the money. The two *kobun* had carefully removed their shiny black leather jackets now and laid them on the table. Underneath they wore tightly tailored white shirts, complete with underarm holsters containing 9mm Llamas. The automatics were back in their briefcases, positioned by the door. Stripped down for action, they were quickly and professionally tallying the certificates, one handling the open cashiers checks and the other the bearer bonds.

Guess they intend to keep a close eye on the details, Vance thought.

Well, screw them. We've still got the protocol. We've got some leverage left.

But he was having trouble focusing on the future. He was still in shock from the sight of Novosty being gunned down in cold blood. Alex's abrupt death was a tragic end to an exceptional, if sometimes dubious, career. He'd really wanted Novosty to make this one last score. The man deserved it. He was an operator who lived at the edge, and Vance had always admired players who put everything on the table, no matter which side.

Well, he told himself, the scenario had come close, damned close. But maybe it was doomed from the start. You only get so many chances to tempt the fates. Today everybody's number came up, Alex's for the last time.

Rest in peace, Aleksei Ilyich.

Then Vera turned back to them. "Now, I want the computer. We know it was moved to the house in Kensington, but our search this morning did not locate it."

So they were on to us from the start, Vance realized.

"Looks like you've got a problem." He strolled over and plopped down in one of the straight-backed chairs along the opposite wall. "Too bad."

"No, *you* have a problem." She examined him confidently. "Because if those materials are not returned to us, we will be forced to take actions you may find harsh."

"Give it your best shot," he went on, glancing at Eva and hoping they could keep up the bravado, "because we've got a few cards in our hand too. Forget the money—that's history now—but we could still be in a position to blow your whole project sky high."

"You two are the only ones outside our organization who know about the protocol. That knowledge will not be allowed to go any farther."

"Don't be so sure. For all you know, we've already stashed a copy somewhere. Left word that if anything happens to either one of us, the package gets sent to the papers. Made public. Think what some premature headlines would do for your little project."

"We have thought about it, Mr. Vance. That contingency has been covered."

"Well, if I don't know what the other player's got, I tend to trust my own cards."

But why play at all? he suddenly found himself musing. Fold this hand and go for the next move.

Before leaving Crete he'd transmitted a copy of the protocol, still in its encrypted form, to his office computer in Nassau. At the time it'd merely seemed like prudence; now it might turn out to be a lifeline. One phone call and it could be transmitted back here this very afternoon. The magic of satellites in space. Knock out another quick translation and they'd only have lost one day. What the hell. Use that as a fallback position. Time, that's all it would take, just a little more time.

"But what does it matter? The game's up anyway." He nodded toward Vera, then turned to Eva, sending her a pointed signal.

"What was it Shakespeare said about discretion and valor," she concurred, understanding exactly what he was thinking.

"The man knew when to fish and when to cut bait."

"True enough. Shall you tell them or shall I?"

"You can do the honors."

She walked over and picked up her briefcase. "You didn't really think we'd leave it, did you, Comrade? So just take it and good riddance. A little gift from the NSA. Who says America's getting stingy with its foreign aid?"

Comrade Karanova motioned for the two *kobun* to take the case. "See if it's there."

As they moved to comply, Vance found himself wondering if this really was going to turn off the heat. Somehow it no longer seemed adequate.

"*Hai so*," he grunted through his teeth as he lifted it, "something is here." Vance noticed that two digits of the little finger on his left hand were missing, along with another digit on his ring finger. Good thing Ken was never a street man, he thought fleetingly. Guess bankers get to pay for their mistakes with something besides sections of finger.

"Then take it out," Vera commanded. "We are running out of time."

You've got that right, lady, Vance thought. Three men were just killed. That personal Boeing of Tanzan Mino's better be warming up its Pratt & Whitney's right now. London's about to get too hot for you.

One of the *kobun* withdrew the Turbo 486. He placed it on the mahogany table, then unlatched the top and lifted it up, only to stare at the blank gray screen, unsure what he was supposed to do next.

Vera knew. She reached for the switch on the side and clicked it on, then stood back and turned to Eva.

"Call up the file. I want to see if you have really broken the encryption, the way you said."

"Truth time," she laughed, then punched up the translation.

Project Daedalus.

And there it was.

Comrade Karanova studied it a moment, as though not quite believing her eyes. But she plainly had seen it before. "Congratulations. We were sure no one would be able to break the encryption, not even you." She glanced around. "You are very clever."

"Okay," Vance interjected, "I'm sure we all have better things to do this morning. So why don't you take the damned thing and get out of here. It's what you wanted. Just go and we'll all try and forget any of this ever happened."

She flipped down the computer's screen, then turned back. "Unfortunately nothing is ever that simple. I'm sorry to have to tell you two that we haven't seen the last of each other." She paused, then continued. "In fact, we are about to become much better acquainted."

"What do you mean?"

"You once told me, back when we met on the plane from Athens, you would welcome that. You should be happy that your wish is now about to be granted. You both are going to be our guests."

"That's kind of you." He stared at her, startled. "But we can probably bear up to the separation."

"No, I must insist. You were right about the difficulties. Your death now would be awkward, for a number of reasons. Alex will be trouble enough to explain, but that is purely an internal Soviet matter. Moscow Narodny can cover it. However, eliminating you two would raise awkward inquiries. On the other hand, you represent a security risk to the project. Consequently we have no option. Surely you understand."

He understood all too well. This was the one turn he hadn't figured on.

Almost eight years. It had been that long ago. But what had Ken said? The Tokyo *oyabun* never forgot. What this really meant was that Tanzan Mino wanted to settle the score first hand. What did he have planned?

Vance had a sudden feeling he didn't want to know. It was going to be a zero-sum game. Everything on the table and winner take all.

The Uzi. The goddam Uzi. Why hadn't they brought it.

It was still back in Kensington, where they'd stashed it in the false bottom of a new suitcase. But if the Mino-gumi had been searching only for a computer, maybe they'd missed it. So Tanzan Mino's hoods could still be in for a surprise. Just make an excuse to go back.

Vera was aware an Uzi had been part of their deal for the limo, but maybe that fact had momentarily slipped her mind, what with all the important things she had to think about. Or maybe she'd assumed Alex had kept it, or maybe she thought it was still in the car. Whatever she thought, things were moving too fast now.

"I get the picture," he said, rising from his chair. With a

carefully feigned nonchalance, he strolled over to the table. "Guess it's time we got our toothbrushes."

"You won't have to bother, Mr. Vance," Vera continued. "Your suitcases were sent to the plane an hour ago. We found them conveniently packed. Don't worry. Everything has already been taken care of."

Okay, scratch the Uzi. Looks like it's now or never. Settle it here.

He shot a glance at Eva, then at Ken, trying to signal them. They caught it, and they knew. She began strolling in the direction of Vera, who was now standing in the doorway, as though readying to depart.

"We appreciate the snappy service," Vance said. He looked down at the computer, then bent over. When he came up, it was in his right hand, sailing in an arc. He brought it around with all his might, aimed for the nearest Japanese *kobun.* He was on target, catching the man squarely in the stomach.

With a startled, disbelieving look the Japanese stumbled backward, crashing over a large chair positioned next to the table. The other *kobun* instantly reached for his holstered Llama, but by then Kenji Nogami had moved, seizing him and momentarily pinning his arms with a powerful embrace.

For her own part, Eva had lunged for Vera and her purse, to neutralize the Walther she carried. Comrade Karanova, however, had already anticipated everything. She whisked back the purse, then plunged her hand in. What she withdrew, though, was not a pistol but a shiny cylindrical object made of glass.

It was three against three, a snapshot of desperation.

We've got a chance, Vance thought. Keep him down. *And get the Llama.*

As the *kobun* tried to rise, gasping, Vance threw himself over the upturned chair, reaching to pin the man's arms. With a bearlike embrace he had him, the body small and muscular in his arms. Out of the corner of his eye he saw Kenji Nogami still grappling with the other *kobun.* The computer now lay on the floor, open and askew.

Where's Eva? He tried to turn and look for her, but

there was no sound to guide him. Then the *kobun* wrenched free one arm and brought a fist against the side of his face, diverting him back to matters at hand.

Hold him down. *Just get the gun.*

He tried to crush his larger frame against the other's slim body, forcing the air out of him. Focus.

But the wiry man was stronger than he looked. With a twist he rolled over and pinned Vance's shoulders against the carpet. Vance felt the shag, soft against his skin, and couldn't believe how chilly it felt. But now he had his hand on the *kobun's* throat, holding him in a powerful grip while jamming a free elbow against the holster.

Cut off his oxygen. Don't let him breathe.

The old moves were coming back, the shortcuts that would bring a more powerful opponent to submission. He pressed a thumb against the man's windpipe, shutting off his air. A look of surprise went through the *kobun's* eyes as he choked, letting his hold on Vance's shoulders slacken.

Now.

He shoved the man's arm aside and reached for the holster. Then his hand closed around the hard grip of the Llama. The Japanese was weaker now, but still forcing his arm away from the gun, preventing him from getting the grip he needed.

He rammed an elbow against the man's chin, then tightened his finger on the grip of the Llama. He almost had it.

With his other hand he shoved the *kobun's* face away, clawing at his eyes, and again they rolled over, with the Japanese once more against the carpet. But now he had the gun and he was turning.

He felt a sharp jab in his back, a flash of pain that seemed to come from nowhere. It was both intense and numbing, as though his spine had been caught in a vise. Then he felt his heart constrict, his orientation spin. He rolled to the side, flailing an arm to try and recover his balance, but the room was in rotation, his vision playing tricks.

The one thing he did see was Vera Karanova standing over him, a blurred image his mind tried vainly to correct. Her face was faltering, the indistinct outlines of a desert mirage. Was she real or was he merely dreaming?

. . . Now the room was growing serene, a slow-motion phantasmagoria of pastel colors and soft, muted sounds. He tried to reach out, but there was nothing. Instead he heard faint music, dulcet beckoning tones. The world had entered another dimension, a seamless void. He wanted to be part of its emptiness, to swathe himself in the cascade of oblivion lifting him up. A perfect repose was drifting through him, a wave of darkness. He heard his own breathing as he was buoyed into a blood-red mist. He was floating, on a journey he had long waited to take, to a place far, far away. . . .

BOOK THREE

CHAPTER SEVENTEEN

Thursday 2:28 P.M.

"The hypersonic test flight must proceed as scheduled," Tanzan Mino said quietly. "Now that all the financial arrangements have been completed, the Coordinating Committee of the LDP has agreed to bring the treaty before the Diet next week. A delay is unthinkable."

"The problem is not technical, Mino-sama," Taro Ikeda, the project director, continued, his tone ripe with deference. "It is the Soviet pilot. Perhaps he should be replaced." He looked down, searching for the right words. "I'm concerned. I think he has discovered the stealth capabilities of the vehicle. Probably accidentally, but all the same, I'm convinced he is now aware of them. Two nights ago he engaged in certain unauthorized maneuvers I believe were intended to verify those capabilities."

"*So deshoo.*" Tanzan Mino's eyes narrowed. "But he has said nothing?"

"No. Not a word. At least to me."

"Then perhaps he was merely behaving erratically. It would not be the first time."

"The maneuvers. They were too explicit," Ikeda continued. "As I said, two nights ago, on the last test fight, he switched off the transponder, then performed a snap roll and took the vehicle into a power dive, all the way to the deck. It was intended to be a radar-evasive action." The project director allowed himself a faint, ironic smile. "At least we now know that the technology works. The vehicle's radar signature immediately disappeared off the tracking monitors at Katsura."

"It met the specifications?"

Ikeda nodded. "Yesterday I ordered a computer analysis of the data tapes. The preliminary report suggests it may even have exceeded them."

Tanzan Mino listened in silence. He was sitting at his desk in the command sector wing of the North Quadrant at the Hokkaido facility. Although the sector was underground, like the rest of the facility, behind his desk was a twenty-foot-long "window" with periscope double mirrors that showed the churning breakers of La Perouse Strait.

His jet had touched down on the facility's runway at 6:48 A.M. and been promptly towed into the hangar. Tanzan Mino intended to be in personal command when *Daedalus I* went hypersonic, in just nineteen hours. The video monitors in his office were hard-wired directly to the main console in Flight Control, replicating its data displays, and all decisions passed across his desk.

"Leave the pilot to me," he said without emotion, revolving to gaze out the wide window, which displayed the midafternoon sun catching the crests of whitecaps far at sea. "What he knows or doesn't know will not disrupt the schedule."

Once again, he thought, I've got to handle a problem personally. Why? Because nobody else here has the determination to make the scenario succeed. First the protocol, and then the money. I had to intervene to resolve both.

But, he reflected with a smile, it turned out that handling those difficulties personally had produced an unexpected dividend.

"As you say, Mino-sama," Ikeda bowed. "I merely wanted to make you aware of my concern about the pilot. He should be monitored more closely from now on."

"Which is precisely what I intend to do." Tanzan Mino's silver hair seemed to blend with the sea beyond. "There is an obvious solution. When he takes the vehicle hypersonic, he will not be alone."

"What are you suggesting? No one else—"

"Merely a simple security precaution. If he is not reliable, then steps must be taken. Two of our people will be in the cockpit with him."

"You mean the scientists from Tsukuba? The cockpit was designed to accommodate a three-man crew, but MITI hasn't yet designated the two researchers."

"No. I mean my personal pilot and copilot. From the Boeing. Then if Androv deviates from the prescribed test program in any way, they will be there, ready to take immediate action. The problem is solved." He revolved back from the window. "That will be all."

Ikeda bowed, then turned and hurriedly made his way toward the door. He didn't like last-minute improvisations, but the CEO was now fully in command. Preparations for two additional life-support systems would have to be started immediately.

After Tanzan Mino watched him depart, he reached down and activated a line of personal video monitors beside his desk.

Thursday 2:34 P.M.

Vance recognized the sound immediately. It was the harplike plucking of a Japanese koto, punctuated by the tinkling of a wind chime. Without opening his eyes, he reached out and touched a hard, textured surface. It was, he realized, a straw mat, and from the firmness of the weave he knew it was *tatami*. Then he felt the soft cotton of the padded mat beneath him and guessed he was lying on a *futon*. The air in the room was faintly spiced with Mahayana Buddhist temple incense.

I'm in Japan, he told himself. Or somebody wants me to *think* I am.

He opened his eyes and found himself looking at a rice-paper lamp on the floor next to his futon. Directly behind it, on the left, was a *tokonoma* art alcove, built next to a set of sliding doors. A small, round *shoji* window in the *toko-noma* shed a mysterious glow on its hanging scroll, the painting an ink sketch of a Zen monk fording a shallow stream.

Then he noticed an insignia that had been painted on the sliding doors with a giant brush. He struggled to focus, and finally grasped that it was the Minoan double ax, logo of the Daedalus Corporation.

Jesus!

He lay a minute, nursing the ache in his head and trying to remember what had happened. All he could recall was London, money, Eva . . .

Eva. Where was she?

He popped erect and surveyed the room. It was traditional Japanese, the standard four-and-a-half *tatami* in size, bare and Spartan. A classic.

But the music. It seemed to be coming through the walls.

The walls. They all looked to be rice paper. He clambered up and headed for the *fusuma* with the double-ax logo. He tested it and realized that the paper was actually painted steel. And it was locked. The room was secure as a vault.

But across, opposite the *tokonoma,* was another set of sliding doors. As he turned to walk over, he noticed he was wearing *tabi,* light cotton stockings split at the toe, and he was clad in a blue-patterned *yukata* robe, cinched at the waist. He'd been stripped and re-dressed.

This door was real, and he shoved it open. A suite of rooms lay beyond, and there on a second futon, still in a drugged sleep, lay Eva. He moved across, bent down, and shook her. She jerked away, her dreaming disrupted, and turned over, but she didn't come out of it.

"Wake up." He shook her again. "The party just got moved. Wait'll you get a load of the decor."

"What . . ." She rolled back and cracked open her bloodshot eyes. Then she rose on one elbow and gazed around the room. It was appointed identically to his, with only the hanging scroll in the *tokonoma* different, hers being an angular, three-level landscape. "My God."

"Welcome to the wonderful world of Tanzan Mino. I don't know where the hell we are, but it's definitely not Kansas, or London."

"My head feels like I was at ground zero when the bomb hit. My whole body aches." She groaned and plopped back down on the *futon*. "What time do you think it is?"

"Haven't a clue. How about starting with what day?" He felt for his watch and realized it was gone. "What does it matter anyway? Nobody has clocks in never-never land."

Satisfied she was okay, he stood up and surveyed the room. Then he saw what he'd expected. There in the center of the ceiling, integrated into the pattern of light-colored woods, was the glass eye of a video camera.

And the music. Still the faint music.

He walked on down to the far end of her room and shoved aside another set of sliding doors, also painted with the double-ax insignia. He found himself looking at a third large space, this one paneled in raw cypress. It was vast, and in the center was a cedar hot tub, sunk into the floor. The water was fresh and steaming, and two tiny stools and rinsing pails were located conveniently nearby on the redwood decking. It was a traditional *o-furo*, one of the finest he'd ever seen.

"You're not going to believe this." He turned back and waved her forward. In the soft rice-paper glow of the lamp she looked rakishly disheveled. Japanese architecture always made him think of lovemaking. "Our host probably figured we'd want to freshen up for the festivities. Check it out."

"What?" She was shakily rising, pulling her *yukata* around her.

"All the comforts of home. Too bad they forgot the geisha."

She came over and stood beside him. "I don't believe this."

"Want to see if it's real, or just a mirage?"

She hesitantly stepped onto the decking, then walked out and bent down to test the water. "Feels wet." She glanced back. "So what the heck. I could use it."

"I'm ready." He kicked off his *tabi* and walked on out.

She pulled off his *yukata*, then picked up one of the pails and began filling it from a spigot on the wall. "Okay, exalted male," she laughed, "I'm going to scrub you. That's how they do it, right?" She stood up and reached for a sponge and soap.

"They know how to live. Here, let me." He picked up a second sponge and began scrubbing her back in turn. "How does it feel?"

"Maybe this is heaven."

"Hope we didn't have to die to get here. But hang on. I've got a feeling the fun is just beginning."

He splashed her off with one of the pails, then watched as she gingerly climbed down into the wooden tub.

"Michael, where do you think we are?" She sighed as the steam enveloped her. "This has got to be Japan, but where?"

"Got a funny feeling I know." He was settling into the water beside her. "But if I told you, you'd probably think I'm hallucinating." Above the tub, he suddenly noticed yet another video camera.

As they lay soaking, the koto music around them abruptly stopped, its poignant twangs disappearing with an electronic click.

"Are you finding the accommodations adequate?"

The voice was coming from a speaker carefully integrated into the raw cypress ceiling.

"All things considered, we'd sooner be in Philadelphia." Vance looked up.

"I'm sorry to hear that," the voice continued. "No expense has been spared. My own personal quarters have been placed at your disposal."

"Mind telling me who's watching me bathe?" Eva splashed a handful of water at the lens.

"You have no secrets from me, Dr. Borodin. However, in the interest of propriety I have switched off the monitor for the bath. I'm afraid my people were somewhat overly zealous, installing one there in the first place." The voice chuckled. "But I should think you'd know. I am CEO of the Daedalus Corporation, an organization not unfamiliar to you."

"All right," she said, "so where are we?"

"Why, you are in the corporation's Hokkaido facility. As my guests. Since you two have taken such an interest in this project, I thought it only fitting you should have an opportunity to see it first hand."

"Mind giving us a preview of the upcoming agenda?" Vance leaned back. "We need to plan our day."

"Quite simply, I thought it was time you and I got reacquainted, Dr. Vance. It's been a long time."

"Eight years."

"Yes. Eight years . . ." There was a pause. "If you would excuse me a moment, I must take a call."

The speaker clicked off.

"Michael, I've got a very bad feeling about all this." She was rising from the bath, her back to the camera. "What do you think he's going to do?"

He's going to kill us, Vance realized. After he's played with us a while. It's really quite simple.

"I don't know," he lied.

Then the speaker clicked on again. "Please forgive me. There are so many demands on my time. However, I was hoping you, Dr. Vance, would consent to join me this afternoon for tea. We have some urgent matters to discuss."

"I'll see if I can work it into my schedule."

"Given the hectic goings-on here at the moment, perhaps a quiet moment would be useful for us both." He paused again, speaking to someone else, then his voice came back. "Shall we say four o'clock."

"What time is it now?"

"Please forgive me. I forgot. Your world is not regimented by time, whereas mine regrettably is measured down to seconds. It is now almost three in the afternoon. I shall expect you in one hour. Your clothes are in the closet in your room. Now, if you will allow me. Affairs . . ."

And the voice was gone.

"Michael, are you really going to talk with that criminal?"

"Wouldn't miss it for the world. There's a game going on here, and we have to stay in. Everybody's got a score to settle. We're about to see who settles up first."

Thursday 3:29 P.M.

"Zero minus eighteen hours." Yuri Andreevich Androv stared at the green screen, its numbers scrolling the computerized countdown. "Eighteen fucking hours."

As he wheeled around, gazing over the beehive of activity in Flight Control, he could already feel the adrenaline beginning to build. Everything depended on him now. The vehicle was as ready as it was going to be: all the wind tunnel tests, all the computer simulations, even the supersonic test flights—everything said go. *Daedalus I* was going to make history tomorrow morning.

Except, he told himself, it's going to be a very different history from the one everybody expects.

"Major Yuri Andreevich Androv, please report to Hangar Quadrant immediately."

The stridency of the facility's paging system always annoyed him. He glanced at the long line of computer screens one last time, then shrugged and checked his watch. Who wanted him?

Well, a new planeload of Soviet VIPs reportedly had flown in yesterday, though he hadn't seen any of them yet. He figured now that everything looked ready, the *nomenklatura* were flooding in to bask in triumph. Maybe after a day of vodka drinking and back slapping with the officials in Project Management, they'd sobered up and realized they were expected to file reports. So they were finally getting around to talking to the people who were doing the actual work. They'd summon in a few staffers who had hands-on knowledge of the project and commission a draft report, which they'd then file, unread, under their own names. Typical.

He reached for his leather flight jacket, deciding on a brisk walk to work off the tension. The long corridor leading from the East Quadrant to the Hangar Quadrant took him directly past Checkpoint Central and the entry to West Quadrant, the Soviet sector, which also contained the flight simulator and the main wind tunnel, or Number One, both now quiet.

As he walked, he thought again about the new rumor he'd heard in the commissary at lunch. Gossip kept the Soviet staff going—an instinct from the old days—but this one just might be true. Some lower-level staffers even claimed they'd seen him. The Chief.

Word was Tanzan Mino himself—none other than the CEO of the Daedalus Corporation—had flown in this morning, together with his personal bodyguards and aides. The story was he wanted hands-on control of the first hypersonic test flight, wanted to be calling the shots in Flight Control when *Daedalus I* made history.

Finally. The Big Man has decided to show his face.

"Yuri Andreevich, just a minute. Slow down."

He recognized the voice immediately and glanced around to see Nikolai Vasilevich Grishkov, the portly Soviet chief mechanic, just emerging from the West Quadrant. His bushy eyebrows hung like a pair of Siberian musk-ox horns above his gleaming dark eyes.

"Have you seen her?" Grishkov was shuffling toward him.

"Seen who?" He examined the mechanic's spotless white coveralls. Jesus! Even the support crews on this project were all sanitized, high-tech.

"The new woman. *Kracevia, moi droog. Ochen kracevia.* Beautiful beyond words. And she is important. You can tell just by looking."

"Nikolai, there's never been a woman in this facility." He laughed and continued on toward Security. "It's worse than a goddam troop ship. You've finally started hallucinating from lack of *pezdyonka.*"

"Yuri Andreevich, she's here and she's Soviet." The chief mechanic followed him. "Some believe she arrived this morning with the CEO, but nobody knows who she is. One rumor is she's Vera Karanova."

"Who?" The name was vaguely familiar.

"T-Directorate. Like I said, no one knows for sure, but that's what we've heard."

"Impossible." He halted and turned back, frowning.

"That's just it, Yuri Andreevich," he sighed. "Those KGB bastards are not *supposed* to even know about this project.

That was everybody's strict understanding. We were to be free of them here. But now . . ." He caught the sleeve of Androv's flight jacket and pulled him aside, out of the flow of pedestrian traffic in the hallway. "My men were wondering. Maybe you could find a way to check her out? You have better access. Everybody wants to know what's going on."

"KGB? It doesn't make any sense."

"If she's really . . . I just talked to the project *kurirovat*, Ivan Semenovich, and he told me Karanova's now number three in T-Directorate."

"Well, there's nothing we can do now, so the hell with her." He waved his hand and tried to move on. "We've both got better things to worry about."

"Just keep your antenna tuned, my friend, that's all. Let me know if you can find out anything. Is she really Karanova? Because if she is, we damned well need to know the inside story."

"Nikolai, if I see her, I'll be sure and ask." He winked. "And if she's the hot number you say, maybe I'll find time to warm her up a little. Get her to drop her . . . guard."

"If you succeed in *that, moi droog*," he said as his heavy eyebrows lifted with a sly grin, "you'll be the envy of the facility. You've got to see her."

"I can't wait." He shrugged and moved on toward the Hangar Security station, at the end of the long corridor. When he flashed his A-level priority ID for the two Japanese guards, he noticed they nervously made a show of scrutinizing it, even though they both knew him perfectly well, before saluting and authorizing entry.

That nails it, he told himself. Out of nowhere we suddenly have all this rule-book crap. These guys are nervous as hell. No doubt about it, the big *nachalnik* is on the scene.

Great. Let all those assholes on the Soviet staff see the expression on his face when the truth comes out. *That's* the real history we're about to make here.

As he walked into the glare of neon, the cavernous space had never seemed more vast, more imposing. He'd seen a lot of hangars, flown a lot of experimental planes over the years, but nothing to match this. Still, he always reminded himself, *Daedalus* was only hardware, just more fancy iron. What really counted was the balls of the pilot holding the flight stick.

That's when he saw them, clustered around the vehicle and gazing up. He immediately recognized Colonel-General of Aviation Anatoly Savitsky, whose humorless face appeared almost weekly in *Soviet Military Review;* Major-General Igor Mikhailov, whose picture routinely graced the pages of *Air Defense Herald;* and also Colonel-General Pavel Ogarkov, a marshal of the Soviet air force before that rank was abolished by the general secretary.

What are those Air Force neanderthals doing here? They're all notorious hardliners, the "bomb first, ask questions later" boys. And *Daedalus* is supposed to be for space research, right? Guess the bullshit is about to be over. We're finally getting down to the real scenario.

And there in the middle, clearly the man in charge, was a tall, silver-haired Japanese in a charcoal silk suit. He was showing off the vehicles as though he owned them, and he carried himself with an authority that made all the hovering Soviet generals look like bellboys waiting for a tip.

Well, Yuri Andreevich thought, for the time being he does own them. They're bought and paid for, just like us.

"Tovarisch, Major Androv, *kak pazhavatye,"* came a voice behind him. He turned and realized it belonged to General Valentin Sokolov, commander of the MiG 31 wing at the Dolinsk air base on Sakhalin. Sokolov was three star, top man in all the Soviet Far East. Flanking him were half a dozen colonels and lieutenant colonels.

"Comrade General Sokolov." He whipped off a quick salute. Brass. Brass everywhere. Shit. What in hell was this all about?

Now the project director, Taro Ikeda, had broken away from the Soviet group and was approaching. "Yuri Andreevich, thank you for coming." He bowed deferentially. "You are about to receive a great honor. The CEO has asked for a private conference with you."

Yuri stared over Ikeda's shoulder at the Man-in-Charge. All this right-wing brass standing around kissing his ass counted for nothing. *He* was the one calling the shots. Who was everybody kidding?

Now the CEO looked his way, sizing him up with a quick glance. Yuri Androv assessed him in turn. It was one look, but they both knew there was trouble ahead.

Then Tanzan Mino patted a colonel-general on the shoulder and headed over. "Yuri Andreevich Androv, I presume," he said in flawless Russian, bowing lightly. "A genuine pleasure to meet you at last. There's a most urgent matter we have to discuss."

Thursday 4:00 P.M.

At the precise hour, the *tokonoma* alcove off Vance's bedroom rotated ninety degrees, as though moved by an unseen hand, and what awaited beyond was a traditional Japanese sand-and-stone garden. It was, of course, lit artificially, but the clusters of green shrubs seemed to be thriving on the fluorescents. Through the garden's grassy center was a curving pathway of flat stepping stones placed artfully in irregular curves, and situated on either side of the walkway were towering rocks nestled in glistening sand that had been raked to represent ocean waves. The rocks were reminiscent of the soaring mountains in Chinese Sung landscape paintings.

Vance's attention, however, was riveted on what awaited at the end of the stony walkway. It was a traditional teahouse, set in a grove of flowering azaleas. And standing in the doorway was a silver-haired figure dressed in a formal black kimono. He was beckoning.

"Did I neglect to tell you I prefer Japanese *cha-no-yu* to the usual British afternoon tea?" Tanzan Mino announced. "It is a ritual designed to renew the spirit, to cleanse the mind. It goes back hundreds of years. I always enjoy it in the afternoon, and I find it has marvelously restorative powers. This seemed the ideal occasion for us to meet and chat."

"Don't want to slight tradition." Vance slipped on the

pair of wooden clogs that awaited at the bottom of the path.

"My feelings entirely," the CEO continued, smiling as he watched him approach. "You understand the Japanese way, Dr. Vance, which is one reason we have so much to discuss."

He bowed a greeting as Vance deposited his clogs on the stepping stone by the teahouse door. Together they stooped to enter.

A light murmur of boiling water came from a brazier set into the *tatami*-matted floor, but otherwise the room was caught in an ethereal silence. The decor was more modern than most teahouses, with fresh cedar and pine for the ceiling and walls rather than the customary reed, bark, and bamboo.

Tanzan Mino gestured for him to sit opposite as he immediately began the formalities of ritually cleaning the bamboo scoop, then elevating the rugged white tea bowl like an ancient chalance and ceremonially wiping it. All the while his eyes were emotionless, betraying no hint of what was in his mind.

After the utensils were ceremonially cleansed, he wordlessly scooped a portion of pale-green powdered tea into the bowl, then lifted a dipperful of boiling water from the kettle and poured it in. Finally he picked up a bamboo whisk and began to whip the mixture, continuing until it had acquired the consistency of green foam.

Authority, control, and—above all—discipline. Those things, Vance knew, were what this was really about. As was traditional and proper, not a word was spoken. This was the Zen equivalent of High Mass, and Tanzan Mino was silently letting him know he was a true master—of himself, of his world.

Then the *oyabun* reached over and formally presented the bowl, placing it on the *tatami* in front of his guest.

Vance lifted it up, rotated it a half turn in his hand, and took a reserved sip. As the bitter beverage assaulted his mouth, he found himself thinking this was probably intended to be his Last Supper. He hoped he remembered enough to get the moves right.

He sipped one more time, then wiped the rim, formally repositioned the bowl on the *tatami*, and leaned back.

"Perfectly done," Tanzan Mino smiled as he broke the silence. "I'm impressed." He nodded toward the white bowl. "Incidentally, you were just handling one of the finest pieces in all Japan."

"Shino ware. Mino region, late sixteenth century. Remarkably fine glaze, considering those kilns had just started firing *chawan*."

"You have a learned eye, Dr. Vance." He smiled again, glancing down to admire the rough, cracked surface of the rim. "The experts disagree on the age, some saying very early seventeenth century, but I think your assessment is correct. In any case, just handling it always soothes my spirit. The discipline of the samurai is in a *chawan* like this. And in the *cha-no-yu* ceremony itself. It's a test I frequently give my Western friends. To see if they can grasp its spirituality. I'm pleased to say that you handled the bowl exactly as you should have. You understand that Japanese culture is about shaping the randomness of human actions to a refined perfection. That's what we really should be discussing here this afternoon, not the world of affairs, but I'm afraid time is short. I often think of life in terms of a famous Haiku by the poet Shiki:

> *Hira-hira to*
> *Kaze ni nigarete*
> *Cho hitotsu.*

"Sounds more like your new airplane," Vance observed, then translated:

> *A mortal butterfly*
> *Fluttering and drifting*
> *In the wind.*

"A passable enough rendering, if I may say, though I don't necessarily accept your analogy." He reached down and lifted a bottle of warmed sake from beside the brazier. "By the way, I know you prefer tequila, one of your odd quirks, but there was no time to acquire any. Perhaps this will suffice."

He set down two black raku saucers and began to pour. "Now, alas, we must proceed."

Post time, Vance thought.

"Dr. Michael Vance." He lifted his saucer in a toast. "A scholar of the lost Aegean civilizations, a former operative of the Central Intelligence Agency, and finally a private consultant affiliated with a group of mercenaries. I had your file updated when I first heard you were involved. I see you have not been entirely idle since our last encounter."

"You haven't done too bad yourself." Vance toasted him back. "This new project is a big step up from the old days. Has a lot of style."

"It does indeed," he nodded. "I'm quite proud of our achievement here."

"You always thought big." Vance sipped again at his sake, warm and soothing.

"It's kind of you to have remembered." Mino drank once more, then settled his saucer on the *tatami* and looked up. "Of course, any questions you have, I would be—"

"Okay, how's this. What do you expect to get out of me?"

He laughed. "Why nothing at all. Our reunion here is merely intended to serve as a tutorial. To remind you and others how upsetting I find intrusions into my affairs."

"Then how about starting off this 'tutorial' with a look at your new plane?" Vance glanced around. "Guess I should call it *Daedalus*."

"*Daedalus I* and *II*. There actually are two prototypes, although only one is currently certified to operate in the hypersonic regime. Yes, I expected the *Daedalus* would intrigue you. You are a man of insatiable intellectual appetite."

"I'm not sure that's necessarily a compliment."

"It wasn't necessarily meant to be. Sometimes curiosity needs to be curbed. But if we can agree on certain matters, I shall enjoy providing you a personal tour, to satisfy that curiosity. You are a man who can well appreciate both my technological achievement and my strategic coup."

The old boy's finally gone off the deep end, Vance told himself. Megalomania. "Incidentally, by 'strategic coup' I suppose you're referring to the fact you've got them exactly where you want them. The Soviets."

"What do you mean?" His eyes hardened slightly.

"You know what I mean. They probably don't realize it yet, but you're going to end up with the Soviet Far East in your wallet. For the price of a hot airplane, you get to plunder the region. They're even going to be thanking you while you reclaim Sakhalin for Japan. This *Daedalus* spaceship is going to cost them the ranch. Have to admit it's brilliant. Along with financing the whole scheme by swindling Benelux tax dodgers."

"You are too imaginative for your own good, Dr. Vance," he said, a thin smile returning. "Nobody is going to believe your interpretation of the protocol."

"You've got a point. Nobody appreciates the true brilliance of a criminal mind. Or maybe they just haven't known you as long as I have."

"Really, I'd hoped we would not descend to trading insults." He reached to refill Vance's sake saucer. "It's demeaning. Instead I'd hoped we could proceed constructively."

"Why not."

"Well then, perhaps you'll forgive me if I'm somewhat blunt. I'm afraid my time is going to be limited over the next few hours. I may as well tell you now that we are about to have the first hypersonic test of the *Daedalus*. Tomorrow morning we will take her to Mach 25. Seventeen thousand miles per hour. A speed almost ten times greater than any air-breathing vehicle has ever before achieved."

"The sky's the limit," he whistled quietly. Alex hadn't known the half of it. This *was* the ultimate plane.

"Impressive, I think you'll agree." Mino smiled and poured more sake for himself.

"Congratulations."

"Thank you."

"That ought to grease the way in the Diet for your deal. And the protocol's financial grab ought to sail through the Supreme Soviet. You prove this marvel can work and the rest is merely laundering your profits."

"So I would like to think," he nodded. "Of course, one never knows how these things will eventually turn out."

"So when do I get a look at it?"

"Why, that all depends on certain agreements we need to make."

"Then I guess it's time I heard the bottom line."

"Most assuredly." He leaned back. "Dr. Vance, you have just caused me considerable hardship. Nor is this the first occasion you have done so. Yet, I have not achieved what I have to date without becoming something of a judge of men. The financial arrangements you put together in London demonstrated, I thought, remarkable ingenuity. There could be a place for you in my organization, despite all that has happened between us."

"I don't work for the mob, if that's what you're hoping."

"Don't be foolhardy. Those days are well behind me," he went on calmly, despite the flicker of anger in his eyes. "The completion of this project will require financial and strategic skills well beyond those possessed by the people who have worked for me in the past."

"All those petty criminals and hoods, you mean."

"I will choose to ignore that," he continued. "Whatever you may wish to call them, they are not proving entirely adequate to the task at hand. You bested my European people repeatedly and brought me a decided humiliation."

Speaking of which, Vance found himself suddenly wondering, a thought out of the blue, what's happened to Vera? She's been European point woman for this whole scam. Where's she now?

Mino continued. "Therefore I must now either take you into my organization or . . ." He paused. "It's that simple. Which, I wonder, will it be?"

Vance studied him. "A lot depends on what happens to Eva."

"The fate of Dr. Borodin depends largely on your deci-

sion. So perhaps I should give you some time to think it
over." He leaned back. "Or perhaps some inducement."

Vance didn't know what he meant. At first. Then he
turned and looked behind him. There waiting on the stony
walkway of the garden were three of Tanzan Mino's personal *kobun,* two of whom he recognized from London.
The CEO's instructions to them were in rapidfire Japanese, but he needed no translation as they moved forward.

Thursday 5:18 P.M.

Yuri Andreevich was mad as hell. After his one-on-one
with Tanzan Mino, he knew he'd been screwed. Sticking a
couple of "pilots" from Mino Industries in the cockpit. It
was just the old GRU trick, surveillance under the specious
guise of "support." He'd seen it all before.

But he'd had an idea. A flash. What about the woman
Nikolai had seen? The one he said was T-Directorate?

A knockout. That's what Nikolai had claimed, so she
shouldn't be hard to track down. He'd been methodically
working the crowded corridors of the North Quadrant,
checking every open doorway. Although the facility was
huge and sprawling, he figured she'd probably be somewhere here close to Command Sector.

Where the hell could she be?

One thing was sure: Tanzan Mino was as sharp as all the
rumors said. The bastard had been on-site for less than a
day and already he'd suspected that something was brewing. So he'd made his own preemptive strike.

The problem now was, how to outsmart him.

This T-Directorate operative had to be the way. After he
got her into a receptive mood, he'd lay out his case. Point
out he had enough to worry about in the cockpit without
playing flight instructor to a couple of Mino Industries
greenhorns. He'd never flown an experimental plane with
civilian copilots and he damned sure wasn't going to start
now. *Especially* now.

Govno! Where the hell was she?

He continued methodically checking the North Quadrant offices just down from the Command Sector, hoping somebody there had seen her. The whole place was getting hectic now: last-minute briefings right and left. Whenever he'd spot a friendly Russian face, he'd collar its owner to inquire about her. Fortunately he had an A-level pass, so all he had to do was flash it to the security stiffs at each sector checkpoint and they'd wave him past. He'd just talked to a couple of flight engineers coming out of a briefing room who claimed they'd spotted her in the hallway no more than half an hour ago.

But why was she here at all? It made no sense. *Unless* she'd defected, gone to work for Mino Industries. Which was exactly the kind of thing you'd expect from one of those opportunistic KGB bastards.

Konyechnaya! There she was, shapely ass and all, just in front of him, headed for Sector Control and flanked by two Japanese security types. They were striding close by, probably showing her around. Maybe she was worried about safety here with all these sex-starved engineers.

Odd, but her walk wasn't exactly what he'd expected. Seemed a little too knowing. Guess that's what happens when you spend too much time in the decadent capitalist West.

He decided to just make his move right there in the hall. Truthfully she *did* look like a hot number. Nikolai wasn't kidding. This was going to be more interesting than he'd figured.

Zadroka! A piece!

Thursday 5:27 P.M.

"*Strasvetye*," came a voice behind Eva. "*Kak pazhavatye.*"

She whirled around. Moving in fast was a tall and—admit it—not bad-looking Soviet major.

"*Ya* Yuri Andreevich Androv," he declared with a light, debonair bow. His Russian was cultivated, Moscow. "They tell me you just got here. Thought we should meet. You've probably heard of me."

"I have no idea who you are," she heard herself saying.

Where the hell did they take Michael? she was wondering. Right after he met with Tanzan Mino, he'd disappeared. And now she was being moved. She didn't know where, but she did know one thing: all the phony politeness was over. Things had gotten very rough, very fast. She was being relocated to a secure location in the Soviet section, or so she suspected, but she figured project management mainly just wanted to keep her out of the way.

Right now, though, she had an agenda of her own.

"I'm a servant of the people." The major who called himself Yuri Androv winked. "Like you. I'm frequently asked to try and kill myself in their behalf."

"I don't know—" she tried to answer, but the Japanese guards were roughly pulling her on.

"I'm the test pilot for the vehicle," he finally announced.

"How lovely." She glared at him. "I hope it's going to be a smashing success."

"I'm about to find out. Tomorrow morning. Right now all I want to do is try and get back in one piece. Which is why I need to talk to you." He caught her arm, temporarily blocking the two uniformed Mino Industries guards. Then he continued on in Russian. "I've got a problem. *We've* got a problem. I was hoping you could help me out."

When the two security men tried to urge her on, he flashed his A-level at them and told them to lay the fuck off, in explicit Russian. Startled, they froze.

That's when it finally dawned on her. *This idiot must think I'm Vera.*

Now he was withdrawing a white packet of English cigarettes and offering her one. Instinctively, she reached out.

"So how can I help you, Major Androv?" Eva flashed him a smile as he lit her English Oval with a match.

"It's the test flight tomorrow. Nobody should be near that cockpit who hasn't been certified to at least ten G's in the simulator. I tried to tell him, but he wouldn't listen."

"Ten G's?" She was trying to keep him talking. "That's—"

"Damned dangerous. But we need it to bring the

scramjets up to rated thrust, at least the first time. They've never been tested in flight. We just don't *know*."

"And nobody else here has been certified?" She wasn't even sure exactly what "certified" meant, but she tried to look concerned.

"Exactly. Now all of a sudden he wants to stick a couple of his Nips in the cockpit there with me, probably crop-duster screwups from Mino Industries." He finally lit his own cigarette, with a suggestive flourish. Christ, she thought, why do all Soviet pilots think they're God's gift to women. "I tell you it's idiotic." He exhaled through his nose. "You've got to help me make him see that, before it's too late."

She glanced sideways at the two impatient Japanese. From their blank faces she realized they hadn't understood a word.

Well, she thought, right now I've got nothing to lose.

"What you're saying, Major, is very disturbing. Perhaps we should have a word with the CEO right away. We both know time's getting short." She glanced down the hall toward the wide doors at the end: Command Sector. "Why don't we just go in together and see him?" She'd noticed the major's A-level, which seemed to carry clout. "Maybe you can deal with these flunkies." She indicated the Mino-gumi *kobun* posing as her guards. "Since I neglected to bring my pass, they have no idea who I really am."

He laughed. "Guess a few assholes around here are in for a surprise."

No kidding, she thought. Mainly you, flyboy.

God, nobody can strut like a Soviet Air Force pilot. Hard currency stores, scotch from Scotland, American cigarettes, French porno videos. They think they own the world. Bad luck, Romeo. You're about to have Tanzan Mino all over your case. Maybe you'll end up so rattled tomorrow you'll crash and burn.

He turned and waved his pass at the two guards. "Mino-san *wa*. Important business *desu*."

Then he seized her arm and pushed the guards aside. "Come on. Maybe you can get these fuck-ups fired after we're through."

"I'll see what I can do." She smiled again. "By the way, you're confirming that the big test flight is still on? in the morning?" She paused, still not sure exactly what the test was all about.

"Oh-nine-thirty hours. All the way." He was leading the way briskly down the crowded corridor.

"And you're going to . . . ?"

"Take her hypersonic. Mach 25. Straight to the edge. Brush the stars. And believe me, I've got to be alone. I can't be running a flight school." He was striding ahead of her now, talking over his shoulder. "Which is why you've got to help me talk some sense into that old fucker. Excuse me," he said, grinning in mock apology, "the CEO."

The guards at the wide double doors leading into Tanzan Mino's suite just gaped as Yuri Andreevich Androv flourished his A-level at them and then shoved his way past, oblivious to the clamor of Japanese shouts now trailing in his wake.

"Mino-san, *pazhalsta*," he said to the figure standing in the anteroom, scarcely noticing it was a woman, and too expensively dressed for a receptionist. Eva watched Vera Karanova lunge for a button on the desk as he pushed open the teakwood door leading into Tanzan Mino's inner office.

The first thing she noticed was the wide window behind the desk opening on a stunning view of the straits, the setting sun glancing off the tips of the whitecaps. Seated behind the desk, monitoring a line of computer screens, was a silver-haired executive.

So that's what he looks like, she thought. Perfect. Central casting couldn't have done better.

"Yuri Andreevich, what . . . ?" he glanced up, glaring at Eva. "I see you've met one of our American guests."

"American?" Androv stopped, then looked at her, puzzled.

Better make this fast, she told herself. In about five seconds Comrade Karanova's going to take this Soviet hero's head off.

"Listen, you bastard." She was storming the desk. "If you so much as lay a finger on Michael or me, either one of us, the National Security Agency is going to close you down so fast you'll think an H-bomb hit this fucking place. I want to see the American ambassador, and I want my belongings returned."

"Everything is being taken care of, Dr. Borodin." Vera Karanova answered from the doorway. Eva glanced back and saw a platoon of eight Mino-guchi *kobun*, Mino's personal bodyguards, all with automatics. "You will come with us."

Androv was staring blankly at her now, his swagger melting like springtime Georgian snow. "You're American? National Security?"

"They kidnapped us. In London. They're going to screw you, everybody. We found out—"

"We?"

"My name is Eva Borodin. I'm director of Soviet SIGINT for the National Security Agency in Washington. And Mike Vance, CIA, is here too. God knows what these criminals are doing to him right now. But they're about to take you apart too, hotshot. So have a nice day. And while you're at it—"

"*Tovarisch* Androv, you have just done a very foolish thing." Vera's voice was frigid. "I don't think you realize how foolish."

"Dr. Borodin," Mino finally spoke, "you are even more resourceful than I'd expected. Resourcefulness, however, is not prudence. Dr. Vance is currently . . . reviewing a proposal I made him. You should be hoping he will accept. As for the National Security Agency, they believe you are still on holiday. After tomorrow, it will not matter. Nothing you can do will interfere with our schedule."

"We'll see about that."

"Trust me," he smiled. Then his look turned grave and shifted. "Major Androv, you will kindly remain after they have taken her away."

CHAPTER EIGHTEEN

The room was cold. Just cold. That was the first thing he'd noticed when they shoved him in. It still was. For nine hours he'd been sitting on a hard, canvas-covered Soviet cot, shivering.

The place was no larger than a small cell, with a tile floor, ice gray concrete walls, and two bare fluorescent bulbs for lighting. No heat. There was a slight vibration—it seemed to be part of the room itself—emanating from the walls and floor. He'd tracked it to a large wall duct.

Ventilation system could use adjusting, he'd thought, fan housing's loose somewhere. They also could turn up the damned heat.

He was wearing only what he'd had on in London, and this definitely was not London. Hokkaido was a much colder part of the planet.

The room had the feeling of a quick, slapped-together job. But it also looked like it could withstand a medium-sized nuclear detonation. One thing was sure, though: It wasn't built with comfort in mind. The door was steel, the same dull hue as the rest. It was bolted from the outside, naturally.

But if isolation and cold were Tanzan Mino's idea of how to break his spirit, to see how tough he was, the man was in for some disappointment.

What the Mino Industries CEO had unwittingly accomplished by moving him here, however, was to enlighten him about the layout of the place. As he was being escorted down the crowded facility corridors by the three leather-jacketed *kobun*, he'd passed a projection video screen suspended over the center of a main intersection. The location seemed to be some sort of central checkpoint, and the screen displayed a schematic of the whole facility.

He'd faked a stumble and used the recovery time to quickly scan its essential features.

He leaned back on the cot and ran through one more time what he'd seen on the screen, trying to imprint it in his memory.

Insight number one: the facility was organized into four main quadrants, with a layout like a large *X*. Some of the writing was Japanese, but mostly it was Russian Cyrillic characters. He massaged his temples and visualized it again.

The first thing he'd focused on was something called the North Quadrant, whose Russian designation was *Komendant.* It looked to be the command center, with a red-colored area labeled in both Japanese and Russian. Next to that were a lot of little rooms, probably living quarters or barracks. *Kanji* ideograms identified those, so that section was probably where the Japanese staffers bivouacked.

That command section, he'd realized, was where he and Eva had been. They'd been quartered in a part of Tanzan Mino's private suites, the belly of the beast.

It got even more interesting. The other three quadrants were where the real work was going on. On the right side of the screen was East Quadrant, whose label was *Komputer/Kommunekatseon,* which meant it contained the computers and communications set-up. Flight Control. And the South Quadrant, the *Assamblaya,* consisted of a lot of large open bays, probably where the two prototypes had been assembled. Those bays connected directly to a massive sector labeled *Angar,* the hangar. But the bays also had separate access to the runway, probably for delivery of prefabricated sections from somewhere else.

The West Quadrant appeared to house test facilities; the one label he could read was *Laboratoraya.* Probably materials labs, next to a configuration that could have been a large wind tunnel. Made sense. That quadrant also had more small rooms with Russian labels. He'd studied the screen a second longer and . . .

Bingo. He'd realized he was being moved into the Soviet sector, probably the barracks and laboratory area.

This had to be the least used location in the facility now, he told himself. All the wind tunnel testing of sections and the materials research was probably wrapped up, meaning this area was history. Yesterday's news. So the CEO had shunted him to this obscure lock-up in the West Quadrant, the Soviet section. What better spot to discreetly dispose of somebody for a while?

Time to brush up your Russian, comrade.

Problem was—he grimaced at the realization—there wasn't a heck of a lot left to brush. He'd had a year at Yale, just enough to let him struggle along with a dictionary and squeak around some standard language requirement. That was it. He'd never given it a second thought afterward. Instead he'd gone on to his real love—ancient Greek. Then later, in CIA days, the action had been Asia. At one time he'd ended up doing some consulting for Langley's Far Eastern INTEL desk, helping coordinate American and Japanese fieldwork.

He could swing the Japanese, but the Russian . . .

Tanzan Mino probably knew that, yet another reason why he'd decided on this transfer. There'd be fewer people here to communicate with. Smart.

The labyrinth of King Minos, brainchild of Daedalus, that's what he felt trapped in. But Theseus, the Greek prince who killed the monster, got some help from Minos's daughter, Ariadne. A ball of string to help him find his way out of the maze. This time around, though, where was help going to come from? Maybe the first job here was to kill the monster, then worry about what came next.

Partly to generate a little body heat, he turned and braced himself at an angle against the door, starting some half push-ups. With his hands on the door, he also could sense some of the activity in the hallway outside. He figured it had to be after midnight by now, but there were still random comings and goings. Activity, but nothing . . .

He felt a tremor, then heard a loud scraping and the sound of a bolt being slid aside.

He quickly wheeled and flattened himself against the

wall, looking futilely for something to use as a weapon.
Aside from the cot, though, there was nothing.

Okay, this would be hand to hand. He could use the
exercise. Besides, he was mad enough.

The gray steel door slowly began to swing inward; then a
mane of white hair tentatively appeared, followed by a
rugged ancient face as the visitor turned to stare at him
through heavy glasses.

"*Strasvitye,*" the man said finally, uncertainty in his
gravelly voice. "*Ya Doktor* Andrei Petrovich Androv."

Friday 1:20 A.M.

Would the idea work? Yuri still didn't know. As he
walked between the vehicles, the hangar's wide banks of
fluorescents glaring down on the final preflight preps for
Daedalus I, he was sure of only one thing: at this point, the
revised plan was the only option left. Would the American
help?

The woman, the bitch, was no fool: An insight he'd come
by the hard way. But maybe the CIA guy—what had she
said his name was?—Vance?

How the hell did he get here? However it had happened, he was being kept in the West Quadrant. It had
been no trick to find him.

He was a godsend; his help would make the scenario
possible. Now it merely required split-second timing.

He glanced up at the big liquid crystal display screen on
the far wall, noting it read zero minus eight hours ten
minutes. He should be back in the West Quadrant now,
catching some sleep—if Taro Ikeda knew he was here in
the hangar, there'd be hell to pay—but time was running
out.

Tanzan Mino had listened icily to his renewed argu-
ments against additional personnel in the cockpit, then
declared that the viability of the program depended on
having backups. Merely an essential precaution. End of
discussion.

Bullshit. As soon as the political games were played out,

the CEO was planning to get rid of him, probably by some "accident."

Well, screw him. And that's where the American came in. The thing to do was just appear to be proceeding with the countdown normally, keep everything innocent. Then, at the last minute . . .

He stared up at *Daedalus I* one last time, watching as the maintenance crews finished the last of the preflight scramjet preps. And he shook his head in amazement that Andrei Androv and all his damned propulsion engineers could create a genuine technological miracle and still be total bumblers when it came to what in hell was really happening.

These technical types thought they were so brilliant! But if it had taken them all this time to realize they'd been fucked by Mino Industries, then how smart could they really be? Made him wonder how the Baikonur Cosmodrome ever managed to get so much as a turnip into orbit.

Now these same geniuses had to get *Daedalus II* flight-ready in just a few hours, and had to do it without anyone suspecting what they were doing. Finally, they had to be ready to roll into action the instant the "accident" happened. No trial runs.

He checked his watch and realized his father's propulsion team was already gathering at Number One, the final meeting. The question now was, could they really deliver? The American was the key.

Friday 1:21 A.M.

"Your name Vance?" The Russian voice, with its uncertain English, was the last thing he'd expected.

"Who are you?"

"For this vehicle, I am Director Propulsion System," he replied formally, and with pride, pulling at his white lab coat. "I must talk you. Please."

Vance stepped away from the wall and looked the old man over more closely. Then it clicked. Andrei Petrovich

Androv was a living legend. Ten years ago the CIA already had a tech file on him that filled three of those old-time reels of half-inch tape. These days, God knows what they had. He'd been the USSR's great space pioneer, a hero who'd gone virtually unrecognized by his own country. No Order of Lenin. Nothing. *Nada*. But maybe he'd preferred it that way, liked being a recluse. Nobody, least of all the CIA's Soviet specialists, could figure him.

And now he was here in the wilds of northern Hokkaido, building a spaceplane. They'd sent over no less than the Grand Old Man to handle the propulsion. This project *was* top priority.

As it deserved to be. But the immediate question was, What was the dean of Soviet rocket research doing here visiting *him*?

"Sorry I can't offer you a cup of tea. No samovar." He looked out the open door one last time. Several Soviet staffers were glancing in as they walked by, obviously puzzled why the famous *Doktor* Androv himself had come around to talk with some unknown civilian.

"Shto? Ya ne ponemayu. . . . I not understand."

"Tea. *Chai*." He shrugged. "Just a bad joke." He reached over and shoved the door closed, then gestured toward the cot. "In the wrong language. Please. Sit."

"Thank you." The old man settled himself. "I did not come for *chai*." His hands were trembling. "I want—" Abruptly he hesitated, as though searching for words, and then his mind appeared to wander. "Your name is Vance?"

"Mike Vance."

"And you are with American CIA?"

What's going on, he wondered? How did these Soviets find out?

"Uh, right." He glanced away. "That's correct."

"Mr. Vance, my son is test pilot for the *Daedalus*." He continued, running his gnarled hands nervously through his long white hair. "His name is Yuri Andreevich."

"Pozdravleneye." Vance nodded. "Congratulations. Yuri Andreevich is about to make the cover of *Newsweek*. You should be proud."

"We have serious problem, Mr. Vance." He seemed not

to hear. "That is why I am come. I am very worried for my son."

Vance looked him over more closely. Yes, he did appear worried. His severe, penetrating eyes were filled with anguish.

"Got a problem with the CEO? Guess the godfather can be a hard man to warm up to, even for his new allies."

"Mr. Vance, I do not know you, but there is very small time." He continued with a shrug, not understanding. "So please, I will tell you many things in very few minutes."

Vance continued to study him. "Go ahead."

"You may not realize, but this project is to be giant leap for our space program. Many of our best engineers are here. This vehicle, a reusable near-earth space platform, would save billions of rubles over many years. It is air-breathing vehicle that would lift research payloads directly into space. But my son never believe that its real purpose. Perhaps I was idealist, because I believe. I always think he was wrong. But more and more of things I have learned about its electronics—things we had nothing to do with—make me now believe he is right. And yesterday, when certain . . . *chelovek* of the Soviet Air Force come, the worst . . ." He paused, his voice beginning to betray barely concealed rage. "I have work all my life for peaceful exploring of space. And now I have been betrayed. The engineers I bring with me here have been betrayed. I also believe, Mr. Vance, that the Soviet people have been betrayed. And along with them, Mikhail Sergeevich himself. This is part of a plot to . . . I don't know what secretly is plan, but I am now convinced this plane must be destroyed, before it is too late. And the world must be warned. That is why—"

"Then why don't *you* warn somebody?" Vance interrupted him. "Matter of fact, there's a lot more to this setup than an airplane."

"But why do you think I am here, talking to you? The facility now is completely sealed. I would warn Mikhail Sergeevich what is happening, but no communication is possible." He hesitated again, painfully. "They want to put my son in the airplane tomorrow with guards. He has been made prisoner, like you. He does not want to fly the vehicle for tomorrow's test, but the CEO is forcing him to do it." He looked up, his eyes bleary and bloodshot. "Mr. Vance, I think he will be killed as soon as this plane is certified hypersonic. They no longer trust him."

"What about you? They probably won't think you're very trustworthy either if they find out you came to see me."

"That is correct. But the time has come for risks."

"So what do you want from me?" He stood back and looked the white-haired old man over one last time. Was he telling the truth? Were the Soviet engineers actually planning a mutiny?

"We are going to stop it. Tomorrow morning, just before the test flight. It must be done."

"Good luck."

"Mr. Vance, you are with American intelligence. We are only engineers. We know nothing about the kind of things necessary to—"

"Do you have any weapons?"

"Nothing. The guards here are all from the corporation." He lowered his voice. "Frankly, most of them look like criminals."

"They are." Vance laughed in spite of himself.

"I don't understand."

"I know you don't understand. If you did . . . but that's beside the point."

"Then will you help us?" His wrinkled face was fixed in determination. "Do you know anything about explosives?"

"Enough. But are you really sure that's the way you want to go?" He paused. "There's a lot that can go wrong in a big facility like this without anybody knowing what caused it."

"All the sensitive areas are under heavy security now. They are impossible to penetrate."

Terrific, Vance thought. "By the way, how does your son, the test pilot, figure into all this?"

"All along he was planning to . . . I don't know. He refused to tell me. But it doesn't matter. Now that two Mino Industries guards are being put in the cockpit with

him, whatever he was planning is impossible. So we have
to do something here, on the ground."

"Well, where is he?"

"He is in the hangar now."

"I'll need to see him."

For one thing, Vance thought, he probably knows how to
use a gun. All Soviet pilots carry an automatic and two
seven-round clips for protection in case they have to ditch
in the wilderness somewhere. Our first order of business is
to jump some of these Mino-gumi goons who're posing as
security men and get their weapons.

"By the way, do you know where they're keeping the
American woman who was brought here with me?"

The old man's eyes grew vague. "I believe she's somewhere here in the West Quadrant. I think she was transferred here around eighteen hundred hours, and then a
little later her suitcase arrive from hangar."

"Her bag?" His pulse quickened.

"Delivered by the facility's robot carts. The plane that
brought you was being made ready for the CEO's trip back
to Tokyo."

"Where was it left?"

"I don't know. I only—"

"Okay, later. Right now maybe you'd better start by
getting me out of here."

"That is why I brought this." He indicated the brown
paper package he was carrying. It was the first time Vance
had noticed it. "I have in here an air force uniform. It
belongs to my son."

The parcel was carefully secured with white string—a
methodical precision that came from years of engineering.

"You will pose as one of us," the old man continued. "You
do not speak Russian?"

"Maybe enough to fool the Mino-gumi, but nobody
else." He was watching as Androv began unwrapping the
package.

"Then just let me do all talk," he shrugged. "If anybody
wonders who you are, I will be giving you tour of the West
Quadrant. You should pretend to be drunk; it would surprise no one. You will frown a lot and mumble incoherent

questions to me. We will go directly to my office, where I will tell you our plan."

Now Andrei Androv was unfolding a new, form-fitting uniform intended for Yuri Andreevich. The shoulder boards had one wide gold chevron and two small rectangles, signifying the rank of major in the Soviet air force. Also included was a tall lamb's-wool cap, the kind officers wore. Vance took the hat and turned it in his hand. He'd never actually held one before. Nice.

Seems I just got made air force major, and I've never flown anything bigger than a Lear jet.

He slipped off the shirt he'd been wearing in London, happy to be rid of it, and put on the first half of the uniform. Not a bad fit. The trousers also seemed tailor-made. Then he slipped on the wool topper, completing the ensemble.

"You would make a good officer, I think." Andrei Androv stood back and looked him over with a smile. "But you have to act like one too. Remember to be insulting."

After the hours in solitary, freezing confinement, he wasn't sure he looked like anything except a bum. But he'd have no difficulty leading *Doktor* Andrei Androv along in the middle of the night and bombarding him with a steady stream of slurred Russian: *Shto eto? Ve chom sostoet vasha rabota?*

How did the Soviets find out he was here? he wondered. Must have been Eva. She'd got through to them somehow. Which meant she probably was still all right. That, at least, was a relief.

After Andrei Androv clanged the steel door closed and bolted it, they headed together toward the old man's personal office, where he had smuggled drawings of the vehicle's cockpit. The hallways were lit with glaring fluorescents, bustling with technicians, and full of Soviets in uniform. Vance returned a few of the crisp salutes and strutted drunkenly along ahead.

They wanted him to help blow up the plane! He was a little rusty with good old C-4, but he'd be happy to brush up fast. After that, it'd be a whole new ballgame.

Friday 1:47 A.M.

"Will he help?" Yuri Androv surveyed the eleven men in the darkened control room. The wall along the left side consisted entirely of heavy plate glass looking out on Number One. That wind tunnel, the video screens, the instrument panels, everything was dormant now. Aside from a few panel lights, the space was illuminated only by the massive eight-foot-by-twenty-foot liquid crystal screen at the far end now scrolling the launch countdown, green numbers blinking off the seconds. Except for Nikolai Vasilevich Grishkov, the Soviet chief mechanic, all those gathered were young engineers from Andrei Androv's propulsion design team. Grishkov, however, because of his familiarity with the layout of the hangar, was the man in charge.

"I just spoke with *Doktor* Androv, and he believes the American will cooperate," Grishkov nodded. "He will bring him here as soon as he has been briefed."

"I still wonder if I shouldn't just handle it myself."

"It would be too dangerous for you, Yuri Andreevich. He knows about explosives. Besides, you have to be ready to fly the other plane, *Daedalus II*, right after the explosion. Nobody else can take it up."

He laughed. "Steal it, you mean."

"Yuri Andreevich, we have made sure it's fueled and we will get you into the cockpit. Beyond that, we will know nothing about—"

"One other thing," he interjected, "I want it fueled with liquid hydrogen."

"Impossible." Grishkov's expression darkened, his bushy eyebrows lifting. "I categorically refuse."

"I don't care. I want it."

"Absolutely out of the question. The engines on *Daedalus II* haven't been certified in the scramjet mode. You can't attempt to take it hypersonic. It would be too risky." He stopped, then smiled. "Don't worry. You can still outrun any chase plane on earth with those twelve engines in ramjet mode."

"I tell you I want to go to scramjet geometry," Yuri Andreevich insisted, his eyes determined.

If I can't do what I planned, he told himself, nobody's going to believe me. I've got to take one of those vehicles hypersonic tomorrow morning, ready or not.

"Impossible. There's no way we can fuel *Daedalus II* with liquid hydrogen. The Mino Industries ground crews would suspect something immediately. It's out of the question. I forged some orders and had it fueled with JP-7 late last night, at 2300 hours. That's the best I can do."

Chort, Yuri thought. Well, maybe I can fake it. Push it out to Mach 5 with JP-7 and still . . .

"And the two 'pilots' from Mino Industries," he turned back, "what about them?"

"If the American plays his part, they will never suspect." Grishkov flashed a grin.

"Unless somebody here screws up," he said, gazing around the room again, studying the white technician's uniforms, the innocent faces.

"There'll be a lot of confusion. When we start pumping liquid hydrogen into *Daedalus I,* the site will be pandemonium," Grishkov continued. "All you have to do is get into the cockpit of the other plane."

It would be a horrible accident, but accidents happened. They'd all heard whispered stories about the tragedy at Baikonur in October 1960, when almost a hundred men were killed because Nikita Khrushchev wanted a spectacular space shot while he was visiting the United Nations. When a giant rocket, a Mars probe, failed to achieve ignition, instead of taking the delay required to remove the fuel before checking the malfunction, the technicians were ordered to troubleshoot it immediately. Tech crews were swarming over it when it detonated.

"Then I guess we're ready." Yuri Andreevich sighed.

"We are." Grishkov nodded and reached for the phone beside the main console, quickly punching in four numbers. He spoke quietly for a few moments, then replaced the receiver.

"They'll be here in five minutes. *Doktor* Androv has just completed his briefing on the cockpit configuration."

"All right. I'm going now. Just get the hangar doors open, the runway cleared, and the truck-mounted starters ready. This is going to be tricky, so make sure everybody thinks we're merely taking *Daedalus II* onto the runway as a safety precaution after the explosion." Yuri gazed over the group of engineers one last time. Would they do it? Whatever happened, he had to get out of there and start checking the cockpit of *Daedalus II* before the morning's preflight crews arrived. "Good luck, Comrades. By 0900 hours I want everything set."

He gave the room a final salute, out of habit, and headed for the security doors. In moments he'd disappeared into the corridor and was gone.

"Let me do the talking," Grishkov said, turning back to the others. "And let *Doktor* Androv translate. Also remember, he has no idea Yuri Andreevich is going to steal the other plane."

The men stirred, and nodded their assent. From here on, they all were thinking, the less they had to do with this plot the better.

Then the door opened. Standing next to Dr. Andrei Petrovich Androv was a tall man dressed as a Soviet air force major. As Grishkov looked him over, he had the fleeting impression that Yuri Andreevich had unexpectedly returned, so similar was the American *poseur* to Andrei Androv's own son. In height and build, the resemblance was nothing short of miraculous. This was going to be easier than he'd dared to hope. Put the American in a pressure suit, complete with flight helmet, and he could easily pass.

"He has agreed to set the explosives," Andrei said in Russian as he gestured toward the man standing beside him in a tight-fitting uniform. "Meet 'Comrade Major Yuri Andreevich Androv.'"

Friday 7:58 A.M.

The room appeared to be the quarters of a high-ranking member of the Soviet staff, now returned to the USSR. It was comfortably if sparely appointed and even had a computer terminal, a small NEC. She'd switched it on, tried to call up some files, but everything required a password. She could use it, however, as a clock. As she watched the time flashing on the corner of the screen, she tried to remember what the Soviet major had said about the schedule . . . the first hypersonic test of the *Daedalus* was scheduled for 0930. That was only an hour and a half away.

She was wearing her London clothes again, but where the hell was her bag? She walked over and sat down on the side of the single bed, thinking. If she could get her hands on the suitcase, the Uzi might still be there.

That's when she heard the sound of muted but crisp Japanese outside—the changing of the guard. The Mino-gumi *kobun* were keeping a strict schedule, a precision that seemed perfectly in keeping with everything else about the facility. Life here was measured out not in coffee spoons but in scrolling numbers on computers.

The door opened and one of the new *kobun* showed his head. At first she thought it was merely a bed check, but he stared at her mutely for a moment, then beckoned. She rose and walked over. This new goon, black suit and all, was armed with a 9mm Walther P88 automatic in a shoulder holster. Outside, the other Mino-gumi motioned for her to come with them.

That's when she noticed her bag, sitting just outside the door.

There goes my chance, she sighed. They want to keep me moving, make sure I'm not in one place long enough for anybody to get suspicious. This way I'll seem to be just another guest.

Without a word they were directing her along the hallway toward Checkpoint Central. All Tanzan Mino's *kobun* seemed to have free run of the facility, because the uniformed security staff didn't even bother to ask for a pass. They may have been new and alien visitors from outside this closed world, but they represented the CEO. Carte blanche.

Now they were moving down the crowded corridor leading to the South Quadrant. The walls were still gray, but this was a new area, one she hadn't yet been in. No sign this time, however, of the Soviet major named Androv.

Guess he wasn't kidding about an important test flight coming up. *Something* was definitely in the wind. The pace of activity was positively hectic. So why was she being moved, right in the middle of all this chaos? It didn't make sense.

She looked up ahead and realized they were headed toward two massive, heavily guarded doors. What could this sector be? Once again the Japanese security guards merely bowed low and waved her Mino-gumi escorts past.

The wide doors opened onto yet another hallway, and she was overwhelmed by a blast of sound. Motors were blaring, voices were shouting, escaping gasses were hissing. The din, the racket, engulfed her. And then she realized the reason: There was no ceiling! Even the "offices" along the side were merely high-walled cubicles that had been dropped here in the entryway of some vast space.

It was the hangar.

The actual entry at the end was sealed and guarded, but instead of passing through, they stopped at the last door on the right.

Whoever had summoned her, it wasn't Tanzan Mino. His array of personal *kobun* weren't lined up outside. In fact, there were no guards at all.

The leather-jacketed escorts pulled open the door, and one entered ahead of her, one behind. Inside was a large metal desk, equipped with banks of phones and rows of buttons.

Sitting behind the desk was Vera Karanova.

"Did you sleep well?" She glanced up, then immediately signaled for the *kobun* to absent themselves.

"Did *you*?" Eva looked her over—the severe designer suit, black, topped off with a string of gray Mikimoto pearls. It was a striking contrast to the short-haired engineers bustling outside.

What riveted her attention, however, was resting on the desk next to the banks of phones and switches. A Zenith Turbo 486.

"We have some time this morning." Vera ignored the

response as she brushed at her carefully groomed dark hair. "I thought we should use it productively."

"Lots of luck, Comrade."

"It is not in either of our interests to be at cross purposes," she continued, still speaking in Russian. It was a startling change in tone from the evening before. "You and I have much in common. We both have worked at high levels in the security apparatus of our respective countries. Consequently we both understand the importance of strategic thinking. That sets us apart." She reached out and touched the laptop computer. "Now, to begin, I would very much like for you to show me how you managed to break the encryption for the protocol. The CEO was most impressed."

"If he wants to know, he can ask me himself." She helped herself to a metal chair.

"He is very busy at the moment," Vera continued, "occupied elsewhere."

This is a setup, Eva was thinking. She wanted to get me down here for some other reason.

But it was hard to concentrate, given the din of activity filtering in from the open ceiling. Above them banks of floodlights were creating heavy shadows around the office, and out there somewhere, she realized, was the prototype.

"Why don't you tell me what's really on your mind, Comrade? Or better yet, why you decided to throw in your lot with all these Yakuza criminals."

Vera Karanova laughed. "You are a director with the National Security Agency. You obviously are very competent. And yet you and the rest of American intelligence seem completely blind. Oblivious to the significance of what is happening around you. In case you hadn't noticed, the Soviet military is being stripped, practically dismantled in the interest of economic restructuring."

"High time, if you ask me."

"That is a matter of opinion. The Cold War, whether we liked it or not, maintained a predictable structure in the world. Both East and West went out of their way to support and stabilize Third World countries in order to keep them out of each other's camp. But with the Cold War slackening, there's disintegration everywhere. Demilitarization is leading to political and economic anarchy worldwide."

Right, Eva thought. But you left out one other interesting fact: Japan got rich while the superpowers were out there "stabilizing" everybody, squandering resources on matching sets of military toys instead of investing in their own infrastructure. They'd love to keep it going.

"This plane," Vera went on, "can be used to serve the ultimate cause of restoring world order." She paused, then continued. "But only if it is in the hands of our air force, from today forward."

"Purge the new thinking?"

"The Soviet Union is on the verge of economic disaster. *Perestroika* has plunged our country into chaos. The time has come to admit revisionism has failed."

"Where's good old Uncle Joe when you need him?" she smiled. "Stalin made the Gulag trains run on time."

"Our restructuring has gone too far," Vera continued. "There are limits beyond which a society can no longer endure change."

Eva stared at her. "I take it KGB and your military right-wingers are planning to try and stage a coup?"

"There still are responsible people in the Soviet Union, Dr. Borodin, who believe our country is worth saving."

My God, Eva thought, their hard-liners are planning to take control of this plane and use it to reenflame the Cold War? Just like the race for the H-bomb, it'll rejuvenate the Soviet military.

"This is our last chance," Vera continued as she reached down and flicked on the computer. "However, if we are to succeed, the terms of the protocol will require certain revisions."

"Do you really think you can get away with this?"

"That's where you come in," Vera went on. "But first perhaps I should show you something."

She reached down and pushed a button on the desk, causing the set of blinds along the side of the office facing the hangar to slowly rise. "I'd like you to see the *Daedalus*." She pointed out the window. "Perhaps then you will better appreciate its significance."

Through the glass was a massive hangar engulfed in white vapor, as cryogenic liquid hydrogen created clouds of artificial condensate, cold steam, that poured over the army of milling technicians. Above the haze, however, she could just make out two giant aircraft. Their wings started almost at the cockpit, then widened outward to the plane's full length, terminating abruptly just before the high tail assembly. Positioned side by side, they looked like huge gliders, except that beneath the wings were clusters of massive engines larger than any she'd ever seen before.

"So that's the prototype, the vehicle specified in the protocol."

They were stunningly beautiful. Maybe all high-performance aircraft looked sexy, but these possessed a unique elegance. The child's vision of the paper airplane reincarnated as the most powerful machine man had ever created.

"I thought you would like to witness the final preparations for our first hypersonic flight," Vera proceeded. "Thus far one of the planes, that one there on the left"— she pointed—"has been flown to Mach 4.5. Today's test will take it to the hypersonic regime, over fifteen thousand miles per hour."

They've leapfrogged the West, Eva was suddenly realizing. It's the X-30 spaceplane America dreams of building in the next century, except it's here now.

"From the looks of things, I'd say you're on schedule."

Vera clicked something on the desk and a blinking number appeared at the top of a video screen. It was the countdown. Liftoff was less than an hour away.

"Yes, so far there has been no hold. Even though today is overcast, with a low ceiling, we don't experience weather delays like the American space shuttle. In fact, this plane is virtually weather-proof, since it leaves from a runway just like a normal passenger jet."

No wonder the test pilot Androv was swaggering, Eva thought. This must be a flyboy's wet dream.

"One more question. Why are you showing me all this?"

"I told you, there's something I need." She paused, and in the silence Eva listened to the increasing clamor of preparations in the hangar outside. "After the test flight this morning, the prototype is scheduled to be transferred to the Supreme Soviet. However, that cannot be allowed to happen. Consequently, there will need to be alterations in the protocol." She clicked on the laptop computer. It hummed lightly as the hard disk engaged, and then the screen began to glow. "Those revisions need to be kept out of the system computers here at the facility for now, so your copy of the text would be an ideal place to prepare a first draft."

"You're going to pull a fast one." Eva stared at her. "You're going to tinker with the terms of the deal and turn this plane over to your air force. Very inventive."

"That is correct. And you are going to help me, Dr. Borodin. You are going to call up your text and print a copy for me."

Sweetie, you are a piece of work.

"Why bother printing it again? Sorry to tell you, but I've already run off a copy. It's in my suitcase."

"We searched your bag. There's nothing there."

"You didn't look hard enough." Maybe this was her chance. "Send some of your thugs to fetch it."

"Very well." She reached for a button on the desk.

Eva turned to look out again through the white mist. Something was going on now. A motorized cart was pulling up and two men in pressure suits were getting off. Must be the pilots.

The first to step off the cart was already waving his hands imperiously at the Japanese technicians. He had to be the Soviet pilot, Androv. Yep, it was him, swagger and all.

Then the second pressure-suited figure stepped down. That one, she assumed, must be one of the Mino Industries recruits Androv had been complaining about. Guess he didn't get very far with his demand to be in the cockpit alone.

The *walk.*

Memories of a long-ago skin-diving trip to Cozumel flooded back. They were off the northern reefs, wearing oxygen tanks, admiring the multicolored banks of coral.

Then later, as they staggered up the beach, she'd laughed at his frog-footed waddle.

Michael!

CHAPTER NINETEEN

Friday 8:37 A.M.

As Vance stepped off the motorized cart, the hangar around him was shrouded in white vapor. The swirling cloud on the ground, the eerie chiaroscuro of the lights, the amplified voice that ticked off the countdown—all added to the other-worldliness of the scene. And above the turmoil two giant spaceplanes loomed, silver monoliths that seemed to hover atop the pale mist.

Chariots of the gods, he thought, gazing up.

The Russian technicians had carefully suited him exactly as Yuri Androv, right down to his boots. Next to his skin was the dark-blue flight suit and cotton-lined leather cap issued to all Soviet pilots, and over these came a pressurized G-suit fabricated from a heavy synthetic material; it felt like a mixture of nylon and Teflon. This was topped off with the flight helmet, complete with a removable reflecting visor, which conveniently prevented anyone from seeing his face.

Although the helmet restricted his peripheral vision, he still could hear clearly through headphones miked on the outside, although they did make the din of the hangar sound tinny and artificial. A Velcro-backed insignia of the Minoan Double Ax adhered to his chest; he was posing as a Mino Industries pilot.

For all its unfamiliarity, however, his gear felt very much like the rubber wet-suit he donned for scuba diving at depths. The two hoses fastened to his abdomen could have been connectors for compressed air tanks and his helmet the oxygen mask. He felt equally uncomfortable. Only the damned flippers were missing.

Since his RX-10 G-suit was designed for high-altitude flight, intended to do double-duty as an emergency backup in case of cockpit decompression, he had to carry along his own personal environmental-control unit, a white, battery-powered air conditioner the size of a large briefcase. It hummed lightly as it cooled and dehumidified the interior of his suit, keeping his faceplate moisture-free. The recycled air he was breathing smelled stale and vaguely synthetic.

The most uncomfortable part of all, however, not to mention the most nerve-racking, had to be the six sticks of C-4 plastic explosive and their radio-controlled detonators now secured against his chest.

Since the Soviet engineers had suited him up in a separate room, avoiding any contact with the Mino Industries doctors who'd been giving Androv his preflight physical, he'd yet to see Yuri Andreevich Androv clearly. He had a partner and he hadn't even had a good look at him yet.

"The other M-I pilot will be arriving in a few minutes," Androv was announcing to the white-jacketed Japanese technicians standing by the Personnel Module. "He was delayed in the briefing." For their benefit he was speaking English, which, to Vance's surprise and relief, was almost perfect. They nodded as he continued. "We'll just go on up in the module. I want to check over the cockpit one last time, make sure there're no last-minute glitches."

The Personnel Module resembled a small mobile home, except its pneumatic lift could elevate it sixty feet straight into the air, permitting direct access to the cockpit's side hatch. It was worlds away from the fourteen-foot metal ladder used to access a MiG cockpit.

"Flight deck." He was speaking through his helmet mike as he pointed up. "Understand? Cockpit." Then he turned and motioned for Vance to follow as he stepped in.

"*Hai.*" Vance nodded gravely, Japanese style. "*Wakarimasu.*"

Let's hope the haze keeps down visibility, he was thinking. This place is sure to have video monitors everywhere. And this fancy elevator is probably bugged too.

Intelligence from Command Central was that Tanzan Mino's two Yakuza "pilots" were receiving a last-minute briefing from the CEO himself. Still, they were certain to show up soon. This was no time to dawdle.

The technicians closed the door of the module, then activated the lift controls. As it began gliding upward, Androv glanced over and gave Vance a silent thumbs-up. He flashed it back, then set down the heavy air-conditioning unit and shifted his weight from foot to foot, still trying to get the feel of the suit.

Maybe, he told himself, this test pilot game is easier than it looks. But only so long as you never actually have to leave terra firma. Then it's probably more excitement than the average person needs.

The upward motion halted with a lurch and the module door automatically slid open. At first glance the open cockpit of the USSR's latest plane made him think of the inside of a giant computer. Nothing like the eye-soothing green of a MiG interior, it was a dull off-white in color and cylindrical, about ten feet in diameter and sixteen feet long. Three futuristic G-seats equally spaced down the center faced a bank of liquid crystal video screens along one wall, and lighting was provided by pale orange sodium vapor lamps integrated into the ceiling.

The real action was clearly the middle G-seat, which was surrounded by instrument consoles and situated beneath a huge suspended helmet, white enamel and shaped like a bloated moth. Everything about the controls bespoke advanced design philosophy: Instead of the usual flight stick placed between the pilot's knees, it had a multiple-control sidestick, covered with switches and buttons, situated on the pilot's right, something only recently introduced in the ultramodern American F-16 Falcon.

Although the throttle quadrant was still located on the left-hand console, in standard fashion, it, too, had a grip skillfully designed to incorporate crucial avionics: the multiple radars, identification-friend-or-foe (IFF) instrumentation, instrument landing system (ILS), and tactical air navigation (TACAN).

He realized they'd utilized the new Hotas concept—hands on throttle and stick—that located all the important controls directly on the throttle and flight stick, enabling the pilot to command the instruments and flight systems purely by feel, like a virtuoso typist. Even the thin rudder pedals looked futuristic. The whole layout, in severe blacks and grays, was sleek as an arrow.

In the end, however, maybe it was all redundant. According to Andrei Androv this vehicle incorporated an advanced control system called *équipment vocal pour aéronef;* it could be flown entirely by voice interface with an artificial intelligence computer. All flight and avionics interrogations, commands, and readouts could be handled verbally. You just talked to the damn thing and it talked back. The twenty-first century had arrived.

The other two G-seats in the cockpit, intended for research scientists, were positioned on either side of the pilot, about four feet away, with no controls whatsoever. All this baby needed was Androv and his computer.

There was more. The space was cylindrical, which could only mean one thing: It was designed to be rotated, again probably by the computer, adjusting the attitude or inclination of the pilot continuously to make sure the G-forces of acceleration and deceleration would always be acting down on him, like gravity, securing him into that special G-seat. And why not? Since there was no windscreen, the direction the pilot faced was irrelevant—up, down, or even backward; who cared?

And the helmet, that massive space-moth intended to be lowered over the pilot's head. From the briefing, he knew that the screens inside were how the pilot "saw." Through voice command to the central computer he could summon any of the three dozen video terminals along the walls and project them on the liquid crystal displays before his eyes.

"So far, so good," Androv said, stepping in and down. Vance followed, then reached back to secure the hatch. It closed with a tight, reassuring thunk. The silent blinking of computer screens engulfed them.

"By the way, it's up there," Vance said quietly, shifting his head toward the newly installed video camera positioned just above the entry hatch. Androv glanced up, nodded, and together they turned away from it. Then without further conversation they each ripped off their Velcro-secured insignias—Androv's, the Soviet air force red star bordered in white; Vance's, the double ax—and exchanged them.

"How much time?" Androv whispered.

"Just give me ten minutes." He held up his heavy wristwatch. Together they checked and synchronized.

"Good luck." Androv nodded and gave another thumbs-up sign, then clasped him in an awkward Russian hug. Vance braced himself for the traditional male kiss, but thankfully it didn't come. *"Do svidania, moi droog,"* he said finally, standing back and saluting. Then he grinned and continued in accented English, "Everything will be A-okay."

Without another word he swung open the hatch, passed through, and stepped into the personnel module.

Vance watched him depart, then turned back to examine the *Daedalus* cockpit more closely. It was a bona fide marvel.

Screens, banks of screens, all along the wall—almost like a TV station's control room. Everything was there. Looking across, left to right, he saw that the engine readouts were placed on top: white bars showing power level, fan rpm, engine temperatures, core rpm, oil pressure, hydraulics, complete power-plant status. The next row started on the navigation and avionics: the radar altimeter, the airspeed indicator, the attitude-director indicator (AID) for real-time readings of bank and dive angle, the horizontal situation indicator (HSD) for actual heading and actual track, and on and on. All the electronics modules were already operating in standby mode—the slit-scan radar, the scanners, the high-resolution doppler. Other screens showed the view of the hangar as seen by the video cameras on the landing gear, now switched over from their infrared mode to visible light.

The avionics, all digital, were obviously keyed to the

buttons and switches on the sidestick, the throttles, and the two consoles. Those controls, he realized upon closer inspection, could alter their function depending on which display was being addressed, thereby reducing the clutter of separate buttons and toggle switches on the handgrips.

The cockpit was not overdesigned the way so many modern ones tended to be: instead it had been entirely rethought. There were probably two hundred separate system readouts and controls, but the pilot's interface was simple and totally integrated. It was beautiful, a work of pure artistry.

Which made him sad. He'd always been an aviation buff, and the thought of obliterating a creation this spectacular provoked a sigh.

On the other hand, H-bombs were probably beautiful too. This was another vengeful Shiva, Destroyer of Worlds. Ridding the planet of its first hypersonic weapons delivery system would be a public service to all humankind.

But first things first. He had no intention of allowing his next moves to be on TV. The newly installed monitor, part of the "retrofit," was about to get a small adjustment.

Strolling back toward the entry hatch, he quickly detached the reflecting outer visor that was designed to drop down over the front of his flight helmet. Then he reached up and wedged the silvered portion against the lens. The camera would continue to operate, relaying back no malfunction signals, but it would be sending a picture of the ceiling. Next he unzipped his flight suit and carefully unstrapped the package riding against his chest. Inside were the six taffy-colored bars of C-4 plastic explosive, each an inch square and six inches long, all wrapped in clear cellophane. They almost looked like candy, but they could blow this entire plane through the hangar's roof.

The charge had to be set before the two Mino-gumi pilots were delivered by the Personnel Module. When they arrived, he'd simply pretend to be Yuri Androv and say they all had to go back down for a final check of their pressure-suit environmental systems. The moment they were clear, he'd activate the radio and detonate. Then the fun would begin.

There. The two consoles on either side of the central G-seat, that's where he'd wedge the charges. It was the perfect place, the central nervous system. After one last, wistful look at the banks of video displays along the wall, he set to work.

Friday 8:43 A.M.

"Do you understand?" Tanzan Mino asked. It sounded more like a command. They were in the Mino Industries Prep Section, a preflight briefing room that led directly into the hangar. The faceplates of the two pilots' flight helmets were raised, allowing him to see their eyes. "Any deviation from the prescribed maneuver blocks will signal a problem."

"*Hai*, Mino-sama," both men nodded grimly. They had come here in the cockpit of his personal Boeing, and they were not happy with their new assignment. Neither had the slightest desire to risk his life in the service of the *oyabun*'s megalomania. The command to serve as last-minute "co-pilots" in the *Daedalus*, however, was an offer they could not refuse.

"Should anything happen, you will radio Flight Control immediately, and we will use the plane's artificial intelligence system, the AI module, to bring it back and land it."

"*Hai*." They nodded again.

"You will not be expected to take the controls," he went on. "The computer can override all commands from the cockpit. You will merely ensure the prescribed flight sequence is adhered to."

He paused, intending to collect his thoughts, but an oddity on the newly installed cockpit monitor caught his notice. He cursed himself for not having kept an eye on it. He'd been too busy briefing the pilots and now . . .

Something about the picture was strange. The perspective had changed. He reached over and, with the push of a button, transferred the image to the large liquid crystal screen on the side wall. Yes, it was definitely wrong. He couldn't quite tell . . .

Had someone jostled the camera? There was still a full half hour before . . .

Something had happened in the cockpit.

The prep crews were scheduled to be finished by now— he glanced at a screen and confirmed that the checklists had already been punched—so no one had permission to be inside the plane. From this point on, only the pilots were authorized to be there.

Androv. Where was he? He was supposed to be in the Soviet Flight-Prep Sector now, across the hangar.

He turned to Taro Ikeda, who was monitoring a line of video screens. "Check with Flight Prep. Has the Soviet pilot completed his preflight physical? Has it been signed off?"

"Let me see." He moved immediately to comply. After he tapped a keyboard, a number matrix appeared on his computer screen, showing the status of all the preflight sequences. Quickly he called up the pilot sequence.

"His physical has been completed, Mino-sama. Everything is checked off. He logged out fifteen minutes ago."

"Then where is he?"

"I'll try and find out."

He reached for a phone and punched in the main number for the Flight Prep sector. The conversation that followed was quick and, as it continued, caused a look of puzzlement to spread over his already-worried face.

"Hai, domo arigato gozaimashta," he said finally and hung up. As he turned back he was growing pale. "Mino-sama, I think there may be a problem. They say he has already left the sector, but—"

"All right then, where has he gone?"

"Sector Security says he left with one of your pilots, Mino-sama, headed for the hangar."

The room grew ominously silent. They were both now staring at the two Mino Industries pilots, standing directly in front of them.

"There must be some mistake." Tanzan Mino inhaled lightly. "Are you sure you understood correctly?"

"It's obviously impossible. I agree."

"Then what's going on? Whatever it is, I think we'd

better find out. Immediately." He motioned for the two pilots to accompany him as he rose and headed for the door. "Stay close by. We're going to the hangar."

Taro Ikeda briskly followed after them into the corridor. If anything went wrong now, he would be the one held responsible. Some vandal tampering in the cockpit was the last thing he needed. Everything had gone smoothly with the countdown so far this morning; he shuddered at the prospect of a last-minute hold.

Ahead of him, Tanzan Mino was striding down the hallway, *kobun* bodyguards in tow, headed directly for the wide hangar doors.

Friday 8:49 A.M.

She was still having trouble thinking clearly. Michael was in the hangar, was actually in one of the planes. What was he doing here?

She barely noticed when a *kobun* walked in and settled her suitcase on the metal desk. He glanced at it, said something in Japanese, and disappeared out the door.

The case was heavy leather, acquired from a little side-street shop by Victoria Station. It looked just as it had when she and Michael stashed the Uzi back in London. They'd deliberately bought a case heavy enough to conceal a weapon inside. Had Mino's people gone through it? discovered the automatic?

"Is this it?" Vera was asking.

"That's the one." She reached down.

"No," Vera said, staying her hand, "I will open it myself." With a quick motion she pulled around the zipper, then flipped back the heavy leather top. There lay a battered map of Crete, under it Michael's book on the palace, piles of rumpled clothes . . .

This isn't how it's supposed to happen, she was thinking. The automatic's down in the bottom, in a separate section, but if Vera probes a little she'll find it. I've got to make her—

"There's no printout here." Comrade Karanova finished

digging through the clothes and looked up. "But then there never really was, was there, Dr. Borodin? Perhaps what you'd hoped to find was this . . ."

She pulled open the top drawer of the metal desk and lifted out a shiny black automatic. It was an Uzi.

"You didn't really think you could do something as amateurish as smuggle a weapon into this facility." She shoved it back into the drawer.

"Congratulations. You've done your homework." So much for surprising Vera Karanova. Apparently that wasn't something easily managed.

"Now we will print a new copy of the protocol," she said, shoving the suitcase over to one corner of her desk. "I don't want to waste any more time."

"Right. Time is money."

So now it was up to Michael. Maybe if she could stall Vera long enough, whatever he was involved in would start to happen.

Glancing out again at the vapor-shrouded floor of the hangar, she fleetingly wondered if maybe she'd been seeing things. No, she was certain. That walk, that funny walk he always had when he didn't feel in control. She knew it all too well; she knew *him* all too well. He'd arrived on the hangar floor riding on that little motorized cart, together with the Soviet pilot, and they'd both entered the hydraulic personnel carrier and been raised up to the cockpit. Then the carrier had come back down and disgorged the Soviet pilot, who'd immediately disappeared into the haze. Which meant Michael still had to be up there.

What was he doing? Had he somehow thrown in his lot with the Soviets? He certainly wouldn't work for Tanzan Mino, so that meant there had to be a revolt brewing. The thing now was to link up, join forces. It was hard to figure.

Oh, shit.

Coming through the wide hangar doors, headed for the same personnel transporter Vance had taken, was Tanzan Mino and a host of his *kobun* bodyguards, followed by two more men in pressure suits. He looked as though he had every intention of—yes, now he was saying something to the operators of the personnel carrier. They all were going up.

Whatever Michael was doing, Mino-san wasn't going to be pleased. The whole scene was about to get crazy. Did Mike have a weapon? Even if he did, he wouldn't stand a chance.

Friday 8:52 A.M.

"Take it up."

Tanzan Mino was marching up the steps of the Personnel Module, accompanied by six *kobun* in black leather jackets and the M-I pilots.

The operators glanced at each other, then moved to comply. One Japanese pilot had just come down and disappeared into the haze. Now two more had arrived, along with the CEO. Were there *three* Japanese pilots? Things were starting to get peculiar. But then this was no ordinary flight; it was the big one.

The door clicked shut with a quiet, pneumatic whoosh, and the module began its ascent. As they rode, Tanzan Mino reflected that in less than an hour this vehicle would be setting new records for manned flight. The world would hear about it from a press conference he would hold in Tokyo, carried live around the globe. That press briefing would also announce a new alliance between Japan and the Soviet Union. It would be a double coup. The planet's geopolitics would never again be the same.

The module glided to a halt and its door opened.

He'd been right. The cockpit hatch was sealed, which meant somebody was inside. The Soviet pilot must be up to something. But what?

Then, unbidden, the pressure hatch started opening, slowly swinging back and around, and standing there, just inside, was a man in a pressure suit. There was no reflecting visor on his helmet now to hide his face.

Friday 8:53 A.M.

Vance stared at the small army facing him, including Tanzan Mino and his two pilots. This definitely was not the drill. Something had gone very, very wrong. Had some of the Soviet ground crews lost their nerve and talked? Whatever had happened, things were headed off the track.

The C-4 explosive was set. But this was hardly the moment to activate the detonators and blow the place.

"How did you get here?" The CEO's eyes narrowed to slits.

"I decided to take you up on that tour."

"What do you think you're doing?"

"Planning a vacation. Checking out the transportation."

"Very amusing, Dr. Vance," he said, staring at a length of C-4, a glass and metal detonator shoved into its side, wedged next to the sidestick. "But who else is part of your scheme? You didn't arrange this unassisted."

"Why would anybody else be involved? I just thought it'd be fun to kick off today's celebration with a bang."

"I'm afraid you will have to be disappointed." He turned to the *kobun*. "Clear the cockpit. Sweep it. And then," he glanced up, "after Dr. Vance replaces the visor on his flight helmet, we will escort him to my office for a very brief and undoubtedly very illuminating interview."

Friday 9:03 A.M.

"What's happening?" Vera had turned to watch through the white haze as the last *kobun* dismounted from the personnel module, following Tanzan Mino and the three pilots.

"Maybe there's been a glitch in the countdown after all." Eva was trying to sound casual. Vera couldn't know the tall pilot in the middle, the one being helped along by Tanzan Mino's musclemen, was Michael. "Looks like Major Androv has got himself into some trouble."

She could tell Vance was mad as hell. They'd probably roughed him up a little there in the cockpit, just to get started, and now they were intending to really go to work on him. But he must be part of a group, so where was everybody else?

"Androv has to fly the plane today. We have everything scheduled. Why are they taking him away?" Vera turned and stalked for the door. "This cannot be permitted. Whatever the problem is, it has to be solved right here. Now. The flight must go forward. Too much is riding on it."

Eva watched her stride out into the white haze of the hangar. She wanted to follow, but then she thought of something better.

Friday 9:05 A.M.

He was wondering when to try and make a break. But how far could he get, encumbered with the pressure suit?

Where's the backup? Are they going to let me just twist in the wind?

The original scenario had fallen apart, but that didn't mean the game was over. The Soviet engineers he'd seen clearly wouldn't be any help in a crisis, but the test pilot Androv was another story. He'd surely try to pull something back together. *Where was he?* Probably still up in the other cockpit, getting *Daedalus II* ready. So now . . .

That's when he saw her, coming out of an office whose doorway was only half visible through the clouds of mist. It looked like . . . Vera Karanova. She was striding directly toward them, intercepting Tanzan Mino's small procession.

"Where are you taking him?" She pointed toward Vance, glancing at his Red Star insignia, as she addressed the godfather in English.

"Are you attempting to interfere in my affairs now, too?" Tanzan Mino demanded as he paused to stare.

"I just want to know what it is you're doing," she replied.

"I am handling a problem," he said coldly as he examined her. "There is a traitor, or traitors, among the Soviets. I intend to find out who's involved."

"What do you mean?" An edge of nervousness entered her voice.

Vance was coming up. "Sorry I screwed up, Vera," he said in English. "So close yet so far. Somebody must have blown the whistle."

"You're not—" She stared as he lifted the visor of his flight helmet.

"But what the hell," he went on. "We gave it a shot. Nothing ventured, nothing—"

"*We?*" She examined him, puzzled.

"I suspected all along you could not be trusted." Tanzan Mino's calm facade seemed to crack as his face flushed with anger. "But I had no idea you would actually betray the entire project. Sabotage the vehicle."

"I don't know anything about sabotage." She clearly was startled, attempting to maintain calm in her voice. "If Vance has—"

"It appears I'm surrounded by treachery and traitors." His voice quavered as he stepped over to one of the *kobun,* then reached in and withdrew the 9mm Walther automatic from the man's shoulder holster. When he turned back, his eyes were opaque with anger and paranoia. He'd clearly snapped, lost it. "Mr. Vance, I want to know the names of everyone who was involved in this plot. Everyone. If I am satisfied you are telling the truth, then perhaps I will consider sparing your miserable life. Otherwise . . ."

He turned back to Vera. She was staring at the gun, her face ashen, not letting herself believe what her eyes were telling her. The white mists of the hangar swirled around them, creating ghostly shadows across the expressionless faces of the *kobun.*

"You made a very grave error in judgment," he was saying to her. "I don't yet know precisely what you were expecting to accomplish, but whatever it was, I can assure you I am not a man who tolerates disloyalty."

His expression was strangely distant as he raised the pistol and fired, one precise round, a dull thunk barely audible above the din of the hangar.

Vance watched in dismay as Vera Karanova stumbled

backward, her dark eyes uncomprehending. It was a gangland-style execution, quick and preemptory, the time-honored way. No appeals or due process.

He'd been hoping merely to gain some time for Androv, not cause her to be murdered on the spot. Now Tanzan Mino turned to him, still gripping the pistol. His face was distorted in irrational fury. "Perhaps I made a mistake just now, Dr. Vance. What do you think?"

"Probably a pretty serious one."

"Yes, now that I reflect on it, I'm inclined to agree. The culprit we seized red-handed was you. You are the one I should be making an example of." He was raising the Walther again.

It began so quickly he almost didn't realize it was happening. From out of the swirl of mist that engulfed *Daedalus I*'s landing gear a white-haired old man appeared, grasping a pistol. Tanzan Mino turned to stare, just in time to hear him yelling—in Russian.

"Release him. Release my son. I order you." He was closing on the group, about twenty feet in front of them, brandishing the weapon uncertainly. Vance couldn't make out what caliber it was, but he doubted it mattered. Andrei Androv clearly had no idea how to use it. His was an act of desperation.

Then another realization clicked.

He said "my son." He thinks I'm Yuri.

Before anybody could move, a white pressure suit materialized out of the distant haze around *Daedalus II*. It was Yuri Androv, running toward his father, shouting. *"Nyet! Don't—"*

"Release him, I tell you." Andrei Androv didn't hear him as he continued to move menacingly on Tanzan Mino. The outcome was inevitable.

Vance ducked and rolled for the Personnel Module just as the *kobun*'s line of H&K automatics flared.

Andrei Androv lurched, gray hair flying, and managed to get off two rounds. But instead of hitting a *kobun*, he caught one of the Mino Industries pilots, visor up, directly in the face.

Comrade *Doktor* Andrei Petrovich Androv, dean of Soviet propulsion technology, chief designer of the *Daedalus*, died instantly, his eyes still fixed in determination. However, Tanzan Mino's *kobun* weren't tidy. One of them squeezed off a couple more rounds just as Yuri Androv ran up and leaned over his father's crumpled body. With a groan, he spun around and staggered against the huge 22-ply tires of *Daedalus I*'s starboard landing gear.

It still wasn't over. As Vance scrambled against the Personnel Module, he caught a glimpse of something that, faintly visible through the clouds of cryogenic fog, apparently was escaping everybody else. Another woman was standing in the door of the office where Vera Karanova had been. Holding an Uzi.

How had she managed to get her hands on *that*?

Not a second too soon. She can sweep the floor. Just get out of the way and give her an opening. Maybe there's still time.

He began scrambling for the base of the Personnel Module. Now the white mist was obscuring everything, and Tanzan Mino seemed to have enveloped himself in it. He was nowhere to be seen. However, his presence was not missed by his *kobun*, who were still taking care of business.

The next agenda item, Vance realized, was himself. As he tried to roll under the module, one was turning, raising his automatic . . .

Now Eva was yelling, "Michael, stay down."

The *kobun* all whirled back, but she was ready. Stock extended, full auto.

Jesus, he thought, that hood in the back is holding enough C-4 to clear a small arena. If she hits one of the detonators . . .

It was either a lucky or an unlucky shot. After eight rounds, less than a second's worth, a blinding ball of fire erupted where the *kobun* had been, sending a shock wave rolling through the open space of the hangar, knocking over technicians almost a hundred feet away. As Vance was slammed under the Personnel Module, out of the corner of his eye he saw Eva being thrown against the door frame of the office. The air blossomed with the smell of deadly C-4, like acrid Sterno. Not for nothing did the U.S. military swear by it.

Now Yuri Androv was peeling himself off *Daedalus I*'s landing gear, his flight suit blackened and smudged. Blood from a bullet wound was running down the right sleeve.

They'll be coming for us all, Vance thought. Tanzan Mino's probably somewhere radioing for more guards right now.

Eva was stalking through the smoke, still grasping the Uzi.

"Michael, are you all right?"

"Hell of a morning." He was pulling himself out from under the Personnel Module, awkwardly trying to straighten his flight helmet. "You took out the palace guard, everybody but Mr. Big. Congratulations. And I thought CIA had a patent on that kind of operation."

Already emergency alarms had begun a high-pitched whine, blaring through the cavernous hangar. Everything around them was chaos.

"You know," she yelled above the noise, "he's going to kill us immediately. There's no way he's going to—"

"I figure we've got about two minutes to think of something," he yelled back and pointed. "Check on the pilot. His name is Androv."

"I know. I met him last night." She turned and stared. "We had a small misunderstanding."

"Well, let's see if he's still in any condition to fly."

"You mean?"

"How else? You got any better ideas, I'd like to hear them."

Yuri Androv had worked his way through the carnage of the explosion, the scattered remains of Tanzan Mino's phalanx of *kobun*, to again bend over the form of his father. Once more the cloud of obscuring mist was flowing over the scene, blanking it.

At that moment, however, a pale glow laid itself around them, the murky light of overcast dawn. Vance realized the Soviet technicians had thrown open the hangar doors and were scrambling out onto the tarmac.

Good, let them. We might just follow suit.

Now Yuri Andreevich Androv was approaching, clasping his right arm.

"We've got to get him fixed," Vance said briskly, looking him over, "put on a tourniquet."

"Think he can still fly?"

"I say we *make* him fly."

With his left hand Androv peeled back his helmet visor and kissed Eva. *"Spacebo,"* he said in Russian, "you did what I would have done if I'd had a weapon. But now I don't know what—"

"How's your arm?" Vance cut in. "We've got to make a decision right now. When the reinforcements arrive, it's game over. One little Uzi won't handle their firepower."

Androv frowned. "Can you fly?"

"Never handled anything bigger than a Lear," Vance replied. "And then only as copilot."

It didn't seem to matter. Androv glanced at the open door of the Personnel Module and motioned to them.

"Then come on. Let's hurry." Now he was searching the hangar. Finally he spotted the man he wanted.

"Pavel," he yelled in Russian, "have the starter trolleys been engaged yet?"

"Da," came the reply.

"Then prepare *Daedalus I* for power-up and get the hell out. We're go for rpm."

"What do you mean? The tow trucks haven't even been—"

"Forget the tow trucks. It's going to be afterburners, right here. Get the rest of your people in the clear."

Afterburners were rings of nozzles that sprayed fuel into the superheated exhaust gases of a jet engine, creating a burst of power. In military aircraft they were used to produce surges in thrust during takeoff and dogfights.

"Afterburners! In the hangar. Yuri, all the hydrogen storage tanks could blow. You'd destroy *Daedalus II*. Just incinerate it."

"That's the idea." He was already mounting the steps of the Personnel Module, not looking back. "There's only going to be one plane left. The one I take."

"The computer." Eva had started up the steps, but then

she froze and turned back, handing Vance the Uzi. "I have to get it."

"There's no time." He reached for the weapon, its muzzle still hot. "We've got—"

"Michael, I didn't come this far just to let the protocol slip through our fingers." She was running past him now, back down. "Only take a second."

He knew it was pointless to argue. And besides, maybe she was right. Who knew where they'd end up?

Now Androv had faltered and was leaning shakily against the open doorway of the module, the right sleeve of his pressure suit covered in blood. Vance took advantage of the ticking moments to step up and examine it.

"You need a bandage." He started tearing away the synthetic cloth. "Or better yet, a tourniquet."

"No." Androv glanced at his arm and grimaced. "There's not—"

"You're going on adrenaline right now, my friend. But when the shock wears off . . ." He looked around the interior of the module, but there was nothing to cut with, so he just ripped away a large portion of Androv's sleeve and parted the material. A savage furrow was sliced across his bicep.

"I don't want you to pass out." He tore a section of the sleeve into a strip and then, struggling with his heavy gloves, began binding it above the wound. The hangar was still bedlam, people running and yelling on every side, alarms sounding. As he was finishing the tourniquet, Eva came bounding up the metal steps carrying her Zenith. They were ready.

Androv quickly secured the door and activated the controls. Through a smoke-smeared window they watched the bloody hangar floor disappear into the haze. The world suddenly turned dreamlike, an unreality highlighted by the soft whoosh of the pneumatic lift beneath them. Then the module lurched to a halt.

Vance led the way through the open hatch. "Looks like somebody forgot and left the lights on."

"Pavel told me the starter trolleys were engaged," Androv said in Russian as he climbed through, then stepped down. He continued in English. "Petra can initiate power-up."

"Petra?" Vance turned back. "You mean the—"

"Our copilot." He pointed toward a large liquid crystal screen at the far end of the cabin, now blank. "I want to try and use her to override Flight Control for the rest of the sequence."

"Short circuit the countdown?"

"I've never done it, but . . ." He walked over and reached down to flip a square blue switch on the right-hand console. "Let's see if she's awake this morning."

He glanced up as the screen blinked on and a large black-and-white double-ax logo materialized, set against the red and white of a Japanese flag. Next he pushed a button on the sidestick and spoke.

"Petra, report countdown status."

All preflight sequences nominal. The eerie, mechanical sound of a woman's voice, speaking Russian, filled the space. *Do you acknowledge?*

"Affirmative," he answered back. "You will now initiate ignition sequence. Bypass remaining countdown procedure."

That is an override command. Please give authorization code.

"Code P-18. Systems emergency."

The countdown is now T minus nineteen minutes twenty-eight seconds. All systems are nominal. Therefore Code P-18 is not a valid command.

"Shit," he whispered under his breath. "Petra, verify P-18 with Flight Control." He paused for a split second, then pushed a button on the console and commanded, "Abort instruction." Another pause, then, "Repeat verify abort command for N equals one over zero."

"What was that?" Eva was wedging her laptop under the left-hand G-seat.

"I think, I *hope* I just put her command-monitor function into an infinite loop. She'll just continuously start and stop the verification procedure. Maybe it'll render that subroutine incapable of blocking the other system functions."

"You're going to confuse her head? Good luck."

He settled himself in the central seat, then reached up and began unlatching the huge flight helmet. As he did, his eyes were suddenly flooded with grief.

"They killed him." He paused for a moment and just stared. Vance thought he'd finally become befuddled from the shock. But then he choked back his emotion and continued. "We're going on the deck. Under their goddam radar."

"What did you say?" Vance strained to catch his words. The English was slurred.

He seemed to grow faint, his consciousness wane, but he finally revived as he finished yanking the giant helmet down over his head.

Vance's headphones came alive as he heard the Russian. "*Daedalus I* to Control. Do you read? I am now bringing up core rpm for starboard cluster, outboard trident." A second later, he continued, "We have S-O ignition."

"Yuri," came a startled radio voice, "what in hell is going on! You can't—"

"Portside cluster, outboard. Rpm up," he continued in Russian, his voice halting. "We have P-O ignition."

"Yuri, you can't—?"

"Starboard cluster, inboard. Bringing up. Portside cluster, inboard—"

"Androv, for godsake, have you gone mad?"

"Sergei, I told them to clear the hangar. I'm taking her to full power."

"The liquid hydrogen tanks are in there. You could blow the whole hangar to hell if you use afterburners. You must be crazy!"

"The bastards gunned him down, Sergei." He caught a sob. "It was my fault. I should have warned—"

"What are you talking about? Gunned who down?"

But Yuri Androv's mind was already elsewhere, drifting into a grief-obsessed dream state.

"Engine start complete," he continued. "Beginning pretakeoff sequence."

Will he be able to get this thing off the ground? Vance was wondering. He's shot up and now he's falling apart.

Guess we're about to find out. The fuselage cameras are showing an empty hangar. Everybody's run for cover.

"Eva, want to take that seat? I'll take this one. No free drinks in this forward cabin section." He was speaking through his upraised helmet visor as he eased himself into the right-hand G-seat.

"And buckle up for safety." She settled herself in the left. "Let's just hope he can still manage this monster. It's a Saturn V with wings."

"He's got his talking computer, if she'll still cooperate. Do me a favor and translate now and then."

"Machines are supposed to translate for people, not the other way around. We're in space warp."

"I believe it."

As he pulled down the overhead seat straps, he found himself wondering what *Daedalus* would feel like in full afterburner mode. Those turboramjets made a Boeing 747's massive JT-9Ds look like prime movers for a medium-sized lawnmower.

"Power to military thrust." Androv was easing forward the twin throttles, spooling them up past three-quarters power. *Daedalus* had begun to quiver, shaking like a mighty mountain in tectonic upheaval.

"Prepare for brake release."

The screens on the wall above reported fuel consumption edging toward three hundred pounds of JP-7 a second.

"Yuri," the radio crackled, "don't—"

"Pavel's got his men out of the hangar, Sergei. I can see on my screen. I'm going cold mike now. No distractions. Just wish me luck."

There was a click as he switched off the communications in his helmet. He missed a new radio voice by only a second. It was speaking in English.

"Dr. Vance, what is going on? He's just cut his radio link with Flight Control. He's deranged. I order you to halt the flight sequence. He could destroy both planes by going to afterburners in the hangar. I demand this be stopped."

Vance glanced up at the TV monitors. An auxiliary screen showed Tanzan Mino standing at the main Flight Control console, surrounded by more *kobun*, who had

muscled aside the Russian technicians. He also noticed that
a lot of Soviet brass were there too.

"Looks like you've got a problem."

"I'm warning you I will shut you down. I can activate the
automatic AI override three minutes after takeoff. The
plane will return and land automatically."

"Three minutes is a long time." Vance wondered if it was
true, or a bluff. "We'll take our chances."

"You'd leave me no choice."

"May the best man win."

"Petra, brake release." Yuri Androv's voice sounded
from beneath his helmet.

Acknowledged.

Vance looked across to see his left hand signal a thumbs-
up sign, then reach down for the throttle quadrant. The
vehicle was already rolling through the wide doors of the
hangar, so if there were an explosion now, at least they'd
be in the clear.

Androv paused a second, mumbled something in Russian, then shoved the heavy handles forward to Lock, commanding all twelve engines to max afterburner. The JP-7
fuel reading whirled from a feed of three hundred pounds
a second to twenty-one hundred, and an instant thereafter
the cockpit was slammed by the hammer of God as the
monitor image of the hangar dissolved in orange.

CHAPTER TWENTY

Friday 9:31 A.M.

"One small step for man."

Vance felt his lungs curve around his backbone, his face
melt into his skull. He didn't know how many G's of acceleration they were experiencing, but it felt like a shuttle
launch. He gripped the straps of the G-seat and watched
the video feed from the landing-gear cameras, which

showed the tarmac flashing by in a stream of gray. The screen above him had clicked up to 200 knots, and in what seemed only a second the *Daedalus* was a full kilometer down the runway. Then the monitors confirmed they were rotating to takeoff attitude, seven degrees.

They were airborne.

Next the screens reported a hard right-hand bank, five G's. The altimeter had become a whirling blur as attitude increased to twenty degrees, held just below stall-out by Petra's augmented control system.

When the airspeed captured 400 knots, the landing gear cameras showed the wheels begin to fold forward, then rotate to lie flat in the fuselage. Next the doors snapped closed behind them, swallowing them in the underbelly and leaving the nose cameras as their only visual link to the outside. The screens displayed nothing but gray storm clouds.

Landing gear up and locked, came Petra's disembodied voice.

"Acknowledge gear secure," Androv said, quieting a flashing message on one of the screens.

No abort so far, Vance thought. Maybe we're about to get away with this.

The airspeed had already passed 600 knots, accelerating a tenth of a Mach number, about 60 knots, every five seconds.

That's when he noticed they were still receiving wide-band video transmissions from the Flight Center. The screen showing Tanzan Mino remained clear and crisp. Surely not for much longer, but now at least the uplink was intact. And the CEO was returning the favor, monitoring their lift-off via a screen of his own. Vance watched as he turned to some of the Soviet brass standing next to him and barked orders. What was that about?

For now though the bigger question was, What do *we* do?

Androv was still busy talking to Petra, issuing commands. Vance realized they were assuming a vector north by northeast, out over the ocean. They also were probably going to stay on the deck to avoid radar tracking, with only passive systems so that no EM emissions would betray their heading.

He glanced up at the screens and realized he was half right. They were over the ocean now, at a breathtaking altitude of only five hundred meters, but Androv had just switched the phased-array radar altimeter over to start hopping frequencies, using "squirt" emissions. Pure Stealth technology. No conventional radar lock could track it.

"Dr. Vance, I am giving you one more opportunity to reconsider." Tanzan Mino's voice sounded through the headphones. He was still standing at the main Flight Control console, though his image was finally starting to roll and break up. "You must return to base. The consequences of this folly could well be incalculable."

"Why don't you take that up with the pilot?" Vance answered into his helmet mike.

"His receiver has been turned off. It's impossible to communicate with him. He's clearly gone mad. I will give you another sixty seconds before I order the on-board guidance computer switched over to the AI mode. Flight Control here will override the on-board systems and just bring the vehicle back and land it."

Again Vance wondered if he really could.

Then a screen flashed, an emergency strobe, and Petra was speaking. The Russian was simple enough he could decipher it.

Systems advisory. You are too low. Pull up. Acknowledge. Pull up.

Androv tapped the sidestick lightly and boosted their altitude a hundred meters.

"Michael," the voice was Eva's coming through his headphones. "She—it—whoever, said—"

"I figured it out. But did you hear the other news? Mino-san just advised he's going to override Petra. We're about to find out who's really flying this baby."

"No." Androv was raising his flight helmet and gesturing, his wounded arm urging at something in his right pocket. "Please take. Do it quickly. And then . . ."

Vance unstrapped his G-seat harness, rose, and moved

over to the central console. Androv had raised his hydraulic helmet all the way up now and was trying to unzip the right side of his flight suit. Vance reached down and helped him, not sure exactly what he needed.

"There." Yuri was trying to point. "The radio. Please, you must . . ." The English began to fail him again.

"What's this?" Vance took out the transmitter, the size and shape of a small calculator.

The answer was in Russian, complex and garbled. Something about *komputer*.

"He's wired something into the on-board computer, Michael," Eva began translating. "The radio will perform brain surgery on Petra, disabling her AI functions. It's supposed to prevent Flight Control from overriding . . . I didn't quite get it. But he wants you to help."

Vance glanced up at the line of video screens. *Daedalus* was now skimming rapidly over the straits, banking in the direction of the archipelago known as the Kurile Islands, and the image of Tanzan Mino was breaking up, almost gone. Had he heard? Maybe it didn't matter. The allotted sixty seconds was ticking away and he could just make out the image of Tanzan Mino, holding a microphone, preparing to give orders.

By the clock on the screens he saw that forty-one seconds had already passed.

"Dr. Vance, we are preparing to initiate total systems override." The CEO's voice sounded through his headphones. "You have fifteen seconds remaining to acknowledge."

"The code," Androv was saying. "It is one-nine-nine-nine."

Vance stared at the small device in his flight glove. It had a number keypad and a liquid crystal display.

"You have ten seconds," Tanzan Mino said. The image was ghostly, but the voice still rang loud and clear.

He began fumbling with the device, but the numbers kept eluding him, slipping around the thick fingers of his gloves. Finally he caught the *1*. Above him the screens were still scrolling. Eight seconds.

Suddenly the cockpit seemed to sway, an air pocket that

even the *Daedalus*'s advanced structural mode control system couldn't damp out entirely. Now Androv was talking to Petra, going for a sliver more altitude. Seven seconds.

"Michael." Eva was watching, her face still drawn from the acceleration. "Is it—?"

"It's the gloves. The damned gloves. I'm . . ." Then he punched in the first *9*.

In the back of his mind he noted that the cockpit was adjusting as *Daedalus* rotated, increasing attitude . . .

He got another *9*. But his grip on the "calculator" was slipping, pressing toward the floor as the G-forces of acceleration weighed against him. He checked the screens again and saw that three seconds remained.

Now Androv was grappling to keep control of the throttle, while issuing instructions to Petra.

Am I about to disable her? he wondered. If I do, can he manage this nightmare manually? What if Mino was only bluffing?

Two seconds.

A final, bright green *9* appeared on the liquid crystal readout.

Alert. AI system malfunction. It was the toneless voice of Petra. She sounded vaguely annoyed.

Something had happened. Two of the screens on the wall above had just gone blank, but *Daedalus* continued to climb.

"Dr. Vance, we are now going to recall the plane. We have ordered a wing of fighter-interceptors scrambled from the Dolinsk airbase on Sakhalin. They will escort you back."

Whoops. So that was what he was telling the Soviet brass to do. Get up some hardware fast. This could well be the shortest flight since the Wright brothers'.

Then he heard Androv's helmet mike click on.

"This is *Daedalus I*. Do you copy me?"

"Major, you—" Mino began.

"Copy this, you bastard. Fuck you. Repeat. Fuck you. I've disabled your fucking AI module."

"You disabled it?"

"That's a roger. Do you read me, you murdering son-of-a-bitch? FUCK YOU!" He clicked off his mike.

Vance was moving slowly across the cockpit, headed back to his own G-seat. As he settled himself and reached for the straps, he glanced up at the screens to check their flight data—altitude, speed, vector, G-force, fuel consumption. They were still on the deck, with an airspeed just under a thousand knots, about eleven hundred miles per hour. Not quite Mach 2, but already it was risky. And their vector was 085, with coordinates of 46 degrees latitude, 143 degrees longitude.

What now? *Daedalus* had all the active radar systems known to modern avionics. Looking at the screens he saw forward-looking radar, sideways-looking radar, a four-beam multimode pulse-Doppler look-down radar, terrain-following radar, radar altimeter, mapping and navigational radar, and a host of high-powered ECM jammers. The problem was, they all emitted EM, electromagnetic radiation. Switch on any of those and they'd become a flying radio beacon, broadcasting their position.

The next row of screens, however, provided readouts of their passive, nonemitting receivers and analyzers. That clearly was what they would have to use to monitor the threat from Sakhalin, scooping up any EM for lightning-fast computer processing. Surely Petra could spit out a fingerprint of everything in the skies. To begin with, there were the basic Radar Warning Receivers (RWRs) located aft, on the tailplanes, as well as infrared warning receivers (IRWRs) positioned high on the outboard stabilizers. The screens showed she could analyze basic frequency, operating mode, pulse repetition frequency, amplitude of pulse, time of arrival, direction of arrival—the full menu.

"If it's true they've scrambled the base at Dolinsk, it probably means the new MiG 31s." Androv was now busy switching on all the passive systems, just the way Vance figured he would. "We have to decide what to do. But first I want to take her up and do a quick recon. Buckle in."

"The latest Foxhound has a multimode pulse-Doppler look-down, shoot-down capability that's as good as any in the world," Vance heard himself saying. "We're the biggest target in the skies, and we're unarmed. We'd be a sitting duck for one of their AA-9 active homing missiles. They're launch-and-leave."

"Let's check it out before we get too worried," Androv replied. "But this has to be fast. You're about to see a Mach 3 Immelmann. Don't try this in a 747." He laughed, then began lowering his high-tech helmet. "I hope I can still manage it."

There was a surge of acceleration as he shoved forward the throttles, then yanked back on the sidestick. The *Daedalus* seemed to kick straight up. And up. And up. The instruments showed they were traveling skyward in a thin arc, as though sliding up the curve of an archer's bow. Now the altimeter was spinning, and in eighteen seconds they had already reached twenty thousand feet. But still Androv kept the stick in, and during the next five seconds, as *Daedalus* continued tracing the archer's curve, they almost began to fly upside down.

At the last moment he performed an aileron half-roll and righted them. The Immelmann had, in effect, taken them straight up and headed their powerful forward-looking IR detectors and radar in the direction of Sakhalin. Vance glanced at the screens and realized they'd climbed thirty thousand feet in twenty-seven seconds. They'd just waxed the standing forty-eight-second time-to-climb record of the USAF F-15 Eagle, and *Daedalus* wasn't even breathing hard. Even though Androv had now chopped the power, they still were cruising at Mach 2. Effortlessly.

No wonder he loves this bird.

The only downside was, the fuel reading showed they'd burned twenty-three thousand pounds of JP-7 during the climb out.

"Petra," Androv said into his helmet mike, "take VSD to standby and give me infrared laser."

Petra's interrogation revealed a wing of eight MiG 31 interceptors, flying in formation at twenty-five thousand feet and closing. At Mach 2.4.

Friday 9:43 A.M.

"Ya ponemaiyu," Colonel-General Gregori Edmundo-vich Mochanov said into the secure phone, the pride of Dolinsk's Command Central. "I ordered a wing of the Fifteenth Squadron scrambled at 0938 hours. Fortunately we were planning an exercise this morning."

He paused for the party at the other end, General Valentin Sokolov on a microwave link from the Hokkaido facility.

"Da, if Androv maintains his altitude below six hundred meters, then he will probably have to keep her near Mach 2. The vehicle, as I understand it, is not designed for that operating regime. So with the MiG 31s on full afterburner, we can make up the distance. But we need his vector."

He paused and listened. "Yes, they are fully armed. AA-9s. A kill perimeter of—" He listened again. "Of course, active homing radar *and* infrared, on the underfuse-lage—" He was impatiently gripping the receiver. *"Da,* but I can't work miracles. I *must* have a vector." He paused again. *"Da,* but I don't want to accidentally shoot down another KAL 747. I must have a confirmed target. I'm not going to order them to fire without it."

He listened a second longer, then said, "Good," and slammed down the phone.

Friday 9:44 A.M.

"Guess we'd better start playing hide-and-seek in earnest," Vance observed.

"Stealth, my American friend," Androv replied. "The hostile radar signature of this fuselage is almost nothing. And we can defeat their infrared by taking her back on the deck, so the engines are masked from their look-down IR. Back we go. We'll pull out at five hundred meters, but it'll mean about three negative G's—blood to the brain, a red-out. Very dangerous. Be ready."

Then he shoved the sidestick forward and *Daedalus* plunged into a Mach 3 power dive. The infrared cameras showed the sea plunging toward them. The dive took even less time than the climb, with the altimeter scrolling. Suddenly the voice of Petra sounded.

Pull up. Warning. Pull up. Pilot must acknowledge or auto-override will commence.

A ton of empty space slammed into them as Petra automatically righted the vehicle, pulling out of the dive at an altitude of four hundred meters.

Vance looked over and saw Yuri Andreevich Androv's bandaged arm lying limp on the sidestick, lightly hemorrhaging. He'd passed out from the upward rush of blood.

Friday 9:58 A.M.

"He has disappeared from the Katsura radar again, Mino-sama. I think he has taken the vehicle back on the deck." Ikeda's face was ashen as he typed in the computer AI override command one last time, still hoping. The Flight Control operations screen above him was reading "System Malfunction," while the engineers standing behind were exchanging worried glances. Who was going to be held responsible? The master screen above, the one with the Katsura radar, no longer showed the *Daedalus*. Androv had taken it to thirty thousand feet, then down again. He was playing games.

Tanzan Mino was not wasting time marveling at the plane's performance specs. He turned and nodded to General Sokolov, who was holding a red phone in his hand. The MiG 31 wing wasn't flying military power; it was full afterburners, which was pushing them to Mach 2.4. If *Daedalus* stayed on the deck, they might still intercept.

"We have no choice," he said in Russian. "Order them to give him a chance to turn back, and tell him if he refuses, they will shoot him down. Maybe the threat will be enough."

Sokolov nodded gravely. But what if Androv was as insane as every indication suggested he was? What if he disobeyed the commands from the Sakhalin interceptors? What then? Who was going to give the command that unleashed AAMs to bring down the most magnificent airplane—make that spacecraft—the world had ever seen. The MiG 31, with its long-range Acrid AA-9 missiles, had a stand-off kill capability that matched the American F-14 Tomcat and its deadly AIM-54 Phoenix. Since the AA-9 had its own guidance system, the pilot need not even see his target. One of those could easily bring down an unarmed behemoth like the *Daedalus* as long as it was still in the supersonic mode, which it would have to be at that low altitude.

A pall of sadness entered his voice as he issued the command. Androv, of all people, knew the look-down shootdown capabilities of the MiG 31. Maybe there was still a chance to reason with him. The *Daedalus* had no pilot-ejection capability. His choice was to obey or die.

Reports from the hangar said he'd taken some automatic-weapons fire from the CEO's bodyguards. How badly wounded was he?

Hard to tell, but he'd got *Daedalus* off the runway, then done an Immelmann to take her to ten thousand meters, followed by a power dive back to the deck. He was frolicking like a drunken dolphin. Pure Androv. How much longer could he last?

Sokolov glanced at the screen in front of him. The computer was extrapolating, telling him that a due-east heading by *Daedalus* would soon take her over international waters. If Androv kept that vector, at least there'd be no messy questions about violating foreign airspace.

"How long before they can intercept?" Tanzan Mino asked, not taking his eyes from the screens. Now the Soviet interceptors were on the Katsura radar, speeding toward *Daedalus*'s last known vector coordinates. It should only be a matter of time.

"In five minutes they will be within air-to-air range," Sokolov replied. He paused, then asked the question weighing on his mind. "If he refuses to turn back, do you really want that vehicle blown from the skies?"

Now Tanzan Mino was thinking about the Stealth capabilities of the *Daedalus*. Was the design good enough to defeat the MiG-31s' pulse-Doppler radar? He suddenly found himself wishing the plane hadn't been so well designed. The stupid Soviets, of course, had no idea—yet—that it could just disappear.

"He could be headed for Alaskan air space. That's what the computer is projecting. You understand the ramifications if this vehicle falls into the hands of the Americans."

The Soviet nodded gravely. That was, of course, unthinkable. There would be no going home again.

Friday 9:57 A.M.

"Yuri!" Eva was up like a shot. "Lean back. Breathe." She was pushing the button that raised the huge flight helmet. As she watched, his open eyes gradually resumed their focus. Then he snapped his head and looked around.

"*Shto* . . . what happened?"

"I don't think you can handle heavy G-loads. You're weak from the wound, the tourniquet."

He straightened up, then glanced again at the altimeter. They were cruising at three hundred meters, smooth as silk. And they were burning six hundred pounds of JP-7 a second.

"Nothing has gone the way I planned." He rubbed at his temples, trying to clear the blood from his brain. "We're just buying a little breathing space now by staying down here. I think the radar noise of the choppy sea, together with all our Stealth capability, will keep us safe. But at this low altitude we're using fuel almost as though we were dumping it. If we continue to hold on the deck, we've got maybe half an hour's flying time left."

"If we gained altitude," Vance wondered, "could we stretch it enough to make Alaska?"

"Probably," Androv replied. "If we took her above fifty thousand feet, we might have a chance."

"Then we've got no choice. The only solid ground between here and the U.S. is the Kurile Islands, and they're Soviet territory."

"But if we did reach U.S. airspace, then what?" Eva asked. "We'd have to identify ourselves. Who's going to believe our story? Nobody even knows this monster exists."

"Right," he laughed. "A top-secret Soviet hypersonic bomber comes cruising across the Bering Strait at sixty thousand feet and into the USAF's airspace. One hint of this thing and they'd roll out the SAMs."

"Maybe we could talk our way down."

"Maybe."

"There's no other choice."

"You are getting ahead of things, both of you," Androv interrupted, staring at the screens on the wall. "We still have to handle the interceptors from Dolinsk. If we went for altitude, we'd show enough infrared signature to make us an easy target during ascent. Before we even reached two thousand meters, they'd have a lock on us."

Vance glanced at the IRWR. *Daedalus*'s infrared laser scanners were still tracking the wing of MiG interceptors, now at twenty-two thousand feet and closing.

"It doesn't matter," he said. "We've got to get off the deck soon, while we still have fuel. Either that or we'll have to ditch at sea."

"Comrade Vance, the *Daedalus* is a marvelous platform, but when we go for altitude, we're going to be vulnerable. There's no getting around it. This vehicle was intended to perform best at the edge of space, not down here."

"All right," he said slowly. "Then why not take her there? Use the scramjets. We may be running out of JP-7, but we have a load of liquid hydrogen. Maybe this is the moment to finally find out if this thing can burn it."

"I'm—I'm afraid. After what happened when we pulled out of the power dive, I'm not sure I could handle the G-load necessary to power in the scramjets." Yuri paused. "The tourniquet has almost paralyzed my arm. I don't have the kind of control and timing we'd need. If I thought I could—but no. I hate to say it, even think it, but maybe we have no choice but to give up and turn back."

"Not yet," Vance said. "Maybe there's one other possibility."

Friday 10:01 A.M.

"They still are not acknowledging," Tanzan Mino said grimly. "We don't know their exact vector, but they will have to gain altitude soon. When they do . . ." He turned to General Sokolov. "Radio Dolinsk and confirm the order."

This was the moment Valentin Sokolov had been dreading. The AA-9 missile, which was carried on the MiG 31s' recessed underfuselage stations, came in two versions: the active radar homing model and the heat-seeking infrared design. He suspected that *Daedalus* had enough Stealth and ECM capabilities to partially defeat radar, but Stealth couldn't mask IR.

Sooner or later, Androv would have to make his move, come off the deck. And when he did, the MiGs would pick him up and it would be over.

But that was still preferable to letting *Daedalus* fall into the hands of the Americans. So if Androv refused to answer his radio and comply with the call-back, there'd be no choice.

Friday 10:02 A.M.

"What do you mean?" Androv asked, wiping at his brow.

Vance took a deep breath. "We've got no choice. You know what I'm thinking."

"We'll need ten G's of acceleration to power in the scramjets, my friend." He leaned back in the seat and closed his eyes. His face was now drawn with pain, but the bleeding had stopped. Above them, Petra silently flew the plane and flashed messages on the screens. "I've trained for years," he continued finally. "Even with your inflatable G-suit, you couldn't possibly take the G-loads and stay conscious."

"What other choice is there? Either I try, or we ditch down there in the Sea of Okhotsk. Personally, I'd rather go out like a shooting star, taking our chances."

"It's not that simple. The scramjets are designed to be

powered in at Mach 4.8. We dare not risk that below at least forty thousand feet. There are aerodynamic reasons. In fact, they're not really intended to be used below sixty thousand."

"Well," Vance said, "if we started our ascent at max throttle, what kind of airspeed could we capture by forty thousand? Could we achieve Mach 4.8?"

"Only if we used afterburners. Which means we'd probably have only about ten minutes of JP-7 left for landing later." He laughed sadly. "Assuming there's anywhere we could land."

"How about Heathrow? I know a Japanese banker who'd probably love to have this vehicle as collateral for a few billion in Eurodollar debentures he's being forced to underwrite. He's a friend of mine and I owe him a favor."

"You want to turn this plane over to some banker?" He was visibly startled. "We can't ignore the fact that it still belongs, technically, to Mino Industries."

"My friend's a big boy. He'll work it out, Yakuza-style. Don't worry." He glanced up at the fuel gauges. They now had twenty minutes left. Just enough to get back to the facility and give up? Or go all the way.

"Eva, what do you say. Want to give it a shot?"

"I'm game. One thing's for sure; I have no intention of going back to get ourselves murdered by Tanzan Mino. If we can make it to the other side of the world by burning hydrogen, then . . ."

"Maybe, just maybe Petra could help enough for you to manage it." Androv paused to collect his strength. "I don't know if you can stay conscious through the ten G's of acceleration needed to initiate the scramjets. But I know for sure I can't, not in my current state. You might as well give it a try." He turned to Eva and continued in Russian. "There's an emergency back-up pressure suit in that locker beneath Petra's main screen. See if you can put it on. You'll still probably pass out, but don't worry, the 'event' is only temporary. After we go through the hypersonic barrier, acceleration will subside. Down to three, maybe four G's."

"I'll get the suit," she said, starting to unbuckle her straps.

"Okay, we'd better get started." Vance was crossing the cabin. The nose cameras were showing the spray of whitecaps directly below them. If they'd passed any fishing vessels, he mused, there were probably stories of flying saucers already going around. The passive IRWR scanner was still tracking the wing of MiG 31s, now at a hundred and thirty kilometers, approximately eighty miles, and closing. *Daedalus* was almost within the kill perimeter of the MiG 31s and their AA-9 missiles.

The radio crackled, something in Russian. Yuri Androv stared at the flight helmet, then looked down at the console and flipped a switch.

"I copy you, Firefight One," he replied in Russian. "Over."

"Androv, you idiot. What in hell are you doing? Defecting to the capitalists?" The voice laughed. "We don't know what the devil you're flying, but when you pulled that Immelmann, my IR thought you were an An-124 Condor transport turned into a high-performance *Foxbat*. One incredible son-of-a-bitch."

"It's a spaceship, Arkadi. Excuse me, Colonel Arkadi. Congratulations on the promotion."

"*Spacebo*," he said, laughing again. Then he sobered. "Yuri, I don't know what this is all about, but I'm instructed by General Sokolov to escort you and that thing you're flying back to Hokkaido. If you're stupid enough to refuse, then I have orders to shoot you down."

"Is that any way to treat an old friend?"

"Yuri Andreevich, we go back a long way. To the Ramenskoye Flight Test Center. You were the best we ever had. Don't make me do this."

"I'm thinking I may spare you the trouble."

"Thank God."

"Give me five minutes. If I don't turn back by then, give it your best."

"Pull up. Show yourself on IR. We have no idea what your vector is."

"I'll take her to three thousand meters. You'll have a lock on me. But I still want five minutes."

"That's all I can give you, Yuri. After that . . ." His voice trailed off.

"I'm going off this frequency. Talk to you in five."

"Five minutes. Starting now."

Androv pushed a switch on the console, then said, "Petra, stabilize at three thousand."

Three thousand, she repeated. *Confirmed.*

He rose from the pilot's seat, motioning for Vance. There was a surge of acceleration as the vehicle changed pitch, the cockpit rotating to adjust for the G-forces. The weight of two and a half G's weighed against them as the altimeter screen started scrolling upward.

Vance walked across to the central seat, studying the console. The throttle quadrant and sidestick he understood, but most of the other controls were new to him. Maybe it didn't matter.

"Does Petra understand English?"

"Of course," Androv nodded. "Russian, Japanese, and English. Interchangeable. She's programmed such that if you command her in Russian, she replies in Russian. If you use English, that's what you get back."

"So far, so good." He looked at the large screen at the end of cabin, the one that displayed Petra's mindstate. She was dutifully announcing that she'd just taken the vehicle to three thousand meters. She also was reporting the IR interrogation of a wing of MIG 31s flying at twenty thousand feet, with a closure rate of three hundred knots. When Daedalus made her move, would she be able to outdistance their air-to-air missiles?

We're about to find out, he thought, in—he glanced at the screens—three and a half minutes. Eva was zipping up her pressure suit now, readying to strap herself back into her seat. The helmet made her look like an ungainly astronaut.

"Like I said, the scramjets become operable at Mach 4.8," Androv went on. "At forty thousand feet, that's about three thousand miles per hour. I've never taken her past Mach 4.5." He was grasping the side of the console to brace himself. "You probably know that scramjets require a modification in engine geometry. In the turboramjet mode, these engines have a fan that acts as a compressor, just like a conventional jet. However, when we switch them over to scramjet geometry, the turbines are shut down and their blades set to a neutral pitch. Next the aft section of each engine is constricted to form a combustion chamber—the shock wave inside becomes the 'compressor.'" He paused. "The unknown part comes when the fans are cut out and the engine geometry is modified. I've unstarted the fans and reconfigured, but I've never fed in the hydrogen. We simply don't know what will happen. Those damned turbines could just explode."

"So we take the risk."

"There's more," he continued. "The frictional heat at hypersonic speeds. Our liquid hydrogen is supposed to act as a heat sink, to dissipate thermal buildup on the leading edges, but who the hell knows if it'll work. We're now flying at about fifteen hundred miles per hour. When you give Petra the go-ahead, we could accelerate to ten, even fifteen *thousand* miles per hour. God help us, we may just melt."

"If you were willing to give it a shot, then I am." Vance looked up at the screens. "We're now at ten thousand feet. I kick over to scramjets at forty thousand?"

"The computer simulations all said that if we go hypersonic below sixty thousand feet, we could seriously overheat. But maybe if we climb out fast enough . . ."

"We'll have to take our chances. We need to minimize that window of AAM vulnerability."

"I agree." Androv gestured for him to sit, then glanced up at the screens. "We have two and a half minutes. I've set Petra for full auto. All you have to do is just talk her through the key intervals of the sequence."

Vance settled in and examined the huge flight helmet looming above him, making him look like an alien insect from science fiction. Now the cabin had taken on an eerie quiet, with nothing but silent screens flashing data. He'd never talked to an airplane before, and the thought gave him some disquiet.

Two minutes.

"What do I do first?"

"You probably should start by attaching that nozzle there on the legs of your G-suit to the pressure hose on the console. When the G-forces go above eight, tubules in the legs automatically inflate using bleed air from the engines. It's going to squeeze hell out of your lower extremities. If you begin to gray-out, try to grunt as hard as you can. The M-1 maneuver, I think you Americans call it. If your vision begins to go entirely, just try and talk Petra through."

"What else?"

"Once you start pushing through the hypersonic barrier, keep an eye on screens B-5 and B-6, which report engine strut temperature and stress loads. Those are the most important data for the scramjet mode. But first check the C-2 screen. Core rpm has to be zeroed out before the scramjet geometry modification, since the compressors need to be completely shut down. If it's not, then instruct Petra to abort the sequence. It could cause a flameout."

"And that's when I switch over to liquid hydrogen?"

"Exactly. Petra will set the new engine geometry, then sample compression and temperature and tell you the precise moment. But the actual switch-over is manual. I insisted on it." He pointed. "It's those blue toggles right behind the throttle quadrant. Just flip them forward."

"Got it."

"After you toggle her over, just ease the throttle forward, and pray." He settled himself into the right-hand seat, tugging at the tourniquet. "When we enter the hypersonic regime, I don't know what will happen. Above Mach 6 or Mach 7 we may begin to critically overheat. Or the airframe stresses could just tear this damned *samolyot* apart. Whatever happens, though, you've got to keep pushing her right on out, to stabilize the shock wave in the scramjets and bring them to full power."

Vance glanced up at the screen—thirty seconds—and fingered the sidestick and the throttles, trying to get their feel. As he began lowering the massive flight helmet, he noted that with the engines on military power they had exactly eighteen minutes of JP-7 left. When he kicked in the afterburners to push them into the hypersonic regime, the fuel readings would start dropping like a stone. But this was their ball of string, their way out of the maze. Would it work?

"Remember," Androv said with finality, "just talk Petra through any problems you have. And try to capture an attitude of sixty degrees alpha . . ."

"Yuri, are you ready for us to escort you back?" The radio voice, speaking Russian, sounded through the cabin.

"I'm still thinking it over," he answered.

"Don't be a fool. I have orders to down you with AA-9s. My weapons system is already turned on. Warheads are locked. You're as good as dead. If I push the fire button here under my left thumb, you're gone in fifty seconds."

"You just made up my mind," he said, and nodded toward Vance. *"Go."*

"Firing one and two," was the radio response.

Vance grabbed the throttles. "Petra, do you read me?"

Yes, she answered in English.

"Give me alpha sixty." He rammed the throttles forward, clicking them into the Lock position, igniting the afterburners. Next he yanked the sidestick into position.

The cockpit rotated upward, automatically shifting to compensate for the changing G-forces. In front of his eyes now was a wide liquid crystal screen that seemed to be in 3-D. The left side resembled the heads-up display, HUD, common to jet fighters, providing altitude, heading, airspeed, G-forces in a single unified format. The right side showed a voice-activated menu listing all the screens along the wall.

"Read me fuel," he said, testing it.

Immediately the numbers appeared, in pounds of JP-7 and in minutes, with and without afterburners. The G-force was now at 3.5 and climbing, while the digital altimeter was spinning.

Systems alert, Petra announced suddenly, *hostile radar lock. And hostile IR interrogation. Two bogies, closure rate nine hundred sixty knots.*

They weren't kidding, Vance thought. He glanced at the altitude readout. *Daedalus* was hurtling through thirty thousand feet, afterburners sizzling. But an AA-9 had a terminal velocity well over Mach 3. Add that to the *Foxhound*'s 2.4 . . .

"Petra, give me estimated time of impact."

Extrapolating closure rate, I estimate impact in forty-three seconds.

Their acceleration had reached 3.8 G's, but fuel was dwindling rapidly, already down to twelve minutes.

"Give me RWR and IRWR, screen one," he commanded.

The liquid crystal panorama inside the helmet immediately flashed, showing the unfriendly radar and infrared interrogations. The two Acrid AA-9s—that's what they had to be—were gaining altitude, tracking them like bloodhounds. One was radar locked, while the other showed active-homing IR guidance. The exhausts of *Daedalus*'s afterburners must look like a fireball in the sky, he thought.

He scanned the menu for electronic countermeasures (ECM) capabilities.

"Petra, commence radar jamming."

Commenced. Estimated time to impact, thirty-eight seconds.

The missiles were still closing. Even if the radar-guided AAM could be confused, *Daedalus* had no way to defeat infrared homing.

The left-hand display now showed they had accelerated to Mach 4.2. The throttle quadrant was locked into the afterburner mode, but outrunning AAMs was like trying to outspeed a smart bullet.

He watched the dials. Mach 4.3. Mach 4.4.

Estimated time to impact twenty-eight seconds.

"I'm not sure we're going to make it," he said into his helmet mike. "We may have to try initiating the scramjets early."

"No, it would be too risky," Androv replied. "The skin temperatures at this altitude. The air is still so dense the thermal stresses . . ."

Vance checked the screen again. "Altitude is now thirty-eight thousand feet. I'm going to level out some, try and boost our Mach number. One thing's sure, we can't make it if we hold this attitude. Besides, we're burning too much fuel. Either we chance it now, or we get blown to smither-ines. We've got no choice." He shoved the sidestick for-ward. For this he didn't plan to bother with Petra.

Time to impact, twenty seconds, she reported tonelessly.

By trimming pitch, *Daedalus* started accelerating more rapidly. Airspeed scrolled quickly to Mach 4.6.

Time to impact, fifteen seconds.

Nine and a half minutes of JP-7 remained. Just enough to land, he thought, if we ever get the chance.

Mach 4.7.

"Eva, take a deep breath. We're about to try and enter the fourth dimension."

"I . . . can't . . . talk."

Then he remembered Androv had said she might pass out. Now he was starting to wonder if he wouldn't lose consciousness too. He was sensing his vision starting to fade to gray, breaking up into dots. The screen noted that their acceleration had reached eight G's and was still climbing. Fighting for consciousness, he reached down and increased his oxygen feed, then contracted every mus-cle in the lower half of his body, trying to shove the blood upward. The G-indicator on the left-hand screen had scrolled to 9.2.

Time to impact, ten seconds.

Mach 4.8.

He reached down and manually locked the pitch on the compressor fan blades into a neutral configuration. They immediately stalled out, causing *Daedalus* to shudder like a wounded animal. Then he heard the voice of Petra, and a new signal flashed on his helmet screen.

We have nominal scramjet geometry. Commence igni-tion sequence.

She'd reconfigured the turbines, meaning *Daedalus* was go for hypersonic. He grappled blindly behind the throttle quadrant and flicked the large blue switches that initiated the hydrogen feed. But would the supersonic shock wave inside the engines fire it?

Time to impact, six seconds.

"Let's go." Reaching for the throttle quadrant, he de-pressed the side button and then shoved the heavy handles forward, sending a burst of hydrogen into the scramjets' combustion chambers. . . .

Daedalus lurched, then seemed to be tearing apart, literally disintegrating rivet by rivet.

Friday 9:57 A.M.

"We have detonation," Colonel Arkadi reported into his helmet mike. His twin-engine *Foxhound* was already in a steep fifty-degree bank.

"We copy you," General Sokolov replied. "Can you confirm the kill?"

"The target is outside my radar and IR," he said, wishing he had some of the new American over-the-horizon electronics he'd heard about. "But both missiles reported impact. I've ordered the wing to chop power and return to base. We're already on auxiliary tanks as it is."

"Roger," came the voice from Flight Control in Hokkaido.

"We downed her, Comrade General. Whatever she was, there's no way she could have survived those AA-9s. The target is destroyed."

CHAPTER TWENTY-ONE

Friday 10:16 A.M.

Tanzan Mino closed his eyes and sighed. The financial portions of the protocol would still stand on their own; the arrangement could be salvaged somehow; it would merely require finesse.

The shocked faces of the Soviet brass standing behind him told of their dismay. *Daedalus,* the most marvelous vehicle ever created, had literally been within their grasp, and now . . . both prototypes destroyed.

But at least, at least it hadn't fallen into the hands of the

Americans. No more humiliating episodes like that in 1976 when the traitorous Lieutenant Viktor Belenko defected with a MiG 25 *Foxbat*, exposing all its secret electronics to the West.

Friday 10:16 A.M.

A slam of acceleration hit him, and he felt a circle of black close in on his vision. It was the darkness of eternal night, the music of the spheres. His last sight was the airspeed indicator scrolling past Mach 6.1. Almost four thousand miles per hour.

The starship *Daedalus* had just gone hypersonic.

He didn't see it, but look-down radar had shown the two Acrid AA-9s exploding a thousand feet below. When the scramjets powered in, the infrared-homing AAM lost its lock on them and detonated the other missile, sending a supersonic shock wave through *Daedalus*. AAMs, however, were now the least of their problems.

Skin temperature was pushing 2,200 degrees and the cockpit was becoming an incinerator. At forty-eight thousand feet they were rapidly turning into a meteorite.

His vision was gone, but just before losing consciousness he shoved the hydrogen throttles all the way forward and yanked back on the sidestick, sending them straight up into the freezing black above.

Friday 10:19 A.M.

Altitude seventy-three thousand feet. Airspeed nine thousand knots.

"Petra, raise helmet." He was slowly regaining his sight as the G-loads began to recede. The cockpit was an oven, overwhelming its environmental control equipment, clear evidence vehicle skin temperature had exceeded design.

Confirmed. Helmet raising.

Although his vision was still black and white, he started easing back on the throttles and checking around the cockpit. Eva was beginning to stir now, rising and struggling with her safety straps, Androv remained slumped in his G-seat.

"You okay?" He rose and moved toward her. "I think I blacked out there for a second or so."

"I'm going to make it." She shifted her eyes right. "But I'm not so sure about . . ."

"Don't worry." The Russian snapped conscious and immediately reached to begin loosening his straps. "I've been through heavy G-loads before." Suddenly he stared up at the screens, pointed, and yelled. "Hypersonic! *Zoloto!* You didn't tell me. I almost can't believe—"

"We almost lost it. Skin temperatures reached—"

"Japanese ceramic composites, Comrade. No other material could have done it. And now the atmosphere is thinning. When we hit eighty thousand feet, or maybe eighty-five, skin temperature should stabilize down around a thousand degrees. That's 'room temperature' for this vehicle." He paused and grinned. "Liquid hydrogen. It's a fantastic fuel, and a terrific coolant. Of course, if this catches on and we stop using alcohol coolant in our MiGs, I don't know what the Soviet Air Force will all drink before payday."

Vance glanced at their vector. They were over the Bering Sea now, with a heading for who knew where.

Mach 11.3 and climbing. The *Daedalus* was pressing effortlessly toward the darkness above. Time to think about what was next.

"How much of this wonderful liquid hydrogen do we have?"

"Just enough to do what I've been planning for a long time." He edged over and touched Vance's shoulder. "I'm deeply in your debt. You made it possible. Now there's only one thing left. The ultimate!"

Vance looked at him and realized immediately what he meant. Why not!

"Do we have enough oxygen?"

"Extra cannisters were loaded because of the two Mino Industries pilots. I think we have about ten hours."

"Then I vote we give it a shot," he said, turning to Eva. "What do you think?"

"What are you talking about?"

He flipped up his helmet visor. "If we can achieve Mach 25 by around a hundred thousand feet, we can literally insert into orbit. It'd cause a diplomatic flap the size of World War Three."

She slumped back in her G-seat. "Is it really possible?"

"Of course," Androv said. Then he laughed. "Well, I *hope* so. I've been thinking about it for a couple of months now. I actually programmed Petra to compute the precise thrust required, orbital apogee and perigee, everything. The first Sputnik had an apogee of one hundred miles and a perogee of one hundred twenty-five miles. I've calculated that at Mach 25 I could propel this vehicle into roughly that orbit. To get out we can just do a de-orbit burn. Set the compressors on the ramjets for retrofire and cold-start them."

"So we can hold Tanzan Mino's *cojones* hostage for a while and have some fun," Vance smiled. "What do we tell Petra?"

"I'll give her the coordinates, but you've got to handle the stick. We need to hit Mach 25 above 98,600 feet, then shut down the engines with split-second timing. She'll tell you when. If I computed it right, we should just coast over the top."

"Got it." He looked up at the screens on the front wall of the cockpit. Their altitude was now 87,000 feet, and their speed had reached Mach 18, over ten thousand miles per hour. They were cracking world records every millisecond. And the cockpit was starting to cool off again as the thinner atmosphere reduced friction on the leading edges. They'd survived the thermal barrier. Coming up was the emptiness of space.

He watched as Androv called the routine in Petra's silicon memory where he had stored the orbital data, then ordered her to coordinate it with their current acceleration, altitude, and attitude.

Confirmed, she was saying. *Reducing alpha by two degrees*. She'd already begun modifying their flight profile.

You are approximately four minutes and thirty-seven seconds from the calculated orbit. Will fuel controls be manual or automatic?

Vance glanced over at Androv. Here at the edge of space, were they really going to turn their destiny over to a talking computer? This game could turn serious if Petra somehow screwed up.

"Let's keep the throttles on manual."

"I agree," he nodded. "Too much could go wrong."

"If we don't like the looks of anything, we can always abort."

"Petra," Androv commanded, "throttles will be manual."

Affirmative. If she felt slighted, she wasn't saying anything. *Four minutes.*

"We'd all better strap in," Vance said, "till we see how this goes."

The screens above them were still flashing flight data. The strut temperature in the scramjets, where a supersonic shock wave was providing the compression to combust hydrogen and the rush of thin air, had stabilized at 3,100 degrees Fahrenheit. Androv stood staring at the screens, and a moistness entered his eyes.

"If my father could have seen this," he finally said in Russian. "Everything he designed has worked perfectly. He dreamed of this vehicle, talked of it for so many years, and now finally . . . to be murdered on his day of triumph."

Eva looked at him. "Maybe his real dream was for you to fly it. To create something for you."

He paused, as though uncertain how to respond. The look in his eyes said he knew it was true. The pain and anger seemed to flow through him like electricity.

"Before we are finished, the world will know of his achievement. I intend to make sure of it."

Three minutes, Petra announced. *Reducing alpha by three degrees.*

The screen above reported that they'd reached Mach 22.4. Their altitude was now ninety-three thousand feet.

She's leveling out, Vance thought. *Are we going to make it, or just fade in the stretch?*

The scramjets were punching through the isolation of near-space now, the underfuselage scooping in the last fringes of atmosphere. He doubted if there'd be enough oxygen above a hundred thousand feet to enable the engines to continue functioning, but if they could capture the vehicle's design speed, seventeen thousand miles per hour, they still could coast into the perigee curve of a huge orbital elipse.

He looked at the screens again. They were now at Mach 23.7, with two and a half minutes left. The complex calculus being projected on Petra's main display now showed their rate of acceleration was diminishing rapidly as the atmosphere continued to thin. Maybe, he thought, there's a good reason why no one has ever inserted an air-breathing vehicle into orbit before. Maybe all the aerodynamic and propulsion tricks in the world can't compensate for the fact that turbines need to breathe.

Petra seemed to sense they were in trouble. *Constricting venturi by seven point three,* she said. *Reducing alpha by four degrees.*

She was choking down the scramjets and leveling them out even more. Their thrust to weight ratio—which at thirty thousand feet had been greater than one, meaning they could actually fly straight up—was dropping like a stone. It was now down to 0.2. *Daedalus* was slowly smothering.

But now their velocity had reached Mach 24.6. Almost, almost . . .

Thirty seconds, Petra said, as though trying to sound confident. She was busy sampling the combustion ratio in the scramjets and making micro adjustments to the hydrogen feed.

Androv spoke into his helmet mike. "I'm beginning to think we won't make it. Petra is now probably estimating thrust based on faulty assumptions about oxygen intake. There's nothing left up here to burn. There'll be no need to abort. The edge of the atmosphere is going to do it for us." He looked up at the big screen and said, "Petra, project image from the nose camera, rotated to minus ninety."

Confirmed, she replied and flashed an image sprinkled with stars. Then the camera swept around, and the massive screen at the end of their cabin brought into view the edge of a wide globe that seemed to be composed of shimmering blue. It was the North Pacific.

"I just wanted to see this," he said wistfully. "I once took a MiG 25 to seventy-three thousand feet, but it was nothing to compare. We're in space."

"I've been eavesdropping on satellites for years," Eva commented. "But this gives it all a whole new perspective."

Ten seconds. Prepare to terminate hydrogen feeds.

The airspeed indicator now read Mach 24.8. Closing. . . .

Vance reached for the heavy throttle grips, watching the final seconds tick down.

. . . four, three, two, one . . .

Terminate hydrogen feeds.

He yanked back on the handles, feeling a dying tremor flow through the vehicle. The airspeed indicator had just hit 17,108 mph.

In the unearthly silence that followed, Petra's synthetic voice cut through the cabin. *Preliminary orbital coordinates are computed as perigee 101.3 miles, apogee 117.8 miles. Duration is one hour and twenty-seven minutes. Radar altimeter will provide data for second iteration of calculations in thirty-six minutes.*

The engines were completely shut down now as they coasted through the dark. Nothing could be heard but hydraulic pumps, air conditioners, light groans from zero-gravity-induced stresses in the massive fuselage.

"Zadroka!" Androv shouted. "We've done it! Maybe there *is* a God."

Now, as *Daedalus* began to slip sideways, like a liner adrift at sea, the nose camera showed they were passing over the ice-covered wilds of northern Alberta.

Vance felt a sudden rush of fluids from his extremities, where they had been pooling because of the G-forces,

upward into his face and torso. The sensation was one of
falling, hanging on to his seat.

Clumsily he unfastened his G-seat harness and pushed
up to . . .

He sailed. Across the cockpit. At the last instant he
twisted, trying to right himself, but before he could he'd
slammed into the bank of video monitors on the opposite
wall.

"Jesus!"

"Sweetie, you look like a flying fish." Eva drifted back in
her seat, loving him all over again.

"I feel like a newborn deer trying to stand up." He
rotated and carefully pushed himself off the ceiling, re-
pressing the instinct to kick like a scuba diver. "But remember the old Chinese proverb. Don't criticize a man till
you've floated in his shoes for a day."

"Darling, it's a dream come true. I'm finally weightless,"
she laughed. "At last, no more dreading to get on a scale."

"The pain in my arm is gone," Androv spoke up again,
renewed satisfaction in his voice. "We've just performed
our first medical experiment in space. It's good for gunshot
wounds."

"I'd like to perform another experiment," Eva said. She
was slowly extracting herself from the G-seat. "What kind
of electrical system do we have on board?"

"We have a massive battery section, kept charged by the
turbines," Androv replied. "All these electronics require a
lot of power."

"So we could transmit?"

"Of course. We're designed for that."

"What are you planning?" Vance looked over as he
drifted back across the cockpit.

"A small surprise for Tanzan Mino." She was twisting
around as she floated next to her straps. "Let me start
preparing the laptop. I knew there was a reason why I
brought it." She reached down under the seat and pushed
it out, where it floated.

"I want to hook this into Petra." She reached up and
awkwardly retrieved it. "Is there any way I can?"

"There's provision for laptop interface. They worked so

well on the American shuttles, our people installed an identical setup here." Androv swam slowly to the console, then flipped down a panel, revealing a serial port. "You can connect it there. The wiring's in place."

Vance twisted and checked their coordinates. They were now at latitude 56 degrees, longitude 109 degrees, headed over central Canada. "Incidentally, so much for North American air defenses. No radar interrogations whatsoever."

"That's because of our Stealth design," Androv said. "We have almost no radar signature. Not only are we a menace to the world, we're invisible."

Vance floated down and settled into the central G-seat. The more he learned about the *Daedalus,* the more unsettling he found it. What should they do with this monster? Maybe turn it over to the UN as a monument to technology gone amuck, to high-tech excess. At last, he thought, man has achieved the ability to move anywhere on the planet, at speeds as fast as the laws of physics will allow, and do it invisibly. Maybe it should be called the *Shadow.*

"Okay." Eva interrupted his thoughts. "I've finished tying in the 486. We're about to go live from the top, gentlemen, the very top. I'm going to send the protocol to every wire service in the world. What better credibility than to be downlinked live from space?"

Vance looked at the picture from the nose camera. They were over the Atlantic now, which meant they'd soon be passing over the Soviet Union, with line-of-sight horizons that stretched from Europe to Asia.

"Why settle for print?" He had a sudden thought. "How about television? With all this video gear, we should be able to put together something that would transmit. The Baikonur Cosmodrome has receiving facilities. We see Soviet cosmonauts in space all the time. And they'll be directly under us. We also could make the evening news all over Japan if we broadcast to the Katsura tracking facility."

"Good thinking, but I've got an even better idea." She seemed to pirouette in weightlessness. "Japan already has DBS, direct broadcast satellites, and there are home satellite dishes all over the country. It's the Global Village. So why don't we just cut in for a special bulletin?"

"Why not." He pointed to the ill-fated cockpit camera Tanzan Mino's technicians had installed above the entry hatch. "Matter of fact, we probably could just use that, if we could hook it into some of the electronics here on the console."

He floated up, half drifting and half swimming, and inspected the camera, convincing himself that it was still in working condition. And it had to be wired into something. Maybe now all they needed to do was flip the right toggles. The console switches numbered, by his conservative estimate, approximately three hundred.

"Let me see what I can do." Androv floated down and immediately started to work, toggling, testing, watching the display screens as various messages were scrolled.

"Petra," he finally commanded in Russian, "give me a positive connect between UHF display-read and video output terminal 3-K."

Interface confirmed.

Suddenly a video screen fluttered, ran through a test series of colored bars, then threw up a picture of the cockpit as seen from the camera above the hatch. Vance studied the image of three figures floating in a confined space outfitted with electronic hardware and a giant wing-shaped hood over the central seat. On TV their cockpit looked like the flight deck of some alien vessel in *Star Trek IX*.

"We're on." Eva waved at the camera. Her image on the screen waved back.

"Okay," Vance said. "Now for the tricky part. Transmission."

Androv smiled as he drifted up again. "That's actually the easiest of all. Remember this vehicle was originally intended—supposedly—as a near-earth research platform. There're plenty of downlinks, in keeping with the need to transmit data, as well as general propaganda functions. We can use any frequency you want, even commercial broadcast channels."

"So why don't we go live worldwide? Just give everybody an inside look at the planet's first radar-evasive space platform."

"Petra has a listing of all commercial satellite channels, just to make sure she doesn't inadvertently violate one of them with a transmission. Let's pull them up and see what they are." He flipped several toggles on the wide console, then told Petra what he wanted. He'd no sooner finished speaking than the large screen that supplemented her voice was scrolling the off-limits frequencies.

"Okay," Eva said. "Let's start with the data channels belonging to world-wide newsprint organizations— Reuters, the Associated Press, all the rest—and send a copy of the protocol. It'll just appear on every green screen in the world. Then we can pick off frequencies used by television news organizations and broadcast a picture postcard from here in the cockpit."

"Sounds good." Androv turned to look at the screen. Quickly he began selecting numbers from the banned list, moving them to a new file that would be used to specify parameters for the broadcasts.

Vance watched, shifting his glance occasionally to the view from the nose camera. Below them clusters of light from central Europe's largest cities beamed up, twinkling lightly through the haze of atmosphere. He reached over and flipped the camera to infrared and sat watching the back-radiation of the North African deserts, now blots of deep red on the southern horizon; then back to visible again, noticing two parallel ribbons of light that signified habitations along the length of the Nile. The world, he was thinking, really is a Global Village. She was right. There's no longer any place you can hide from the truth.

"Eva, when you feed the protocol to the wire services, note that there'll be a transmission of some live video at—" he glanced up at the digital readouts on the screens, "how about at 0800 hours, GMT?"

"That's in twenty minutes."

"Should be enough time, don't you think?"

"Sounds good to me. And to show you I'm brave, I won't even fix my hair."

"You never looked more beautiful, even that night out at

the palace. Don't change a thing." He turned to Androv. "How about doing the talking? First in Russian and then in English? We'll write the English part for you."

"It will be my pleasure, Comrade. My fucking pleasure."

"*Daedalus*," Vance said, mostly to himself. "He found a way to escape the maze of Mino. We did too. It's easy. You just use your wings and fly."

Friday 8:47 A.M.

Kenji Nogami settled the telephone back into its cradle and reached for the television's remote selector. The set was currently scrolling a special text being distributed over the Reuters financial-service channel. Very interesting.

He shoved aside the pile of new Mino Industries Eurobond debentures, to make room for his feet on the teakwood surface of his desk. BBC had just informed him they'd taped an accompanying video segment and were planning to broadcast it in thirteen minutes, at nine o'clock. At least that's what Sir Cecil Ashton, director general, had just warned. As the London banker for Mino Industries, he had told Sir Cecil he officially had no comment.

No comment was required.

He reached into a drawer and drew out a box of Montecristo Habana No. 2s, noting sadly there were only three left. With a frown he picked up his pocket Dictaphone and made a note to his secretary to stop off at the tobacconists on Threadneedle, just down from the Bank of England, and get another box.

A hypersonic *aircraft*. So that was what it had been about all along. And now some Russian test pilot had stolen it, taken it to orbit, and was planning to land it at Heathrow in three hours, there to turn it over to Westminster Union Bank, the London financial representative of Mino Industries Group.

Perfect timing. The thought immediately occurred to him that this would be ideal collateral for the billions in phony Eurodollar debentures he was being forced to issue for Tanzan Mino. Finally, *finally* he had the man by the bollocks. Who, he wondered, did he have to thank for this godsend?

Yes, it was shaping up to be quite a morning. Perhaps a trifle early for a cigar, but . . .

He flicked the TV off the Reuters text and onto BBC-1.

". . . would appear to be further evidence of the growing technological supremacy of Japanese industry. As this commentator has had occasion to note in times past, the lines between civilian and military technology are rapidly vanishing. That Japan's so-called civilian research sector could create the high-temperature ceramics required for such a vehicle, even as European and American military research has failed to do so, speaks eloquently of the emerging shift in world . . ."

He rolled down the sound a bit. The commentator went on to mention that all Mino Industries representatives—both here in London and in Tokyo—named in the announcement from orbit had refused either to confirm or deny the story.

He noted the time on his Omega, then smiled, leaned back, and snipped the end off his cigar.

Friday 11:00 A.M.

"Mino-sama." The man bowed low. "NHK just telephoned your office in Tokyo, asking for comment."

"Comment about what?"

"They have received some text off a satellite."

"What? What did they receive?"

"It was purportedly the English translation of a secret protocol, an agreement between Mino Industries and the Soviets. Naturally we denied it in the strongest possible terms."

"It has to be some preposterous fabrication. I can't imagine how anything so absurd could have—"

"That's actually the problem, Mino-sama. NHK says they received it from a manned space station, but they've checked with NASDA and have been assured there are currently no astronauts in orbit by any nation."

"In orbit?" My God, he thought. *Daedalus* didn't go down; she went *up*. With the protocol aboard.

How did they manage to get her hypersonic? Androv was wounded. He couldn't possibly have handled the G-forces. Which meant—

Vance.

"Tell NHK if they broadcast one word of this libelous, unsubstantiated hoax, they should be prepared to face legal action." His face had become a stone mask as a sepulchral hush settled over Flight Control.

"I will inform them," the man bowed again. He hadn't had the courage to tell the *oyabun* the rest of what NHK was now receiving . . . along with half of the citizens of Japan via their new direct-broadcast satellite dishes.

Friday 9:00 A.M.

Kenji Nogami thought the picture was a little indistinct at first, the hues slightly off. But then somebody in BBC's technical section corrected the color balance, making the tape's blues and greens and reds all blue and green and red.

Yes, now he could make it out. A cosmonaut was drifting across the camera's view, suspended. It made him ponder briefly the phenomenon of weightlessness. Curious, really, that it was all a matter of where you were.

One wall of the cockpit was lined with video terminals, and at the end was a massive screen currently displaying the Daedalus Corporation logo, a double ax. Nice advertising, he thought. Coca-Cola probably feels envious. Overall it was a classy job, no two ways about it. The *oyabun* didn't do things by halves.

Well, this was one marvel Her Majesty's government would be happy to get their hands on. For his own part, not a bad piece of collateral. Must have cost billions in start-up investment.

Then he got a better look at the figure and realized

something was wrong. One side of his white environment suit was stained red. And he seemed to be nursing a bandaged arm as he drifted up toward the camera.

"*Stradstyve,*" he began, "*Ya Yuri Andreevich Androv. . . .*"

The cosmonaut then proceeded to deliver a long-winded speech in Russian that Nogami could not follow and the BBC had not yet translated. He seemed to be growing angrier and angrier, and at one point he gave a long disquisition about someone named Andrei Petrovich Androv. He was obviously a Soviet test pilot. Who else could fly that creation? Given the looks of the cockpit, it was a quantum advance in high technology.

Nogami leaned back, his match poised. The good part, the part in English, was coming up. That's what Sir Cecil had said. The Russian segment had been for broadcast in the Soviet Union, had the local spin. The English part was for the world. And for Tanzan Mino.

Who was now in deep, deep trouble. Murder, fraud, a global conspiracy—they all were there, and even more damning for the *way* the story had come to light. The medium was the message.

About that time the cosmonaut who'd identified himself as Soviet Air Force Major Yuri Andreevich Androv drifted to the side, permitting a better view of the cockpit. That's when Nogami noticed two other individuals. One appeared to be a woman—leave it to the Soviets, he smiled, to know about good public relations—also wearing an environment suit, her helmet momentarily turned away. The third appeared to be male, also in an environment suit and flight helmet. Sir Cecil hadn't bothered mentioning them, since Air Force Major Androv had done all the talking.

Then the male cosmonaut in the center drifted up and began opening his visor, some kind of curved glass that reflected the yellow sodium lights in the ceiling. He grappled with it a moment, then in annoyance just yanked it off and tossed it to drift across—

Nogami stared at the face. Mother of God!

He was laughing so hard he almost missed his Montecristo when he finally whipped up his match. . . .

ABOUT THE AUTHOR

After writing two non-fiction books on Japan and China, THOMAS HOOVER published a best-selling novel of India, *The Moghul,* now planned for a major TV miniseries. This was followed by *Caribbee,* another historical novel that found a wide audience in the U.S. and Europe. He then turned to contemporary fiction with the Wall Street thriller *The Samurai Strategy* and now *Project Daedalus.* Formerly an executive with an international consulting firm, he lives in New York and is currently completing *Project Cyclops,* set in Europe and the Greek islands.

READ A PREVIEW FROM THOMAS HOOVER'S NEXT THRILLER:
PROJECT CYCLOPS

A privately owned spaceport is seized by a chillingly proficient group of terrorists headed by a mastermind named Sabri Ramirez. After a lifetime of international terrorism, Ramirez is immune to all but two emotions: intense hatred of the U.S.A., and greed for huge sums of money. With a Pakistani warhead in his possession, and the spaceport from which to launch it, all that's left to do is for Ramirez to put in a call to the President of the United States. Regarding extortion.

In this breakneck-paced opening scene, Ramirez's goal is to knock out the U.S. frigate *Glover,* making the navy helpless to track his ICBM. . . .

"Keep her above three hundred meters when we make the approach." Ramirez's hard voice cut through the roar of the 2,200-hp Isotov turboshafts. Down below, the cold, dusk-shrouded Aegean churned with a late-autumn storm. "Any lower and there'll be surface effect."

"I'm well aware of that," the Iranian pilot muttered, a sullen response barely audible above the helicopter's noise and vibration. It stopped just short of open disrespect.

Sabri Ramirez didn't mind. The man had been an unfortunate necessity, but in three days he would be dead. The others, the professionals, were the ones who counted. When he hand-picked the European terrorists now resting on the four litters in the main cabin, he had gone for the best. Each man had a track record and a purpose. Ramirez, however, was the leader, fully in control. He had planned, financed, and now commanded the operation.

In the ghostly light of late evening, his sleek cheeks, iron-shaded temples, trim mustache gave no hint of the extensive plastic surgery that had created this, his latest face. He wore a black jumpsuit, just as the others, but under his was a $2,000 Brioni charcoal double-breasted— perhaps more suited for a three-star dinner in Paris, at L'Ambroisie or La Tour d'Argent, than the operation at hand. All the same, he felt comfortably at home in this Hind-D helicopter gunship, the most lethal assault machine ever. Their operation had two objectives, and the first had just appeared on the bright green cockpit radar.

It was the 2,600-ton U.S. frigate *Glover*, Garcia class, which had been converted to a Mideast spy platform for the National Security Agency. Loaded with missile-tracking and communications-monitoring antennae, it had to go.

Ramirez expected no difficulties. Like the USS *Stark*, the frigate disabled by Iraqi Exocet missiles in the Persian Gulf in 1988, it was a perfect target. With only one gun, it would be child's play for a fully armed Hind.

"Activate IFF," he ordered, glancing back at the instrument panels. "They should acquire us on radar within two minutes now."

"IFF on." Salim Aziz, the still-brooding Iranian, nodded and reached for the interrogator/responsor in the panel on his right. They were using the NATO Identification System, a low-band interrogator, into which the false Israeli Identification Friend or Foe code had been programmed. The gray box would receive the electronic query "Are you a friend?" and it would automatically reply, "Yes, this aircraft is friendly."

Ramirez watched with satisfaction as the green numbers flashed. Deception, he thought. The key to everything.

In the intelligence dossiers of the CIA, the KGB, Mossad, he was known as the Hyena, killer of hundreds in Europe and the Middle East. But the most cherished recent fact in those dossiers was that his private organization had been disbanded. And he had thankfully been written off. Of course, the self-important analysts reasoned over their pipes and printouts, of course the chimera named Sabri Ramirez must be dead. His unmistakable touch had not been on a bombing in years. The playboy terrorist who flaunted silk suits, had cellars of rare vintage wines in Tripoli, Damascus, Baghdad, and Beirut . . . that man wouldn't just retire. He had to be *gone.*

They were half-right. He had wearied of the squabbles and disputes of a far-flung organization; however, he had not lost his taste for money. Or his hatred of the United States.

Now that NATO was disbanding, America had moved its entire army to the Middle East—aided by its European lackeys. But he had put together a plan that would end America's military intimidation once and for all. Not coincidentally, he was going to acquire $800 million in the process.

"We'll be exposed," he continued, "but only for about three minutes. They only have one gun, a .38-caliber DP Mk 30, mounted on the forward deck. It is in plain view. Remember, I need a clear ten-second window for the

Swatter. After we take out their ordnance, we come about and strafe the communications gear."

He hoped this dense Iranian understood the approach profile. He had briefed the man over and over, but still he wasn't sure it had sunk in. He looked Salim Aziz over one last time—the bulky face was sunken, almost depressed eyes—and stifled a sigh of exasperation. Iranians.

"The most important part of the approach," Ramirez went on, "is to make sure we're ID'd by their VIS, their Visual Identification System. It's crucial they make our Israeli markings."

The Soviet Hind-D looked like nothing else in the world, one of a kind. Its visual profile, dark green against the sunset hues of the sky, should be unmistakable. Or so he hoped. Almost sixty feet long and over twenty feet high, it had a main rotor fifty-five feet in diameter and heavy, retractable landing gear. The tandem stations in the nose for the weapons operator, and pilot above him, had individual canopies, with the rear seat raised to give the pilot an unobstructed forward view. Any schoolboy should be able to identify one a mile away, as well as its Israeli markings—the blue Star of David in a white circle.

"They just acquired us on radar," the Iranian announced as a high-pitched alert sounded from the instrument panel and a line of green warning diodes turned red.

"Right on schedule." Ramirez nodded. "The U.S. Navy never sleeps." He turned and motioned to one of the men crouched on a litter in the main cabin, shouting above the noise. "Peretz, it's time to start earning your share."

Dore Peretz had spent five years training with the crack Israeli antiterrorist unit Sayaret Matkal and then had served with the hostage rescue unit of the Israeli Border Police. Now he was free-lance. Ramirez had picked him for his technical skills, and for his greed.

He rose and made his way forward, working carefully through the jumble of legs and automatic weapons. He was younger than he appeared; his prematurely salt-and-pepper hair made him look to be in his late forties, though he actually was only thirty-nine. He settled into the weapons station below Salim, pulling down his black turtleneck the better to accommodate a flight helmet, and switched the radio to 121.50 megahertz, the military emergency channel.

"Mayday. Mayday. Israeli Hawk One requesting permission for emergency approach." He then repeated the announcement in Hebrew. It was, of course, a pointless gesture for the illiterate Americans, but for now verisimilitude counted.

"We copy you, Hawk One. This is USS Glover. *We've acquired you on radar,"* came back the response, a southern drawl, young and slightly nervous. *"What seems to be the problem?"*

"One of our turboshafts has started losing oil pressure. We could use a visual check. What's your position?" Peretz glanced down at the green radar screen and grinned. It showed the frigate's coordinates to within meters.

The radioman complied, then continued. *Could be a problem, Hawk One. The storm's just pushed the sea over four feet. It's a helluva—"*

"Permission to approach. We have a situation here," he continued in English.

"Have to check that with the CO. We've got a perimeter," came back the uneasy answer.

"Fuck your perimeter, sailor." Peretz's voice was harder now. "This is Lieutenant Colonel Leon Daniel, Israeli Air Force. We've got an emergency and we're coming in. Tell *that* to your CO, and get us perimeter clearance. We're coming by." He switched off his mike.

"Well done." Ramirez nodded his approval. "Just the right combination of entreaty and bravado. I think the Americans will be stymied. The good-neighbor policy they like to talk about."

He leaned back and wished he had a cigar. . . .

"Conditional clearance granted," crackled the radio voice. *"But we have to visual-ID you first. Approach from vector 0320. Emergency rescue op being readied, just in case."*

"Roger, USS *Glover*," Peretz spoke back sharply, in his best military style. "Keep the coffee hot."

"It's always hot, sir. This is the U.S. Navy."

"Appreciated."

"Glad to be of help, Hawk One."

Peretz clicked off the radio and turned around. "I think they bought it."

"So far so good," Ramirez nodded.

He descended the three steps into the lower cockpit, the weapons station, and stood behind Peretz, looking it over again. The Hind's offensive capability included a four-barrel Gatling-type 12.7mm machine gun in a turret under the nose. The stubby auxiliary wings each had hard points for thirty-two-round packs of 57mm rockets and the wingtips carried four Swatter homing antitank missiles, two on each side. Plenty of firepower.

"Remember," he said to Salim as he moved back up, "no hint of hostile action until after they make the ID."

He checked his watch. Four and a half minutes should take them inside the VIS range. The altimeter showed that they were now at 1,100 meters, and so far the Iranian was bringing her in perfectly.

7:28 P.M.

"Sir, we got an RQ from the *Glover*." Alfred Konwitz, a twenty-year-old Oklahoman with a thirty-eight-inch waist known to the evening radio shift affectionately as "Big Al," lifted off his headphones and reached for his coffee, extra cream and sugar, which he kept in a special Thermos-insulated cup.

The United States has two bases on the southern Mediterranean island of Crete, strategically close to Libya and the Middle East in general. They are the naval and air base at Souda Bay, which is large enough to accommodate the entire Mediterranean Sixth Fleet, and the communications base at Gournes, in the southern outskirts of Iráklion.

He and Staff Sergeant Jack Mulhoney were at Gournes, on the fourth floor of the faceless gray building that housed operations for the massive battery of antennae. They both knew the *Glover* was a Garcia-class frigate, technically part of the Sixth Fleet, that was on a routine but classified intelligence-gathering assignment a hundred kilometers northwest of Souda Bay.

"They've got an Israeli chopper Mayday," Konwitz continued. "They need a verify. See if it's a scheduled op or what."

Jack Mulhoney was busy with paperwork—more damned forms every day—and didn't really want to be bothered. He got off at midnight, and the staff officer had ordered it completed and on his desk, by God, by 0800 tomorrow. Or else.

"Then run it by Traffic," he said without looking up. Forms. "Maybe it's some exercise. You could call down to the Mole and see if it's on his schedule."

The Mole was Charlie Molinsky, who ran the Traffic Section on the second floor. If the Israeli chopper was on a regular op, he'd have it in the computer.

"Roger." Konwitz punched in the number and asked Molinsky to check it out. As he waited he found himself wishing he were back in Oklahoma, hunting whitetail deer on his uncle's ranch. They were thick as jackrabbits . . .

Suddenly he came alive. "He's got a negative, sir. He's asking if we could get *Glover* to reconfirm."

"Christ, switch me on." Mulhoney shoved aside the pile of paper and reached for his headset. *"Glover,* this is Gournes. Do you copy? Over."

He listened a second, then continued: "Roger. We have no ID on that bogey. Repeat, negative ID. Can you reconfirm?"

While he was waiting he punched up a computer screen and studied it. The *Glover* had reported a position at 36°20' latitude and 25°10' longitude at 1800 hours. And their bearing was last reported to be two-five-zero. Nothing else was in the vicinity.

Damn. He didn't like the feel of this one. His instincts were telling him something was wrong.

Then his headphones crackled. *"Verified IFF. Definitely Israeli code. Do you copy?"*

"I copy but I don't buy it. Proceed with caution. Configure for a bogey unless you can get a good visual."

"Roger. But can you get through to Israeli Control? There's a hell of a storm coming down out here right now, and visuals don't really cut it."

"I copy you, *Glover.* Hang on and we'll try to get something for you." Mulhoney flipped off the headset and revolved in his chair, concern seeping into his ruddy features. "Al, see if the people downstairs can get through on their hot line to Israeli Air Control. Military. Tell them we need a response *now.* Priority. Could be we've got a bogey closing on one of ours, maybe using a phoney IFF. I want them to clear it."

"Aye, aye, sir," he said crisply, then reached for the phone again. He spoke quickly, then waited, drumming his fingers on the vinyl desk. . . .

7.25 P.M.

"Do you read me, Odyssey II? *Come in."* The radio crackled on channel sixteen, the ocean mariner's open line. *Goddammit Mike, do you copy? Over."*

Michael Vance had the salty taste of the Aegean in his mouth as he reached for the black mike of his radio, still gripping the starboard tiller. His waterproof Ross DSC 800 was topside, since there was no other place for it.

He was lean, with leathery skin and taut cheeks, that were more tanned than usual from his having spent the last three days fighting the Aegean. He had dark brown hair, with a high forehead above eyebrows that set off inquiring blue eyes.

"Is that you, Bill? Good to hear your voice, but this is a hell of a time—"

"Who else would it be, you loony gringo. Hey, I'm getting a damned lot of static. How about switching channels? Over to seventy."

"Seventy, confirmed." He pushed in the code, his fingers

slippery and wet. The wind was already gusting up to thirty knots, while his boat was crabbing across the growing swell. "Okay, Lotus-eater, you're on."

"Listen old buddy," the voice continued, clearer now that it was digital, *"our weather radar shows a squall building in the north, up in the Sporades, and it looks like it could be a real bear. It's going to be all over your butt in no time. Thought I'd better let you know. You ought to try and hole up down on the south side of Kíthira."*

Kíthira was an island just off the southeast tip of Greece's Peloponnesus. It was now looming off Vance's starboard bow, barren mountains and sheer cliffs.

"I've been watching it," he yelled back into the mike, holding it close to shield it from the howl of wind. The gale was coming in at an angle to the waves, creating two swells running at ninety degrees, and the sea was getting short and confused. "But I think I can ride it out. I'm making probably seven or eight knots. Just a little rock and roll."

"That's horseshit, friend. This thing's for real. You'd better head for cover." It was the profane, oversmoked voice of Bill Bates, CEO of SatCom, who'd been monitoring his trip with the awesome electronics he'd installed on the little island of Andikíthira, fifteen kilometers south of Kíthira. *"Remember that inlet on the south side of the island, that little harbor at Kapsali? We put in once for a drink last year. I respectfully suggest you get your ass over there and drop anchor as soon as possible."*

"And let you win? No way, José." He was jamming his weight against the starboard tiller and the radio was distracting. As far as he was concerned, the wager with Bates was ironclad: retrace Ulysses's route in a fortnight and do it without ever touching land. "I just think you're getting worried. You suddenly remembered we've got ten large riding on this."

"You're a headstrong idiot, Michael," Bates sputtered. *"Fuck the ten grand. I don't want it and you don't need it. I'm hereby going on record as taking no responsibility for this idiotic stunt, from here on out. You're really pushing your luck."*

"We both know this ain't about money. I've got a reputation to live up to." Vance paused to secure the linen sail line to a wooden cleat.

"Well, for once in your life use some sense. The risk isn't worth it. Our weather radar here at the facility tells no lies, and you should see it. This is going to be a granddaddy. I've triangulated your position and you're only about four klicks off the east side of Kíthira. You could still run for that little harbor down south before it hits."

"I know where I am. I can just make out the island off my starboard bow. About two o'clock." The truth was, he was starting to get worried.

"Then go for it." Bates coughed. *"Listen, you crazy nutcake, I have to get back out to Control. We've got a major run-up of the Cyclops laser system scheduled tonight for 2100 hours. So use your head for once, goddammit, and make for that anchorage."*

"Your views are taken under advisement. But a great American philosopher once said it ain't over till it's over." He pushed the thumb switch on the microphone, clicking it off. Then he switched it on again. "By the way, amigo, good luck with the test." The Cyclops was going to power the world's first laser-driven space vehicle. Who knew if it would work. . . .

"Thanks, we may need it. Talk to you again at 2300."

"See you then." If I'm still around, Vance thought. He clicked off his mike, then switched back to channel sixteen.

Odyssey II was a thirty-eight-foot wooden bark, planked construction of cypress on oak, that no sane man would have taken out of a marina. But Michael Vance was going to prove to the world that the fabled voyage of Ulysses from Troy back to Greece *could* have happened. Unlike anything seen afloat for almost three thousand years, his "yacht" was, in fact, an authentic replica of a single-masted Mycenean warship. Painted lavender and gold—the ancient Greeks loved bold colors—she could have been a theme-park ride. But every time he looked her over he felt proud.

His browned, cracked fingers gripped the wet wood as

the sea churned ever higher, now blotting out the dim line of the horizon. The storm was arriving just as daylight faded—the worst moment. He was tired, and he was thirsty, but there was no time for even a sip of water. With the sea rising, waves were pounding over the primitive sideboards and soaking him to the skin. Next the squalls would come . . . though maybe a little rain would feel good. He hadn't had a shower for four days and he knew he smelled like . . .

Then it happened. Without warning the winds abruptly switched around to the north, going from thirty knots to what seemed like sixty, and the patchwork linen sail started to strain to the limit. He instinctively heaved harder against the tiller, hoping to bring her about and keep her on course. . . .

"Odyssey II, *come in,*" the radio crackled again, and he recognized Bates's voice. *"Do you read?"*

He reached down and picked up the small black mike, then yelled against the howl of wind. "I copy you, but make this quick. No time to chat."

"I had another look-see at the radar, Mike, and I just noticed something else you should know about. We show you at almost the same position as a U.S. Navy ship of some kind. Maybe part of the Sixth Fleet. Take care you miss her."

He clicked the mike to transmit. This time he didn't want to bother switching channels. "Some kind of exercise, probably. What's her class?"

"Can't tell. But she's still a hell of a lot bigger than you are, buddy. They may pick you up on their radar, but again maybe not. Just take care."

"I'll keep an eye out for lights. Thanks." He clicked off the mike again, then looked around. But the Aegean, what he could see of it, was dark and empty.

He leaned his weight back into the tiller, still trying to hold as much of the wind in the sail as possible. The waves had begun lashing him, cold and relentless. He reached for the life jacket he had secured to the mast, a new Switlik

Fastnet Crew Vest MKII. Just another half hour, tops, and—

Christ! Bill was right. A massive hulk was looming dead ahead, running with no lights! It was . . . long as a football field, the bow towering up forward like a battering ram, and she was moving in off his portside stern—she looked to be making at least fifteen knots. High above the bridge, antennas and communications gear were just visible against the twilight gloom, gray and huge. She could shear the *Odyssey II* in half and never even notice. But there was still time to tack and give her a wide berth.

He threw his weight against the tiller, veering to leeward. When he was clear, he'd bring the bow about and let the cutwater top her wake like a surfboard, keeping him from taking water. Then he'd be on his way, into the storm and the night.

He was leaning on the tiller, watching the monolithic hulk skim silently past, when he noticed a throaty roar beginning to drown out the slap of the ship's wake against the side of *Odyssey II*'s hull. After a few moments, as it grew in foreboding intensity, he realized it was coming in from the south. What in hell!

He whirled to look. It was some kind of chopper, altitude about eight hundred meters. What was it doing here? Damn Bill. Had he decided to send SatCom's little Bell to . . .

No, it was way too big. Had to be . . . what! He finally saw it clearly, the stubby wings and rocket pods. It was a Soviet MiL-24D, a Hind. Over the mottled camouflage paint was the blue star and white background of the Israeli Air Force. Odd.

He knew they had captured one once, an export model from the Syrian Air Force, but they would never fly it this far into international airspace. It was a prize. What's more, this bird was fully armed—with dual heat-seeking missiles secured at the tips of each stubby wing, just beyond the twin rocket pods—and the way it was coming in . . .

He lunged for the radio, already afraid he would be too late.

Ramirez stepped down to the weapons station again, gazed out through the huge bubble, and smiled. "Shut down the radar. Their IWR must not have any reason for alarm. They're probably running our IFF through Gournes right now."

The Israeli nodded, then reached over to switch off all systems that might be interpreted as weapons guidance. Next he clicked on the low-light TV. Unlike radar, it was a passive system that would not tip off the ship that she was being ranged.

Ramirez knew that the Control Room of the USS *Glover* would now be crowded with curious young seamen glued to their monitoring screens, probably happy to have a little excitement. Their IFF would be reporting an Israeli chopper. But the minute the visual ID came through, all hell would break loose.

So far, he told himself, it had been a textbook approach. Airspeed was down to ninety-five knots and altitude eight hundred meters. Carefully, carefully. Don't spook the quarry. First rule. We don't need radar. We'll be passive, heat-seeking. No ECM they can throw at us will make any difference.

"Under two minutes now," he said. "It's time."

"No pain, no gain." Peretz flipped on the radio. "USS *Glover*, we're going to have to ditch. We have a crew of three—pilot, co-pilot, and navigation trainee."

"We have emergency crews on starboard side, ready to pick you up. Do you have Mae Wests?"

"Life jackets on. Standard-issue yellow. With dye markers and saltwater-activated beacons. We'll—"

"Hawk One, our Traffic Section at Gournes can't verify you."

"Tell them to check again," Peretz suggested matter-of-factly. "Maybe they screwed up in—"

"We'll have to run it by one more time. Just routine security. Keep a three-thousand-meter perimeter till—"

"Dammit sailor, oil pressure's in the red. We're taking her by your starboard bow. Ready your crews."

Suddenly another voice came on the radio. It was older. *"Israeli Hawk One, this is Captain Vince Bradley. Who the hell are you? We visual-ID you as a Soviet MiL-24 gunship."*

Peretz had switched off his mike and was loosening his helmet strap. "You got it right, asshole."

"Perfect timing," Ramirez said, moving down to the weapons station and taking Peretz's place. "We're inside forty-five seconds. Now just keep her on the deck. First we take out the forward gun turret."

"Taking airspeed to fifty knots." Salim was praying now. *"Allau Akbar!"*

"USS *Glover*." Ramirez had switched on the helmet mike again. "We have a confirmed ditch. Oil pressure just went entirely. We'll be taking her by the bow."

"I repeat, who the hell are you?" the captain's voice came back on the radio. *"We still have no confirmed ID. If you make a pass, I'll assume hostile intent."*

"Sorry. No time to play this by the book," he replied. "We're ditching."

He immediately clicked on the radar. In less then ten seconds he'd be in position to lay a Swatter directly into the forward gun turret. Command on the *Glover* knew it, and at that moment the gun was swiveling, coming around.

Suddenly there was a blaze past them in the sky as the forward gun fired and a telltale tracer ripped by. It was meant to be a warning.

But now the gun glowed on the IR interrogation screen.

Thank you very much, Ramirez thought, and flipped a switch, activating the starboard Swatter's heat-seeking guidance system.

7:32 P.M.

"Right." Alfred Konwitz snapped to attention. "Yes, *sir*." He slammed down the phone and whirled around to

Jack Mulhoney. "Full denial, sir. Israeli Control says they have no military aircraft operating anywhere in that sector of the Aegean. They double-confirm. That's Class A. Hard."

"We're in the shit. Some son of a bitch is closing on one of ours, and we don't even know who he is." He picked up the headphones, then switched on the scrambler. *"Glover, do you read me? I think it's a bogey. I can't tell you that officially, but you'd better inform your CO in the next five seconds or it'll be your ass, sailor."*

"This is Bradley," came back the captain's voice. *"We just—Jesus!"*

"Glover, what—"

"Hostile action . . . do you copy? We've got a hostile."

"How many?"

"It's visual-ID'd as a Soviet MiL 24-D. With Israeli markings. We're taking fire forward—"

"What are—?"

Sounds behind the radio voice had erupted in turmoil. Something catastrophic was going on.

"Al." Mulhoney turned quickly. "Get Command. I think we've got an Israeli ID'd Hind taking hostile action on the *Glover.*"

He didn't realize it, but with those words he'd just given Sabri Ramirez a full half day of extra time. And just as planned, it would make all the difference.

When Jack Mulhoney turned back to his radio, he only heard static.

Look for Thomas Hoover's *Project Cyclops* in the summer of 1992.

"Virtually impossible to put aside until the final horrifying showdown." -- *People*

Edgar Award winner Jonathan Kellerman once more explores the corruption of California's golden dream and produces a novel of complex characterization and non-stop suspense.

TIME BOMB
by Jonathan Kellerman
author of **Silent Partner**

By the time psychologist Dr. Alex Delaware reached the school the damage was done: A sniper had opened fire on a crowded playground, but was gunned down before any children were hurt.

While the TV news crews feasted on the scene and Alex began his therapy sessions with the traumatized children, he couldn't escape the image of a slight teenager clutching an oversized rifle. What was the identity behind the name and face: a would-be assassin, or just another victim beneath an indifferent California sky?

Intrigued by a request from the sniper's father to conduct a "psychological autopsy" of his child, Alex begins to uncover a strange pattern of innocence, neglect, and loss. Then suddenly it is more than a pattern -- it is a trail of blood. In the dead sniper's past was a dark and vicious plot. And in Alex Delaware's future is the stuff of grown-up nightmares: the face of real human evil.

TIME BOMB. On sale wherever Bantam Books are sold.

AN300 -- 8/91

THE ASSASSINI
by Thomas Gifford

"A monumental thriller. Gifford's masterpiece." -- Ira Levin, author of *The Boys from Brazil*

It is 1982. In the Vatican, priestly vultures gather around the dying Pope, whispering the names of possible successors. In a forgotten monastery on Ireland's gale-swept coast, a dangerous document is hidden, waiting to be claimed. And in a family chapel in Princeton, New Jersey, a nun is murdered at her prayers.

Sister Valentine was an outspoken activist, a thorn in the Church's side. When her brother, lawyer Ben Driskill, realizes the Church will never investigate her death, he sets out to find the murderer himself -- and uncovers an explosive secret. The assassini. An age-old brotherhood of killers. Once they were hired by princes of the Church to protect it in dangerous times. But whose orders do they now obey?

The Assassini marks the triumphant return of a master at the peak of his powers -- the first novel in more than a decade from the acclaimed author of *The Wind Chill Factor*.

Available wherever Bantam Books are sold.

AN309 -- 8/91

THRILLERS

Gripping suspense...explosive action...dynamic characters...international settings...these are the elements that
make for great thrillers. Books guaranteed to keep you
riveted to your seat.

Robert Ludlum:

☐	26256	THE AQUITAINE PROGRESSION	$5.95
☐	26011	THE BOURNE IDENTITY	$5.95
☐	26322	THE BOURNE SUPREMACY	$5.95
☐	26094	THE CHANCELLOR MANUSCRIPT	$5.95
☐	28209	THE GEMINI CONTENDERS	$5.95
☐	26019	THE HOLCROFT COVENANT	$5.95
☐	27800	THE ICARUS AGENDA	$5.95
☐	25899	THE MATERESE CIRCLE	$5.95
☐	27960	THE MATLOCK PAPER	$5.95
☐	26430	THE OSTERMAN WEEKEND	$5.95
☐	25270	THE PARSIFAL MOSAIC	$5.95
☐	28063	THE RHINEMANN EXCHANGE	$5.95
☐	27109	THE ROAD TO GANDOLOFO	$5.95
☐	27146	THE SCARLATTI INHERITANCE	$5.95
☐	28179	TREVAYNE	$5.95

Frederick Forsyth:

☐	28393	THE NEGOTIATOR	$5.95
☐	26630	DAY OF THE JACKAL	$5.95
☐	26490	THE DEVIL'S ALTERNATIE	$5.95
☐	26846	THE DOGS OF WAR	$5.95
☐	25113	THE FOURTH PROTOCOL	$5.95
☐	27673	NO COMEBACKS	$5.95
☐	27198	THE ODESSA FILE	$5.95

Buy them at your local bookstore or use this page to order.

Bantam Books, Dept. TH, 414 East Golf Road, Des Plaines, IL 60016

Please send me the items I have checked above. I am enclosing $_____
(please add $2.00 to cover postage and handling). Send check or money
order, no cash or C.O.D.s please.

Mr/Ms _____

Address _____

City/State _____ Zip _____

TH–11/90

Please allow four to six weeks for delivery.
Prices and availability subject to change without notice.